"The only thing more fun than an October Daye book is an In-Cryptid book. Swift narrative, charm, great world-building . . . all the McGuire trademarks."
—Charlaine Harris, #1 *New York Times* bestselling author

"Seanan McGuire's *Discount Amageddon* is an urban fantasy triple threat—smart and sexy and funny. The Aeslin mice alone are worth the price of the book, so consider a cast of truly ORIGINAL characters, a plot where weird never overwhelms logic, and some serious kickass world-building as a bonus."
—Tanya Huff, bestselling author of *The Wild Ways*

"McGuire kicks off a new series with a smart-mouthed, engaging heroine and a city full of fantastical creatures. This may seem like familiar ground to McGuire fans, but she makes New York her own, twisting the city and its residents into curious shapes that will leave you wanting more. Verity's voice is strong and sure as McGuire hints at a deeper history, one that future volumes will hopefully explore."
—*RT Book Reviews*

"Verity is a winning protagonist, and her snarky but loving observations on her world of bogeyman strip club owners, Japanese demon badger bartenders, and dragon princess waitresses make for a delightful read."
—*Publishers Weekly*

"*Discount Armageddon* is an exceptionally well-written tale with a unique premise, fantastic character work, and a plot that just pulls you along until you finish. This is one for the urban fantasy enthusiasts out there—as well as for anyone who wants something different from most anything else on shelves today. Easily one of my favorite books of 2012."
—*Ranting Dragon*

"Smart, whimsical and bitingly funny, Verity Price is a kick-ass heroine that readers will love. Just when I thought she couldn't surprise me again, she would pull some new trick out of her hat –or, in the case of her throwing knives, out of her corset. I would send Verity and my Jane Jameson on a girl's night out, but I'm afraid of the damage bill they would rack up!"
—Molly Harper, author of *Nice Girls Don't Have Fangs*

"*Discount Armageddon* is a quick-witted, sharp-edged look at what makes a monster monstrous, and at how closely our urban fantasy protagonists walk—or dance—that line. The pacing never lets up, and when the end comes, you're left wanting more. I can't wait for the next book!" —C

**DAW Books presents the finest in urban fantasy
from Seanan McGuire:**

InCryptid **Novels:**

DISCOUNT ARMAGEDDON

MIDNIGHT BLUE-LIGHT SPECIAL

October Daye **Novels:**

ROSEMARY AND RUE

A LOCAL HABITATION

AN ARTIFICIAL NIGHT

LATE ECLIPSES

ONE SALT SEA

ASHES OF HONOR

CHIMES AT MIDNIGHT*

* Coming soon from DAW Books

MIDNIGHT BLUE-LIGHT SPECIAL

AN INCRYPTID NOVEL

SEANAN McGUIRE

WITHDRAWN

DAW BOOKS, INC.

DONALD A. WOLLHEIM, FOUNDER

375 Hudson Street, New York, NY 10014

ELIZABETH R. WOLLHEIM
SHEILA E. GILBERT
PUBLISHERS

http://www.dawbooks.com

First Printing, March 2013
1 2 3 4 5 6 7 8 9

For Betsy Tinney.
You are the best steampunk pixie godmother a girl
could want.
Thank you, forever.

Price Family Tree

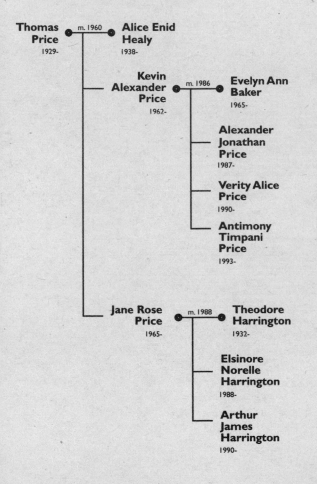

Thomas Price 1929-

m. 1960

Alice Enid Healy 1938-

Kevin Alexander Price 1962-

m. 1986

Evelyn Ann Baker 1965-

Alexander Jonathan Price 1987-

Verity Alice Price 1990-

Antimony Timpani Price 1993-

Jane Rose Price 1965-

m. 1988

Theodore Harrington 1932-

Elsinore Norelle Harrington 1988-

Arthur James Harrington 1990-

Cryptid, noun:

1. Any creature whose existence has been suggested but not proved scientifically. Term officially coined by cryptozoologist John E. Wall in 1983.

2. That thing that's getting ready to eat your head.

3. See also "monster."

Prologue

"Well, that's not something you see every day. Go tell your father that Grandma needs the grenades."

—Enid Healy

A small survivalist compound about an hour's drive east of Portland, Oregon

Thirteen years ago

VERITY STOOD WITH HER HANDS FOLDED in front of her and her feet turned out in first position, watching her father read her report card. They were alone in his study. That was something she would normally have relished, given how hard it was to get her father's attention all to herself. At the moment, she would rather have been just about anywhere else, including playing hide-and-seek with Antimony. (Annie was just six, and she was already beating both her older siblings at hide-and-seek on a regular basis. It was embarrassing. It would still have been better than this.)

Kevin Price stared at the report card a little *too* long before lowering it, meeting Verity's grave stare with one of his own. "Verity. You need to understand that blending in with the rest of the students is essential. We send you to school so you can learn to fit in."

"Yes, Daddy. I know."

"We can never attract too much attention to ourselves. If we do, things could get very bad for us. The Covenant is still out there."

"I know, Daddy." Most of the kids in third grade were afraid of the bogeyman. Verity didn't mind bogeymen — they were pretty nice, mostly, if you didn't let them talk you into doing anything you weren't supposed to do — but there was one monster that she *was* afraid of, one you couldn't argue with or shoot. It was called "Covenant," and one day it was going to come and carry them all away.

"So why have you been fighting with the other students?"

Verity looked down at her feet. "I'm bored. They're all so *slow*, and I never get to do anything fun."

"I see." Kevin put the offending report card down on his desk, half covering a report on the New Mexico jackalope migration. He cleared his throat, and said, "We're enrolling you in gymnastics. You'll be keeping your dance lessons, for now, but I want you to have a way to work off that extra energy. And Verity?"

"Yes, Daddy?"

"Play nicely with the other children, or you won't be taking any more ballet classes. Am I clear?"

Relief flooded through her. It wasn't victory — victory would have been more dance lessons, not stupid gymnastics — but it was closer than she'd been willing to hope for. "Absolutely. I won't let you down again, I promise."

"I'll hold you to that." Kevin leaned forward to hug his older daughter, mind still half on the teacher comments from her report card. If she couldn't learn to blend in, she was going to need to find a way to stand out that wouldn't get them all killed ... and she needed to do it fast, before they all ran out of time.

One

"The best thing I ever did was figure out how to hide a pistol in my brassiere. The second best thing I ever did was let Thomas figure out how to find it, but that's a story for another day."

—Alice Healy

The subbasement of St. Catherine's Hospital, Manhattan, New York

Now

THE AIR IN THE SUBBASEMENT smelled like disinfectant and decay—the worst aspects of hospital life— overlaid with a fine dusting of mildew, just to make sure it was as unpleasant as possible. Only about a quarter of the lights worked, which was almost worse than none of them working at all. Our flashlights would have been more useful in total darkness. All they could do in this weird half-light was scramble the shadows, making them seem even deeper and more dangerous.

"I think there are rats down here," Sarah whispered, sounding disgusted. "Why did you take me someplace where there are *rats*? I *hate* rats."

"It was this or the movies, and the rats seemed cheaper," I whispered back. "Now be quiet. If that thing is down here with us, we don't want to let it know we're coming."

Sarah's glare somehow managed to be visible despite the shadows. The irony of telling the telepath to shut the hell up didn't escape me. Unfortunately for Sarah and her need to complain endlessly about our surroundings, I needed her to stay focused. We were looking for something so different from the human norm that we weren't even sure she'd be able to "see" it. That meant not dividing her telepathy just for the sake of whining without being heard.

(Sarah is a cuckoo—a breed of human-looking cryptid that's biologically more like a giant wasp than any sort of primate, and telepathic to boot. Evolution is funky sometimes.)

To be fair, Sarah hadn't exactly volunteered for this little mission. Sarah rarely volunteers for *any* mission, little or otherwise, and was much happier staying at home, doing her math homework, and chatting with my cousin Artie on her computer. I'm pretty sure that much peace and quiet is bad for you, so I drag her out whenever I can find an excuse. Besides, there's something to be said for having a telepath with you when you go hunting for things that want to eat your head.

"Wait." Sarah grabbed my arm. I stopped where I was, glancing back at her. Her glare was still visible, less because of its ferocity and more because her eyes had started to glow white. It would have been unnerving as hell if I hadn't been hoping that was going to happen.

"What?" I whispered.

"Up ahead," she said. "We're here." She pointed toward one of the deeper patches of shadow with her free hand—a patch of shadow that I'd been instinctively avoiding. I nodded my appreciation and started in that direction, Sarah following half a step behind me. The shadows seemed to darken as we approached, spreading out to swallow the thin beams of our flashlights.

"I love my job," I muttered, and stepped into the dark.

Fortunately for my desire not to spend eternity wandering in a lightless hell, Sarah was right: we had reached our destination. The darkness extended for no more than

three steps before we emerged into a clean, well-lit hallway with cheerful posters lining the walls. At least they
seemed cheerful, anyway, as long as you didn't look at
them too closely. I pride myself on having a strong stomach, and one glance at the poster on gorgon hygiene was
enough to make me want to skip dinner for the next
week. (Here's a hint: All those snakes have to eat, and
anything that eats has to excrete. This, and other horrify-
ing images, brought to you by Mother Nature. Proof that
if she really exists, the lady has got a sick sense of humor.)

A white-haired woman dressed in cheerful pink hospital scrubs was standing by the admissions desk. She
would have looked like any other attending nurse if it
weren't for her yellow-rimmed pigeon's eyes and the
wings sprouting from her shoulders, feathers as white as
her hair. Her feet were bare, and her toenails were long
enough to be suggestive of talons. She looked up at the
sound of our footsteps, and her expression passed rapidly
from polite greeting to confusion before finally settling
on cautious relief.

"Verity Price?" she ventured, putting down her clipboard and taking a step in our direction. Her voice had
a flutelike quality that blurred the edges of her accent,
making it impossible to place her origins as anything
more precise than "somewhere in Europe."

"That's me," I agreed. "This is my cousin, Sarah Zellaby."

"Hi," said Sarah, waving one hand in a short wave.

The white-haired woman gave Sarah a quick once-
over, one wing flicking half-open before snapping shut
again. She looked puzzled. "Dr. Morrow didn't tell me
you would be bringing an assistant, Miss Price," she said
slowly.

"He probably forgot," I said. I was telling the truth.
People have a tendency to forget about Sarah unless
she's standing directly in front of them, and sometimes
even then. It's all part of the low-grade telepathic masking field she inherited from her biological parents.
There's a reason we consider her species of cryptid one
of the most dangerous things in the world.

"Nice to meet you," said Sarah. "I never knew there was a hospital down here."

As usual, it was exactly the right thing to say. The white-haired woman smiled, both wings flicking open this time in visible pleasure. "It required a very complicated piece of sorcery to conceal it here, but it's more than worth the cost of maintenance. We have access to the whole of St. Catherine's when we require it, which prevents our needing to acquire some of the more specialized equipment for ourselves."

"Clever," I said. Inwardly, I was salivating over the idea of getting, say, an MRI film of a lamia. There'd be time for that later. This was the time for business. "When Dr. Morrow contacted me, he said you were having trouble."

"Yes." The white-haired woman nodded, expression growing grim. "It's started again."

"Show me," I said.

🐾

St. Catherine's was one of five hospitals located within a two-mile radius. That might seem excessive, but two were privately owned, one was more properly termed a hospice, and one—St. Giles'—was constructed under the subbasement at St. Catherine's. St. Giles' didn't appear on any map, and wasn't covered by any medical insurance plan. That was because, for the most part, their patients weren't human.

Over the centuries, humanity has had a lot of names for the sort of people who go to places like St. Giles' Hospital. There's the ever-popular "monsters," and the almost as enduring "freaks of nature." Or you could go with "abominations," if that's what floats your boat. My family has always been fond of the slightly less pejorative "cryptids." They're still people, men and women with thoughts and feelings of their own. They just happen to be people with tails, or scales, or pretty white wings, like the woman who was now leading us down the hall toward the maternity ward.

Sarah caught me studying our guide and shot me an

amused look, accompanied by an arrow of audible thought: *She's a Caladrius. She's wondering if you'll notice, and a little bit afraid you'll start demanding feathers.*

Whoa, I replied, trying not to stare. Caladrius are some of the best doctors in the world. Their feathers have a supernatural healing quality that no one's ever been able to duplicate. That's why there are so few Caladrius left. They used to volunteer to help with any sick or injured creature they encountered, regardless of the dangers to themselves. It took them a long time, and the slaughter of most of their species, before they learned to be cautious around humanity.

"Here," said the nurse, stopping in front of a doorway. It was blocked off with plastic sheeting, lending it an ominous air. She gestured to it with one hand, but made no move to pull the plastic aside. "I'm sorry. I can't go in with you."

"I understand," I said. I did, really. If Dr. Morrow's report was correct, we were about to walk into a slaughterhouse. Caladrius will heal the wounded if they possibly can, but they can't bear the sight of the dead. Dead people look like failure to them. "Thanks for showing us the way."

"If you need anything . . ." she began.

Sarah smiled. "We'll call," she said. "Loudly."

That is so much nicer than "we'll scream until you send backup," I thought.

Sarah's smile widened.

Looking relieved, the Caladrius nodded. "I'll be at my desk if you need me." Then she turned, hurrying away before we could think of a reason to need her to stay. Sarah and I watched her go. Then Sarah turned to me, a wordless question in her expression.

"I'll go first," I said as I turned and drew the plastic veil aside.

The smell that came wafting out into the hall was enough to make my stomach turn. I'd been the one to request that the room be sealed off without cleaning, to give me a better idea of what I was dealing with. Suddenly, I thought I might regret that decision.

Streaks of long-dried blood warred with cheerful pastels for ownership of the walls inside the maternity ward. Most of it was red, although there were a few streaks of green, purple, and even shiny-clear breaking up the crimson monotony. Patches of the original cartoon murals showed through the gore, representing a cartoon cryptid wonderland, with dozens of happy cryptid and human children gamboling through a paradise of acceptance that hadn't existed in millennia, if it ever existed at all. Sarah blanched.

"Verity . . ."

"I know." Even the thickest splotches of blood had been given time to dry. I touched one, and it flaked away on my fingertips. "If the pattern holds, it's still nearby."

"Oh, goody. Have I mentioned recently how much I hate it when you say things like that?" Sarah glanced nervously around. "I'm not picking up on any other minds in this room. We're alone in here."

"That's a start." There was a closed door on the far wall. I pulled the pistol from the back of my jeans, holding it in front of me as I walked cautiously forward. "Stay where you are."

"You don't need to tell me twice," said Sarah.

The door swung gently open when I twisted the knob, revealing the darker, seemingly empty room beyond. I squinted into the gloom, seeing nothing but a few sheet-draped tables and what looked like an old-style apothecary's cabinet. My flashlight beam bounced off the glass, refracting into the room where Sarah and I stood.

"Looks like it's all clear," I said, starting to turn back to Sarah. "We should keep on movi—"

Something roughly the size of a Golden Retriever—assuming Golden Retrievers had massive, batlike wings—burst out of the dark behind the door and soared into the room, shrieking loudly. Sarah added her own screaming to the din, ducking and scrambling to get under one of the gore-soaked tables. I stopped worrying about her as soon as she was out of sight. The creature would forget she was there almost instantly, if it had managed to notice her in the first place. The cuckoo: nature's ultimate stealth predator, and also, when necessary, nature's ultimate coward.

The creature continued its flight across the room, giving me time to take solid aim on the space between its wings, and get a good enough view to make a hopefully accurate guess at what it was. It could have been your average attractive older Filipino woman, assuming you liked your attractive older women with wings, claws, fangs, and—oh, right—nothing below the navel. Where her lower body should have been was only a thin, pulsing layer of skin, providing me with a nauseatingly clear view of her internal organs.

My brother owed me five bucks. When I'd described the thing that was supposedly attacking downtown maternity wards to him over the phone, he'd barely paused before saying, "There's no way you're dealing with a manananggal. They're not native to the region." Well, if the thing that was flying around the room wasn't a manananggal, nature was even crueler than I'd originally thought.

"Hey, *ugly!*" I shouted, and fired. Shrieking, the manananggal hit the wall, using her momentum to flip herself around and start coming back toward me. I fired twice more. As far as I could tell, I hit her both times. It didn't slow her down one bit. I dove to the side just as she sliced through the air where I'd been standing, that unearthly shriek issuing from her throat the entire time.

"I fucking hate things that can't be killed," I muttered, rolling back to my feet. The manananggal was coming back for another pass. That was, in a messed-up kind of way, a good thing. Mentally, I shouted, *Sarah! Go find her legs!*

My cousin stuck her head out from under the table, eyes wide. *You're kidding, right?* came the telepathic demand.

No! Hurry! I fired at the manananggal again, keeping her attention on me. It wasn't hard to do. Most things focus on the person with the gun.

I hate you, said Sarah, and slid out from under the

table, using the sound of gunfire and screaming to cover her as she slipped through the open doorway, into the dark beyond.

The manananggal are native to the Philippines, where they live disguised among the human population, using them for shelter and sustenance at the same time. They spend the days looking just like everyone else. It's only when the sun goes down that they open their wings and separate their torsos from their lower bodies. That's when they fly into the night, looking for prey. Even that could be forgiven— humanity has made peace with stranger things—if it weren't for *what* they prey on.

Infants, both newly-born and just about to be born. The manananggal will also feed on the mothers, but only if they're still carrying or have given birth within the last twenty-four hours. Weak prey. Innocent prey. Prey that, in this modern world, is conveniently herded into maternity wards and hospital beds, making it easy for the manananggal to come in and eat its fill. As this one had been doing, moving in a rough circle through the local maternity wards, slaughtering humans and cryptids with equal abandon.

She'd been getting sloppier, and her kills had been getting more obvious. That was a bad sign. That meant the manananggal was getting ready to find a mate and make a nest . . . and that was something I couldn't allow to happen.

I'm a cryptozoologist. It's my job to protect the monsters of the world. But when those monsters become too dangerous to be allowed to roam free, I'm also a hunter. I don't enjoy that side of my work. That doesn't mean I get to stop doing it.

The manananggal seemed to realize that her tactics weren't getting her anywhere. With a ringing scream, she hit the wall again, and then turned to fly straight at me, her arms held out in front of her as she went for a choke-hold. I ducked. Not fast enough. Her claws raked across the top of my left bicep, slicing through the fabric of my shirt and down into my flesh. I couldn't bite back my yelp of pain, which seemed to delight the manananggal; her scream became a cackle as she flew past me, flipped around, and came back for another strike.

I put two bullets into her throat. That barely slowed her down . . . but it slowed her enough for me to get out of her path. She slammed into the wall, hard. I tensed, expecting another pass. It never came. Instead, her wings thrashed once, twice, and she sank to the floor in a glassy-eyed heap, brackish blood oozing from the gunshot wounds peppering her body.

Breathing shallowly, I moved toward the body. She didn't move. I prodded her with the toe of my shoe. She didn't move. I shot her three more times, just to be sure. (Saving ammunition is for other people. People who aren't bleeding.) She didn't move.

"I hate you," announced Sarah from the doorway behind me.

I turned. She held up the canister of garlic salt I'd ordered her to bring, turning it upside-down to show that it was empty.

"Legs are toast," she said. "As soon as I poured this stuff down her feeding tube, the lower body collapsed."

"Oh. Good. That's a note for the field guide." I touched my wounded arm gingerly. "This stings. Do you remember anything about manananggal being venomous?"

Sarah grimaced. "How about we ask the nurse?"

"Good idea," I said, and let her take my arm and lead me away from the fallen manananggal, and the remains of the last infants she would ever slaughter.

This is how I spend my Saturday nights. And sadly, these are the nights I feel are most successful.

Two

"Treat your weapons like you treat your children. That means cleaning them, caring for them, counting on them to do the best they can for you, and forgiving them when they can't."

—Enid Healy

The Freakshow, a highly specialized nightclub somewhere in Manhattan

A WEEK HAD PASSED since the manananggal incident, giving me sufficient time to file my reports, update the family field guide (this just in: manananggal *are* venomous), and pay two follow-up visits to St. Giles' Hospital, where Dr. Morrow and the Caladrius nurse (whose name turned out to be Lauren) were happy to patch me up free of charge. The manananggal's claws didn't even leave a scar. I had resolved a threat, and saved a bunch of babies—and their mothers—from being eaten. Not bad for a ballroom dancer from Portland.

I hit the stairs leading down from the nightclub roof almost five whole minutes before my shift was scheduled to start. For me, that's practically getting to work early, especially these days. We had a little snake cult incident last year, and the city's cryptids are still all worked up about it. That's meant more mediation, more handholding through interactions with the human world, and, unfortunately, more hunting, since some of the more predatory types of cryptid took the destabilization of

Manhattan as an invitation to move in and start chowing down on the locals. It seems like I'm out on the streets every other night, teaching some idiot that you don't act like that in my city.

Candy was standing by the base of the stairs, eating a ham and gold leaf sandwich. (It's a house special. Angel calls it "the Adam Lambert," and serves it with a pickle and a shot of Goldschläger. Bartenders are weird.) "You're late," she called, as I went blowing past her like my shoes were on fire.

"I have five minutes!" I shouted back, and kept on running until I hit the dressing room, and dove into chaos.

Picture a medium-sized room, maybe twenty feet by twenty feet square. Now add standing lockers cannibalized from a high school gym, with the requisite long wooden benches stretching between the rows. Great. Now add half a dozen women, all of them jockeying for position at the single long mirror lining one wall, and you'll have some idea of what I was walking into.

Sometimes I think I'd rather deal with a herd of angry unicorns than a bunch of women trying to get themselves ready for work. "I'm here," I announced to no one in particular as I walked past the throng and made my way between two racks of lockers to my assigned spot. The "real world skills" I've learned from my years of struggling to launch a dance career are mostly limited to things like putting on mascara on a moving bus, but I definitely know better than to come between an amateur kick-line and their own reflections.

I opened my locker and tossed in my bag before starting to squirm out of my street clothes. Five minutes was cutting it close for getting into my uniform and putting on my makeup. I'd done it before, but that didn't mean I could waste time watching the clown car antics unfolding in front of the mirror.

The dancers and cocktail waitresses fighting for space squabbled like wet hens as they applied lip gloss, fixed their eye makeup, and tried to keep from being bitten by Carol's hair, which was making its usual attempt to es-

cape from her elaborate beehive wig. Carol stuffed the
tiny serpents back into the weave as quickly as they slithered free, but it was a hopeless fight—like all lesser gorgons, she was seriously outnumbered by her own hair.

Under normal circumstances, Carol would have had at
least three feet on either side of her, since only Marcy was
willing to sit any closer. Marcy's an Oread, and her skin is
way too thick to be punctured by anything as plebeian as
a snake bite. That was under normal circumstances, not
during shift change. During shift change—especially shift
change to the night shift—real estate at the mirror was
too valuable to leave open just because you might wind
up getting chomped on by a cocktail waitress' hairdo.

Distraction makes you careless. One of the new girls
squealed and jerked away from Carol, clutching her
hand to her chest. I sighed as I fastened the last few
snaps on my uniform bodice and pulled on my ruffled
cancan skirt. Once that was done, I grabbed the at-work
first aid kit from my locker and walked over to the mirror.

"I'm *so* sorry, tomorrow's feeding day, they're all
cranky," Carol was saying to the girl her hair had taken
a chunk out of—a wide-eyed human whose normally
coppery complexion was underscored with a sudden
sickly pallor. Carol kept stuffing as she spoke, trying to
get the snakes back into her wig. They weren't cooperat-
ing. Her agitation was transmitting itself to them, and
they were beginning to writhe and snap wildly, making
her blonde beehive wig pulse like a prop from a bad horror movie.

"Here, Carol." I pressed my emergency can of Mom's
gorgon hair treatment into Carol's hand. She shot me a
grateful look. Neither of us really understands why a mix
of concrete dust, eggshells, and powdered antivenin has a
sedative effect on the snakes, but it doesn't hurt them,
and it keeps them calmer than anything else we've been
able to come up with. Carol gets three cans a month. I get
one in the same shipment, for emergencies just like this
one.

The new girl was still sitting there, looking terrified. I

tried to remember who'd recommended that we hire her. Humans are great dancers, but most of them really aren't all that comfortable with the cryptid world—and there's good reason for that. You need to worry about a lot in a normal chorus line; being bitten by the other girls' hair isn't on the list.

"You." I pointed to another of the new girls, a green-haired siren with eyes only a few shades lighter than her heavily hairsprayed curls. "Take her to the manager's office. There's antivenin in the fridge there."

"Okay," said the siren, the whistling sweetness of her voice betraying her anxiety. She took the bitten girl by the elbow, pulling her away from the mirror. "Come on, Nye. Let's get that taken care of."

The bubble of silence that followed their departure held for only a few seconds before the room exploded back into its previous level of chaos. The hole at the mirror left by the siren and her human friend was almost instantly filled. That's show business for you.

Marcy dusted Carol's hair with sedative powder as Carol shoved the suddenly-passive little snakes back into her wig.

A quarter of the mirror had been claimed by four of the gorgeous blondes we spent centuries calling "dragon princesses" before we learned that, no, they were just the female of the dragon species. Three equally gorgeous Chinese girls were crammed in there with them, all of them doing their makeup with grim precision. They were visiting representatives of another dragon subspecies. They were in town to grill William—the dragon who lives under downtown Manhattan, and yeah, I'm still pretty flipped out about that—about whether any of *their* males might have survived, and, like all dragons, they were happy to spend their off hours making a few extra bucks by waiting tables.

(Dragons take avarice to a religious level, but they have good reason; their health and reproduction depend on the presence of certain precious materials. European dragons need gold. Their Chinese counterparts seemed to have a similar affection for jade and pearls, although some of what I'd been able to overhear implied that they actually *created* pearls somehow, which definitely gave them a financial leg up. What can I say? I'm a cryptozoologist, and we didn't write our books on cryptid biology by being too polite to eavesdrop.)

"Are we good?" I asked.

"We're good," said Marcy, shoving the last of the sedated snakes under Carol's wig. "Thanks for the save."

"It's no big deal," I said, although a quick glance at the clock told me that it was actually a very big deal indeed. I was due on stage with the rest of the chorus in less than three minutes. I stuck two fingers in my mouth and whistled sharply before shouting, "This is not a drill, people! Hairspray down, high heels on, and anyone who breaks a leg before intermission is going to answer to me!"

The already hectic dressing room exploded into motion as everyone scrambled, double-time, to get ready for the cue that was about to crash down on us. I dashed back to my locker, grabbing the few pieces of costume still in need of application, and took off for the stage. Anything I couldn't put on while I was running was just going to have to wait until I got a break.

There's no business like show business. And thank God for that.

A little background, in case it's still needed: my name is Verity Price, and I'm a journeyman cryptozoologist, currently studying the sentient cryptid population of New York City and the surrounding area. This turns out to pay surprisingly poorly, since most people don't believe cryptids exist, and those who *do* believe in them usually fall into one of two camps—either "kill it with fire" or "I wonder how I can use that freak of nature to make myself buckets and buckets of money." Neither of these is helpful when what you're trying to do is observe and assist a cryptid population, and so I, like every other member of my family, make do with whatever jobs my admittedly non-standard skill set can help me hold onto.

That brought me, in a roundabout way, to Dave's Fish and Strips, a tits-and-ass bar that was billed as a "nightclub for discerning gentlemen."

Dave was a bogeyman. He probably still is, since no one's managed to kill him yet—at least as far as I know, and given how we parted ways, I would expect his killers to send me a nice "you're welcome" card. Anyway, when I came to town looking for gainful employment, serving cocktails in a cryptid-owned establishment seemed like the best of all possible worlds. I could study the urban cryptid population both in and out of the workplace, allowing me an unparalleled view of their social structure, and I could make a little money at the same time.

I mean, really, it was all going pretty great until Dave decided to sell me to a snake cult before skipping town. They say nobody's perfect, but there's having a few flaws, and then there's selling your employees as human sacrifices. That sort of thing is just uncool.

The whole "human sacrifice" thing didn't pan out, and I returned to find Dave gone and the strip club abandoned. Since he wasn't technically dead—not until I get my hands on him, anyway, and who knows when that might be?—the rest of the city's bogeymen got to decide what would be done with his property, and they settled for turning it over to his niece, Kitty. She'd been touring with her boyfriend's band when things really got nasty, and didn't find out that her uncle was missing until she came to ask for her old job back. Maybe Dave left the deed in her name, or else her boyfriend was really good at fabricating paperwork, but either way, talk about your welcome home presents.

None of us had expected too much of Kitty, but she proved to have a good head for business and, better still, a good sense of showmanship. Dave operated the club on a sort of "If we put hot naked girls on stage, they will come" theory. Kitty looked at that and said, "Well, yes, but how are we going to get them to come *back*?" Dave's Fish and Strips closed its doors for good a week after Kitty took it over. Two months after that, the Freakshow was born.

Have a prehensile tail? Wear a miniskirt and use it to carry an extra tray when you're serving drinks. Got wings? How do you feel about swinging on a perch suspended from the ceiling? Cryptids of every race and creed were invited to come and show off the things that divided them from the human race—and every one of them who did just helped to raise the Freakshow's cred a little higher. There was even a review in the New Yorker, calling it a "cunning use of smoke and mirrors," and "a fantastic example of the misuses one can manage with a degree in theatrical makeup and costuming." In short, it was so in-your-face that everyone assumed it had to be fake, and the human populace of the city was all but busting down the doors for the chance to dance with the monsters they still didn't believe in.

Still, every gimmick has its shelf life, and Kitty knew that if she wanted to keep the Freakshow running, she would need to have more than just a few strange but pretty faces on staff. She'd need actual *entertainment*. Well, that, and some of the stiffest drinks in the city, courtesy of our bartenders, Ryan and Angel.

All of which goes to explain why I scrambled to the middle of the stage less than a minute before curtain, wearing a corset, a ruffled black-and-red cancan skirt, high heels, and enough glitter to start my own David Bowie tribute band. In the end, no matter how tight the timing, the show must always go on.

"Ladies and gentlemen, honored guests and less-than-honored neighbors, the Freakshow welcomes you to a night of thrills, chills, and sweet surprises that can be found nowhere else in this fairest of all fair cities." Kitty always did her ringmaster act from the center of the stage, despite the fact that she's a bogeyman, and should hence want to avoid the light whenever possible. I guess she never got to that page of the bogeyman edition of *Our Bodies, Ourselves*. She strutted back and forth between two precisely placed marks as she used her womanly wiles to get the attention of a rowdy crowd.

Her luck was usually good in that regard. Something about her wearing an outfit that looks like a classic ringmaster's attire as reinterpreted by a designer who specializes in high-end fetish gear just managed to catch the eye. It didn't hurt that she had the subtly inhuman proportions shared by all bogeymen, making her difficult to look away from.

I said Kitty changed the place after Dave left. I never said she made it *classy*.

"—and now, my beloved guests, if you would put your hands together for our sweet sugarplums, our cancan belles, our Freakshow dancers, the Scarionettes!" Kitty finished our introduction with a flourish, her heels hitting the floor with gunshot precision as she walked off the main stage half a step ahead of the opening curtain. Floodlights splashed down from the rafters, revealing eleven dancers in corsets and short ruffled skirts, all frozen in perfect clockwork doll poses as we waited for the music to begin.

The tapping of an unseen conductor's baton echoed from the speakers, catching the attention of those patrons who had learned to ignore Kitty's posturing in favor of sucking down cocktails while they waited for the floorshow to begin. Then Emilie Autumn's "I Know Where You Sleep" blasted out, and we started to dance.

Kitty was being generous when she called the floorshow's first number a "cancan." I've danced the cancan, although never professionally, and while it does involve a lot of girls hiking their skirts to heaven, they're usually doing it wearing outfits that look less like they came from the remainder bin at Hot Topic. Still, it was athletic, enthusiastic, and involved cute girls in high heels and corsets bouncing up and down for five minutes without stopping for air, which was more than sufficient for our clientele.

We whirled and spun around the stage, kicking, prancing, thrusting our chests out, and somehow managing to look like we were both classier and naughtier than your average stripper. A lot of the credit for that goes to my choreography, if I do say so myself. My specialty is Latin ballroom, which is all about pouring a whole lot of sexy into a very small amount of suggestive.

Off to one side of the stage, a chorus girl was deviating from the routine to snatch dollar bills from a leering man in a baseball jersey. Okay, so maybe the transition from stripper to dancer was still a work in process for some of my coworkers. I was happy to work with them as much as I had to, since failure might mean going back to cocktail waitressing. Any amount of coaching our slower learners was worth it if it meant I could avoid that particular fate. Even if I had to do my coaching in a corset.

🦡

The nicest thing about working in a bar with aspirations of growing up to be a burlesque joint: I might have to shake my tail feathers if I wanted to bring home a paycheck, but the rotation of the acts and the solo numbers in-between meant that I was only on stage once every ninety minutes during the busy periods.

I congratulated the rest of the chorus as they stampeded off the stage, narrowly avoiding the snake dancer who was shoving her way up the backstage steps with a large wicker basket in her arms. The basket hissed companionably as it passed me. I hissed back, trying to keep my tone respectful. It never pays to piss off a wadjet.

The main room was packed with bodies by the time I stripped off my chorus girl outfit—trading it for a much more demure lacy blouse-and-petticoat combination, and yes, moments like that are the only times when I miss the tacky little uniforms Dave used to make us wear—and pushed my way out of the dressing room into the crowd. A few men leered in my direction, but none of them made a move toward me. Proof that men of any sentient species can be taught.

Also proof that having a bad-ass tanuki bouncer who sometimes fills in behind the bar can work wonders for the female employees of a place like the Freakshow. I waded my way through bodies to the bar, where luck, timing, and the willingness to cut people off won me an open stool. The man I'd ducked under to get the seat glared at me. I flashed a bright smile and blew him a kiss, then turned my attention to the bartender currently mixing drinks for my side of the room.

"Ryan, I require something so horrifically alcoholic that it makes livers tremble with fear and run for their lives when its name is uttered," I said solemnly.

Ryan raised an eyebrow. "Or I could get you a martini glass filled with club soda and garnished with something that makes it look like you're actually drinking liquor for a change. That way when you left the bar, you might not fall off the nearest available rooftop."

I grinned. "That sounds good. Let's do that."

"Why am I not surprised?" asked Ryan—but he was laughing as he said it, and he kept laughing as he moved to get me my drink. A woman bellied up to the bar next to me, giving his ass an appreciative look. Now, I'm happy to admit that Ryan has a fantastic rear end. He not only works out, he's a therianthrope, a shapeshifter who gets his connection to the wild side through magic and genetics, not a curse-turned-infection. Plus, how many six-five half-Japanese hotties do you find on the street, even in Manhattan? Ryan was prime man-flesh on the hoof.

There was one small complication: "His girlfriend works here," I informed the woman, blithely.

She turned the measuring look she'd been applying to Ryan's ass on me, expression clearly telegraphing my failure to live up to whatever rating system she was using. "Oh, really?"

"Yes, really," I said, stung. I may be short, but five-two is a respectable height, and I don't have any unpleasant birth defects, or share my little sister's taste in clothes. I'm a natural blonde, even though my particular line of work means I have to keep my hair cut Mia Farrow-short, and spending three hours a day at dance practice has guaranteed me the kind of figure that stops salsa judges in their tracks. Sure, I was covered in glitter and wearing what looked like Victorian underwear, but there are a lot of men who'd find that a plus. Ryan among them: Istas believes in glitter and petticoats the way some people believe in God.

The woman sniffed. "I'll take my chances."

I narrowed my eyes. "Uh-huh." There was a moment when I considered abandoning my efforts to warn her, but quite honestly, a little snottiness wasn't enough to earn her a broken arm. Maybe a sprain or something. "I'm not the girlfriend in question. She is." I indicated Istas, who was bussing tables on the other side of the room. She was dressed in her gothic Lolita best, a fashion statement that didn't stand out nearly as much as it used to now that the whole club was done in steampunk-meets-Hot Topic circus style. "Just a friendly warning. She's the jealous type."

"She should be," said the woman, giving Ryan's ass one more approving glance. Then, with a final sneering look at me, she turned and blended back into the crowd.

I was still looking sulkily in her direction when Ryan waved a hand in front of my eyes, calling my attention back to him. "Earth to Verity, come in, Verity. You checked out on me for a minute there. Have the mice been letting you sleep?"

"I think letting me sleep is against their religion."

"You *are* their religion."

"And in their cosmology, the gods have no need for silly little things like 'sufficient rest.'" I picked up the club soda Ryan set in front of me. Tonight's garnish involved a lemon wedge, a chunk of mango, and yes, a little paper umbrella. "Seriously, though, I've been interviewing hidebehinds all week, and I'm a little worn out."

Ryan started to answer me, but stopped himself before the first word could form. Straightening to his full height, he fixed his eyes on a point just behind me in the crowd, all but glowering. "You have company."

There's only one man I know in New York City who can get that kind of rise out of Ryan. I took a deliberate sip of my club soda before removing the paper umbrella from the glass, drying its toothpick handle on my napkin, and sticking it jauntily behind one ear. Then I turned, cocking my head and directing a winsome smile at the man standing there.

"Want a drink?" I asked. "I'm buying."

"We need to talk," replied Dominic.

That's the Covenant for you: never using five words when four extremely ominous ones will do. I slid off my hard-won bar stool, taking one more drink from my club soda before putting it down on the bar. "I'll get my coat," I said, and stalked toward the dressing room door, leaving Dominic De Luca waiting alone in the crowd that clustered around the bar.

I couldn't even get a little peace and quiet in a cryptid-owned burlesque club. What's the world coming to these days?

Three

"Any man who doesn't believe in carrying
weapons on a first date is not a man worth
knowing."

—Frances Brown

The halls of the Freakshow, a burlesque club for the adventurous soul

THE HALL OUTSIDE the dressing room and employee
break room was briefly deserted, thanks to the shift
change. One shift's-worth of dancers and floor staff were
out in the main club, working, while the other employees
were taking their scheduled opportunity to grab a drink,
a smoke, or whatever else their biology demanded. The
dragon girls were probably doing Goldschläger shots at
the bar. It sounded more extravagant than it was, since
they never paid for anything. What's the point of being a
preternaturally hot chick in a club full of men if you can't
get someone to buy you the occasional drink? Carol was
almost certainly in Kitty's office, drinking a cobra-venom
cocktail while she waited for her hair to wake up. That's
how it goes when you work in a cryptid-owned establishment. I've had time to get used to it. Honestly, it's even
sort of fun. I mean, how many people have jobs where
they can say "I didn't sleep last night because the mice
wouldn't stop talking" and get sympathy rather than a
referral to a psychiatrist?

I walked briskly through the empty dressing room to
my locker. If I was going to have a chat with Dominic, I

wanted to do it while I was wearing pants, and more heavily armed than it was possible to be in lace and petticoats. In addition to being a waitress and Ryan's girlfriend, Istas served as Kitty's costume designer, and she believed firmly in snaps and zippers and quick releases. Being a waheela—a type of Inuit therianthrope—meant she understood that sometimes people need to get out of their clothes in a hurry. That made them practical for work-wear, but not so much for the sort of things I was likely to get up to with Dominic De Luca.

Well. *Some* of the sort of things I was likely to get up to with Dominic De Luca, maybe. My work clothes would definitely be practical for the sweaty, naked things I sometimes wound up doing with Dominic, since I'd be able to strip in something approaching record time. That would be a nice change. During our last opportunity for naked fun times, I'd been wearing a Kevlar vest and a pair of cargo pants that practically had to be removed with the Jaws of Life. Getting naked before he had a chance to change his mind would be awesome.

I had just pulled my shirt on and was checking my hair in the tiny mirror inside my locker when the locker door slammed shut, nearly catching my fingers in the process. "Hey!" I yelped, turning to face whoever had interrupted my styling regime. "I was using that!"

Kitty looked at me coolly, one eyebrow arched in an almost perfect impression of my younger sister (who always said she was impersonating Mr. Spock, so that's probably what my boss was actually trying to do). She was still wearing her ringmaster's gear, which didn't look quite as spectacular in the empty dressing room as it did on the carefully-lit stage. People with a naturally gray skin tone shouldn't wear black leather unless they want to look like they've been standing in a smokestack for an hour or so. I'm just saying.

"Your Covenant boy is here again," she informed me.

"I know. That's why I'm leaving." I reopened my locker, grabbing a brush from the top shelf and starting to rake it through my hairspray-stiffened hair. "What's up, Kitty?"

"I thought I told you that I didn't want him here."

"You did. And I told him. Unfortunately, because I am not actually the boss of the Covenant of St. George, he chose to ignore me. I don't know *why* he decided to ignore me this time, hence the putting on pants and going to talk with him." I squinted at my reflection. I either looked pleasantly punky, if you were willing to squint and be generous with your definition of "pleasantly," or like a bleached hedgehog. Given that I was about to go have a clandestine chat with my not-a-boyfriend no-really-honest, I decided to vote for "pleasantly punky."

"You need to tell him again. He upsets the dancers."

"Uh, no, he doesn't, not really. I mean, Ryan isn't too keen on him, but that's just because he thinks Dominic is going to turn me in to the Covenant and kill everyone who works here. The dragons love him, Istas tolerates him, and even Carol says he's basically okay, for a homicidal maniac."

Kitty glowered at me. "He upsets *me*."

"That's different." I replaced my brush on the shelf, removed my backpack from its hook, and shut the locker door. "Look, I'll talk to him, but you know Dominic. He never makes a phone call when an ominous, Batman-like appearance will do. Unless you want to start posting men with guns on all the doors and windows, he's going to keep showing up."

"Like a cockroach," she muttered darkly.

"Not the most complimentary comparison ever, but I can't refute it." I turned to face her, offering a sympathetic smile. "I understand that the Covenant stresses you out, Kitty. I mean, honestly, the Covenant stresses *me* out, what with their whole 'line of traitors' approach to my family. But as long as Dominic and I are on good terms, I don't think you need to worry about this place getting purged."

Kitty didn't look particularly reassured. "And when you're not on good terms anymore?"

"Then one of us is probably dead." I shrugged. "That's the best I can do. I'm taking my break now."

"Will you be back tonight?"

"I don't know. I'm sorry."

"I should fire you."

"I know. But you won't."

Kitty's glower became a full-on scowl. "Why's that?"

"Because if you didn't have me here, you wouldn't know what the local Covenant was doing. Later, boss." I flashed her a quick smile—it wasn't returned—and scooted for the door before she could say anything about cutting my pay for the night. My mama may have raised a generation of thrill-seeking cryptid-chasers, but she didn't raise no fools.

Now for a little bit more background, since no one should ever go into a potentially sticky situation blind, and anything involving the Covenant of St. George is a potentially sticky situation. The Covenant is your classic secret organization of scholars, warriors, and assholes, dedicated to eradicating the world's "monster" population. Who decides whether something is a monster? Why, they do, which is why totally innocent cryptids have been finding themselves on the wrong end of Covenant swords for centuries. My family doesn't like them very much. Which is only fair, because they don't like *us* very much either.

Then again, that may have something to do with the fact that we were members of the Covenant until about three generations ago, when my great-great-grandfather— Alexander Healy, Sr., my brother's namesake—told them to stuff their protocols where the sun didn't shine. He took his family and decamped to North America, where they'd be reasonably out of the way. The Covenant gave them a few decades to sulk before they started sending field agents to lure the prodigals back to the fold. The family sent the first one packing. The second, Thomas Price, submitted his letter of resignation and married one of the prodigals in question—my grandmother, Alice Healy. The Covenant has had a "kill on sight" order out for my family ever since.

Or they would, if they weren't reasonably sure that we, like many breeds of cryptid, had gone extinct. We managed to disappear from their radar two generations ago, when my grandfather opened a portal to hell and messed everything up. It was a bad time. The Covenant's belief that we all died when things went wrong is about the only good thing to come out of it.

Anonymity has proven to be convenient and irritating at the same time. On the one hand, it keeps us from getting shot at—much—while we're trying to do our jobs. On the other hand, it means that we've had to find alternate means of training to protect the cryptids of the world—like my combat applications of ballroom dance, or my sister Antimony's tumbling and trapeze classes. And no matter how hard we try, we can't completely avoid encounters with the Covenant. I give you Exhibit A: Dominic De Luca, who may or may not be my boyfriend, depending on the day of the week and which one of us you decide to ask. (Hint: Normally, I'm the one disavowing all knowledge of our assignation, on account of the part where my maybe-boyfriend can be a truly massive asshole when he wants to.) We met when I stepped into a snare-trap he'd set to catch arboreal cryptids. In his defense, he didn't really expect to snag a cocktail waitress who was taking the scenic route across Manhattan. And to counter that defense, he shouldn't have been setting snares on my rooftops.

I've managed to break him of that habit. Mostly. Dominic was raised Covenant, and some habits die hard. Including, as we'd both discovered, the habit of mistrusting people you've been raised to regard as "the enemy." To him, I was the latest daughter in a long line of traitors. To me, he was the latest in an even longer line of cold-blooded killers. I mean, if it weren't for the mind-blowing sex, and the part where he saved my life six months ago—that snake cult thing again—we'd have absolutely nothing in common. Then again, my cousin Sarah says that's probably part of the appeal. He's forbidden fruit in hot brooding Italian man form, and just like Eve before me, I can't resist taking a bite or two.

Dominic was waiting for me on the roof of the club, standing silhouetted against the night sky. I stopped for a moment to admire his profile—being a cold-blooded killer may not be good for your karma, but man, does it do amazing things for your physique—before letting the stairway door swing shut behind me with a clang. "S'up?"

"The English language is beautiful, versatile, and capable of poetry that steals men's breath away from them," said Dominic, turning to face me. "Is that really the best you can manage?"

"Yup," I replied, with a sunny smile. "I went to public school."

"There are times when I listen to you and feel that the reputation of your family is completely overblown," said Dominic.

"What about the rest of the time?"

Dominic shook his head as he walked away from the edge of the roof. He stopped in front of me, turning to face me. "The rest of the time, I think my elders made a tactical error when they didn't respond to your forefathers' defection by destroying the continent."

"You say the sweetest things." I cocked my head, trying to make out his expression through the gloom. "What's up? You know Kitty doesn't like it when you visit me at work."

"I don't much care for it, either. This is not an appropriate venue for a young woman's employment."

"Why, because of all the cryptids, or because of the uniforms?"

"Is that what you call them now?"

"Hey, I wear less when I'm competing."

Dominic sighed. "Yes. I know. But at least that's to a purpose beyond coaxing cash from the unwary."

I gave him an affronted look, not particularly concerned with whether or not he'd be able to see it. "Hey, now. It's not like I'm *stripping*. I'm a respectable dancer."

"Yes, of course," he said dryly. "Whatever was I thinking?"

"I do not know." I've wanted to be a professional dancer since I was six years old—a calling that has managed to interfere with my involvement in the family business several times over the years. It's hard to find the time to spend a summer on a Greenpeace vessel concealing the plesiosaur migration from oceanographers when I need to be practicing for half a dozen upcoming competitions. Ballroom dance is a cutthroat world, and if you take so much as a long trip to Disney World, it can trash your standing for years.

Dancing for Kitty was a long way from the rarified heights of the World Tango Championships, but hell, it was dancing, and I was getting paid for it. That was close enough for me, especially where paying my rent was concerned.

Dominic frowned a little as he studied me, his expression barely visible through the dark. Finally, he asked, "Is there someplace we could go, for a brief while, where we wouldn't be observed? I have matters I need to discuss with you."

"Well, we can't go to your place, because you've never let me see where you live. And we can't go to the coffee shop, because you always get all weird when I want to 'discuss' things in public," I said slowly. "You realize what that means."

"Yes, unfortunately." Dominic sighed. "I don't suppose there's a chance that they're currently involved in some religious observance involving total silence and secluded meditation?"

I laughed. Maybe it was cruel, but I couldn't help myself. "You really don't know Aeslin mice very well, do you?"

"It was an idle hope," said Dominic. "Well. If the mice are not engaged in ritual silence, can I throw myself upon your mercy and request that we take a cab to your apartment, rather than indulging in your customary suicidal approach?"

"Nope." I leaned up onto my toes, pressing a quick kiss to his cheek. Dominic looked suitably flustered in response. Sometimes I wonder if I'd be as attracted to him if he weren't so much fun to torment. That's probably one of those things I shouldn't think about too hard. "*You* can take a cab, if you want, but I'm going to be taking the overland route."

Dominic sighed again, more deeply this time. "You're going to plummet to your demise one day, and I'm going to have to beg your cousin to notify your family, as I'm reasonably sure they'd shoot me for having been in the city when you lost your unending battle against gravity."

"And again, you say the sweetest things," I said. "Bye, now. See you at the apartment." I offered him a little wave before turning and sprinting for the edge of the roof. One step carried me onto the low retaining wall, and another step carried me over it, dropping down into the dark on the other side.

Manhattan is a city built almost entirely on the principle that you can never have too much straight up. This makes the city a free-runner's paradise and a death trap at the same time, since one moment of carelessness can result in fifteen stories of free fall, concluding with a painful introduction to the street. I've managed to avoid doing anything quite that dramatic, but I've had more than a few close calls.

The thing to remember about free-running is that energy has to go somewhere. Your momentum can either be translated into going where you want to go, or it can be taken away from you and used to send you where *gravity* wants you to go . . . and you probably don't want to go where gravity wants you to go. Continual motion reduces the chances of a fall, assuming you have the training and physical skill necessary to keep that motion under control.

I dropped like a stone for the first two stories, plummeting almost all the way back to the club before I grabbed hold of a ledge and used the energy from my fall to fling myself, hard, onto the nearby fire escape. From there, I slid down the ladder and dropped to the street below, landing with my weight balanced on my toes. The world seemed to stop for a moment, everything falling into the sweet, familiar pattern of the run. And then I was off, racing for the next building, where the dumpster would lead to the fire escape would lead to the roof would lead to the next step in my journey home . . .

Free-running in a city as vertical as Manhattan means a lot of going up just so I can go down again. It may look inefficient, but familiarity and speed make it the fastest way for me to get almost anywhere. There's rarely traffic on the rooftops, and what there is consists almost entirely of cryptids and cryptid sympathizers, almost all of whom are happy to step aside and let me pass. I'm a Price girl, after all; I'm their defender, even if I am sleeping with the enemy. But when I'm running, that doesn't matter. When I'm running, everything is simple, even the risk of a permanent fall.

I wouldn't change it for the world.

Dominic was waiting outside the door to my semilegal sublet apartment when I came trotting up the stairs. He looked calm, cool, and collected, as always. I, on the other hand, was a sweaty mess, although the endorphins generated by my run had me flying high enough that I really didn't care.

"How is it you can always get in here without me?" I asked, slowing to a walk. "I thought this building was supposed to have security."

"I have my ways."

"You stole somebody's keys, didn't you?" I used my own key to unlock the door.

Dominic looked affronted. "I did nothing of the sort," he said. "I bribed the building manager with a tale of woe concerning our lovers' spat."

"Uh-huh. Was this before or after we actually *had* one?"

"Oh, considerably before."

"Why am I not in any way surprised? Come on. Time to face the inquisition." I pocketed my keys as I pushed the door open, took a deep breath, and stepped into the apartment. Dominic followed quickly. He'd been over often enough to know what was coming, and that we needed to have the door closed before it got fully underway.

The latch had barely clicked into place when the mice filling the apartment's short entrance hall began to cheer wildly, waving their tiny banners and ritual implements in the air. "HAIL! HAIL! HAIL THE HOMECOMING OF THE ARBOREAL PRIESTESS!"

"Yeah, guys," I said, dropping my bag on the little table that was meant to hold the mail. "I'm home. Dominic's here, too, so could you maybe chill out for a while?"

"HAIL!" shouted the mice, overcome with ecstasy at the idea of having *two* humans they could cheer at. "HAIL THE VISITATION OF THE GOD OF QUESTIONABLE MOTIVATIONS!"

Dominic raised his eyebrows. "Is that my divinity this week?"

"Apparently so." My family has been living with Aeslin mice for generations. They're tiny, furry religious fanatics, and they worship us as their gods. No, I'm not quite sure how it started, but it's pretty standard for the Aeslin; every colony anyone has ever encountered has been deeply, religiously devoted to something . . . and there's no law requiring that the "something" make any sense whatsoever. We put up with them because they're cute, and because they're useful. Aeslin mice turn everything they witness into religious ritual, and their oral history is impeccable.

According to the Aeslin, all the women in my family are priestesses, connecting them directly to the divine, and all the men are gods. Maybe that's a little sexist of them, but hey, they're talking mice. If they want to enforce their own weird ideas of human gender roles, we're willing to let them, if only to avoid the necessity of answering their questions about human sexuality. Believe me, there are worse things in this world than being considered a priestess. Since Dominic's been sleeping with me, the mice have been trying various labels on him, looking for the one that fits. My personal favorite was the week they spent calling him "the God of Absolutely Never Smiling, No, Not Ever." They did it because they felt it was accurate. I enjoyed it because it annoyed the crap out of him.

The mice were still cheering, although it was less uniform than it had been when we first arrived. I hunkered down, scanning the throng until I spotted the pigeon-skull hat worn by the current leader of the colony. "Dominic and I need to talk, and we need to do it without interruptions," I said. "What's the price for an hour of privacy?"

"An Offering must be Made!" replied the mouse priest, without hesitation. I could actually hear the capital letters in the middle of the sentence.

I thought about what was in the fridge for a moment before saying, "Tomorrow's grocery day. Will you accept a box of Hostess cupcakes and some sharp cheddar for now?"

This required a quick conference with the mice around him before he looked up and nodded, banging his kitten-bone staff against the floor to signal his acceptance. "It will suffice," he intoned.

"Great. Dominic, I'll meet you in the living room."

"Naturally." He was only shuddering a little as he turned and beat a hasty retreat away from the colony. That was a big improvement. Dominic might be tolerant of my cryptid-loving lifestyle, but the Aeslin mice still creeped him right the hell out, maybe because they insisted on staring at him constantly, waiting for him to prove his godhood. And this is why neither I nor my siblings ever brought home any dates during high school.

It took me about five minutes to get the mice sufficiently placated, and hence out of our hair for at least the next half hour. They were still doing their rapturous dance in celebration of the Coming of Cheese and Cake when I left the kitchen and walked down the short hall to the living room. Dominic was sitting on the side of the couch that wasn't completely covered by my dance costumes.

"All done," I said, moving to lean up against an open patch of wall. "So what did we need all this privacy for?"

"Verity . . ." Dominic hesitated. Then he stood, looking at me solemnly. "I must ask—no, I must *beg*—that you not become upset until you have heard everything I need to say. It is very important that you understand everything I have come here to tell you, and why this discussion needed to happen both immediately and in secret. May I have your assurance that you will remain calm?"

"Dominic, what's going on?" I straightened, unconsciously trying to match the seriousness in his stance. "Is everything okay?"

"Please. Your assurance."

"Yeah, sure. I'm a pretty calm person, you know that."

It was a sign of how concerned he was that he didn't even roll his eyes at such a blatant lie. Instead, he continued, "I have become fond of you, frustrating and impossible as you are, and I have learned a great deal about the unnatural races with which we share this planet through our association. It's difficult to view them all as monsters when so many of them seem to be genuinely decent individuals, damned solely by the accident of their birth."

"I'll be sure to tell Sarah you said so," I said dryly.

Dominic ignored me. "I do not wish any harm to you, or to the people—and yes, I admit now that they *are* people—to whom you have introduced me. Please understand that."

"Dominic?" I bit my lip, looking at him warily. "You're starting to freak me out a little bit here."

"Good," he said, with surprising fervency. "You *should* be 'freaked out.' You need to leave, Verity. You need to take your mice, and your cousin, and anything and anyone else you care about in this city, and *leave*."

My eyes widened. "What?"

"Get out of here. Please, while you still can."

"What the *hell* are you talking about?" I took a step forward, shock fading into anger as I scowled at him. "Stop talking like Covenant and start speaking English, or I swear to God, I will start introducing you to my knives."

"I've already met most of them," said Dominic, and sighed, shoulders slumping. He reached out one hand, pressing his fingers against my cheek. "Verity, the Covenant is coming. They're coming here. They want to check my work. They want to verify my reports."

"What . . . ?" I breathed.

Dominic nodded very slightly, like the gesture pained him. "They're coming to see how close I am to beginning the purge. Run, Verity. Run now, while you still can. If you're here when they arrive, they'll kill you."

Four

"The question you have to ask yourself before you run away is this: am I running because I have no choice, or am I running because I'm afraid? And if I'm running because I'm afraid, will I actually escape, or will I just delay the inevitable?"

—Evelyn Baker

A semilegal sublet in Greenwich Village, about thirty seconds later

"WHAT?" I REPEATED, loudly enough that the mice actually stopped celebrating for a few seconds. They've lived with my family long enough to learn that, sometimes, shouting means it's time to scramble for the nearest hidey-hole.

Their exultations resumed when my question wasn't followed by gunfire. The mice may have learned some self-preservation, but there's nothing in this world or any other that can interrupt Aeslin religious rites for very long.

Dominic, on the other hand, looked genuinely upset. "This wasn't my idea, Verity, you have to believe me. I tried to convince them that there was no reason for them to send a team to check up on me, but my superiors feel that this is too large a territory for me to control on my own. They want to see for themselves that things are going as well as I've claimed."

"And are they? Going as well as you claimed? How

many cryptids do they think you've killed?" I couldn't
quite keep the edge out of my tone. It wasn't his fault, and
I knew it—if Dominic had wanted to sell me out to the
Covenant, he would never have warned me that they
were on their way. That didn't stop all the old demons
from rearing their heads, the ones that said this was always going to be the way things ended. That Covenant
boys don't change what they are just because Price girls
are occasionally stupid enough to fall into bed with them,
and I'd been a fool for trying to tell myself otherwise.

"That's not fair," he said quietly.

"When are they going to get here?"

"Soon."

"Could you be a little more precise? Tomorrow? Next
week? Next month? Should I even bother to run?"

"Goddammit, Verity, can you stop being angry with
me for one second and just *think?* I'm not telling you this
because I want to gloat! I'm trying to help. I'm trying to
give you a chance—"

"You can't." My anger was suddenly gone, replaced
by a resignation so deep it felt like it ran all the way
down to my bones. "There's no way I can evacuate the
entire cryptid population of Manhattan. Even if I wanted
to try, they'd have nowhere to go. It would be chaos. And
if I can't get them all out, I can't go."

"Verity. They're not—" He stopped speaking so
abruptly that for a moment, I thought he might have actually bitten his tongue. Somehow, that just made me feel
even more resigned.

"You were about to say that they weren't worth staying here and maybe getting myself killed over, weren't
you?" He didn't answer me. "Come on, Dominic. Tell me
that I'm wrong. All I'm asking you to do is look me in the
eye and tell me that I'm wrong."

"I can't," he said, very quietly.

I nodded. "I sort of figured that was what you were
going to say. Did you really think I could run and leave
them all here to die? Did you think I was that much of a
coward?"

He didn't say anything. He didn't have to. The look on

his face was all the answer that I needed from him, and it broke my heart a little bit to see it.

"I see." I took a breath, drawing myself as upright as I could. It helped if I told myself that this was another form of Paso Doble, the only form of Latin dance whose competitive form was as much a battle as anything else. "Thank you for the warning. I'll take it from here."

Dominic's eyes widened in visible alarm. "Verity, please. Don't do anything rash."

"I'm a Price girl, remember? We specialize in rash, with the occasional side order of outright stupid." I straightened a little. "I think you'd better go."

"I wish you wouldn't be like this."

"If wishes were horses, we'd have a way easier time feeding the chupacabras. Now please. Go."

The mice were still celebrating in the kitchen, but that sound seemed to drop away, leaving nothing but Dominic, and me, and the sudden silence stretching out between us. I'd always known that we came from different worlds, and that we'd have to go back to them someday. I'd just been telling myself that we'd have longer than this. And I'd been wrong.

"Very well," he said finally. He walked back to the door, shoulders ramrod-straight beneath that damn pretentious duster he was so fond of. The mice cheered louder as he approached them, and he nodded genially in their direction—a small kindness, but one that showed how much he'd grown. How much I *thought* he'd grown. I was starting to realize I'd never known him at all.

He only looked back once, dark brown eyes pained above a mouth that was set as firmly as his shoulders. Then he opened the apartment door, and he was gone, leaving me alone.

The sound of a door swinging shut had never seemed so final.

It felt like I was moving in slow motion as I walked across the living room to where I'd dropped my bag. My cell phone was tucked safely into the front pocket. It took me three tries to make the zipper work, and another five tries before I could successfully access my contact list and call the one number that had a prayer of helping: Home.

Covenant "purges" are legendary in most cryptid circles, including the ones my family moves in. The Covenant of Saint George sends in a team of their best men, and when the dust clears and the blood has been hosed off the streets, nothing inhuman remains standing. When Dominic had first arrived in Manhattan, I'd asked my father to look up any historical records relating to purges in the New York area. The things he'd been able to find were bad enough to give me nightmares for weeks, and that was saying something, given all the other nightmare fodder that particular summer had offered me.

Some people call the Covenant "monster hunters," and if there's anything that demonstrates how wrong that label really is, it's the way they purge a city. True hunters spare the children and the pregnant females, allowing the population to remain stable. That's how they ensure that they'll always have something to hunt. The Covenant has no such concerns. They don't *want* to ensure that they'll always have something to hunt. They want to wipe every breathing cryptid off the face of the planet. I don't *know* that they give out merit badges for confirmed extinctions, but I wouldn't be surprised.

The members of the Covenant aren't monster hunters. They're exterminators.

The phone rang for what seemed like forever but was probably only a few seconds. Then my father's voice was in my ear, asking in that warm, familiar tone, "Why shouldn't I hang up on you? You have five seconds."

My family has been answering the home phone as rudely as possible for as long as I can remember. It's a mechanism for screening calls without raising suspicion from the wrong quarters. As far as we're concerned, that's pretty much everyone who isn't a relative or on the extremely short list labeled "allies."

"Dad, it's me," I said.

"Verity!" he said, delighted. "That's an excellent reason not to hang up on you. Hello, sweetheart. What's going on? Shouldn't you be at work?"

"Yes. Normally, I would be. Daddy, there's a problem."

His tone sobered in an instant. "Are you all right?"

"I'm fine."

"Honey, you don't *sound* fine. Is it Sarah?"

"Not yet." Any purge of Manhattan would naturally affect her . . . assuming the Covenant could find her. There's nothing in this world or any other that hides as well as a cuckoo that doesn't want to be found, and that includes the hidebehinds.

"Then what's going on?"

"It's the Covenant, Daddy." I walked back to the couch and sat down, covering my face with my free hand. That helped, a little. Maybe if I stuck my head under something and waited patiently, the Covenant would go away. "Dominic says they're coming to check his work. They want to see how far along he is in preparing the city for a purge. Which means the next step is either them figuring out that he isn't prepared at all, or the Covenant starting the purge."

There was a long pause before my father asked, "Did he tell you this?"

"Yes."

"Is he there with you now?"

"No. I asked him to leave."

There was another, longer pause. Finally, my father said, "I don't think you should have done that."

"What?" I straightened, pulling my hand away from my face. "Who are you, and what have you done with my father?"

"If he was willing to tell you that the team was coming—"

"—but not willing to stand up to the Covenant! Not willing to stop them from—"

"—then he may be willing to work with you to minimize the damage to the population." My father's tone was firm, and left little room for argument. He's been in charge of our branch of the family since before I was born, and that means he's had time to get very, very good at giving orders to people who aren't very good at taking them. "I know it's hard. I can tell that you feel betrayed right now."

"Um, just a little. Why are you on his side?" I stood, pacing across the living room to the hallway door. The mice were finishing up their celebration. I stopped there, leaning against the wall and watching them. At least the mice could still find things to be happy about. "I thought we hated the Covenant."

"I also thought you'd decided that Dominic deserved to be judged as an individual."

I didn't say anything.

Dad sighed. "Verity. Please. I'm glad you called me. That was the right thing to do, and I'll do my best to get you some backup. But that doesn't mean you can neglect the resources that you already have at hand. I'm not telling you to trust him. I'm telling you to use him, for as long as you possibly can."

"Hold on a second," I said, my stomach sinking. "Are you telling me that you *might* be able to send me backup, and that until then, I have to work with the man who may or may not be in the process of selling me out to the people we've been hiding from since before I was born?" I paused. "I lost track of that sentence somewhere in the middle. Dad, you *can't*. You can't expect me to work with him. Not now."

"You have to."

"I won't."

"Are you saying that because you think it's the right thing to do, or because he hurt your feelings by not cutting ties with everything he's ever known as soon as it came into conflict with what you wanted?" I didn't have an answer for that, so I didn't even try. Dad kept talking: "I know this is hard. I will do everything I can to get you the help you need. But Dominic is right there, Very, and he wouldn't have told you if he didn't want to help, at least a little."

My voice was very small as I asked, "What if he

doesn't want to help me anymore? I turned him down hard."

"Then we'll figure something else out."

"Okay." I pushed away from the wall, turning my back on the mice. "What do I tell Sarah?"

"Tell her that she should come home. She has no business staying in that city while a purge is going on."

I wanted to make a snarky comment about how he'd leave me to die while he evacuated my adopted cousin for her own good. I couldn't do it because he was right. I was raised fighting, whether I wanted to or not. Sarah was raised doing her homework, obeying curfew, and trying to pass for human without constantly rearranging the brains of the people around her. She could keep herself out of sight better than damn near anyone else in the world, but she wouldn't be any help if things got really bad.

"I'll tell her," I said, quietly. "I can't promise that she'll listen."

"Of course not," he said, and laughed. "She's a member of this family, isn't she?"

"Yeah," I agreed. "She is."

Dad and I talked for a few minutes after that, but if anything of substance was discussed, I didn't remember it after I hung up. All I really remembered was the tone of his voice, struggling to reassure me without letting his own panic show. It's times like that that make me wish my parents were just a little better at lying to me. It would be nice to have them say, "Don't worry, honey, everything's under control," and actually be able to make myself believe them.

I found myself back in the kitchen doorway, watching the mouse acolytes as they dutifully cleaned up the remains of their celebration. I don't really understand the full details of the Aeslin religious structure. I don't think anyone human—or even demi-human, like Sarah or my

Uncle Ted—can. The logic of the Aeslin is not like our Earth logic.

One of the acolytes noticed my observation and straightened, tiny oil-drop eyes fixed on me in rapt fascination. "Priestess," it said, solemnly. "I am Blessed by your Observance."

Nobody pronounces capital letters like an Aeslin mouse. "Hey," I said. "Do you know when the night prayers will be over? I need to talk to the Head Priest at some point."

"The Catechism of the Patient Priestess is to be recited tonight," said the acolyte. "It should conclude with the sunrise. Would you like me to go to the Head Priest, and request his Attendance upon your Holiness?"

The Patient Priestess was their name for my great-great-grandmother, Enid Healy, who belonged to the Covenant of St. George, once upon a time, before she and her husband wised up, quit, and moved to America. According to the mice, she was a really awesome lady. I wish I'd had the opportunity to meet her, but, well. My family isn't exactly the "live long and die peacefully in your bed" sort. She was killed a long time before my parents were born.

"That's okay," I said, crouching down to put myself more on the acolyte's level. "I can talk to him when the catechism is over. Have you been to this recitation before?"

"No, Priestess," said the acolyte, with obvious reverence. "I am very excited by the knowledge that this will be a night filled with Revelations and Enlightenments."

My family's colony of Aeslin have so many religious rituals at this point that even the supposedly yearly rites don't actually come around on a yearly basis anymore. There was a ten-year gap between recitations of the Catechism of the Violent Priestess—my great-grandmother, Frances Healy. Then again, that may have been because Mom yelled at the mice about the property damage every time they performed those particular devotions.

At least the revelations and enlightenments offered by Enid's life story weren't as likely to hurt the apartment's security deposit. The Sasquatch I was subletting from probably wouldn't take "but the mice had religious needs" as much of an excuse.

Crap. I needed to call her answering service and tell her that there might be a purge coming. If I died trying to stop it, she could come home to a very, very bad situation. Considering I'd been living out of her apartment for almost a year, that didn't seem fair.

"Well, if you see the Head Priest before the services begin, and he doesn't look too busy, can you let him know that I'll be coming to see him sometime around dawn?"

"Yes, Priestess," said the acolyte.

"Cool. Thanks." I straightened, picking up my backpack in the process. "I'll be back later. Don't burn down the apartment."

The small audience of previously unnoticed mice that had come to watch with rapt attention as I spoke to the acolyte suddenly cheered. Loudly. "HAIL THE COMMITMENT TO NOT IGNITE THE DOMICILE!"

"Uh, yeah," I agreed. "No fire."

"HAIL THE ABSENCE OF FIRE!"

"I'll just be going now," I said, and fled, before the mice could launch fully into some sort of ritualized fire-safety lesson. Sometimes being one of the holy figures of my own personal church was more trouble than it was worth.

Dominic didn't pick up when I called his cell phone. I didn't have his home number, assuming he even had one; I'd never seen the place where he lived. He could have been emulating Sarah, and just moving from hotel to hotel, keeping a roof over his head without tying himself to a permanent address. The more I thought about it, the more it seemed like I'd been deluding myself all along. There was no way he'd ever really trusted me.

Still, I needed to put that aside, at least for right now, and figure out how I was going to deal with the very real threat of a Covenant purge. I broke into a run as I pushed my phone deep into the front pocket of my jeans, building to a full-out sprint. I needed to find Dominic. I needed to start warning people. And there was nothing saying I couldn't combine the two.

Gravity took over once I stepped off the edge of the roof, and I was able to push other concerns aside in favor of the pressing need to keep myself from splashing on the pavement. That's one of the nice things about free-running; it's very distracting when I need it to be. I'm focused enough on my surroundings that I can usually avoid things that present an actual danger, like pissed-off cryptids or booby-traps, but I don't need to think about my faltering dance career, or the fact that the man I'd been starting to think about as maybe being my boyfriend wasn't really boyfriend material, or the upcoming Covenant purge. All I have to think about is the run.

My first destination was a little café called Gingerbread Pudding. Going there wouldn't help me find Dominic. It *would* help me begin the process of warning the city's cryptids that they needed to keep their heads down and maybe consider taking that California vacation they'd been dreaming about. I was telling the truth when I told Dominic that there was no way I could evacuate the entire city. That didn't mean I had to leave the people I considered my friends unprepared for what was coming.

Letting go of the last rooftop between me and my destination, I dropped down, into the dark beyond.

🐀

The hours posted outside of the Gingerbread Pudding storefront said that they were open until nine PM, and a cheery sign in the window told me to come back tomorrow for fresh sweets and the best hot chocolate in New York. I can testify to the quality of both the baked goods and the hot drinks, but coming back tomorrow wasn't an option. I banged on the door. Politely. When five minutes passed without anyone coming to let me in, I banged again, impolitely this time.

"Hey!" I half-whispered, half-shouted, pressing my mouth up to the crack in the door. "Sunil! Rochak! Come let me in, I need to talk to you!"

I was starting to consider breaking and entering when I heard the bolt on the door being undone, and the door swung soundlessly open, revealing a smoking-hot Indian man in his mid-twenties. Note that the word "human" was nowhere in that sentence. Sunil was a Madhura, a type of humanoid cryptid. His skin was a rich, medium brown, and his hair was a few shades darker, distinguishable from black only because his brother, Rochak, had hair that was even darker. Their sister Piyusha's coloring had been somewhere in-between, with lighter brown eyes like Sunil's and true black hair like Rochak's.

Piyusha had been sacrificed by the snake cult that was trying to wake the dragon sleeping under the city. I tried to save her. I hadn't been fast enough. There were reasons I thought warning her brothers about the coming purge was really the least that I could do.

Sunil didn't look surprised to see me. "It's late," he said.

"I know. I'm as diurnal as you are, but this is sort of an emergency. Did I wake you? Can I come in?"

"No, you didn't wake me, and yes, you can come in. Rochak is in the café kitchen heating up some gingerbread." Sunil stepped to one side, waving for me to enter. I did, blinking at him.

"Were you expecting me?"

"Yes," said Dominic. I snapped my head around so fast it made my ears ring. He was standing in the doorway to the private dining alcove, a festively-decorated little nook with a single table and no windows opening on the outside. That was how I'd been able to miss the light. "I was hoping you'd come here after you finished calling your family. Did you convey my regards to your father?"

"Not this time," I said. Sunil closed the door behind me, pulling the shade a little tighter. I barely noticed. My attention was focused on Dominic. "Why are you here?"

"Because I knew you would come." He smiled a little, indicating Sunil with one hand. "You are a deeply infuriating woman, but you're also a dependable one. I knew you'd start by warning your friends. The dragons will panic. Then they will demand explanations and protection, all of which will take a great deal of time. You were going to begin either here or with your cousin."

"And she can wait," I said softly. "Dominic . . ."

"Why don't you go sit down?" asked Sunil. "I'll help Rochak in the kitchen." He looked uncomfortable, maybe because very few cryptids who've seen a one-on-one meeting between a Price and a member of the Covenant have walked away unwounded.

"Thanks, Sunil," I said. He flashed me a smile, and left.

Dominic, meanwhile, gestured for me to follow him into the dining nook. He'd clearly been there for a while; a half-empty cup of hot cocoa was sitting in front of one seat, and his duster was hanging from a hook on the wall. He didn't say anything as he sat, picked up his cup, and looked at me.

"I'm sorry about before," I said awkwardly, sitting down across from him. "I know you were trying to help. My reaction was out of line."

Dominic sipped his cocoa. "Yes," he agreed. "It was. To be fair, however, it was unexpected information. You had good reason to react as you did. I may have hoped that you would respond better, but I knew not to place all my faith in hoping."

"Dad said . . . I mean, he thinks, and maybe I think, too . . . I mean . . ." I stopped, sighing, and took a deep breath before I continued. "Dominic, there's no way we can evacuate this entire city before the Covenant gets here. And there's no way for you to prevent them from coming. I'm going to need help making sure they do as little damage as possible. Please. I need your help."

Dominic's answer was delayed by Rochak's arrival. He was carrying a plate of the café's rightfully famous gingerbread. He also had a cup of hot cocoa for me. "Hello, Verity," he said, with an honest smile.

"Hey, Rochak." For a man who accused me of killing

his sister the first time we met, Rochak has mellowed a lot where I'm concerned. I stood as he put the dishes down, giving him a quick hug. "How is everything?"

"It's been better." His eyes darted toward Dominic as he pulled away from me. "Is there really a purge coming?"

"Yes." There was no percentage in sugarcoating things. So to speak. "That's what we're talking about now."

"Sunil and I won't leave."

I bit back a sigh as I settled into my seat. "I didn't think you would. So I guess we'll just have to keep you under the radar."

"I guess so," said Rochak, and smiled again before he turned to slip out of the nook.

I looked back to Dominic, who was watching me with unguarded affection. "You are insane, infuriating, and in dire need of aid if you're going to survive this," he said. "My help was always yours. All you had to do was ask for it."

"I'm asking," I said.

"Then I'm yours." He nudged the plate of gingerbread toward me. "Gingerbread?"

"Gingerbread and tactics," I agreed, picking up a piece of piping-hot baked goodness. "Now that's a date that I can really get behind."

Dominic laughed. After a moment, I joined in.

Five

"The Covenant of St. George isn't evil, simply misguided. This doesn't mean you can't shoot them, but it does mean you should apologize to their next of kin, should the opportunity ever arise."

—Enid Healy

Downtown Manhattan, approaching the Port Hope Hotel

WE ATE HALF A PLATE of gingerbread and drank all the cocoa before coming to the conclusion that our next stop, tactically speaking, was Sarah's place. She was family, which meant she had to be warned about what was coming. Beyond that, she was the fastest way for us to tell the dragons about the situation.

No one—and I mean *no one*, my family included—hates the Covenant of St. George like the dragons do. William is the last known male of their species, largely because of the Covenant's fondness for dragon slaying. When they heard that a purge was coming, they were going to freak out. My family used to belong to the Covenant a long time ago, and the dragons have never quite forgiven us for that. If they got the news from me, things could turn ugly.

Sarah, on the other hand, is a cryptid, which makes her automatically more trustworthy than a human. It doesn't hurt that everybody wants to trust a cuckoo, right up until the cuckoo stabs them in the back, steals their wallet, and runs away to Acapulco with their life savings. She'd have a better chance of explaining what was going on than I would . . . and sending her to explain things to the dragons would put her safely underground, in William's nest, where I wouldn't have to worry about her for a little while.

In deference to Dominic's dislike of falling—and my own desire to finish eating my gingerbread, which was just as good as the sign on the door had promised it would be—I allowed him to flag down a taxi on the corner in front of Gingerbread Pudding. After checking my phone to be sure that I hadn't forgotten where Sarah was staying, I gave the driver the address for the Port Hope Hotel and settled in my seat, ignoring my dislike of New York taxis in favor of enjoying my Madhura-concocted treats.

We were about halfway there when Dominic raised his head, gave me a bewildered look, and asked, "Where are we going again?"

"To see my cousin Sarah." He still had some gingerbread left. I leaned over, snatching the last bite from his fingers before he could object. "She just changed hotels last week; that's why you can't remember where we're going. Don't worry about it."

Dominic's bewilderment lasted a few more seconds before it cleared away, replaced first by understanding, and then by an irritated scowl. "I hate the way she does that."

"I know. But she doesn't mean to, so you should really just shrug it off and wait until she stops hitting you so hard." Given sufficient exposure to Sarah, he'd develop more resistance to her passive defenses, even as she got better at reading his mind. It's a trade-off, and one that most of the family has been more than happy to make, since it means we don't literally forget that she's in the house when we can't see her.

Dominic didn't say anything. He just kept scowling.

To be honest, I understood his irritation. Camouflage is the cuckoo's primary weapon; they become a part of their surroundings, disappearing from casual view by fitting in so perfectly that it's impossible to think of them as unusual. Sarah's periodic disappearing acts were the result of instinct telling her not to stay in one place long enough to get caught—that, and hotel security systems refusing to be telepathically influenced into ignoring the fact that she was essentially a squatter. Unfortunately, the amount of telepathic static kicked up by a cuckoo in the process of changing nests has a tendency to make even allies forget what's going on, which is why I made sure to keep her latest hotel address in my phone memos.

(I encrypted the addresses, naturally, using a code key that requires intimate knowledge of the Argentine tango to break. Paranoia is a way of life when they're genuinely out to get you.)

My Grandma Angela—also a cuckoo, in addition to being both Sarah and Mom's adopted mother—says Sarah's relocations make us forget where she is because normal cuckoos don't *have* any allies. They just have enemies who happen to not be trying to kill them at that particular moment. So periodically disappearing from absolutely everybody's radar is the only way most ordinary cuckoos survive long enough to ruin the lives of everyone around them. Sarah may eventually be able to stop that from happening, but it's going to take years of practice. Luckily, she doesn't have any natural predators or catch human diseases, so unless she walks in front of a bus, she's going to live a long, long time. Cuckoos are lucky that way.

They're a charming species, the cuckoos. Except for the two that I'm technically related to, they're the only cryptid race I can think of that should really be shot on sight—assuming you'd know one when you saw one, which is questionable. As it stands, they're the only race that has absolutely no good ecological reason to exist. They're not true apex predators and they're not true parasites. They practice brood parasitism, but they usually do it in empty nests, so it's not even like they're reducing the human population (something that does occasionally need to be considered, no matter how distasteful I may find the idea).

Near as anyone can tell, the cuckoos don't serve an

otherwise unfilled purpose in any ecosystem. They just kill, and destroy, and break things for the pleasure of seeing the shards come raining down. Oh, and they do algebra. For fun. Their universal fascination with higher mathematics may be the least human thing about them.

The taxi let us off in front of the Port Hope Hotel. Dominic paid the cabbie—tipping generously, I was pleased to note—before turning to join me in studying the building. It was modest by Sarah's usual four-star standards, although it wasn't run-down by any means. For a moment, I couldn't imagine what she was doing here. Then I spotted a sign in the hotel window, and had to bite my lip to stop myself from laughing.

Dominic frowned at me. "What is it?"

"Sarah has finally returned to the Mothership," I said, pointing to the sign. He followed my finger, and then, to my surprise, Dominic De Luca laughed out loud.

Visit the Manhattan Museum of Mathematics! cajoled the sign. *Only four blocks away on East 26th Street. Math can be fun!*

"I wonder if they have souvenir postcards," Dominic said.

"I wonder if she left them any after she hit the gift shop," I countered. He laughed again. This time I joined him, and together we walked into the light of the hotel's lobby.

The telepathic static signaling Sarah's presence hit as soon as we were inside. To my surprise, it was coming from the other side of the lobby. I turned to see her waving cheerfully from the hotel's restaurant, one of those modern things where the tables also serve as the restaurant wall. It's supposed to seem homey and welcoming. I think it's a good way to cut down on the amount of cover in a firefight. My standards are perhaps not those of the people who build hotels.

Sarah was dressed in her going-to-school best—a bulky brown sweater that did absolutely nothing for her porcelain-pale complexion, and a calf-length green skirt that looked like she'd stolen it from one of the Brady Bunch kids—and her long black hair was tied into a ponytail. She had a glass of something that looked like over-thick cherry soda in the hand that wasn't busy waving.

It's ketchup and tonic water, she informed me blithely, about a half-second after my eyes hit her glass. *Delicious and a good preventative against malaria.*

"Sarah, you don't have blood as most mammals understand it. Why would you need to worry about malaria?" Dominic shot me a startled glance, and I realized that I'd spoken aloud. Dammit. "Stupid telepaths," I mumbled, chagrined.

Sorry!

No, you're not, I thought back at her, starting across the lobby toward the restaurant.

No, I'm not, Sarah agreed. She stood as we came closer, putting her ketchup soda down on the table. "What are you guys doing here? Are you hungry? They make a really fabulous lasagna here. The kitchen's technically closed, but if I asked—"

"Can we go up to your room? It's sort of important, and I'd rather not talk about it down here."

Sarah blinked, expression going momentarily confused. Then she nodded. "Sure. I was pretty much done here anyway." She picked up her soda and stepped around the table, passing over the line between the restaurant's carpet and the lobby's hardwood floor.

She didn't leave any money on the table as she toasted the hostess on duty with her glass and started toward the elevator. If I'd tried that, I would have wound up with an irritated hostess chasing me down for a signature. Sarah just got a blissful smile and an enthusiastic wave, like she was the Queen of England or something.

"Stupid telepaths," I said again, and followed Sarah.

As always, Sarah was staying in the nicest suite in the hotel, although this one was, at least, only slightly larger than my apartment. She'd been there for three days. It was already a disaster zone that would have made my mother clutch her head and weep for the future of our family.

Dominic looked around the room, frowning for a moment before he said, as delicately as he could, "You might do well by allowing the maids access to your room."

"Oh, they were just here this morning," said Sarah guilelessly. She looked at Dominic, improbably blue eyes wide, and asked, "Don't you think they did a good job?"

Dominic sputtered. Sarah giggled, hiding it behind her hand.

"Sarah, don't toy with the Covenant boy," I said sternly. "He and I have both had a long night, and it's not going to get any better from here."

"What's going on?" Sarah took a sip of her tomato soda, frowning at me. "You're reading awfully serious."

Cuckoos don't really have telepathic ethics, unless you count "loot first, *then* burn" as an ethical approach to reading someone else's mind. Grandma Angela got past this by encouraging Sarah to watch every episode, ever, of *Star Trek: the Next Generation* and *Babylon 5*. Sarah went on to augment her education with lots of comic books and classic science fiction. End result, a very polite psychic geek who won't invade your brain without permission. Most of the time.

I took a breath, trying to figure out how to word what I needed to tell her. Then I looked helplessly at Dominic. He frowned, squared his shoulders, and turned to Sarah.

"Please read my mind," he said. "It will be the simplest way to convince you both of the urgency of this situation and my role in it. In this one instance, I give you my consent."

Sarah's eyes widened. "Uh." The Covenant of St. George specializes in hating cryptids, and Dominic was still a member of the Covenant, no matter how relaxed he was becoming about associating with "monsters" like my cousin. Him giving her permission to read his mind was huge, and she had no idea how to deal with it. Finally, she went with the easy option: "Okay. Um, just clear your mind of everything but what you want me to see, and try not to think about Verity naked, okay?"

Dominic reddened. I smirked. Telling people not to think about nudity is the best way to make *sure* they think about nudity. That was intentional. If you're busy trying frantically not to picture someone's tits, you're not thinking about keeping the telepath out of your head. Sarah says it's a good way to get around a person's natural defenses.

Sarah's eyes began to glow white. The brightness rapidly increased, until her pupils and irises had been completely obscured. Then her eyes widened again, mouth falling open in a horrified "oh." "They're coming *here*?" she demanded, in a voice that couldn't decide whether it wanted to be a whisper or a squeak, and wound up demonstrating the attributes of both.

"Yes," said Dominic gravely.

"They—you—how can you let them do these things?" The glow in Sarah's eyes went off as she broke contact with Dominic's mind. Her entire body seemed to shudder, and she took a long step backward, away from him. "You know what they're coming here to do. I know you know. I *saw* it."

"And you also know that I did not invite them, and that I am here to help." Dominic sighed deeply. "Believe me, Sarah, I was raised to want nothing more than to be able to join my brethren in cleansing this city without remorse. Part of me still wants to be sure in my mission, confident in the righteousness of the Covenant's purpose. But I can't. I can't be that man anymore."

"This is why they call you people dangerous, you know," Sarah said, looking at me. "He's telling the truth." She paused, gaze swinging back to Dominic. "That's really why you wanted me to go into your head, isn't it? So I could tell Very that you were being sincere when you said you wanted to help us not wind up dead."

"I told her myself; I doubt that she fully believed me," said Dominic calmly. "This seemed the simplest way to answer everyone's questions."

"You let a cryptid poke around inside your head, so

I'd believe that you wanted to be a good guy?" I asked. "Wow. You really have learned a lot."

"That, or you truly are the foul, corrupting beast that my elders would make you out to be." Somehow, Dominic managed to make that sound like an endearment. He looked toward Sarah. "We need your help."

"I know. I picked that up, too. You seriously want me to go into the Nest and tell the dragons that the Covenant is en route? I mean, that's how you think I should be spending my night? I have class in the morning, you know."

I smiled a little. "You mean you have a chat date with Artie in a few hours. Can't you reschedule?"

Sarah didn't blush—she's not physiologically capable of blushing, since she doesn't have hemoglobin in her blood—but she did wrinkle her nose and scowl at me before relenting and saying, "I'll email him. Can we not tell him there's supposed to be a purge coming? I don't want to freak him out."

"You know he's going to find out from Dad, and then he's going to be pissed that you didn't tell him yourself."

"I know. But I'd rather he be pissed at me later, when this is over, than panicking at me now, when I have other things to worry about." Sarah sighed. "I guess I'm going to miss class too, huh?"

"Depends. Do you think the dragons will finish freaking out in time for you to get a decent night's sleep? It's only eleven-thirty."

Sarah gave me a withering look. She didn't say anything aloud, but in my head I heard, *Dominic is really worried about you. Me, too, a little bit, but mostly you. I think you should be cautious.*

Why? I asked. *Do you think he's going to hand me to the Covenant?*

No. But I think there's a pretty good chance that he'll drug your drink and you'll wake up on a Greyhound bus bound for somewhere in the Midwest. He doesn't want you to get hurt.

On a scale of one to ten . . .

If he's not playing straight, he's got shields I can't break past without a lot of effort. For right now, I'm assuming he's telling us the truth.

The subject of our furtive mental discussion was looking at us with weary annoyance. "I can tell when you're discussing me telepathically, you know," he said. "Despite my never having sought to develop this particular skill, I've learned to recognize the signs."

"We're educational," I said blithely. "Sarah's afraid you're going to drug me and dump me on a bus to get me out of town."

"I'll admit, the thought did cross my—" Dominic stopped and scowled. "I do not appreciate the violation of my privacy."

"You invited me in," Sarah countered. "I can't help what I see while I'm in there. I wasn't snooping, but the image of getting Verity the hell out of Dodge was pretty prominent in your thoughts."

"And I'm not in the mood to play the fainting flower and get shipped off," I said. "We all clear on that point?"

Dominic sighed. "Sadly, yes."

"Good. Sarah, can you please get to the dragons tonight? Let them know the Covenant is coming, and we don't know anything more than that, but that they have my word that we'll do everything we possibly can to keep William safe." Female dragons are the ultimate pragmatists. William's wives would be perfectly happy to die if that was what it took for him to survive the purge. I guess that's one of the perks that comes with being the last known male of your species.

"Just let me email Artie and I'll head right down."

"That works. As soon as you're done at the Nest, I want you to head for the airport and catch the next plane home." Sarah wouldn't need a ticket. That was one more bonus of being a cuckoo. She could waltz past security without showing ID, and the airline would mysteriously find her an unclaimed First Class seat.

"No," said Sarah calmly.

I blinked. "No? What do you mean, no?"

"I mean no. The Covenant isn't going to find me. You need me, Verity. I'm the ultimate spy. Dominic was thinking it, even though he was trying not to, because he didn't want to upset you. You need me to stay here and help. I'll do it, because if I let you get killed, your mother's going to be *so* mad." Sarah looked at me calmly. "You can argue if you want, but I'll just change hotels and not tell you where I am."

"I hate you sometimes," I said.

"I know."

I sighed. "But also I love you. I do appreciate this, Sarah."

Sarah smiled. "I know that, too."

"Dominic and I are going back to the Freakshow. I need to tell the staff we're about to have issues and make sure everyone knows what to do when the Covenant comes to town."

"Okay."

"Okay," I echoed, and moved to hug her before heading toward the door. "Don't be a hero, Sarah."

She laughed at that. "I'm the last person in the world you need to worry about there. I'll call if I hear anything."

The convenient thing about having a telepath in the family: she never runs out of batteries, and she doesn't depend on the cell towers for service. "Gotcha. Good luck down there."

"Miss Zellaby," said Dominic, with a small nod. Then he turned, and followed me to the door, out to the hall, and into the elevator.

"That went surprisingly well," I said.

"Yes," he agreed blandly. "Now let's go figure out what can go surprisingly poorly."

"Don't worry," I said, as the elevator doors closed. "I'm sure we can find something."

Six

"We aren't exiles from the Covenant of St. George. We're natives in our own country, and when that country is endangered, it's our duty to dig in our heels and fight. If we aren't willing to save ourselves, how can we expect anyone else to save us?"

—Alice Healy

The Freakshow, a highly specialized nightclub somewhere in Manhattan

"So this is what the street-level entrance looks like these days," I said, as Dominic and I approached the front door of the Freakshow.

It was painted to look like the mouth of a tent, with old-fashioned "carnival posters" pasted to the wall all around the ticket booth. I recognized myself in the middle of a cancan lineup, one painted leg eternally cocked at a come-hither angle that I hoped never to have to explain to my father. Sometimes I think the dangers of my mundane career outweigh the dangers of the career that's more likely to get me actually killed. Vivisection hurts, but it can't hold a candle to parental disapproval.

Dominic followed my gaze to the poster in question, quirking an eyebrow before he said, "Surely this can't be the first time you've approached from the ground."

"I hate taxis, subways freak me right the hell out, I don't have a car, and no one who isn't a bike messenger, certifiable, or both tries to ride a bike in Manhattan." I shrugged. "I stick to the rooftops. It's worked out pretty well for me so far."

"You mean you haven't reduced yourself to a street pancake due to a misjudged leap."

"That's what I said, isn't it? It's worked out pretty well so far." I flashed my ID at the girl in the ticket booth, another dragon I didn't recognize. She looked up from filing her nails only long enough to confirm that I didn't need to pay admission—and that, by extension, Dominic didn't either—before rolling her eyes in disgust and pointing toward the door.

"One day you will have to tell me where you acquired this aversion to walking on solid ground," said Dominic.

"Try having a baby sister whose idea of a good time involves pit traps and land mines," I advised. The bouncer on duty opened the club door for us, and I smiled at him as we walked on through. "It's amazing how fast that sort of thing will make you think it's time for a return to the trees."

The entry hall was decorated to match the door: green canvas tent fabric draped with strings of Christmas lights and little triangular banners obscured the walls and ceiling, making it seem like we were heading into the big top. Even the floor was covered in a layer of sweet-scented sawdust, reinforcing the carnival theme. I had to admire it as a cost-cutting measure. The cedar shavings were probably saving Kitty a fortune in air fresheners, and she could buy them from the Abatwa who lived under Broadway, which would save her even more. If you need a corner cut, talk to a bogeyman.

Ryan was on duty at the interior door, less to check the work of the first two gatekeepers and more to make it clear to any drunk businessmen looking for a little grab-ass that we were a respectable establishment that would kick your nuts into your nasal cavity if you so much as looked at one of the girls wrong. He blinked when he saw me come walking down the hall. He blinked again when he saw Dominic walking behind me.

"Verity?" he said, an uncertain note in his voice.

"You're on the ground. Are you okay?" His eyes flicked to my feet, not-too-subtly checking for a limp.

Dominic snorted. "You really were serious." He stepped up next to me, offering Ryan a nod. "Hello again."

"Twice in one night," Ryan said, with a nod of his own. "You're becoming a bad habit, De Luca. Very? Is this guy bothering you?" From his tone, he was hoping I'd say yes, giving him the excuse he wanted to kick Dominic's ass.

I didn't have the heart to tell Ryan that in a fight between him and Dominic, he was probably going to lose. Sure, he was a shapeshifting badass who could turn into a giant raccoon-dog-monster-thing and render his flesh practically impermeable, but Dominic was a heavily armed monster hunter. And when it's supernatural powers versus cold, hard steel, I vote for the knives every time.

"He's not bothering me, but we're here to bother Kitty," I said. "Do you think you could get somebody to take the door for you? I'd sort of like you to be there for this."

Ryan blinked again. Then he nodded. "Sure. Why don't you head on back, and I'll see if I can get one of the other bouncers to come take over. Can Istas come, too, or is this a private party?"

"Istas should be in on this meeting, I think." Istas and Ryan represented most of the club's serious physical defenses. There was no reason not to include them as early as we could.

"Okay. We'll be right there."

I reached out to squeeze his elbow, offering a small smile, and led Dominic past him into the Freakshow proper.

The entry put us onto a low catwalk about five feet above the floor, providing a brief but panoramic view of the chaos below. I must have spent half my waking hours in the Freakshow, but that was as an employee. Now I was seeing it the way that a patron would, and that changed everything.

Girls in circus-themed outfits slithered through the crowd, in some cases literally, their cryptid attributes out in the open for everyone to see. Maybe some people thought the wings on the gargoyle girls were prosthetics, or that the sirens were into dyeing their hair, but the harpies? The bogeymen? It took an incredibly charitable—and potentially intoxicated—mind to mistake them for human women. On the stage, Jahi the wadjet was involved in a complicated dance with his snake dancer, Maibe. She gyrated her hips to the beat, seeming entirely unconcerned by the fact that she wasn't wearing much beyond a fourteen-foot cobra.

Humans mixed freely with cryptids everywhere I looked. It was exactly the sort of scene the Covenant of St. George was dedicated to preventing. "We are so screwed," I said, in a hushed tone.

"Almost certainly," Dominic agreed. "This will trigger a purge of Biblical proportions."

I shot him a look. "Way to be encouraging there, buddy."

"I'm not here to be encouraging, Verity. I'm here to make sure you get through this alive. If that means a few more lives are preserved in the bargain, then so be it." Dominic shrugged. "I am learning to accept your idiosyncrasies."

"What's sad is that for you, that's really sweet." Istas was passing through the crowd, heading back to the bar with an empty tray. I trotted quickly down the stairs, moving to intercept her before I could lose sight of her. "Istas!"

Istas turned at the sound of her name, a quizzical look on her face. The impression of utter confusion was assisted by her hair, which was up in two carefully curled pigtails, with clips of bright blue artificial hair wound through her natural glossy black. "Verity? I thought your shift ended."

"It did." I jerked a thumb toward Dominic. "He came to get me. It's been an interesting night. Think you can take your break and come back to Kitty's office? Ryan's going to be there in a minute."

Istas' confusion faded, replaced by guarded hope. "Is this meeting a prelude to carnage?"

"Yeah, I'm afraid it probably is."

"I will be right there," Istas assured me, and turned to finish heading for the bar, a definite spring in her step. I sighed, shaking my head, and motioned for Dominic to follow me to the employee door on the far wall.

"She seems excited about the prospect of a slaughter," murmured Dominic as we walked. His voice was barely audible above the thudding music coming from the club speakers.

"Yeah, well, that's a waheela for you. She likes introducing people to their insides. Only when they deserve it," I hastened to add. "I've never seen her actually get violent with someone who didn't, you know, try to sacrifice me to a snake cult. Or grab her tits while she was bussing tables."

"Absolutely equal crimes," said Dominic, with the hint of a smile tugging at his lips.

"They are if you ask most cocktail waitresses," I said. The employee door at the Freakshow was never locked, since most people, even drunk, weren't stupid enough to follow the monsters into their lair. I pushed it open, holding it for Dominic. "After you."

Kitty was still using her uncle's old office, since it was well located and already had a desk and a functioning computer. Bogeymen aren't as inclined toward pennypinching as dragons are, but there was really no point in remodeling if it wasn't necessary. That wasn't all that she'd kept of her uncle's. I stopped in the hall, sighing as I saw the solid bank of darkness that blocked the office door.

"She has the darks on," I said.

Dominic frowned. "The what?"

I glanced at him. "Have you ever noticed how some cryptids manage to live shrouded in eternal darkness, even in the middle of the day in Alaska? Caves with pools of unexplainable shadow, houses where the lights never seem to come all the way on, that sort of thing?"

"Yes . . ."

"Darks. Diurnal species turn on lights, and nocturnal species turn on darks. Witches make a lot of money off these things." I pitched my voice a little louder as I added, "And if Kitty thinks I'm coming in there while she has the darks on, she's as crazy as her uncle."

"Oh, come on, Verity," said Kitty's voice. It came from somewhere barely inside the door. I didn't jump. It was a close thing. "I've never knocked you out and sold you as a human sacrifice. Have a little faith, why don't you?"

"You make me wear a corset. It's almost as bad."

The darks clicked off, replaced by normal overhead lighting. Kitty looked at us impassively. "Your concept of scale never fails to astonish me." She turned her attention on Dominic. "Covenant. You're on private property, you know."

"I will endeavor to behave myself," Dominic informed her.

I bit my lip to keep from grinning. "Kitty, I know you're trying to be all intimidating and stuff, but that might work a little bit better if you weren't wearing fuzzy Elmo slippers. Just as a tip."

Kitty paused, her gaze following mine to her feet, which were encased in effigies of a particular red-furred Muppet. The slippers matched her flannel pajamas in theme, if not in specific character, and I had to wonder (somewhat enviously) where she'd been able to find Super Grover jammies in an adult size. "Okay," she said finally. "Maybe that does undermine my authority a little bit. But, Verity, you know I don't like him. What the hell would have possessed you to bring him here on purpose?"

"Ryan and Istas are going to be joining us in a minute, and then I'll be happy to explain everything," I said. "I don't want to start without them."

Kitty paused again, this time for substantially longer.

She looked from me to Dominic and back to me before she asked, "How bad?"

"Bad enough that I'm standing in front of your office an hour before closing time with a man from the Covenant of St. George in tow," I said. "Seriously, it would be best if we could go inside and shut the door. I'm trying not to start a panic."

"I remember a time when your boyfriend could start a panic by breathing," said Ryan, walking up behind us. Istas was with him. The only sign that she'd gone off duty was her apron, which was now frilly lace, rather than industrial canvas. "I guess you're a bad influence."

"I *know* she's a bad influence," said Dominic. Now that it was him, me, and three cryptids, he was starting to look less sure about what he was doing.

I grabbed his wrist before he could change his mind. "Into the office. It's conference time."

It took Dominic less than ten minutes to explain what was going on, and what was important enough to bring us back to the Freakshow. It took me another twenty minutes to get everyone to stop yelling. Kitty was demanding answers. Ryan was demanding someone's head on a platter. Istas was just yelling because everyone else was yelling, and it seemed like the thing to do.

Eventually, everyone calmed down. A few questions were asked. A few answers were given. And things proceeded to take a turn for the weird, which is like taking a turn for the worse, but doesn't necessarily involve cleaning your knives afterward.

See, the Covenant of St. George did get one major thing right when they wrote their files on the world's cryptids: all cryptids are essentially different from humans, because they're entirely different *species*. We may be similar enough to work in the same places, watch the same TV shows, and complain about the same tax increases, but we're not the same. We can't be.

So it only goes to reason that cryptids will occasionally have reactions that any reasonable human would view as completely and unequivocally batshit crazy. "You can't be serious," said Dominic, staring at Kitty.

"I'm dead serious," said Kitty.

"Possible stress on the 'dead' there," said Ryan.

Kitty ignored him. "Look. You say the Covenant is sending people to check on you, and that when they find out how little progress you've made, they're probably going to purge Manhattan. Great. Do you have any idea what kind of cryptid population this city has?"

"No, he doesn't, and you're not going to tell him," I said hurriedly. Dominic raised an eyebrow. I patted him on the arm. "You're earning a lot of points tonight, but there are still some things I don't think we should be sharing just yet."

Dominic sighed. "Much as I'd like to argue, with my fellows coming to town, I'm afraid that Verity is correct. If they suspect that I've been . . . compromised . . . they have ways of getting me to reveal any information that they desire."

"You know where the club is located," noted Istas. "We should kill you to preserve that information." She smiled. Somehow, that didn't help.

"There will be no killing of my boyfriend," I said firmly. "I'm not killing yours, you're not allowed to kill mine."

Istas considered this for a moment before allowing, "That seems fair."

"If we could get back to the point here?" said Kitty. "I meant what I said. There are too many cryptids in this city for even the Covenant to kill. I will not run. I will not let them win. And the Freakshow will *not* be closing its doors."

"Kitty—" I began.

"Boss—" Ryan began.

"Surely—" Dominic began.

"QUIET!" Kitty's time as a wanna-be rock star served her well; when she shouted in an enclosed space, you knew damn well and good that somebody was shouting

at you. "Everybody who doesn't own this club, shut the hell up and listen to me. You," she thrust a finger at Dominic, "had no trouble finding this place even before you started fooling around with Verity. You know why? Because my uncle wouldn't know discretion if it bit him on the ass. He advertised too widely, and we got a reputation for having freaky girls. All I've done is build on that reputation."

"Which is why you need to close for the duration," said Dominic.

"Which is exactly why I *don't* need to close for the duration," said Kitty. "Too many people know we're here. If we close, we might as well be putting up a big sign that says, 'Oh, hey, that club that had the fake monsters? They were real monsters.' We'll become the all-you-can-kill cryptid buffet. But if we stay open . . ."

"Hiding in plain sight," I said, finally grasping what she was trying to say. "I'm an idiot. You want to do exactly what I did on TV."

Kitty tapped the side of her nose with one over-long finger. "At last, Miss Verity Price decides to join the party!"

"It's been a long night." Before I came to New York, I went to Los Angeles. Not to study the local cryptids: to appear on reality television. I was a contestant on the nation's highest-rated dance competition show, *Dance or Die*, under the name "Valerie Pryor." I put on a red wig and green contact lenses, and I cha-cha'd my way into America's hearts. Far enough into their hearts to take second place anyway, and while that wasn't as good as winning, it was pretty decent.

"May I have an invitation to this 'party' that you're talking about?" asked Dominic.

"It's important that you guys—the Covenant, I mean—continue thinking that my family died out two generations ago," I said. "That's why when you've seen me at dance competitions, I've been wearing a wig and using a fake name. It's hiding in plain sight."

"We slap some latex on the girls who look mostly human, and we give the girls who look too inhuman to pass a few weeks off," said Kitty. "More importantly, we give people a place to run if they need to."

"And if the Covenant comes looking for cryptids in a place where they have been known to gather?"

"They'll find a bunch of humans in prosthetics and stage makeup." Kitty looked at him calmly. "Bogeymen have a reputation. I'd have to be blind not to see that you expect me to cut and run because my uncle did. But the thing most people forget is that we run from *your* homes. We run from *your* places. We don't run from our own. We stay."

"Perhaps there will be the opportunity for carnage," said Istas.

I sighed. "See, that's what I was hoping to avoid. Carnage is bad for business."

"My business," said Kitty. "If they want to bring the carnage to us, let them. We'll be ready."

Judging by the looks on their faces—Istas anticipatory, Ryan grim, and Kitty just determined, like there was nothing in the world that could sway her—if the Covenant decided to come to the Freakshow, they were going to get a lot more than they had bargained for. I just hoped that the right people would be the ones standing at the end of it all.

Seven

"When everything else fails, smile big, shoot
sharp, and remember that a lady never
needs to say she's sorry."

— Frances Brown

*A semilegal sublet in Greenwich Village, about twenty
minutes later*

EVEN DOMINIC had to admit that expecting me to take
three taxis in one night was pushing things, especially when we were looking at the trip from the Freakshow back to my apartment. There was no one else I
needed to warn immediately, and that meant that it was
time for me to email the rest of the family with an update and maybe get myself some actual sleep for a
change.

Besides, I needed some time to clear my head. Sarah
said that Dominic was on the up-and-up, and I wanted to
believe her—and him—enough that I was going along
with it, for the moment, for as long as it didn't mean taking him anywhere he'd never been before. But I needed
to remember that he was the enemy, whether he wanted
to be or not. I needed to be wary.

Once again, the enemy met me at my front door. "Security is just a joke to you, isn't it?" I asked.

"This building's security is a joke to anyone sufficiently determined to get inside," he replied.

"I suppose your building's security isn't?" I asked
lightly, as I dug my keys out of my pocket. Dominic

didn't answer, but his shoulders stiffened. I sighed. "You know, eventually, this whole 'I am Batman, I can never reveal the location of my secret lair' shtick is going to get real old. Oh, wait. It already did." And it just made me worry more about his motives, which wasn't helping.

"Verity, it's ... complicated. The Covenant ... they would know if I had a woman in my residence. They would know she had been there the moment they crossed my threshold, no matter how little sign she left." Dominic mustered a small smile. "Perhaps I could conceal some women, but you have a way of making your presence known even after you've left a place."

"It's not like they make you guys take an oath of celibacy. Personal experience aside, I have several ancestors who will testify to *that*." I shoved open the apartment door, triggering cheers from the small cluster of mice waiting on the hallway table. I waited until Dominic and I were both inside before frowning at them and asking, "Okay, where's the rest of the colony?"

"In attendance at the Catechism of the Patient Priestess!" announced one of the mice. The rest cheered again in punctuation. "We were selected to bear the great honor of welcoming you back to the domain when your travels ended."

Having a live-in colony of Aeslin mice means never having to come home to a silent house. I paused, the true meaning of what the mouse was saying sinking in. "I have a new honor for you."

"Yes, Priestess?" asked the mouse, whiskers quivering with excitement. I couldn't tell whether it was male or female. It wasn't relevant, and so I didn't ask.

"I need you to stay here in the hall until the catechism is over, so you can tell the rest of the colony that there will be cheese and cake if—and *only* if—they do not enter the bedroom until I open the door. Do you understand?"

The mouse ran one paw over its ears in a thoughtful grooming behavior. Finally, it asked, "Is this a Now-Only Thing?"

For a heady moment I considered saying that no, do

not bother me in the bedroom was now part of scripture. The trouble was that the mice would believe me, and would expect cheese and cake every time I went into my room without being bothered. Aeslin mice are like normal mice in one regard: they'll eat themselves into perfect spheres if you make enough food available to them. "One-time offer," I said. "Leave me alone in the bedroom for now, get cheese and cake when I emerge."

"It Shall Be Done," intoned the mouse, with audible capital letters on every word. The rest of the mice erupted into cheers. I flashed them a quick salute before turning to throw the deadbolt on the door, grabbing Dominic by the wrist, and towing him ignominiously down the apartment's short hall to the bedroom.

"What in the world—?" he asked.

"No talking now. Kissing is more important." I let go of his wrist as I pushed him past me into the bedroom. Once we were both inside, I closed the bedroom door, and locked it for good measure. I didn't bother turning on the light as I turned to face him. Let the moon shining through the window be light enough. This wasn't a time when we needed to see each other clearly. "Kissing *now*."

"And the Covenant?"

"Are they coming tonight?"

Dominic shook his head.

"We've told Sarah. We've told the gang at the Freakshow. I called my family before I came to Gingerbread Pudding. If the Covenant is really going to be keeping that close of an eye on you while they're here, you're not going to be stopping by for sexy naked fun times." I unzipped my hoodie and shrugged it off, hanging it on the doorknob before starting to unbuckle my shoulder harness. "I am thus demanding my sexy naked fun times now, so that I'll remember why I like you and don't start endorsing an all-Covenant shoot on sight rule. Besides. I don't want you getting ideas about that oath of chastity thing."

I wanted to touch him one more time before I knew whether or not he was going to betray me. I wanted him to touch me one more time when I still believed that it was safe to trust him.

"Chastity would be easier than trying to understand you, but not nearly so much fun. I suppose I will yield in this case to your very solid argument." Dominic watched me hang my shoulder harness on the hook next to the door. "Are you still armed?"

I smiled blithely. "Why don't you come over here and find out?"

He came over there and found out.

My grandmother—Alice, the human one who spends most of her time in the Underworld, not Angela, the cuckoo one who spends most of her time in Ohio—always said that when I met the right kind of man for me, I'd know. He'd be the one who wouldn't bat an eye at the fact that I usually had three or more knives in my pants. Instead, he'd start suggesting ways for me to carry even more knives, possibly while wearing less clothing. I always figured she was talking about some crazy ideal, the way dancers dream about big studios with high ceilings and low rents. Then I met Dominic and realized that no, she wasn't fantasizing at all. She was telling me what it would be like to date a boy from the Covenant of St. George.

Dominic found and dispensed with the various holsters and straps holding my weapons in place in short order, either hanging them from the doorknob with my hoodie, tossing them onto the dresser or, as in the case of the collapsible baton in my sock, just throwing them onto the floor. I was too busy responding in kind to argue about the treatment of my things. Dominic didn't usually carry a gun—silly boy—but he had more knives than I did, secured in even more interesting places. If we'd been having a competition, I'm not sure which one of us would have won.

Of course, once we'd finished stripping the obviously deadly toys away, we were down to our underwear, so I'd say that we both won. We stopped for a moment, hands briefly empty, and just looked at each other. Dominic was breathing hard already. The light coming through the open window was bright enough to let me see his expression, but not very much more. That was okay. I've always been good at picturing things with my fingers.

He took a breath, raising his hands like he wanted to ward me away. He didn't lift them all the way. "Verity—"

"They could be here tomorrow. We could be back to being enemies tomorrow. They're not here tonight. Let's have tonight." I stepped closer, to where he could either pull me close or push me away. "We've earned it, don't you think?"

Dominic didn't answer. Instead, he reached out and wrapped his arms around my waist, pulling me close, and kissed me hard. My lips would be bruised in the morning. I didn't mind, because I was giving back as good as I was getting, and we were already halfway tangled together when we fell sideways onto the bed.

Dominic's fingers ran through my hair and down to the nape of my neck, where he took hold, gripping firmly enough to keep me where I was. I made a soft noise in the back of my throat and bent to bite his shoulder. He pulled me closer still, and after that, words and meanings and consequences didn't matter to either one of us. Let the purge come tomorrow. We would have tonight, and while I won't pretend that one night is ever enough, it was still more than some people ever get.

Sunlight came in through the open window, shining into my eyes and pulling me out of the dream that I'd been having. I groaned, rolling over and pressing my face against Dominic's chest. He laughed sleepily.

"If you don't get up, who will protect all the cryptids of your fair city from the big, bad men who are on their way?"

"Don't know," I mumbled, without lifting my head. "Don't care. Somebody else can do it. Lemme 'lone, I'm *sleeping*."

"No, you *were* sleeping. Now you're denying the morning." He leaned down to kiss the top of my head. "That never works. Better men than I have died trying."

I sighed and squirmed around to prop my chin against his chest, looking up at him sulkily. Dominic smiled.

"Good morning, Verity."

"What's good about it?" Even as I asked the question, I knew the answer. What was good about it was that I was waking up—always a bonus in my line of work—in a bed that was toasty warm, thanks to the addition of another body. The mice hadn't come to bother us. We'd actually been able to get a decent night's sleep . . . once we finally fell asleep, anyway, which took quite a while. All in all, this definitely qualified as a good morning.

"Everything," said Dominic, echoing my thoughts in a single word. Then he grinned. "Your hair is sticking in all directions like an electrocuted hedgehog's quills. It's endearing. You should wear it like this more often."

"Mmm. Get out of my apartment," I said.

"No," said Dominic, and sat up, sending me rolling half off of him. He caught me at the last moment, pulling me up into a kiss. Pulling back, he added, "I don't have any trousers on."

"Okay, fair. You don't have a shirt, either. Or boxers." I let my hand slide down the length of his torso, proving my statement with a light touch of my fingertips. "You'd get arrested for indecent exposure for sure if you went out there the way you're not dressed right now."

"Infuriating woman," said Dominic. This time there was no "almost" about it; the words were fond, even affectionate. Then he sobered, and said, "Verity. I have to ask you something."

"I don't know where your pants wound up last night, but I can help you look," I said. Then I paused. "That's not what you were going to ask, is it?"

"Truly, your grasp of the obvious remains monumental in its scope." Dominic sat up a little straighter, dislodging my hand in the process.

I blinked and sat up, clutching the sheets around myself like some sort of soap opera heroine covering herself from the camera. I realized a moment later how stupid that was, and I let the sheets fall. There was nothing about me that Dominic hadn't seen. Not even the scars that my tango costumes normally hid from the rest of the world. My scars are nothing on my father's, or my grandmother's—life in the field is hard on a body, and it gets harder the longer it goes on—but they're mine, and I usually make love in the dark to keep people from seeing them. Not Dominic. He had scars of his own to share.

He watched me as I pulled away, a strange seriousness in his dark eyes. "You said something last night," he said.

"I said a lot of things last night," I replied. "Which thing in specific was the problem?"

"It wasn't a problem, exactly. I just . . ." He paused, and sighed, muttering, "I am so much better at this with women who aren't you," before he asked, in a more normal tone, "Verity, what are we to one another?"

"Uh . . . what?" That wasn't a question I'd been expecting. Not from *him*, not now, and possibly not ever. "What do you mean?"

"You, me . . . this." He waved a hand, encompassing the room, the weapons scattered on the floor, our mutual nudity. "Are we lovers? Are we in a relationship? What are we? The tanuki called me your boyfriend. You didn't deny him. You even used the term yourself."

"He has a name, you know. It's Ryan."

"I know. You're avoiding the question."

"I know." I sighed and ran the fingers of my right hand through my bed-messed hair, using the gesture to buy myself a few seconds to think. "Jeez, Dominic. Most guys start the day by asking the girl if she wants breakfast. Not if they're dating."

Dominic smiled a little. "I am not 'most guys.' No more than you are most girls. You are a fabulous, insane, infuriating creature, and I have never felt that normal was a requirement for this . . . whatever it is. Still. I'd like to know."

"Is this about those vow of chastity jokes? Because I really didn't mean them."

"Verity." Dominic reached out and took hold of my chin, resting his thumb in the hollow just below my lip. "Most of the young knights in my generation have taken lovers as soon as they arrived in a new city. Others hire prostitutes to fulfill their carnal needs. All of them know that one day, they will return to the Covenant and be married to a member of a good Covenant family, to have children of good breeding to join in the cause."

My eyes widened. I pulled away. "So what, I'm your spring fling?"

"No! No." Dominic scowled. "That isn't what I'm saying at all. Verity, I didn't take a lover because I didn't *want* one. I was not looking for distraction from my mission. And so, instead of falling into the arms of a soft American woman who would never ask where I spent the small hours of the morning, I found myself with you, and you, Verity Price, you were so much more than that phantom girl could ever have been. Do you understand me? I did not choose you because you were expected. I did not choose you at all. But now that I have found you . . . please. I just want to understand what you are to me, and what I am to you."

I stared at him. That was the only thing that I could think of to do. "I . . ."

In the pocket of his pants, kicked half under the bed and nearly hidden under the black cotton of my sports bra, Dominic's phone began to ring. We both froze, the rest of the sentence dying before I could force it past my lips. It wasn't a ringtone I'd heard before. Not that I'd heard his phone ring more than once or twice, but that ringtone—

"Is that . . . ?"

"Yes. It is." He rolled away from me, spine suddenly stiff again, like the spine of the wannabe holy warrior who caught me in his rooftop snare. He was still there with me, but he was already gone by the time he found his pants and dug his phone out of the pocket, flicking it open. "De Luca."

There was a long pause as whoever was on the other end spoke. Then Dominic asked, in a light, rhetorical tone, "If God is occupied with the fall of sparrows then who, on Earth, will count the fall of dragons?"

It must have been the right thing to say. There was another pause, and some of the tension went out of his shoulders.

"Yes, of course, sir," he said. "Pier A, in Battery Park.

Two hours. Yes, sir. I have arranged for transportation and housing." He paused again. "Yes, sir, I understand. I will bring all my reports thus far for review during the trip to your residence."

The next pause was longer. Dominic closed his eyes as it stretched on, chin dipping slightly, so that he looked for all the world like he was praying. Finally, he said, "Yes, sir, I understand the scope of the honor that is being afforded to me. I will not question my privilege. I will not doubt my orders. I will do my best to bring glory to the name of the Covenant, and to the family whose name I bear. Yes, sir. I will be on time."

Then he closed the phone. For a moment, he just stood there, eyes still closed, lit by the early morning sun streaming through the window.

I slid out of the bed and walked toward him. "Dominic?" He didn't react. I raised a hand, reaching carefully toward his shoulder. "Dominic?"

"Don't touch me right now, Verity," he said. His voice was low. "I am betraying someone, right now, and I honestly do not know who it is. So please, I beg you. Do not touch me."

"I'm sorry." I pulled my hand away. "That was the Covenant. On your phone." In my apartment. For the first time in a while, I realized just how dangerous my relationship with Dominic really was. All he had to do was say the word . . .

And if he was going to do that, he would never have told me the purge was coming, much less answered the phone in my presence. I couldn't let myself start thinking that way. If I did, I might as well get out of the city right now.

"Yes. They're on their way. I've told you when and where they will arrive. Be careful. Don't let yourself be seen." He grabbed his pants off the floor, yanking them roughly on before looking back at me over his shoulder. I had never seen him look so miserable. "I truly do not know whether I'm doing the right thing. But I know that I don't want you getting hurt, and I know that nothing I can say will make you leave. So, for me, for my sake, be careful."

"I'll try," I said. Where I grew up, "be careful" was a death sentence. From the look in his eyes, he didn't think of it that way.

To my surprise, Dominic laughed. It wasn't a happy sound. "A man from the Covenant of St. George telling a Price woman to be careful. What is this world coming to?"

"I don't know, but we've been here a few times before," I said.

Dominic laughed again, even less happily. "So true." He didn't say anything else as he gathered the rest of his clothes and got dressed, and he didn't look at me on his way out of the room. I heard the front door slam a few minutes later. Once again, I was alone, and feeling more lost than ever.

I stayed in the bedroom long enough to collect my thoughts and give Dominic a chance to get out of the building. Then I dressed, taking my time, concealing as many weapons as I possibly could under camouflage cargo pants and a black tank top. Adding my custom tactical vest—half-corset, half-Kevlar, all military spec material—gave me room for easily a dozen extra knives. If I needed all those weapons, I was probably already dead, but it's better to be prepared for anything.

The mice were waiting in the hall when I opened the bedroom door. They cheered as I emerged, a cry of "CHEESE AND CAKE!" rising from the throng.

I smiled a little. No matter how bad things look, life goes on. "I have to go out for a little while," I said. "Let's get your communion set up."

Praise and exultations followed me into the kitchen. That was nice. I had the distinct feeling that no one else was going to be singing my praises any time soon. It was time to go.

Eight

"Don't be careful. Be couragcous. Don't be
safe. Be strong. Don't be a victim. Be the
one who makes it home."

— Evelyn Baker

The rooftop of the old Department of Docks on Pier A in Manhattan

THE ROOFTOP OF THE OLD Department of Docks building was slanted—something uncommon enough in
Manhattan to be deeply disconcerting, especially when I
was trying to stay out of sight. The angle of the roof was
sharp enough that I couldn't lic flat, but shallow enough
that I couldn't use it for cover. "Avoid really obvious
cover" was one of the rules I'd been raised with, entry
number eight hundred and thirteen in the Gospel of
Staying Alive. I sent up a silent apology to my entire
family tree as I disregarded their advice and slunk into
the shadow of the building's decorative clock tower. It
was a short, mostly useless piece of masonry. It was sufficient for my current needs.

Once I was safely out of view, I settled into a crouch,
and prepared myself to wait.

There's a certain meditative mindset that goes with
long periods of actively doing nothing. That isn't the con-
tradiction that it sounds like. Anyone can passively do
nothing, staring off into space or at the latest mindless
sitcom eating up the hours on their TV. Actively doing
nothing means holding perfectly still while paying atten-

tion to everything around you. It's a skill cultivated by hunters, soldiers, and biologists hoping to get a glimpse of something no one's ever seen before. My training makes me sort of a combination of all three, and I've had time to get very, very good at not moving.

I didn't move as the sun slid slowly across the sky, counting down toward the point when Dominic's superiors were scheduled to arrive. I didn't move when I saw Dominic himself come walking down the pier. He was wearing that stupid leather duster that he had on the night we met. I was too far away to see his face. I didn't need to. His shoulders were locked, and he was walking with the slow, borderline-resentful steps of a man on the way to his own execution.

He stopped at the edge of the pier, hands in the pockets of his duster, and looked out over the water. Then he froze, going as still as I was. I held my position, and the two of us waited, together and apart at the same time.

The Hudson River isn't the sort of thing you mess around with. I'm not sure what I was expecting to see come sailing up to the pier. I certainly wasn't expecting the taxi that drove up behind Dominic and stopped, disgorging three black-clad figures onto the sidewalk. Each of them had a satchel. The driver emerged long enough to help them remove two suitcases from the trunk. Then the tallest of the figures handed him a stack of bills, and he climbed back into the cab and was gone, leaving Dominic and the trio behind.

Dominic still didn't turn. The shortest of the three—a woman, with long brown hair pulled into a ponytail—stepped up to him, putting a hand on his shoulder. There was a pause while none of them moved; the brunette was probably speaking. Dominic nodded once, not turning. One of the others raised his hand to shoulder-height in a gesture that looked like a benediction or a summons, or possibly both. Dominic nodded again.

This time he turned to face the three, and bowed to them deeply. The brunette woman bowed back, as did the shorter of the two men. The taller man simply stood there with his hand raised, watching. It should have looked ridiculous, an old-fashioned dumb show being carried out in front of a semi-abandoned pier, with a pile of luggage just begging to be stolen. Instead, it was positively chilling. These were Covenant agents. Three of them, in *my* city. Dominic didn't count. He hadn't been Covenant to me since the day we found William.

Dominic gestured toward their bags, probably saying something else that I was too far away to hear. I found myself wishing Sarah was with me. She's not usually very good at getting clean telepathic reads off people she's never met, but anything would have been better than nothing. The three Covenant operatives nodded, and the tall man finally lowered his hand.

They followed Dominic as he walked down the side of the pier to the rental car he had parked illegally in a nearby loading zone. It was a black Crown Vic—of course it was—and from the way he held the doors open for them, he could almost have been mistaken for their chauffeur. He even loaded the suitcases into the trunk without assistance. All three kept hold of their satchels. Dominic never even reached for them. There were apparently some things that simply were not done.

Once the others were safely in the car, he walked around to the driver's side door and pulled it open, taking what must have looked like a natural pause while he looked up to the nearby rooftops. I remained frozen where I was, using the shadow of the clock tower for cover. His eyes skated over me without pausing, and as he climbed into the car and drove away, I still wasn't sure whether I'd been seen.

I would normally have tried to follow the car, but the selection of the old Department of Docks building hadn't been an accident. It was detached, set far enough out on the pier that there was nothing I could jump to or grab hold of. Even getting to the nearest buildings would have required running across level ground, and that would have left me visible. I did follow them as far as the roof's edge, straightening up while I watched them disappear into the flow of traffic.

The Covenant was in Manhattan. All I could do now was try to keep myself—and everyone else—alive.

The Department of Docks roof was as good a place as any to make a phone call, and the cell reception was surprisingly good, maybe because it was one of the few spots in the city without multiple skyscrapers looming directly over it. I retreated back to the shadow of the clock tower to dial, propping myself in the space created where the tower wall met the angle of the roof.

The logical person to call would have been my father, who was probably worrying himself sick while he waited to hear what was going on. Instead, I dialed someone who stood a better chance of actually helping me. "Sarah? Hi, it's Verity."

"Oh, hey." Sarah yawned, barely making an effort to hide it. "What do you want? It's, like . . . jeez, Very, what time is it?"

"About eleven," I said. "Don't you have morning classes?"

"I was at the Nest until almost five-thirty," she said, and yawned again. "Besides, it's not like I'm actually enrolled in any of my classes. Nobody's going to notice if I don't show up."

"Fair," I allowed. Sarah probably had the equivalent of three math degrees, but she didn't have anything on paper. Her natural camouflage meant she could show up for any class and be accepted as someone who belonged—and yet she'd never enrolled in a single college course. She hadn't even gone to a public high school, since being a telepath in a building full of confused teenagers trying to figure out what to do with their hormones was something she and Grandma Angela both regarded as just this side of hell. Actual Hell, I mean, where the border imps live, and those bastards can strip the meat off a cow faster than a swarm of horror movie piranha.

"The dragons were pretty calm," said Sarah, still audibly waking up. "I mean, for dragons. Bill breathed fire on the girls when they got rowdy, and that settled them right down."

Male dragons breathe fire; female dragons are fireproof. Evolution works in mysterious ways. "What are they going to do?"

"Circle the wagons and stay underground until we give them the all clear. Even if they could move Bill, they can't shift the eggs." Sarah paused. When she spoke again, she sounded sharper—good. I needed her sharp. "Verity, why are you calling me? Shouldn't you be off saving the world or something? Or at least sleeping?"

"I need a favor."

"You always need a favor."

"I need a favor from Artie."

I could practically hear Sarah's double take. "You need a what?"

"I need you to call Artie and get him to trace a rental car for me."

"Uh . . . Verity, I don't know who you've been talking to, but real life doesn't work like television. You can't just say 'trace a rental car in Manhattan' and have your helpful neighborhood computer guy find you a name and address before the next commercial break. Remember? We went over this when you wanted us to trace Antimony via her cell phone GPS. Please stop taking your technology tips from *Criminal Minds*."

I ignored her. "The car is a black Crown Victoria, looked like either a 2006 or a 2007, rented to Dominic De Luca. He'll have been using a foreign ID, but the card he used will have a billing address somewhere in Manhattan."

Silence greeted this statement.

I kept going: "The Covenant called him this morning while we were at my apartment. I watched him make the pickup. There are three of them, two male and one female. I didn't get a good look at their faces, but one of the men was pretty obviously in charge."

More silence.

"I don't know when the next time Dominic is going to

be able to get away from them will be. He made sure I was there to see the pickup. They didn't see me."

"Very . . ." Sarah took a breath. "If you're that sure he'll be easy to find, why didn't he give you an address? It would have been easier."

"Because he's still trying to figure out who he's going to betray—me, or the Covenant." I shook my head, not caring that she couldn't see the gesture. "I honestly don't know which way he's going to go, either. Maybe he'll turn his back on the only life he's ever known. Maybe he'll sell me out. I guess we'll find out sooner or later."

"If you really think there's a chance that he might turn you in, you need to get out of there. We don't know if the Covenant taught him to hide things from telepaths." Sarah sounded alarmed, and rightfully so. "You can come stay with me. Bring the mice, we'll make it a slumber party."

"And when Dominic decides I'm the next one on the 'betray me now' list and comes looking for me? I can't disappear completely, Sarah. If they start looking for me, they'll find me, and they'll follow me straight to you." More silence from her end of the phone. I sighed. "Yeah, I thought so. Look, Sarah, there's no good answer here. I wish there was one. Just call Artie for me, okay?"

"What do you want me to tell him? I'm not going to be the one to say, 'Oh, hey, the Covenant's throwing a purge on the island of Manhattan and me and Verity are both invited.' I'm just *not*."

"Tell him I need to know, and that I'll explain later." If I'd called Artie myself, I would have been explaining *now*, because otherwise he would never have done it. If the request came from Sarah, he'd go ahead, minimal questions asked. And then the two of them wonder why the rest of the family is betting on when they'll just go ahead and start dating already.

"Verity . . ."

"I'm not leaving New York while the Covenant's here, and you're not leaving while I'm here, so will you just call Artie? Please, for me?"

Sarah sighed. "Okay. I'll call him. But I'm really not sure this is the way to go about things."

"I'll tell you what: if you come up with any better ideas, you be sure and let me know." I hung up before she could say anything else, and sank down against the roof, briefly closing my eyes. This was one hell of a mess, and it was going to get a lot worse before it got any better.

I stomped up the stairs to my apartment, taking my frustrations out on the poor, innocent banister, which had never done anything bad to anyone. None of my neighbors poked their heads out to see what the ruckus was about. Most of them probably had respectable jobs that kept them away from home during the day. That just served to make me grumpier. New York was about to be a battleground, and the rest of my building wasn't even going to notice unless the Covenant decided to firebomb me while I slept.

Somehow, that particular thought didn't do anything to help. I dug my keys out of my pocket, grumbling as I jabbed them into the lock—

—and froze as the doorknob shifted under my hand. The door wasn't locked. But the door had *been* locked when I left the apartment. I'd locked it from the inside, and I'd left via the kitchen window, like I normally did.

Moving carefully now, I slipped my keys back into my pocket and pulled the pistol from the back of my pants. I pressed myself to the side of the door, reached over, and twisted the knob, shoving the door open in the same gesture. It banged against the wall, and I spun into the doorway, pistol in front of me in a shooter's stance.

There was a tall, neatly-groomed man standing in my hall with an automatic crossbow in his hands. It was loaded, and aimed at my stomach. He raised an eyebrow questioningly. "Is that how you say hello now?" he asked.

"Uncle Mike!" I didn't lower my pistol. "What's the password?"

"There is no password," he replied. "If you need a password, you're probably already dead, and that makes it a moot point. Now get in here before you scare the neighbors."

I beamed, clicking the safety on my pistol into place before replacing it in its holster and stepping through the open door. The mice—who had been obeying my edict never to let themselves be seen from the hall, and were consequentially plastered against the wall just inside—cheered loudly. "What are you *doing* here?" I asked, while I closed and locked the door. I sniffed the air. "Is that pot roast?"

Uncle Mike just looked at me, eyebrow still raised.

Oh, right. "Before you scare the neighbors" was the first half of the family passcode. "I mean, the neighbors don't scare easy," I said. "I'm pretty sure they've seen it all before."

"Your father called me and said you needed backup," he said, finally lowering his crossbow. "And yes, it's pot roast. I figured you'd be going largely nocturnal for the duration of the shit that's about to hit the fan, and there's no such thing as too much readily available protein."

"Hail!" chorused the mice. "Hail the High Priest of Goddammit Eat Something Already!"

I grinned. "See, I almost didn't need to get a passcode from you. The pot roast would have been effective proof of identity."

"Yes, but if you hadn't confirmed my identity, I would have shot you on general principle," said Uncle Mike. Then he smiled. "Come over here and give me a hug, or I may shoot you anyway."

I went over there and gave him a hug. It wasn't an unpleasant experience. Uncle Mike—full name Michael Gucciard, a cryptozoologist from the Chicago area who specializes in water-based cryptids—was large, solid, and an excellent hugger. He also wasn't related to the family in any biological sense, but anyone who puts up with as much of our crap as he does should get to be an honorary relation, or at least get hazard pay. (Being an *honorary* relation is why he's only a High Priest, and not a

God. If you want to be a God, you need to bang a Priest-ess, and Aunt Lea wouldn't approve.)

"Where's Aunt Lea?" I asked, pulling away. I paused. "Please tell me she stayed home."

"She stayed home," he said reassuringly. "I love your family, and you know there's nothing I wouldn't do for your father, but the day I bring my wife into the path of a Covenant purge is the day the papers report on my mysterious drowning."

I relaxed slightly. "Good." Like so many cryptozoologists, Uncle Mike had fallen in love with his work—specifically with an Oceanid he met in Palm Beach. The Covenant had a history with Oceanids. It wasn't a pretty one. Then again, the Covenant didn't have a pretty history with anyone, so far as I could tell.

"Your security is terrible," Uncle Mike informed me, pleasantries apparently completed. "I picked the locks in under a minute. No one came out to see what I was doing. I even passed someone in the downstairs hall, and he asked if I was heading for the second floor, since he didn't want to carry a misdelivered newspaper all the way up the stairs." He scowled briefly. "It's a miracle you're still alive."

"I tell myself that every day," I said. "Where are you staying?"

"Here, at least for tonight," he said, in a tone that left no room for arguing.

I looked around my postage stamp of an apartment and considered arguing anyway. "*Where*?" I asked.

"There's a couch," he said. "I fold."

"Uncle Mike—"

"Your father gave me a précis on the whole situation, Verity, including your on-again, off-again boyfriend." He fixed me with a stern eye. "I'm the last person who's going to tell you who you should be dating—"

"Yeah, at this point, everybody else has already had their shot," I muttered.

"—but if you think I'm going to leave you alone while he and his compatriots run loose in this city, you got another think coming. If it were up to me, we'd be relocating to somewhere more secure. We may have to do that anyway, but I figured I'd hear your game plan before I started packing your bags for you."

"That's very considerate, thank you," I said dryly. "Do you want the update, or do you want to lecture me some more about how lousy my apartment is?"

To my surprise, he grinned. "Honey, I live in Chicago. I understand that this is a perfectly reasonable apartment for someone on your budget. But your security is shit, your neighbors are basically cannon fodder, and there's no one close enough to help if things get bad. We shouldn't stay here."

"You're right." Even the admission hurt. Not as much as the one that came after it: "Dominic knows where I live. He's known for a while now. I can't trust him not to tell the Covenant where to find me."

There was a pause while Mike looked at me, trying to figure out whether I was serious. Finally, deciding that I meant what I was saying, he asked, "There a reason you haven't moved house already? Aside from wanting to be here to see my smiling face—and that's a lousy reason, by the way, since you didn't know that I was coming. I don't recommend trying to convince me of that one."

"This has all happened really fast, and I didn't totally believe it until this morning," I said. I shrugged. "Besides, where are we supposed to go? I can't stay with Sarah, that'll just put her in the line of fire. The dragons won't have me, and I'm pretty sure my boss would kill me herself if I tried sleeping at work."

"Don't you still dance with that goat-sucker guy?"

"You mean James?" In my alternate identity as Valerie Pryor, professional ballroom dancer, I was usually partnered with a very sweet, very gay chupacabra. He didn't mind that I kept guns under my tango costume, and I didn't mind that he occasionally turned into a semi-reptilian quadruped and went hunting deer in the New Jersey Pine Barrens. Like any partnership, our association was based on mutual trust. I trusted him not to sell me out to the Covenant. He trusted me not to shoot him in the head.

"Yeah. He lives around here, doesn't he?"

"Yes, he does, and if I tried to hide at his place when I potentially had the Covenant of St. George on my tail, his husband would kill us both. Dennis puts up with a lot for James' sake, but there are limits." I paused. "I need to call him anyway, and tell them both to get out of town."

Mike sighed. "You've made a pretty good mess for yourself, kiddo. Isn't there *anywhere* you could go that the Covenant doesn't know about?"

"Wait—maybe." I started toward the living room, mice dodging out of the way of my feet as I walked. "The dragons used to have a Nest in the old meatpacking district. They'd been living there for more than a century, and that means they must have managed to ride out previous purges. The place is essentially a fortress."

"Sounds great," he allowed. "But where are the dragons now?"

"They couldn't get their husband out of the cavern he was asleep in, so they've relocated to be closer to him," I said. "They seem perfectly happy down there." Then again, they were female dragons in the presence of the first male anyone had seen in centuries. Between that and the heaps of gold they'd been amassing since they arrived in North America, they had everything they could possibly have needed.

"Great. You think they'll let you use this Nest?"

"I may have to sell a kidney to pay what they're going to ask for it, but there's a chance." I ran a hand through my hair, leaving it sticking up in untidy spikes. "I need to call home and give Dad an update on the situation. You want to listen in, so I don't have to do it twice?"

"Just put the phone on speaker," he said. "I'll take care of the pot roast while you deliver the bad news."

"Thanks, Uncle Mike," I said—and I meant it. Having another person with combat training standing next to me made the odds feel a little less imbalanced, and a little more survivable. Maybe I was kidding myself. But there's nothing wrong with some healthy self-delusion once in a while, especially when there's an ancient organization of monster hunters involved. Since my boyfriend was one of the monster hunters, and they considered my family a type of monster, I figured I was entitled to a double dose.

With the mice swarming around my feet and periodically cheering for no good reason that I could see, I finished trekking to the living room. It was time to bring the rest of the family up to speed. And when that was done, I could start packing.

Nine

"I know that we're supposed to be the better people and all, but sometimes I just want to stop playing nice and start playing for keeps."

— Alice Healy

A semilegal sublet in Greenwich Village, twenty minutes and a lot of shouting later

"OKAY, DADDY," I said, over the sound of my mother and father yelling at each other, and my little sister yelling at no one in particular. Sometimes I think Antimony yells just so she won't feel left out. "Daddy? Okay. I'm hanging up now. Uncle Mike says the pot roast is almost ready, and I haven't had anything to eat today."

"Why are you eating pot roast?" demanded Antimony. "It's not even lunchtime yet!"

"We're probably going nocturnal for the duration, and shut up. You think cold pizza is a breakfast food," I said.

"Only if you put Captain Crunch on it," she replied.

There was a moment of silence as all of us considered this. Even the mice stopped their chattering, although they were probably less horrified than reverent. Finally, my mother said, "I want you to listen to your uncle, Verity. I know you're supposed to be doing your journeyman studies, and I wouldn't dream of impinging on your independence, but there's being independent, and then there's being stupid. If you get yourself killed, I'll never forgive you."

The idea that she wanted me to just hand my city over to Uncle Mike stung. Still, she was probably right, and so I forced the rancor from my voice as I said, "I know, Mom. We're going to relocate soon—and no, I'm not telling you where we're going. I'll keep in touch via email as much as I can."

"I've left a message for your grandmother, but I haven't heard back yet. She's in one of the border worlds right now, and she may not get back in time to help you," said Dad. He didn't push the issue of where we were going. He knew as well as I did that when you try to drop off the grid, the fewer people who know your location, the better. "The same goes for your Aunt Mary. The routewitches say they'll notify her if she pops up on their radar, but . . ."

"It's okay, Daddy. I have Sarah, the gang from work, and Uncle Mike. We'll be fine." My paternal grandmother, Alice Price-Healy, spends most of her time wandering around various parallel dimensions looking for her missing husband, Thomas Price. The rest of us are pretty sure he's dead, but try telling that to a woman who's abandoned everything she ever cared about for the sake of bringing her true love home. As for Aunt Mary, we *know* she's dead—she's been a crossroads ghost since she was run off the road in 1937. Not that it's slowed her down any. Like Uncle Mike and Aunt Lea, she's not actually a relative, but she fills the same ecological niche, and ghosts are always fun at Halloween parties.

"I'm still not happy about leaving you there on your own," Mom said.

"I know, Mom, but I really do need to go, or we're not going to have time to eat before we have to go and negotiate for a new place to hole up. Email if you're sending anyone else. I won't be here to meet them."

We exchanged our farewells—even Antimony sounded worried about my well-being, which was sort of terrifying—and I ended the call, triggering more cheering from the mice. This discussion was probably about to become a permanent part of their religious canon—the Holy Ritual of the Phone Call Home. I sighed, but I didn't tell them to shut up. This sort of thing was the whole reason I had a colony in Manhattan with me.

Mice—especially intelligent, tool-using mice—are hard to kill, and it would practically take a nuclear strike to wipe out the entire colony. If things went wrong and I didn't make it out of the city, the Aeslin mice who lived with me would be my little black box. They would tell my family what happened, because they would be the only ones who'd been there.

With that particularly cheerful thought in mind, I turned and walked back to the kitchen, where Uncle Mike was busy carving his roast. I stopped in the doorway, not wanting to crowd the large man with the knife. "Did you hear all that?"

"Every word," he said, and held his knife out toward me, a chunk of steaming red meat impaled on the tip. "It's too bad we can't get Mary out here. She'd be great for recon work."

"Right up until she got exorcised," I replied, and plucked the piece of roast from the knife, popping it into my mouth. I made appreciative noises as I chewed, and flashed him a thumbs up.

"Pot roast is easy," he said, dismissing the praise. He still looked pleased. "You should try my lasagna."

I swallowed. "Maybe next time we have a few days in the same place without the specter of imminent death looming overhead."

"That'd be a change, huh?" He opened a cupboard, and frowned. "Where do you keep your Tupperware?"

"I mostly live out of takeout containers," I said. "I don't even know if there *is* Tupperware."

"I don't know how you haven't starved to death, I honestly don't." He pulled a roll of tin foil from the cabinet above the stove. "What's our next move?"

"Head for the Freakshow. A bunch of the dragons work there. I can ask them about renting the old Nest."

"How much authority do they have?"

I smiled a little, leaning over to snatch another piece of roast. "Well, one of them is the current Nest-mother and first wife of their male, so I'd say they have plenty of authority."

Mike paused and blinked at me. Finally, he said, "When you decide to mess with the status quo, you don't think small, do you?"

"Not really." Prior to discovering William asleep under Manhattan, everyone in the cryptozoological community had assumed that the dragons were extinct, and that the dragon princesses were the cryptid equivalent of oxpecker birds—a species of symbiotic hangers-on who had evolved to live alongside the dragons, and didn't know what to do with themselves once their hosts died off. Finding out that dragon princesses were really female dragons changed everything . . . except for the dragons themselves, who continued on their single-minded path toward total control of the world's gold supply.

Now that the old Nest wasn't necessary for the safety of the Manhattan colony, Candy would probably let us use it, as long as we paid what she considered a fair price. If we talked to her at the Freakshow, I could get Kitty to arbitrate, and make sure that Candy's "fair price" didn't wind up being something that would bankrupt my entire family for the next hundred years.

"You Price girls, I swear." Mike produced a loaf of bread from one of the brown paper bags clustered on the counter. "I'm going to pack some roast to go and make a few sandwiches. You're too thin. Then we should get moving. I want to be out of here by nightfall."

"Works for me." We'd have to come back to the apartment at least once. I wouldn't be crushed if I wound up leaving the majority of my possessions behind—it would sting, but I've done worse. There was no way that we could move the mice without having a place to move them *to*.

And there was no way we could move the mice at all without their permission. I turned and walked down the hall to the linen closet, leaving Mike to his roast. The mice who had been in the living room followed me, cheering again as I opened the closet door.

Most of the closet was taken up by a modified Barbie Dream House. All the windows had been punched out and replaced by wooden scaffolding, which twisted around and around the house like a ribbon around a maypole. The pink paint was entirely gone, covered by a thick coat of gunmetal gray nail polish. The mice had done that part themselves. All I provided was the heavy lifting.

I knelt, putting myself on a level with the top windows of the Pantheistic Cryptid Mouse Dream House. "I request audience with the Head Priest," I said. "I don't have any cheese, or cake, but there's pot roast in the kitchen, and we'll share."

For once, there was no cheering. Instead, the mice sat silently, and more tiny rodent faces appeared in the other windows, all of them waiting to see what was going to happen next. Finally, a white-whiskered mouse with a squirrel's skull atop his head stepped laboriously out onto the scaffold in front of that top window.

"Your audience is granted," he squeaked, in a voice that used to be sonorous—by mouse standards, anyway—and now barely carried past the lintel of the closet. "What do you require, O Arboreal Priestess?"

Aeslin mice live a long time by normal rodent standards, but their lives are short by human standards. I remembered when this Head Priest was young and vital, and full of potentially blasphemous ideals. I grew up, and he grew old. There would be a new Head Priest soon. That knowledge made me deeply sad. "The Covenant of St. George is here," I said.

He nodded. "I know. The God of Questionable Motivations is one of theirs, at least in body, if not in heart or mind."

I decided not to think about that too hard. "They know where we live. They have this address."

"Ah," he said, sagely. "You are here to tell me that we

must leave this pleasant home and move to somewhere new, that we might survive to carry the gospel to another generation."

"Something like that," I said. "Can the colony pack up and be ready by tonight? We want to move as soon as possible. It's not safe here anymore."

"If I tell them we must go, they will be ready," he said. He reached out one grizzled paw, clearly beckoning. I held my hand out to him, and he placed his paw gently on the tip of my index finger. "Do not trouble yourself with us, Priestess. We exist only to serve."

"You do a damn good job," I said. "Get them ready. I'll leave the pot roast outside the closet, so you can provision yourselves for the trip."

"So shall it be," he said, and pulled his paw away. I withdrew my hand and stood, recognizing a dismissal when I saw one. The rest of the mice ran into the closet before I could close the door, swarming up the scaffolding as they fought to get into the best position to hear the coming sermon.

He was already beginning to speak when I shut the closet door and turned away. I couldn't hear what he was saying, but from the cheers of the other mice, it was something stirring and inspirational, at least to them. I shook my head and walked back to the kitchen.

"That seemed to go well," said Mike, handing me a roast beef sandwich.

"We're going to get them all killed," I replied. "I don't know where they get that much faith in us."

"Same place anybody gets faith in anything, I guess," he said, and shrugged. "You ready?"

"As I'll ever be. Come on. Let's go see a dragon about an apartment."

Mike's car was parked a block down the street from my apartment, where I would have seen it if I hadn't come in via the rooftops. It was a black Lincoln sedan, and it would be practically invisible in the traffic of any major city. I paused, eyeing it.

"Did you trade in the other car?" I asked.

"Always stay two years behind the times," he replied, clicking the button to unlock the doors. "Any newer, looks like you've got money, you become a viable target. Any older, you risk sticking out. Two years is the sweet spot."

"I'm assuming that means 'yes,'" I guessed. "See, I avoid that problem by never driving anywhere."

"Not all of us want to be Batgirl when we grow up," said Mike, and got into the driver's seat. There was nothing to do at that point but get in on my side, and trust him not to kill us horribly.

(To be fair, Uncle Mike is an excellent driver. He has to be, if he wants to stay alive in Chicago, which seems to have been outfitted with more than its fair share of hitch-hiking ghosts, phantom roadsters, demonically possessed convertibles, and idiots who don't know how to use their turn signals. There are cities that just reinforce my decision not to get a driver's license. Chicago may not be at the top of the list, but it's right on up there. The first two cities on the list are Los Angeles, for obvious reasons, and Warsaw, Indiana, for less obvious ones.)

"So how's things with the dancing?" asked Mike, as he steered us around a double-decker bus full of tourists who were gawking, for no apparent reason, at a street mime. Tourists are weird. If you can accept that, everything about New York starts making infinitely more sense. "Lea and I both voted for you every night while you were on TV, you know."

"No, I didn't know," I said, touched. "That's really sweet of you. Thank you."

"Hey, it was our pleasure. You're pretty good, you know that?"

"I'm aware." I wasn't bragging. I just wasn't arguing with him. There was no point in false modesty: pretending you don't understand your own skills is a good way to get yourself killed when you're out in the field, and once you've given up on underestimating yourself in one area, you might as well give it up entirely. "The dancing is going . . . I mean, it's going, I guess. I spend as much time on it as I can, but other things keep getting in the way, and a lot of the time, they seem way more important. So I guess it's not going as well as I hoped it would be by now, you know?"

"Yeah, I do." He made a right turn, following the silent instructions of his car's GPS. "I used to want to be a bartender, you know."

I blinked. "You did?"

"Oh, yeah. It's the perfect job. You mix a few drinks, you listen to people's problems, you get smiled at by pretty girls, and at the end of the night, unless you have a drinking problem, you get to leave it all behind and go back to a nice little apartment where nothing's lurking in your closet to rip your guts out. It seemed pretty much ideal if you asked me."

Like most of us, Uncle Mike is a hereditary cryptozoologist. His family didn't start with the Covenant—in fact, they didn't even know that cryptids existed until after they'd settled in Chicago, when there was some sort of an incident involving his great-grandfather, a hungry river hag, and my great-grandparents, Frances and Jonathan Healy. At the end of it, they had a dead river hag and a new associate, Arturo Gucciard. He raised his kids knowing about the cryptozoological world, and his kids did the same with theirs, leading us, three generations later, to me and Mike, driving through downtown Manhattan.

"I didn't know this wasn't always what you wanted," I admitted. "What changed?"

"I met Lea. Realized I couldn't trust that other people would always keep her safe—no offense to you or your family, but since you split out of Michigan, it's not like you're exactly the folks next door, you know?"

"No offense taken."

"I wanted to make sure things stayed safe for her, and that meant staying a part of the community. Besides, it turns out that I'm pretty good at monster hunting and cryptid social work. It's hard to fit on a résumé. It still keeps the bills paid, and it keeps my wife nice and breathing, which is a priority for me."

"Yeah." I leaned back in my seat, sighing. This seemed like an odd time for a heart-to-heart—Covenant, eminent danger, possible purge—but Manhattan traffic doesn't respect dramatic tension. We'd get there when we got there, and not a minute before. "I want to dance. I mean, it's what I've wanted my whole life. But it's a daylight career, and so much of what we do happens at night. I've missed three competitions, I've had to stop working as a dance instructor . . . I don't know. I'm just not seeing how I can make both things work at the same time, and if I have to choose one over the other . . ." I stopped.

Mike chose cryptozoology for Lea. I could do the same for Sarah and Ryan and Istas and the mice—all the people that I cared about who didn't fall on the "human" side of the fence. Even my cousin Artie and Uncle Ted, although they had Aunt Jane to make sure nothing came after them. But dance was what I loved. How long would I be able to go without resenting everyone I cared about if I felt like they had forced me to give up the thing that I loved most in the world?

Uncle Mike patted my knee as he pulled into a parking space that had just opened up on the block across from the Freakshow. He neatly cut off a taxi in the process, and the driver leaned hard on his horn, shouting obscenities that were drowned out by the noise. I smiled a little. Uncle Mike smiled back.

"You'll figure it out, Very," he said, turning off the engine. "You think you're the first one who didn't want to grow up and take over the family business? Hell, your daddy didn't always want it. He was going to teach history. And my grandpa used to say that your great-grandpa Johnny wanted to be a librarian."

"Great-Grandpa *was* a librarian," I said.

"That was his daytime job. He never made it out of Buckley, because his real job was in those woods, with your great-grandma. They figured it out. So will you."

I frowned. "Has anyone ever figured out that what they really want to do is walk away and have that daylight job all by itself, forever?"

"No," said Mike. "Come on. Let's go meet your boss."

The dragon from before was no longer in the ticket booth. She had been replaced by a more familiar, less friendly face: Istas, who was sitting calmly behind the glass, stitching another layer of lace onto the edge of her parasol as she waited for a paying customer to demand her attention. I rapped on the edge of the booth. She lifted her head and frowned, eyes narrowing.

"Why are you on the ground?" she demanded. Her gaze flicked to Uncle Mike, who was standing behind me and trying politely not to loom. He wasn't doing a very good job of it. I'm five-two, and almost any adult male will wind up looming over me if he stands too close. "Who is this man?" Her expression brightened slightly, although the frown remained, which was a neat trick. "Are you being held against your will?"

"No," I said quickly, skipping pleasantries in favor of stopping Istas before she could decide to disembowel my uncle. "Istas, this is Mike Gucciard, a friend, associate, and honorary member of my family. Uncle Mike, this is Istas, one of my coworkers."

"It's a pleasure," said Mike, giving Istas a thoughtful look. Istas looked unflinchingly back.

This is Istas: picture a drop-dead gorgeous Inuit girl, about five-six, and roughly an American size sixteen. Now give her a wardrobe entirely based on the concept that one can never have too much lace, too many ribbons, or too many puffy skirts. She's possibly the only waheela in the world devoted to the Gothic Lolita school of fashion, which means she's almost certainly the only waheela in the world who regularly wears her hair in spiral-curled pigtails.

"Waheela?" he asked finally.

"Yes," replied Istas, without batting an eye. "Human?"

Waheela come from the upper reaches of Canada, where they normally spend their days running around in the shape of huge man-eating wolf-bear things, and view dried blood, unspecified muck, and the occasional half-tanned hide as perfectly acceptable wardrobe choices. They aren't very friendly, and no one really gets too upset about that. As members of her species go, Istas is practically a social butterfly. There are days when she not only talks to six whole people, she manages not to threaten any of them.

Uncle Mike nodded. "At least that's what my parents tell me."

"We're going to go inside," I said, before the two of them could start comparing family trees. "Is Kitty in her office?"

"I believe so." Istas resumed stitching lace to her parasol. From a predator, that was a serious compliment. She didn't feel the need to watch me while we talked. Insisting on eye contact would have been a lot more worrisome. Sometimes, dealing with cryptids is all about understanding the social cues they *don't* share with the human race. "She has said that she will be remaining here as much as possible while she prepares for a siege. Angel is at the Costco, buying things."

"That makes sense," I said. "See you."

"Probably," Istas agreed, and kept sewing.

"Come on," I said, and led Mike past the bouncer on the door, into the canvas-draped hallway beyond. He came quietly, looking around as we walked. I felt the sudden urge to start justifying my place of work, explaining how it wasn't as bad as it looked and how really, Kitty's design choices were completely reasonable and understandable. I swallowed it and kept walking. The Freakshow was what it was. If Mike had a problem with that, nothing I said would change it.

We stepped through the last doorway into the main club. Mike stopped, blinking. I followed his gaze to the floor. The lunch rush was over; the people who were left were the truly devoted, the deeply bored, and the ones with no place better to go. A few waitresses circulated,

but most of them were clustered near the bar, where
Ryan and Daisy were busily setting out the remains of
the appetizers they'd over-prepared for the lunch crowd.
Marcy was eating a bowl of gravel with whipped cream
and what looked like kitty litter on top. Carol was taking
mincing bites from a buffalo wing. She'd given several
bones to her hair, and the tiny serpents were fighting
over them.

"Wow," said Mike, finally. "You know, Very, from what
your mother told me, this isn't what I was expecting."

I winced. "It's not?"

"No. This is amazing." He shook his head, turning
toward me. "Lea would love this place."

"Well, once New York is no longer being threatened by
the Covenant, you'll have to bring her for a visit. I can
even let you guys use my staff discount. Come on." I
started down the stairs, waving to the crowd at the bar.
Most of them waved back, but kept eating. Breaks are
rare, precious things in food service; breaks that come
with free snacks are only to be surrendered if you have no
other choice.

Ryan cast a wary look toward Uncle Mike and raised
his voice to call across the music, "Hey, Very. You need
anything?"

"That's concerned friend-ese for 'do I need to break
this guy's legs for you,'" I said, just loud enough for Uncle Mike to hear me. Louder, I called, "No, I'm good. I'll
come back for introductions in a sec. Is Kitty in her office?" A few of the patrons looked our way, and then
turned disinterestedly back to their drinks or their pe-
rusal of the bored-looking dancers on the main stage. I
made a mental note to talk to Kitty about punching up
the quality of our midday entertainment.

"I think so," said Ryan, still watching Mike with suspicion.

I decided to cut this off before there could be some
kind of "emergency" that caused him to come charging
in to Kitty's office while we were trying to explain what
I needed from the dragons. I gestured for Mike to follow
as I approached the bar. Once I was close enough that I

no longer needed to raise my voice, I gestured to Mike, and said, "Ryan, this is my Uncle Mike, who is *not* with the Covenant, but *is* here to help me keep us all from getting killed. Also, he made me a pot roast, and stood over me while I ate a sandwich."

"An entire sandwich?" asked Ryan, who knew far too much about my occasionally spotty eating habits.

"Yup." I looked toward Mike. "Uncle Mike, this is Ryan, our bartender and bouncer. He's also Istas' boyfriend, which means he's either insane or preternaturally patient, and he makes a mean cocktail."

"We'll have to trade tips some time." Mike extended his hand to Ryan, who took it, too surprised to do anything else. They shook. "Nice establishment you've got here. Now if you'll excuse us, my niece and I have to see a bogeyman about a room."

Carol gave another bone to her hair, which hissed happily and set about stripping off the last shreds of meat. "Your family's coming to town?" she asked. "Are things that serious?"

I realized that all the other waitresses were staring at me—and that none of them were human. I owed them the truth. "Not yet," I said. "Uncle Mike's my only backup so far, because we don't know that I'm going to need any more than that. We just want to talk to Kitty about some tactical issues. I promise, nobody's going to start killing anybody else without me giving you a heads-up about things. Okay?"

Carol and the other waitresses looked dubious, but finally she nodded, and the others followed suit. The only ones who didn't look unhappy about the situation were the snakes that made up Carol's hair. They kept stripping the meat off of chicken bones, entirely oblivious to the danger that we were all in.

"Come on, Uncle Mike," I said, and waved to Ryan before grabbing Mike's wrist and pulling him with me toward the door to the staff area. He'd stay if I let him, trying to put everyone at ease and get them all comfortable with the idea of his presence. That was just the kind of guy he was. It was part of what made him so good at his job, and why he and Lea could hold Chicago essentially on their own. The trouble was we didn't have time.

He knew it, too, because he let himself be pulled out of the main club and into the staff area. I was getting pretty tired of making this particular trek. Hopefully, I wouldn't have to do it too many more times. Somehow, I wasn't going to bank on that.

It felt like everyone who worked in the Freakshow was in the building, even the ones who weren't supposed to be on duty for hours. Some of them were carrying backpacks, coolers, and even camping gear. They were settling in for the long haul. I didn't see any dragons, but everyone else seemed to be present, from the near-human to the barely-there. It was like walking through one of George Lucas' fever dreams, only a little more coherent, and a lot less prone to head-tentacles.

"Was that a Pliny's gorgon?" muttered Mike, as we walked toward Kitty's office.

"Yup," I said mildly. "His name's Joe. Don't let him make you coffee." I kept walking. (There are three major subspecies of gorgon. Representatives of two of them worked at the Freakshow. If Kitty ever hired a greater gorgon, she'd be able to declare some form of weird cryptid bingo and win absolutely nothing but the knowledge that she had a lot of venomous people on her staff.)

Kitty was sitting at her desk with the door open when we reached her office. She didn't have her darks on, maybe because with this many people around, she would have just been turning them off every five seconds anyway. I knocked on the doorframe. She looked up, and blinked twice—first at the sight of me, and then at the sight of Uncle Mike. Unfamiliar humans weren't exactly what you'd call "common" in the back halls of the Freakshow. "Can I help you with something?" she asked. There was a wary note in her voice, and she didn't stand up. One of her out-of-sight hands was probably on the panic button, ready to summon security if I looked even a little bit distressed.

Funny as that would have been, I liked all our bouncers too much to pit them against my uncle. "Kitty, this is my Uncle Mike. He's in town to help with the Covenant situation. We need to ask you for a favor."

Kitty blinked again. Then she stood, revealing the bright yellow robe she'd put on over her Super Grover pajamas, and walked to the office door to offer Mike her hand. He took it and shook, not flinching at the strange way her fingers bent. (Bogeymen have extra knuckles, the better to creep you right the hell out when they grab your ankles in the dark. It makes shaking hands with them a little bit disturbing, since it feels like you're breaking fingers no matter how many times you adjust your grip.)

"Katherine Smith," she said. "You can call me 'Kitty,' everyone else does."

"Michael Gucciard," he responded. "You can call me Mike. Thank you for having me here."

She raised an eyebrow. "I had a choice?"

Mike laughed, reclaiming his hand. "Well, ma'am, technically I suppose you could tell me that my services were not required at this time and follow it up by asking me to get the hell out of your city. But that might be a bad idea, given the rest of the situation. I don't think the Covenant of St. George is going to be that easy to get rid of."

"If only," said Kitty. She turned to me. "What's the favor?"

"The Covenant knows where I live," I said, not bothering with prevarication. "I need to move someplace secure, where I won't be endangering anyone else—which means I can't stay here. Can you help me convince Candy to let me rent the old Nest for the duration?"

"What?" Kitty stared at me. "This is your favor? You want me to help you negotiate with a dragon? Are you planning to sell a few kidneys to help finance this little plan?"

"I found them the first male they've seen in centuries.

I'm hoping that will keep the interest rates down. As for the rest, that's where you come in. They'll give me a fairer deal if you're sitting in on the negotiations."

Kitty snorted. "Says you. I know bogeymen have a reputation for striking a hard bargain, but there's loansharking, and then there's whatever it is the dragons do."

"You employ most of the dragons in the city. If they piss you off enough, they don't get paid anymore. Besides which, if the Covenant catches me and starts putting me through information extraction, they might find out where the new Nest is. More importantly, they might find out about William." I bared my teeth in something that bore very little resemblance to a smile. "I think the dragons would really prefer that I not be that easy to catch, don't you?"

"Remind me never to play poker with you," said Kitty. She turned and walked back to her desk, where she hit a button on her phone. "Daisy? It's Kitty. Can you please find Candy and send her to my office? Verity's here, and we need to talk about something."

"Sure thing, Kitty," said Daisy.

Kitty removed her finger from the phone. "All done," she said. "Now we just have to wait."

We didn't have to wait for long. Invoking my name and the phrase "we need to talk" in the same sentence had obviously been enough to light a fire under Candy, because she came speed walking down the hall toward Kitty's office less than five minutes later. She was wearing street clothes, rather than her waitressing gear: yoga pants, an Old Navy tank top, and a pair of scuffed sneakers that were probably bought off the back of a truck somewhere in the Garment District. Dragons don't believe in spending money on things like brand name clothing. Not when they could be spending money on more important things, like gold.

Not that they need nice clothes to be devastatingly gorgeous. Whatever quirk of evolution decided that dragon females should look like human women really went all-out on their physical design: I've never seen a dragon who didn't look like a super model, although they tend to be a modern size ten to fourteen, which makes them a little less high fashion than they were fifty or five hundred years ago. Since dragons only want to attract human men long enough to empty their wallets, I'm not sure the dragons have noticed—or that they really care. Candy was characteristic for her species, with a curvy figure, long, naturally golden hair, enormous blue eyes, and the sort of roses-and-cream complexion that has launched a thousand cosmetic campaigns.

She was also, judging by the way her belly curved under her tank top, at least two months pregnant. "That's why you've been keeping your corset on all the time lately, isn't it?" I asked, indicating her middle. "You don't want it to interfere with your tips."

Candy glared at me. From her, that was practically a warm welcome. "Who is this?" she demanded, jabbing a finger at Mike. Then she turned her glare on Kitty. "I'm not on duty yet. You have no right to claim my time."

"I started paying you for today as soon as I called for you," Kitty smoothly replied. "And any time you spend talking to Verity is not coming out of your breaks or lunchtime. Talk long enough, you could get paid for *hours* of doing basically nothing. Don't you think that's worth coming on the clock a little early?"

"Normally, I would love to improve relations with the dragons by helping you get money for nothing and your kicks for free, but I don't have hours to do basically nothing," I said, flashing Kitty a grateful look. "Candy, this is Michael Gucciard, my uncle. He's here from Chicago to help me deal with the Covenant while they're in town. We'd like to get them *out* of town before anybody gets hurt. I need your help."

Candy eyed me suspiciously. "What kind of help did you have in mind?"

"I want to rent the old Nest."

Whatever answer Candy had been expecting, it wasn't that: her eyes widened, genuine shock showing through before her expression hardened again and she snapped, "Absolutely not. It's out of the question."

"Why?"

"What if the Covenant follows you there? Then what?"

"It's not connected to your new Nest in any way. There's not even a tunnel between the two of them. You're not going to move back there, not with William stuck under the city, and you're not going to find a way to move William while the Covenant is in town. Dominic knows where I live, Candy, and that means that the Covenant knows—I hope he won't tell them, but I can't be sure." I looked at her earnestly. "If you want me to be here to fight the Covenant for you, I need to be sure that they can't just stroll in and take me out. That means I need to be somewhere safe. Secure. Solid. I need the Nest."

"It's *ours*," she snapped.

"I don't want to buy it. I just want to rent it."

"And you're going to rent it to her, Candy, for a reasonable amount," said Kitty suddenly. We both turned to look at her. "It's a large building, entirely uninhabited— say five thousand a month? Would that be acceptable to the both of you?"

"Well—" I began, doing a quick mental review of my finances. I was supposed to be self-sufficient while I was in New York, but this was the sort of thing where I could get money from my family if I needed it. The only question was how much, and how fast.

"It's fine," said Mike.

I felt a flash of resentment. I should be grateful that he was helping with my plan, but this was *my* city, and I didn't need him taking over. I forced the resentment down just as quickly as it came. Pride is for people who can afford it.

"Good," said Kitty. "Candy? You're the Nest-mother. Is five thousand a month acceptable?"

Candy glowered. "She can't stay forever," she said.

"Six-month lease with an option to renew if the Covenant is still in town at the end of that period," said Kitty.

If the Covenant was still in town in six months, there wouldn't be a Nest for me to rent. That kind of stay would mean that the purge was well and truly in prog-

ress. The dragons might survive, if they went underground fast enough, sealed all the doors and got lucky in
every possible way—because they couldn't run, could
they? Out of all the dragons in the world, the dragons of
Manhattan were the ones with something they had to
defend.

"No," said Candy coldly. "No, she can't have our Nest.
Six months is too long. Six *hours* is too long."

Something inside of me snapped. Without a safe place
to go, I was as good as done—and while I'm not quite
arrogant enough to think that Manhattan was doomed
without me, the cryptid population was going to be in a
lot more trouble if they had to wait for the next wave of
defense to arrive. Assuming the family even sent another
team. Assuming they didn't just call one ally and one
daughter a big enough price to pay, pull Sarah out, and
wash their hands of the matter.

We're not heroes. We're not gods, no matter what the
mice may think. We're just people trying to do a job, and
that sometimes means admitting that the job is too big
to finish. I'd be added to the family history as one more
soul we couldn't save, and the rest of them would go on
trying to survive. That's what we do. That's what we've
been doing since Alexander and Enid Healy walked
away from the Covenant of St. George.

Sometimes I get awfully tired of just surviving.

"How far along are you, Candy?" I asked quietly.
She flinched. "I'm guessing you're about eight weeks.
Nearing the end of your first trimester. Do dragons
have trimesters?"

"We carry the eggs for six months, and then we incu-
bate them for six more," she said, voice just above a
whisper.

"Do you want the Covenant to find your eggs? I bet
they'd be fascinated. They haven't had dragon eggs to
play with in so long. Oh, and there's your sisters to think
about. I mean, back in the day, there was no way to really
tie you guys biologically to the males of your species.
That level of sexual dimorphism is really unusual outside
of deep sea fish. But science doesn't play favorites. The

Covenant has science, too. They'll crack a couple of those eggs open, find some scaly little boys and pink-skinned little girls, and then they'll figure it out. You've survived because they haven't been hunting you. They haven't considered you worth hunting. How do you think the league of dragon hunters will take it when they find out that they've been ignoring their mission statement all these years? I think it'll be like Christmas for their twisted little hearts."

Candy glanced frantically at Kitty, who shook her head.

"You want me to tell her to stop being mean, I can tell," she said. "I'm not going to do that, because she's not being mean. Mean would be threatening to call the Covenant on you if you didn't do what she wants. She's just pointing out that being stubborn for the sake of being stubborn doesn't get you anything but killed."

"Why are you on *her* side?" demanded Candy.

"Because, Candice, I'd like to live," said Kitty. She planted her hands on her hips and glared. Her Sesame Street pajamas undermined her intimidation factor a bit, but her gray skin and subtly inhuman bone structure balanced it. "I know you don't like the Prices, although I sort of thought we were getting past that, with the whole 'here, have your scaly Prince Charming' stunt they pulled last year. I don't care. You're going to let Verity use your Nest as long as she needs it, as long as the Covenant is here in town. I'm going to pay you five thousand dollars for every month that she's there. And you're not going to say one more bad word about it. You're just going to go back to your sisters and your husband and let them know that the Prices are moving in."

Candy stared at her. Then she stiffened, and said coldly, "I never thought you'd side with humans over your own kind, Kitty."

Much to everyone's surprise, Kitty burst out laughing. "Seriously, Candy? *Seriously?* You're going to pull the cryptid solidarity card on me? Honey, you're not even a *mammal.* Verity is a closer relative of mine than you are, and frankly, I will side with whoever keeps me, and the rest of the city's bogey community, breathing. Understand me?"

"Yes," said Candy coldly. She turned to me. "I'll go get you the keys. It may take a while. I hope you don't shoot me for making you wait." Then she turned and stomped off down the hall, not looking back.

I sighed. "That could have gone better."

"I've done a lot of negotiating with dragons," said Kitty. "Trust me, no, it couldn't have. Besides, now you've got a place to go. That's what you wanted, isn't it?"

"Yeah," I said. "Can you send Ryan over with the keys when Candy finally comes back? I need to go pack."

"Sure," said Kitty. "And Verity—trust me. It's going to be okay."

I laughed a little. "At least one of us thinks so."

Ten

"Bang bang. You're dead."

— Frances Brown

The Meatpacking District, which is nicer than it sounds, inside a converted warehouse (which is a more pleasant way of saying "slaughterhouse")

THE HIDEBEHIND GLAMOUR that had once hidden the true contents of the converted slaughterhouse that held the dragons' Nest was gone. We had been able to see the true structure of the building from the minute we walked through the front door. (This had been more difficult than I expected it to be, since the dragons' overpriced bodega was also gone, and that was the only easy ground floor entrance to the slaughterhouse courtyard. Luckily, Mike and I had both been picking locks since before we could tie our shoes, but it would have been nice to have a little warning.)

The power still worked—that made sense, since it wasn't like the dragons had ever been paying for it in the first place—and after flipping a few dozen switches, we were able to get a good idea of what we were dealing with: a huge, two-story building with a ground floor that consisted almost entirely of one enormous room. The gold that used to fill the place was gone, taken by the dragons when they moved to their new home beneath the city. The patched-together carpet was still on the floor, but that was about it. There was no furniture, and whatever illusion the building might have possessed of being something other than a part of the industrial wasteland had departed with the dragons.

Stairs led to the offices on the second floor, which were arrayed all the way around the edges of the room. The layout was left over from the original slaughter-house design, letting the occupants of those offices look out on the livestock waiting to be put to death below. Charming stuff, and the reason I was vaguely afraid of being haunted by the ghosts of hamburgers past while we were staying at the Nest. A waist-high rail ran along the walkway to keep people from plummeting to their deaths, presumably out of sorrow for the cows, sheep, and other victims of the slaughterhouse assembly line. There were enough offices that we could each have one as a bedroom, with another to use as an armory, and an-other for the mice. Even after all that, there were easily half a dozen offices standing empty, and we hadn't even looked at the basement.

The mice were thrilled about having an entire office for their Barbie Nightmare House. It must have been an incredible step up after being confined in a single closet. They had started arranging raiding parties as soon as I put them down. All the raiding parties were armed with tiny spears, crossbows, and swords. There would be no rats left in the slaughterhouse by morning, and the mice would feast for days.

It can be easy to forget that Aeslin aren't cute Disney cartoons come to life. They're vicious fighters when they have to be, and they've survived in a world filled with bigger, meaner, better-armed creatures by being smart and absolutely ruthless. That's something else they have in common with our family. Prices and Aeslin always, *always* shoot to kill.

"Verity!"

"Coming!" I stepped out of the office we'd given to the mice, walking to the rail and looking down. Ryan and Mike were on the main floor of the slaughterhouse, pil-ing my meager possessions—mostly weapons and clothing—around the coolers and gear boxes Mike had brought with him from Chicago. "What'cha need?"

"Do you own a bed?" asked Mike. He somehow managed to shout without sounding like he was shouting. Probably a skill developed to make it easier to talk to sea monsters who didn't feel like coming to shore, but didn't want to be yelled at, either.

"Not here," I said. I sat down on the walkway, squeezing through the gap between the bars intended to keep us from plummeting to our deaths. Then I turned, hooking my toes against the base of the rail, and leaned backward. This resulted in my dangling about eight feet off the floor. Mike and Ryan watched this process without comment. "I left my bed back in Portland."

"Got it. We're going to want to pick up some inflatables, maybe a bean bag chair or something. Things we can carry in without attracting attention." Mike returned to surveying my belongings, for all the world like I wasn't dangling from the walkway behind him. I leaned forward again, grabbed the lowest bar of the railing, and tucked my knees, bracing against the side of the walkway in a sort of horizontal squat before letting my feet drop. "I think we've got enough food to hold out for a few days—did you know there's a full kitchen?"

"I guess they couldn't replace that with gold," I said, hand-walking my way over to the nearest of the support beams holding up the walkway. It was like the monkey bars on my elementary school playground, only without as many yard monitors waiting to tell me that it wasn't ladylike to climb. "Thanks again for helping us get moved in, Ryan."

"Yeah, about that—it wasn't purely altruistic." The therianthrope bartender moved toward me as he spoke, lacking Uncle Mike's skill at shouting without shouting. "I wanted to ask you for a favor."

"Name it." I had reached the pillar. I grasped it firmly with my knees and let go of the rail, flipping so that I was facing toward the floor. With this accomplished, I began climbing carefully down.

"Istas and I were wondering if maybe—what the *hell* are you doing?"

"I'm going to assume that wasn't your original question. What I'm doing is figuring out the tactical shape of the room. Most of the time, if I can't shoot something in the first thirty seconds of dealing with it, my style of staying alive involves being able to go up as much as possible. So knowing what will and won't support my weight is important." It was also fun, and extremely relaxing. I needed to relax. This wasn't going to end overnight.

"Oh. That's weird, Very."

"I know."

"Anyway, Istas and I were wondering if we could come and stay here with you. You know, until all this is taken care of. Kitty says we can crash at the Freakshow if we want, but Istas really can't do crowds twenty-four seven. I'm afraid she'd take somebody's head off. And then she'd eat it, which would probably get her fired."

"You want to crash with us?" I grabbed the pillar and flipped myself around again, landing with my feet neatly on the floor. Then I blinked at Ryan. "You realize that if the Covenant finds out about this place, it's going to be open season."

"I don't think any place in this city is safe now that they're here. I'd rather be unsafe with you than unsafe on my own, and I don't want Istas eating one of the barmaids without a really good reason."

I glanced toward Mike. He put his hands up, and said, "Ryan already said he was going to ask you. I told him it was your call."

"But what do you think?" I asked. He'd acknowledged that this was my operation. I could be magnanimous.

Mike lowered his hands, looking serious. "I think we need all the muscle we can get, and I can cook for four as easy as I can cook for two."

Given that Ryan and Istas were both therianthropes, I was pretty sure Mike was going to regret saying that. This wasn't the time to point that out. I turned back to Ryan. "As long as you can be subtle about moving your stuff over here, you and Istas are both welcome to stay."

Part of me wanted to add "and so is anybody else who wants to come." The sensible part of me—the one that

understood that this was about to become a war zone—
stepped in, and didn't let the words get out.

Ryan grinned, relief obvious. "I'll go tell Istas. Thanks
a lot, Very."

"Don't thank me until you've spent your first night
trying to sleep through the mice," I said—but I let him
hug me when he stepped closer, and I hugged him back
with equal fervor. There's something to be said for keeping your friends around you when things get bad. It may
not be good for their life expectancies, but it's sure as
hell easier on the heart.

My phone rang. I pulled away from Ryan, offering
him one last smile, and dug the phone out of my pocket.
The call was coming from a blocked number. "Hello?"

"Verity, it's Sarah. You owe me. Do you understand
how much you owe me? Does your tiny, fluff-filled little
head have the capacity to comprehend the volume of
'owe' that you now bear on your skinny little shoulders?"

I laughed. "Artie found the address?"

"Artie found the address," Sarah confirmed. "Artie
then spent an hour grilling me about why I wanted to
know. Do you have any idea how bad I am at lying to
him?"

"You're probably the only cuckoo in the world who
can say 'I'm a bad liar' with a straight face, you know." I
sat down on top of an ammo box. "What did you tell
him?"

"That you'd explain later. About twelve times. And
then I told him that if he didn't stop pushing, I was going
to start crying, and then neither of us would get anything
done. He's really unhappy, Very."

"I'm sorry. I really am. But you said he found the address?"

Sarah made a frustrated sound. "I'm texting it to you
now. You were right—the credit card used for the rental
is registered to an address downtown. It's an apartment,
though, about the size of yours. I don't think Dominic's
going to be keeping the entire Covenant there."

"No, but he may have left something that we can use
to figure out where he's gone." I paused. "Speaking of

which, don't bother going by my apartment. We just finished moving my stuff out of there. I'm going to see if I can get the Internet working where I am now, and I have cell service."

"Wait, 'we'?" said Sarah, voice going suddenly suspicious. "Who's with you?"

"Uncle Mike's here from Chicago." I had to hold the phone away from my ear to keep her delighted squeal from piercing my eardrum. "Sarah! Volume!"

"Sorry! Sorry sorry, but tell Uncle Mike I say hi, okay? I'd ask where you were, but you probably shouldn't tell me over the phone, so I'll just beg you to be at least a little bit careful, and try not to get killed."

"I'll do my best." I briefly considered telling her to get out of the Port Hope, but decided against it. No one who wasn't attuned to her would be able to remember where she was, and much as I hated to consider it, that included Dominic. She was safest if she didn't move. "Stay inside tonight, okay?"

"Okay." She sounded relieved.

That made two of us. We exchanged good-byes, and I hung up. The little yellow envelope that meant I had a text message appeared at the top of my screen two seconds later. I tapped it with my thumb, and it opened, displaying a midtown address. According to the clock, it was almost six. The sun would be setting soon. I straightened, slipping the phone into my pocket.

"Hey, Uncle Mike? I think I need to go out for a little while. Can you get things set up here?"

"Depends. Are you going to go do something stupid that your folks would want me to forbid you to do?"

"Nope. And it's not like you can forbid me to do anything anyway." I smiled winningly. "I'm just going to break into Dominic's apartment and see if I can find anything to tell me where he's keeping the Covenant while they're in town."

"Oh, is that all?" Mike waved a hand dismissively. "Pick up some eggs while you're out. I'll make omelets in the morning. Also, write down the address and leave it by the door. If you're not back in an hour, I'll go over to have a chat with your young man." Any "chat" Uncle Mike described in those terms would probably involve a crowbar.

"Sure thing, Uncle Mike," I said, and turned to head for the nearest stairway. If I was going to do this, I was going to do it my way, and that meant that step one was getting myself away from ground level.

The dragons had been living in the Meatpacking District for so long that their renovated slaughterhouse was surrounded on all sides by buildings whose tenants probably had no idea what was in that sealed-off courtyard. New York is an old enough city that it has more than its share of odd architectural quirks like that, little streets that lead to nowhere, little courtyards that technically aren't accessible unless you know the secret steps to get you there. I stopped on the edge of the slaughterhouse roof, looking around me as I assessed my position.

This was my neighborhood now. I might never see the apartment I'd been illegally subletting again. The thought was oddly sobering. Even if I survived, my time in New York was almost up. The deal I'd made with my family was for a year. At the end of that, I was supposed to choose between cryptozoology and dancing. I had one month left in my original plan.

When this ended, I was either cutting ties with the cryptid community, or I was going home.

I tried not to think about that too hard as I backed up to the middle of the roof, got myself a running start, and leaped.

Some people will tell you that gravity is a cruel mistress. I think they're missing the point. Gravity isn't cruel. Gravity is exactly the same for everybody, Covenant, Price, or neutral party. Gravity doesn't *care*. Once you give yourself over to the essential forces that govern the universe, your choices are plummet or learn how to control your fall. After years of effort, I had learned control.

The buildings around the old Nest were still mostly

unfamiliar to me—I'd never been what you'd call a regular guest back when the dragons lived here, and I certainly hadn't been swinging by on a regular basis since—but I'd been free running through New York long enough by that point to be at least a little comfortable traveling blind. I grabbed hold of a fire escape as I fell, letting my own momentum snap me to a stop and then send me swinging upward. Energy likes to be used, and so I used it, turning the half swing into a full swing that deposited me neatly on the next level of the fire escape. From there, it was just a matter of running along the building ledge until I could leap again, landing safely on the next roof.

I gathered speed and certainty with every transition. My muscles were loosening, body falling into the familiar dance of playing chicken with gravity. I've been free running since puberty was just a scary specter in the rearview mirror of my life, running up on me like T. Rex in the first *Jurassic Park*. I've long since passed puberty, and a bunch more milestones I wasn't looking for, and through everything that's changed, free running has always stayed the same. I appreciate that.

I also appreciated the fact that getting to Dominic's address involved several stretches of city that I was comfortable with, allowing me to take the time to confuse my route by doubling back, using unnecessary shortcuts and longcuts (like shortcuts, but designed to make the trip longer and more confusing), and generally messing around. If someone tried to follow me, or tried to use some kind of tracking spell to figure out where I'd started from, they were going to find it a much taller order than originally assumed.

New York is seen as a pretty big city, especially by people who look at the population size and try to imagine a world where all those people actually *fit*. In reality, the island of Manhattan is fairly small. It's just compact, with enough people for a dozen cities all stacked on top of each other. That makes it a free runner's dream and a monster hunter's nightmare. The city's cryptid population would know the rooftops and sewers as well as or better than I did, leaving the Covenant of St. George grasping at shadows as they tried to figure out where their targets were going to stop.

Home field advantage is a good thing, if you know how to use it, and if you're not overly committed to the idea of playing fair. Personally, I've always thought that "playing fair" was another way of saying "play to lose." I'm more a fan of my grandmother's motto: play for keeps. If I was going to get involved in the Covenant's little game, I was going to come out the winner, or I was going to die trying.

The address Artie had provided was to a nondescript live-work building that looked like it had last been renovated sometime in the early nineties, when all the dotcom kids were totally in love with the idea of working themselves into an early, if lucrative, grave. Dominic's apartment was on the nineteenth floor. That worked out well for me, since the building was only twenty-three stories high. A little air is a nice thing to have. A lot of air can lead to plummeting.

Most of the time, I prefer to do my running without a net; nets just slow you down. Sometimes, however, even I have to admit the wisdom of having a little something to hold onto. That's why I always carried a climbing harness when I thought I might need to perform a little friendly breaking and entering. I measured off my rope based on the floor where the apartment was supposedly located, leaving myself a few extra feet for maneuverability. Once that was done and the rope was set, I tied it to one of the building's heat vents, checked the climbing belt twice to make sure it was secure, and stepped off the edge of the roof onto the empty air.

The air obligingly failed to support my weight, and I dropped forty feet straight down, only to be brought up short by the elastic ties connecting the rope to my harness. I went limp, letting gravity have its way with me. That was the best way to avoid any unwanted broken bones or dislocated shoulders. Physics can play nice, as long as it feels like you're playing along.

(Antimony calls that particular move "pulling a Gwen Stacy," and mutters imprecations about how she's going to wind up short a sister one of these days. Antimony reads too many comic books.)

Once the rope stopped swaying, I sat up and looked around. I was dangling about two feet below the floor level of a nearby balcony. I swung myself over that way, reaching out to grab the rails as soon as they came close enough. Then I pulled myself laboriously upward, finally sliding myself onto the balcony.

The small child who was standing behind the sliding glass door leading into the apartment blinked at me. I blinked back, too surprised to do anything else. Slowly, he opened the sliding glass door.

I said the first thing that popped into my head: "Didn't your parents tell you never to open the door for a stranger?"

"Superheroes aren't strangers," he said, with calm matter-of-factness. I must have looked puzzled, because he explained, "You flew onto the balcony. Strangers don't fly. If strangers could fly, I'd *never* be allowed outside. So you're a superhero. Like the man next door."

Like the . . . "See, that's who I was coming here to see," I said quickly. "We're supposed to be having a team-up. Can you tell me which way his balcony is? It's sort of hard to aim precisely when you're heading for something the size of a building."

The little boy pointed solemnly to the balcony to the right.

"Great, thank you." I boosted myself back onto the banister, intending to jump. Then I paused. "Oh, and hey, kid? There are bad superheroes, too. So you really shouldn't open the door, even for people who *can* fly." Most human threats were unlikely to attack from above. That didn't do much to eliminate the cryptid ones.

"Okay," said the boy, and closed the door. I guess when a superhero tells you to do something, you do it.

Leave it to Dominic to preach secrecy and caution to

me, and forget to consider whether or not his neighbors could see him from their balcony. I smirked as I jumped back down and swung over to his apartment, grabbing hold of the balcony rails and pulling myself up for a second time. This time, no small children greeted me. Instead, the sliding glass doors granted me a view of a sparsely furnished, utterly deserted apartment.

"Jackpot," I murmured, and started squirming out of my climbing harness.

After the last of the buckles was undone, I used a carabiner to snap the harness to the balcony rail. That way, I'd still be able to reach my rope if I needed to make a quick escape, but I wouldn't be wandering around the apartment looking like the victim of badly-considered bondage. The kid from next door hadn't reappeared on his balcony. I decided that was a good thing—no one wants people watching their breaking and entering, especially not when they're as rusty as I am—and moved to try the door.

It slid open easily. I stopped, blinking. "Okay, that was . . . anticlimactic," I muttered. Dominic must not have considered the need for exterior nineteenth floor security. If we both survived this, and were on speaking terms when everything was said and done, he and I were going to have some serious talks about that.

That, or this was all a trap. I stayed where I was for several seconds, weighing the possibility that he was playing me against my need to know what was inside. In the end, common sense was solidly voted down by the rest of me.

I stepped inside.

My father always says that you can tell a lot about a person by the way they live when no one's watching. My brother Alex, for example, didn't do laundry for three months when he went away to college, because that was how long it took for him to run out of clean shirts. Sarah generally lived like she was totally unaware that the physical world existed. Antimony alphabetized her knives.

Apparently, Dominic lived like he was expecting to be gone tomorrow, and didn't want to leave too much of a mess for the next people who passed through. There was something almost tragic about the bare wood floor and the empty, Ikea-issue shelves. What little furniture he had was clearly window dressing, purchased because it was expected of him, and then practically unused.

I moved through the apartment like a ghost, opening every drawer and cabinet that I passed. The coat closet was filled with weapons, ranging from a longbow and three quivers of arrows to an assortment of pole arms that had clearly become part of the standard equipment back during the Covenant's dragon slaying days. The pantry held nothing but ramen noodles, canned chicken, and generic macaroni and cheese, the kind that never looked like food, no matter what you did to it. The fridge was a little better—at least it had a few cartons of take-out Chinese food. I recognized them as coming from the Chinese place we always went to together, on our rare "date nights." Maybe he didn't know anything closer.

The medicine cabinet in the bathroom was packed with first aid supplies both mundane and magical. Band-Aids and gauze pads, over-the-counter painkillers and powdered basilisk bones, antibiotics and antivenin, even some Tylenol 3 with codeine—all the things your modern monster hunter needs if he's going to keep fighting.

Once I had exhausted the rest of the apartment, I moved on to the bedroom. Dominic's bed was a twin-sized futon mattress without a frame, shoved up against the wall like an afterthought. Looking at it broke my heart a little bit. The Covenant gave him resources and access to knowledge stretching back for centuries. What it didn't give him was a single person willing to make sure he slept in a real bed, and ate something more nutritious than shrimp-flavored ramen.

"Dammit, Dominic," I murmured, and began searching the bedroom.

I found what I was looking for under the futon: a sheet of paper on which was written a dockside address, the number for a car rental service—labeled—and another number, unlabeled. I straightened, folding the paper and slipping it into my belt.

"I couldn't tell you, but I could count on you finding a way to come and get it for yourself," said Dominic.

I stiffened. Then I turned, slowly, half-convinced that he'd be holding a crossbow with his finger on the trigger.

Instead, he was just standing there, hands in his pockets, looking faintly defeated. "They're getting settled into our temporary residence," he said quietly. "I've been sent out for food. If you can recommend an 'authentic Italian' restaurant that does takeout, I'd be very grateful. None of the places I go will meet their standards."

"Dominic . . ." I began, and stopped, not sure how to continue. "I'm sorry I broke into your apartment" probably wasn't going to cut it.

A very small smile crossed his face. "You found the place faster than I expected you to. I was actually stopping by to pick up a few things."

"Like what?" I asked, before I could stop myself. "There's nothing here to pick up. You might as well be living out of cardboard boxes."

"I threw those out months ago." His smile faded, expression composing itself. "Verity . . ."

"Are you okay? Those people from the Covenant, they're not hurting you or anything, are they?" It was a stupid question. I didn't know what else to ask.

"Why would they hurt me? They think I'm one of them."

"Are you?"

Another smile crossed his face. This one was sadder, and died even faster than its predecessor. "I don't know, Verity. I wish I did."

"I'm not in my apartment anymore."

"Good. I'm glad. You weren't safe there."

"You wouldn't tell them where to find me, would you?"

Dominic sighed. "I don't know. If I knew . . . there are

a great many things that I don't know, right now. It's not a pleasant sensation."

"I'm sorry." I stepped toward him, offering my hands. After a moment's hesitation, he took them. "If you need me, call. I'll try to come."

"If I call you, run. There's no guarantee I'll be doing it for the right reasons—or of my own free will." He leaned forward to rest his forehead against mine. "Either I'll have betrayed you, or they'll have compelled me. It's not worth the risk."

"I wish—"

"I know." He ducked his head enough to bring his mouth to mine. The kiss was long, and slow, and sweet in a way that was difficult to describe. Kisses on the eve of battle almost always are. When he pulled away again, it was only to murmur, "I have something I need to tell you. I should have told you before. I shouldn't tell you at all."

"What?" I blinked at him, puzzled.

"I love you, Verity Price. Regardless of how things go from here, please remember that. There was a time, however short, where I was a boy, and you were a girl, and I allowed myself to love you." He smiled ruefully. "I'm sorry."

"Don't be sorry." This time, I was the one leaning in. I kissed him hard, hard enough that when I pulled away, my lips felt bruised. "Covenant boys and Price girls . . . it's sort of the natural order of things at this point, don't you think?"

"Nature is cruel," Dominic murmured, and tugged his hands free of mine. I let him go. "You can't come here again. Once they're settled, they'll begin patrolling, and this is technically Covenant property. They'll feel free to come and go here as they like. I can't risk them stumbling over you because they stopped to resupply themselves."

"I don't suppose you can give me their names, can you? Just so I can find out who we're dealing with."

Dominic hesitated.

"Come on," I said, a bit more sharply. "I'm the one

who's standing solo here. It's not betraying the Covenant
to tell me who I'm going to be fighting against."

He sighed. "All three are from the British arm of the
Covenant, possibly because that was where I had the bulk
of my training, after my parents died. The men are Peter
Brandt and Robert Bullard. The woman . . . Verity, please
understand that I had absolutely no influence in choosing
who would be sent with this team."

"I know that." I frowned. "Why?"

"The woman's name is Margaret Healy. She's your
third cousin. And if there is anyone in the Covenant who
hates your branch of the family more than she does, I
have yet to have the misfortune of meeting them."

I stared at him. "Oh," I said, finally. "Well, shit."

Dominic sighed again. "My thought exactly."

Eleven

"Nobody loves you like family. Nobody hates you like family, either. That's why it's so important for us to stick together. If we don't, we're going to wind up hunting each other down."

—Enid Healy

The rooftops of Manhattan, heading back toward the Meatpacking District

I RAN ACROSS the rooftops faster than I ever had before, managing to make the leaps and changes in elevation needed through a combination of skill and raw terror. Terror is a powerful motivator toward perfection. Even so, it was something of a miracle when I reached the Meatpacking District without falling to my death.

Margaret Healy. The woman who was almost certainly going to kill me was named Margaret Healy. Her friends probably called her "Peggy" or something—if being a member of the Covenant of St. George left her any time for making friends. She was probably a really nice person in her off hours. And she had all the training, resources, and focus she needed to take me down.

I was so screwed.

That thought clung to the front of my mind like a Pacific Northwest tree octopus clings to a branch as I grabbed the rail of the nearest fire escape and jumped off the slaughterhouse roof. By swinging hand over hand, I was able to make it to a low enough point to let me safely drop down to the brick courtyard attached to the Nest. I landed harder than I would have liked, still too distracted by my encounter with Dominic to balance myself right. Pain shot up my heels and into my calves as my legs protested the impact.

"Walk it off," I muttered, and straightened, starting toward the slaughterhouse door. The pain lingered for the first few steps, but then it faded, except for a few distant grumbles that would probably be bruises in the morning. There's a reason I buy my Tiger Balm in bulk.

When I was sure that the pain was on the way out, I broke into a run, and kept running until I was inside the Nest. The door echoed as it slammed closed behind me. There was no one there.

"Uncle Mike?" I looked around before cupping my hands and shouting, "Uncle Mike! If you're here, we need to talk!"

"He is not present." The voice came from behind me. I whirled to find Istas standing less than two feet away, her head cocked to the side, a quizzical expression in her dark brown eyes. She was wearing her hair loose for once, hanging around her round face in heavy black waves, and had a bright blue feather fascinator clipped above one ear. She was probably the most stylish waheela in the world, for certain values of "stylish."

She was still a waheela. I took a step back. "Personal space, Istas, remember? We've talked about this."

"My apologies." She also took a step back, creating an acceptable bubble of emptiness between us. Istas was a coworker, a friend, and someone I was perfectly happy to share a converted slaughterhouse with. Sometimes, she was also a giant, man-eating wolf-bear from the primal heart of humanity's nightmares. I like her a lot, but having her stand too close can still remind my reptile hindbrain that part of her will always view me as prey. "Your not-relation and Ryan are currently not present."

"Where are they? I have news."

"They said we required provisions, and Ryan wanted to inform Kitty that we would be accessible via telephone only for the duration of the crisis." Istas suddenly smiled, showing teeth that were too sharp to be entirely human. "I am very pleased that we will be staying here. It makes Ryan feel better, and increases the potential for carnage."

"Oh, trust me, the potential for carnage is *very* high right now," I muttered. Then I paused, an unpleasant thought striking me. "Uh, Istas? Not to be indelicate or anything, but what is it that you, you know, eat?"

"I can eat all types of human food, although I am very fond of pizza and chicken wings. They're crunchy."

"Oh, good—" I began.

But Istas wasn't done. "I am also fond of alley cats, small dogs, and urban rodents. I make an excellent rat casserole. Ryan says I am a natural." Istas perked up. "Would you like me to prepare dinner?"

"No," I said, wincing. "But there are some people I think you need to meet before we do anything else."

Freed from the confines of their front hall closet, the Aeslin mice had been busy. Their raiding parties had returned with several dead rats and a coatl—a feathered snake four feet long. It was probably a tohil, one of the smaller, less venomous varieties of feathered serpent, judging by the color of its plumage. The mice had been in the process of skinning the thing when Istas and I arrived, and I didn't feel like interrupting dinner preparations to find out.

It was funny, in a way. If Dominic had killed the coatl, I would have lectured him for days about harming cryptid wildlife that wasn't dangerous to the human population. But the coatl was one of the natural predators of the Aeslin mice, and if they wanted to eat it before it could eat them, I wasn't going to hold it against them.

The entire colony stopped their preparations for the moving feast when Istas and I walked into the office, and a sea of tiny heads turned in our direction, tiny black eyes glittering in the overhead light. More heads poked out of the walls and the converted Barbie house—which was now surrounded, I saw, with smaller lean-tos and half-built ceremonial buildings. This wasn't just a feast. It was a barn raising, Aeslin style.

All the more reason for me to get this taken care of quickly. "Hello, colony," I said.

"HAIL!" replied the mice, with one voice. Istas jumped.

"Verity . . ." She stepped closer to me. This time, I didn't remind her about personal space. "There are *mice*."

"Yes. I don't want you to eat them, so it seemed to me that introductions were in order."

She gave me a sidelong look, expression clearly implying that I might well be insane. I'd been seeing that face since I was old enough to get sent home from kindergarten for telling fibs. (To their credit, my parents had grounded me, not for telling fibs—I hadn't—but for being stupid enough to tell my teacher about the time my grandmother shot the Boob Fairy with a load of buckshot. All my teacher heard was that things were taken care of. And they were. I became a much better liar after that.)

"The mice are *talking*," said Istas patiently, in case I had somehow failed to notice.

"True," I agreed. "Colony, this is Istas."

"HAIL ISTAS!" declared the mice.

Istas jumped again. Then she turned and glared at me, like this was all an elaborate trick that I was staging for her benefit. "Make them stop *talking*," she demanded.

"I can't. No one can. If I had that power, my sex life would be a lot less complicated." I decided to take mercy on her—always show mercy to the apex predators when possible—and cleared my throat before saying, "In the interests of maintaining local harmony, I invoke Conversation for Cake."

The mice cheered once before going eerily silent. Istas stepped closer still, until I could feel the heat of her skin. I managed not to step away.

A small figure appeared on one of the wooden paths winding around the former Barbie Dream House. It made its slow way up to the very top of the structure, leaning heavily on its staff with every step. I didn't offer to help. The High Priest was proud. If he wasn't, he would already have stepped down, letting a younger, more enthusiastic mouse take his place. I wouldn't shame him by acting like he couldn't make the walk on his own.

When he reached the top of the house, he stopped, coiling his tail tightly around his feet as he turned to face us. He kept hold of his kitten bone staff, letting it support his weight. His whiskers were forward, signaling his curiosity. "What do you wish, O Priestess?" he squeaked.

"Hello, my friend," I said. I indicated Istas. "This is Istas, of the waheela. She'll be staying with us here while we take care of things. I wanted her to meet the colony."

"Before there could be Bad Decisions," said the High Priest. He bowed to Istas. "Milady Carnivore. Welcome to our Home."

The other mice took this as an invitation to cheer. The High Priest silenced them all with a stern glare, and one rap of his kitten bone staff against the roof. He might be old, but he still ruled his people with an iron paw.

Istas, meanwhile, was looking at him with unabashed curiosity. "You are talking mice," she said. "Mice are not meant to talk."

"Yet talk we do," said the High Priest. "Truly, you are wise, to approach such a complicated theological question on your very first introduction." He rapped his staff again. This time it was a cue, and the colony's cheering went unabated.

"They're hyper-religious," I explained to Istas, quietly. "They worship my family."

"Oh," said Istas, looking puzzled. She looked at the High Priest. "If you worship her, what do you do with me?"

"We ask that you do not eat us, Milady Carnivore, and offer to share the spoils of our hunt with you," said the High Priest. "We will feast well this night, on rat and bat and feathered snake."

"I would like that," said Istas. "Do you *always* talk?"

"Sadly," I muttered.

The High Priest pressed his whiskers forward. "You

are truly a lover of complex theological debate," he said, sounding delighted. "We will enjoy your company."

"As long as that company doesn't involve eating my family's mice," I said, to get us back on message. "Istas, please don't eat my mice. They're very important to me, and besides, it's rude to eat anything you've been introduced to."

Istas pondered this for a moment before she said, "I will not eat any mouse that speaks to me, or that is caught within this room."

"Thank you," I said.

"May I stay here and partake of the dead rats which they have offered me?"

I grimaced. "Maybe." I looked to the High Priest. "Istas is not human, and does not share my dietary restrictions. If she dines with you, will you make this a religious ritual? Because I won't eat rat for you, no matter how important you think it is."

The High Priest slicked his ears back in evident amusement. "No, Priestess," he said. "This will be the Feast of the Waheela With Religious Questions, and will be celebrated only when a waheela is present to dine with us."

"In that case, yes, Istas, you can stay and eat dead rats with the mice."

Istas beamed, evidently delighted. "Perhaps I can help with the gutting."

General cheers, and the sound of Istas' laughter, followed me out of the room. Sometimes my life really is indescribably weird.

With Mike and Ryan off getting supplies and Istas eating dinner with the mice, there wasn't much that I could do with myself. I went to the office I'd claimed as a temporary bedroom and finished unpacking my weapons, lining them up along the walls until I stopped feeling quite so transitory. A Price girl can live anywhere as long as she has her boots, her knives, and her guns. That's a lesson we picked up from my great-grandmother, Frances Healy, but near as I can tell, it's been true for every generation of our family since the dawn of time. Our last name may have changed, but our essential nature has always remained the same.

Even I could only spend so much time fussing with the placement of ammo boxes and throwing knives. Once that was over, it was time to turn to the much less pleasant of my planned chores: making some calls.

Not every cryptid has a telephone, or wants one, but all smart urban cryptids are plugged into the local gossip network. The bogeys and the dragons knew about the impending purge. That was a start; between them, they had connections to two thirds of the city's cryptid population. With a few calls, I was able to tip off the harpies—for the aerial cryptids—and the nixies—for the aquatic ones. I couldn't reach any of the gorgons in my contact list, but hopefully between Carol and Joe, they'd hear what was coming.

(There are three species of gorgon. Carol could warn the lesser gorgons. Joe could warn the Pliny's gorgons. No one was going to warn the greater gorgons, but then again, greater gorgons are generally what you're warning people *about*. They'd be okay if the Covenant was armed with anything short of a tactical nuke.)

Once I was out of numbers and tired of being screamed at by people who were convinced that this was my fault, I went out into the main room and spent another twenty minutes placing dart boards around the area, hanging them off support beams and at odd angles on the walls. They'd work for target practice in a pinch, and this was not the time to let myself start getting sloppy.

The slaughterhouse didn't have many windows. The windows it did have were narrow things set high to the ceiling, where even the most industrious burglar—or assassin—would have to really work for the kill. Even so, I found myself wishing Antimony were there. Not to stay; this situation was too dangerous to wish on my little sister, no matter how many times she'd tied me up when we were kids. I just wanted her around long enough to set trip wires and alarms on all the unexpected entrances. She had an eye for that sort of thing.

Without her, I was going to have to improvise. So improvise I did, scaling bits of exposed pipe and doorframes to place mason jars full of nails in front of every window I could possibly reach, and a few I probably should have left alone, since a fall at that angle could have left me with broken bones—or worse. (It seems to be an immutable fact of nature that any time you move into an empty building, no matter how recently it was vacated or how thoroughly it was cleaned, you'll find roughly a dozen forgotten glass jars in cabinets and closets. No one knows why. It's a mystery that may never be solved.)

I was trying to figure out what to do with myself next when my phone rang. I jumped before checking the readout—it was a blocked number, which meant Sarah—and answering. "Hello?"

"I thought you were going to turn the Internet on." Sarah sounded peevish. "You haven't checked in, you haven't been online, and I was starting to worry."

I sighed. "Mom put you up to this, didn't she?"

"Your father, actually, but it's still true. I hadn't heard from you, the Covenant's in town, I was worried. Then I thought, 'Wait, there are these magical pocket telepathy machines that we all carry,' and I dialed your phone. Ta-da." The last was delivered, not with a flourish, but in a dust-dry deadpan.

"You're a real comedian, Sarah." I produced a throwing knife from inside my shirt and flicked it at the nearest dart board. It hit a little left of center. "What's really on your mind?"

"How did it go with Dominic?"

My second throw went wild as her words forced me to finally think about what I'd been trying to avoid thinking about. I hate circuitous logic. Closing my eyes, I said, "Good and bad."

"Good how?"

"He loves me."

Sarah paused. "That's good, right?"

"I just said it was good."

"Do you love him?"

"That is a large and complicated question, affected by a great many outside factors, most of which are beyond my control."

"Gosh." She sounded almost impressed. Then: "That's pretty much bullshit. I mean, even *I* can tell that's pretty much bullshit, and I have the relationship sense of a wombat."

"You just have biology issues. Your own species is made up entirely of sociopathic assholes, and Artie doesn't know what to do with a girl who actually likes him, rather than just liking his pheromones."

Sarah sighed deeply. "Tell me about it. Dominic loves you? Like, he said he loves you? In those words?"

"He told me he loved me, right before he told me to run, because he wouldn't be able to protect me if the Covenant came back. Oh, and it gets better."

"How does it get better than that?"

"There are three Covenant representatives in town. I should call Dad to get him to run dossiers on them." That would mean telling him who they were, and *that* would mean telling him that we were up against family. "Two of them, I didn't recognize their names. They're not from any Covenant family I know."

"Uh-huh," said Sarah slowly. "Why do I get the feeling that behind door number three is something that's going to explain your sudden radio silence?"

"The third is Margaret Healy."

There was a long moment of awed silence before Sarah said, "Wow. When you decide to get into a bad situation, you don't mess around, like, *at all*. Your boyfriend, who loves you, is totally hanging out with your evil cousin."

"She's not necessarily evil. Just misguided."

"I'm on her magical hunter 'kill it on sight' list, so I think I get to call her evil if I want to," Sarah countered.

I sighed, but I didn't argue. She had a point.

According to the family record, there was a time when the Healys were the pride of the Covenant of St. George.

They were faithful, they were devout, they bred like rabbits, and once they were aimed at a target, they killed without hesitation. They were the perfect monster hunting assassins. Dozens of my ancestors were canonized in the annals of the Covenant, heroes and heroines of the war they fought on mankind's behalf.

They were demonized at the same time, recorded as monsters in the history of the world's cryptids. There are two sides to every story, and history is a story like any other.

It wasn't until my maternal great-great-grandfather came along that any of the Healys questioned the party line — and when they decided to start asking questions, they did it the way the Healys had been doing things for centuries: enthusiastically, and with suicidal levels of commitment.

It's funny, but I sometimes wonder what the hell Great-Great-Grandpa Alexander was thinking. Every other defector we know of was motivated by something, love or death or a great epiphany in the field that changed everything. Great-Great-Grandpa did some research. That was all. He was trying to learn better ways to kill monsters, and what he found was something entirely different. He researched further, and when he didn't like the things he found, he did more research. And then he not only threw away everything he'd ever worked for, he convinced my great-great-grandmother to do the same thing. We may be the only people in history to defect from their religious order not over a point of faith, but over footnotes.

Great-Great-Grandpa was able to convince his wife to leave the Covenant with him, but he couldn't convince his parents, or his siblings, or his cousins. The Healys in America were never more than a tiny group of exiles, one that eventually changed its name; there are no Healys anymore, just Prices and Harringtons. The Healys in Europe, on the other hand, are legion, and they hated us right up until they stopped believing we existed. We were the ones who besmirched the family name. We were the ones who had to pay.

Sarah's voice brought me out of the family history and back into the present. "You realize this means they suspect you're here."

"What?" I shook my head vigorously, not caring that she couldn't see me. "Dominic didn't tell them. If he had, they would have taken me already."

"He didn't tell them, but they suspect something. The Healys haven't been in the Covenant's good graces since the defection. So why would they send one on this kind of mission, unless they wanted her to look for signs that the family was still around?"

"You sure do know how to make a girl feel safe," I muttered.

"Feeling safe isn't what matters right now. Staying alive is." I heard something beep behind her. "That's my alarm. I need to get to class—do you want to come by my hotel tonight? We can talk about what to do next, order too much room service, and try not to freak out."

"It's a date," I said, and hung up. It was time to give in to the inevitable. It was time to call my father.

❧

The less said about my call home, the better. By the end of it, I knew that the Brandts were an old Covenant family from Wales, and were mostly men of action, which meant that I didn't need to worry about Peter hatching any clever plans against me. The Bullards were more recent additions to the fight, having signed up shortly before the Healys left. We didn't have much data—most of what we did have came in with Grandpa Thomas, who referred to Darren and Cassandra Bullard as "right twats." Somehow, I didn't find that encouraging.

And Margaret Healy was, of course, likely to recognize me as a relative and shoot me on sight. Not in the head. That would have been too easy, and Healy women have always been good at resource management. She would shoot me in the kneecaps, and be able to grill me at length about the location and strength of the family in North America. And then she would hunt us down, one by one, and finally finish what the Covenant failed to accomplish in my grandparents' time. She would be the one who killed the traitors. As one of the traitors in question, this didn't strike me as a good way to spend my time.

The end of the call was as predictable as the rest of it. "This changes things, Very," said Dad. "With your cousin in town . . ."

"You mean my biological cousin, not Sarah."

"Yes, exactly. With your cousin—"

"And not my uncle-by-adoption, since you're the reason Uncle Mike is here."

"Verity—"

"Oh, and not all the people who depend on me. The ones I promised not to run out on, because they were going to need my help with the Covenant in town. The only one who matters is Margaret. Right? None of the rest of them. Just her."

Dad sighed heavily. "I'm worried about you, pumpkin. I'm not ready to add you to the family history."

"You *won't*, Dad. I have good people here with me, and some of them are even human." Mike and Ryan walked in just in time to catch that comment. They looked at me quizzically, their arms loaded down with bags of groceries. I waved for them to give me a second. "I can't run out on New York. I'm needed, and what kind of Price would I be if I ran the second it looked like things were getting bad? I have to stay, and you have to stay far away."

"I wish you weren't there, Verity." The misery dripping off his words was palpable. "I wish we'd told you 'no' when you said you wanted to go and spend a year dancing. We should have told you that you couldn't go."

"I'm a grown woman, Daddy. I would have gone anyway. At least this way, you know what's going on. Uncle Mike just got back, and I need to fill him in. Can you catch Mom up?"

"I can, and Very—if things get really bad, come home. Don't worry about whether you're followed. We can handle it if you are. Just get Sarah, and get out." He paused before adding, "If you can't get Sarah, trust her to follow on her own. You just run." He sounded guilty. I couldn't blame him. The idea of leaving her behind had never even crossed my mind.

"I'll be careful," I said, and hung up before he could say anything else. Tucking my phone back into my pocket, I turned toward Mike and Ryan, who were watching me with almost matching expressions of bemusement on their faces.

"What was that?" asked Mike.

"Dad sounding the horns for Judgment Day," I said. "Istas is upstairs having a celebratory feast with the mice. I just spoke to Sarah. She's fine, and I'm supposed to go check on her later tonight."

"So what's the problem?" asked Ryan.

"The problem is that I'm no longer the only biological member of my family in this city," I said, and turned to focus my attention more on Mike, who would understand the importance—and the danger—of what I was about to say. "One of the Covenant representatives is a woman named Margaret Healy. She's a cousin."

"Oh," he said. "Crap."

I nodded. "Yeah. There's a lot of that particular sentiment going around. So now the question is . . . what are we going to do?"

Twelve

> "If you get yourself turned to stone, you are grounded for a *week*. No TV, no dessert, and no trips to the range. Do I make myself clear?"
>
> — Evelyn Baker

The Meatpacking District, which is nicer than it sounds, inside a converted warehouse, trying to come up with a plan that doesn't get everyone killed

"I DON'T GET what the problem is," said Ryan. "Verity's this chick's cousin, right? So why can't she just explain that this city is her territory, and that the Covenant needs to leave? Family should respect family, even if they're on opposite sides of a war."

Tanuki have always been very family-oriented. Large portions of their culture were based around tracking who was related to who and through what sort of path, although that had less to do with filial affection and more with their having a limited gene pool. No one wants to find out after the fact that the cute guy you've invited back to your den is actually a first cousin. It was that devotion to family that got a lot of tanuki killed when the Covenant came to Japan. The tanuki just kept rushing in to save the ones who'd been captured, and got themselves slaughtered in the process. Being able to turn yourself to stone doesn't stop the men with sledgehammers.

"It doesn't work like that for humans, Ryan," I said,

and chucked another throwing knife at the nearest dart board. It embedded itself deep into the cork. "We keep track of our relatives more so we'll know where to send Christmas cards and who to hate than because we're planning to help each other out."

"Hey, now." Uncle Mike stopped cutting the lasagna long enough to shake his spatula at me. It was store-bought—the lasagna, not the spatula, although the spatula probably came from a store somewhere—and the smell rising off the baked meat-and-cheese concoction was heavenly. "Family is a good thing, too. Don't you forget about that just because you're busy being freaked out over some cousin you didn't even know existed before yesterday."

"Even knowing that the Covenant probably sent her *because* she's family? Nobody sniffs out a Healy like a Healy, and we've only been Prices for two generations." If I was going by Grandma Alice and the pictures I'd seen of Great-Grandma Fran, I could call myself a Price as much as I wanted; I was still going to be an obvious Healy girl to anyone with eyes.

"Even knowing that she's here because she's family. Being a Healy doesn't give you magic powers or anything. Maybe makes you a little stubborn. The stubborn has to be genetic. And then there's the luck thing. But none of that guarantees that she's going to trip over your hiding place, and you've got a lot more allies in this town than she does." Uncle Mike dished a healthy serving of lasagna onto a paper plate. "Now eat. You're too thin, and you're going to worry yourself into getting even thinner."

"I'm a professional ballroom dancer," I said. "Thinner is a good thing." I still took the lasagna, moving to sit down at the nearby table. The dragons had been living in this Nest for long enough to have paid—probably grudgingly—for converting the employee break room into a serviceable kitchen. Between the stove, the fridge, and the microwave Ryan and Istas had brought with them, we had sufficient facilities to keep us all fed for the duration of the siege.

"Not when you have to wrestle a lindworm out of its hole, it isn't. Eat." Uncle Mike turned and pressed another plate into Ryan's hands. "You, too. Is that girlfriend of yours going to want some when she finishes partying with the mice?"

"Probably," said Ryan. "Istas is a black hole in a lacy pinafore."

"And other phrases that have never before been uttered." I stabbed my lasagna with my fork. It wasn't as satisfying as certain other kinds of stabbing would have been, but it was what I had available at the moment. "We need a plan."

"Don't die," suggested Ryan.

"We need a better plan."

"Don't get seriously injured," said Uncle Mike.

I eyed him. "Are you going to take this seriously? This is serious. This is a serious situation." I paused, scowling. "Only now I've said 'serious' so many times that it's starting to sound funny to me. Dammit. We need a *plan*."

"The Covenant doesn't know where this place is, so that's a start," said Mike.

"Dominic has never been here, and he doesn't like free running, so he's unlikely to have ever followed me," I agreed. "The others don't know yet that I'm someone they *should* be following, so that buys us a little time. We'll need to be careful coming and going, but we were already planning on that. And the mice make remarkably good spies. If anyone comes sniffing around here, we'll know."

For the first time, Ryan looked faintly uncomfortable. "They're not going to be, you know, announcing themselves to people on the sidewalk or anything, are they? Because talking mice will convince the Covenant that there's something up with this place pretty darn quick."

"They're actually better at being subtle than anyone gives them credit for," I assured him. "When you see them around me, they're in a safe place. They know they can be themselves here. Out in the world, they practice stealth and actual cunning. If they didn't, we would have long since run out of Aeslin mice."

"That's a relief," said Ryan.

I paused. "Actually . . . there's something to be said for using Aeslin mice as spies. We've done it before, when we felt that we really had to. The mice are happy to have something they can do to help the gods." And some of them inevitably wouldn't make it back from their "holy mission," because they were *mice*, and what I was contemplating involved sending them out into a world where practically everything was bigger than they were.

It was still one of the best ideas I'd had so far, and from the thoughtful look on Uncle Mike's face, he thought so, too. He brought his plate and sat down next to me. "It would be a good way to find out what the Covenant was up to, if we could find a way to sneak some mice into their headquarters," he said. "Didn't the mice come before your family left the Covenant, though?"

"Yeah, but they came with my great-great-grandmother, Enid, when she married into the Healys," I said. "Margaret might not know about the mice."

"There's an awful lot of wiggle room in 'might.'"

I didn't have an answer for that. I was saved from needing one when Istas appeared in the kitchen doorway. "I smell lasagna," she announced. "You will share."

"Hi, sweetie." Ryan waved his fork in her direction. "Food's on the stove. Did you have a good time with the mice?"

"Yes." Istas started toward the lasagna, detouring only long enough to kiss Ryan on the cheek. "They are very pleasant company."

"You have rat breath," said Ryan, wrinkling his nose.

Istas looked pleased. "Yes," she said. "I know." She dished half the remaining lasagna onto a plate, bringing it with her as she moved to sit down next to Ryan. "Have we determined the best method for driving the Covenant from our territory yet? Will carnage be involved?"

"We're still working on that," I said. "We have numbers . . . now. But if this whole team disappears without a trace, the odds are good that the Covenant will send more people to find out what happened to them.

Maybe we can disappear a second team, but can we manage a third? Or a fourth? Eventually, we're going to wind up being the ones who don't have the numbers in our favor." And then the purge of New York would be able to begin in earnest.

"So what do we do right now?"

"Right now? I guess we watch and see what *they* do. Once we know what we're up against, we'll be able to counter it." I jammed my fork into my lasagna. "I hate waiting."

"Doesn't everyone?" asked Mike.

I sighed heavily. "That's what I'm afraid of. We're waiting because we want to minimize the damage. Well, the Covenant doesn't have anything like that to worry about. They can move whenever they want to, and we have no way of seeing them coming."

Ryan took care of the dishes while Uncle Mike walked around the slaughterhouse, double-checking my traps and doubtless setting a few of his own. We'd all need to walk carefully from now on. That was good. It would keep us on our toes. As for me, I collected all the knives I'd thrown at the various dart boards—it was a surprisingly high number, given how little time I'd had, but I guess stress makes me stabby—and returned to the small office that was going to be my bedroom for the foreseeable future. My "bed" was an air mattress on the floor with a quilt I didn't recognize and a pile of pillows that I did. I threw myself onto it with more force than was necessarily safe and rolled onto my back, staring at the ceiling.

My lease was almost up. The Sasquatch whose apartment I'd been using was going to be home soon, which was supposed to be my cue to go back to Oregon (assuming she came back at all, after the message I'd left for her). Mom and Dad would understand that I couldn't leave while the threat of a purge was hanging over the city—we've always done fieldwork in emergency situations, and the Covenant was the next best thing to a natural disaster as far as most cryptids were concerned. But what was going to happen after that?

I came to Manhattan to prove that I could make it as a professional ballroom dancer. Only things didn't exactly work out that way. I hadn't managed to win a single major competition; the times I'd placed, it had always been local, and the prize money I'd received barely paid for the cost of my registration. It didn't touch my costumes, or the hours of studio time I had to beg, borrow, and steal whenever I could. Most people in my tier of the profession supplemented their income teaching classes, but I couldn't even do that anymore. Trying to be a cocktail waitress *and* a cryptozoologist took up too much time. Quit bussing tables and I couldn't afford to eat. Quit taking care of cryptids . . .

If I quit taking care of cryptids, I wouldn't even know who I was anymore. I pulled a throwing knife out of my shirt without thinking about it, flicking it toward the ceiling. It flew in a satisfyingly straight line, embedding itself in the wood with a soft "thunk" sound. The fact that throwing knives into the air while I was on top of an air mattress was maybe not the smartest idea barely even crossed my mind. I was too busy thinking.

I came to New York to dance. The cryptozoology was supposed to be a sideline, something I did to keep my parents happy while I proved that I could have a career if I wanted one. But somewhere along the way, the proportions got reversed. I started spending more and more time with the cryptids who needed my help, and less and less time fighting my way through the cutthroat world of ballroom dance. My partner, James, had to chase me down for rehearsals. If it weren't for the fact that he was cutting back his own availability while he prepared for chupacabra mating season, he would probably have talked to me about seeing other partners by now. As it was, I was braced for that conversation.

(James was decidedly gay, and extremely devoted to his husband, Dennis, who put up with more than any human married to a goat-sucker could reasonably be expected to endure. But sexual preference didn't matter during mating season. Chupacabra never raise their young in the presence of both biological parents— something about it increasing the odds of the pups being eaten before they get old enough to become intelligent. The ways of chupacabra biology are strange, and not for me to understand. Yet.)

I was about to lose my apartment, my partner, and my chance at ever having the kind of career I dreamed of when I was a kid. As a professional dancer, I was on the cusp of failing. At the same time, the Covenant of St. George was in my city, I'd been forced to go into hiding to avoid having them find me, and I had no game plan for getting rid of them. As a cryptozoologist, I wasn't doing much better. All I could really swear to doing correctly was being a member of my family: too pigheaded to know when I was beat, and too contrary to admit when it was time to run away.

I sat up, tucking the knife I'd been about to throw at the ceiling back into my shirt. That was the answer I'd been looking for. It didn't matter if my dancing career was over, or if I decided to put on a red wig and become Valerie Pryor full time. No matter what, I was a Price girl. And if there's one thing no Price girl has ever voluntarily done, it's back down from a fight.

I'd been living alone long enough that it was weird to need to tell people where I was going. I still tracked Mike down and made sure he knew I was heading for Sarah's before I left the slaughterhouse. He asked when I'd be back. I barely managed to bite back the urge to tell him that I didn't have a curfew, and stomped up the stairs to the roof.

The night air was cool and smelled like big city, that heady mix of human bodies, cooling pavement, and a thousand clubs and restaurants venting their private atmospheres into the greater ecosystem of the metropolis. A city the size of Manhattan is like a rain forest or a desert: it has its own ecology, its own secrets, and its own dangers—its own predators.

Good thing that I was one of them.

It didn't take long for me to reach Sarah's hotel, even with the necessary detours and slowdowns created by the variable architecture of Manhattan. I maintained a dead run all the way, burning off the barest edge of my frustration.

The Port Hope was the lowest building on its part of the block, being only five stories high. That was useful for my purposes, especially since Sarah was staying on the top floor. I couldn't jump straight from the roof of the high-rise next to it, so I got out a climbing hook and lowered myself one floor at a time, pausing on the narrow brick lips that marked the base of each new floor to adjust my rope. Once I had a good grip, I'd start down again.

When I finally reached the floor slightly above the roof of the Port Hope, I unhooked the rope and jumped. I hit the roof as gracefully as can be expected for a human girl leaping six feet straight down. The best landings only happen when there's no one there to see them. (Paradoxically, the same is true for the worst ones. If you're going to break an ankle or something, you're probably going to do it when there's no one around to hear you shouting for help.) I held my crouch for a few seconds, indulging my paranoia as I waited to see whether I'd been followed. No one appeared. I straightened, and walked to the roof door.

It was locked. Naturally. But the faint static that told me I was in the presence of a telepath who knew me was crackling at the back of my mind—Sarah was home. I paused to center myself, trying to clear my head of any useless thoughts. *Sarah? Are you there?*

Very? Her answer was tinted with a strong feeling of confusion, like she couldn't figure out where my thoughts were coming from. Understanding—her understanding—washed over me a split second before she added, *What are you doing on the* roof? *How did you even get up there?*

I jumped, I replied. *Can you come and let me in? The door is locked, and this place is low enough that the only other way for me to get out of here involves rappelling down the side of the hotel.* Which wasn't something I was opposed to under normal circumstances, but it might lead to some awkward questions, especially since I'd be going inside right after I reached the sidewalk.

I'll be right there, thought Sarah firmly. The feeling of connection died, although the static remained. "Telepath here" is a signal she can't stop sending, no matter how hard she tries. Much as I love her, I actually find that a little bit reassuring. It proves there's one thing the cuckoos can't control, and given how many advantages they have, I appreciate knowing that they're not perfect.

I'd been waiting on the roof for less than five minutes when the door swung open, revealing Sarah. She was in her usual "I am a normal college student" attire: orange sweater, jeans, and scuffed-up white sneakers. Sarah is a natural Daphne, designed by nature to be boy-bait, but you'd never know it from the way she dresses. I think she'd rather be a Velma. Sadly, nature didn't give her a vote in the matter.

"You were supposed to call," Sarah chided me, as she stepped out of the way to let me into the stairwell. "There are these things called doors that normal people use."

"I'm using a door right now," I protested, half-laughing.

"Yeah, because I had to let you off the *roof*," Sarah shot back.

"And you did a fabulous job of it," I said, patting her shoulder before I started down the stairs. "I seem to remember a promise of room service."

"Room service and not freaking out," Sarah agreed. "Also, Artie may call at some point. He wants to talk to you—and no," she put her hands up, "I don't know why, it may be for something totally unrelated."

"Well, yes. But I think it's a little more likely that he wants to yell at me, don't you?"

"Probably," Sarah agreed.

We were still laughing when I opened the door at the bottom of the stairs, stepped out, and found myself nose-to-nose with Margaret Healy. I'd never seen her up close before. I didn't need to, because there was no one else she could have been. This woman was family.

Her hair was the same shade of chestnut-verging-on-red as my sister Antimony's. She still had it pulled it into a ponytail, showing the cheekbones we had inherited from our mutual ancestors. Her eyes were a clear shade of hazel—Antimony's eyes are blue, like mine—but aside from that, Margaret could have been mistaken for my sister.

She blinked at me. I blinked at her. Sarah, still laughing, crowded up behind me. "Why are you just standing he—oh." Her laughter died like a switch had been flipped, replaced by a look of utter bafflement. "Oh. Hello." *Verity, I didn't know you had company. Why can't I see her?*

There was no sign in her voice that she recognized Margaret as a Healy. That, sadly, made sense: cuckoos recognize people by thought, not by appearance. To her, all humans look essentially the same. She can tell races, genders, hair colors, and that's about it.

"Hello," said Margaret. Her accent was British. She looked past us to the stairs. "Is the roof of this hotel a hopping night spot, then?"

"No, we're just stargazers," I said, taking hold of Sarah's arm and tugging her with me as I stepped out of the stairwell, into the hall. I kept my eyes on Margaret, and kept a smile plastered across my face. If Sarah couldn't "see" her, she must have been wearing some sort of telepathy blocker. Not a good sign. "I wanted to show Sandy here the Pleiades."

Sarah looked even more confused but nodded enthusiastically, saying, "They were shiny."

I shot her a sharp look. I didn't need to bother. Margaret was nodding in time with Sarah. There was a faintly glazed look in her eyes. Sarah was freaking out in her own quiet way, and that meant that her natural camouflage was kicking in. Anti-telepathy charm or not, it's *hard* to counter a cuckoo who's actively putting the whammy on you, and Sarah's survival depended on Margaret accepting her as a natural part of the setting.

It seemed to be working, thank God. If Sarah said she'd been looking at stars well, then, she *must* have been looking at stars. My backpack was large enough to hold a telescope. The story made total sense.

"Is there anyone else up there?" asked Margaret.

"No," I said.

"Then I think I'll give these stars a look myself. Thank you for letting me know they were good tonight." Margaret stepped into the stairwell, closing the door behind her, and Sarah and I were alone.

I made a small squeaking noise in the back of my throat and started towing Sarah down the hall toward her room.

"What's going on?" she asked.

"No talking," I said. "This is walking time, not talking time."

Sarah, wisely, shut up until we reached her suite, where she unlocked the door and let us both inside. I followed her inside. Then I shut the door, locked the deadbolt, and resisted the urge—barely—to shove a chair under the knob. Sarah watched this whole process, her bewildered expression deepening.

"Verity, who was that woman? Why couldn't I see her properly?"

"That was Margaret Healy." What was she doing at the Port Hope? There are hundreds of hotels in Manhattan, maybe even thousands. So why would the Covenant pick *this* one? They weren't going to be interested in the math museum. So why—

Unless someone told them I might be here. Someone like Dominic De Luca, who had been to the Port Hope before, and who had been around Sarah often enough that he might have been able to remember the location, even if he forgot why it was important. I felt myself go cold. Here, then: this was what I'd been waiting for. He'd betrayed us. He was the enemy. I didn't have to feel conflicted anymore.

So why didn't that help?

"The brunette?" asked Sarah, gaping. "She's a *Healy*?"

"Yeah." If I could recognize Margaret as a relative, it was only a matter of time before she was going to start thinking that I looked oddly familiar. Like a picture she'd seen once in a history book, next to a paragraph titled "Traitor."

"But . . . but what's she doing?"

"I don't know, Sarah. Probably assessing the roof for tactical defense purposes." Which meant—assuming she had any training at all, which she must, or they wouldn't have sent her—that Margaret was going to notice the scuffs in the gravel that marked the place where I'd hit the roof from above. She'd be able to read those marks like a hunter reading a deer's tracks in the wood. Something humanoid had jumped from the next building over; it had recovered without injury; it had gotten off the roof somehow. And she'd encountered two women coming out of the stairwell.

Sarah's cuckoo camouflage might slow Margaret down for a little while, make her second-guess what she was thinking and try to come up with other reasons for us to have been up there, but that couldn't work forever. Cuckoos work best when they stay near their targets, and we'd moved away from Margaret as quickly as we could. Factor in Margaret's anti-telepathy charm, and I had no idea how long she'd be confused.

"What do we do now?"

"Get your things. We're getting you out of here."

Sarah's eyes widened. "But I just got here."

"She *saw* me!" I didn't realize I was going to shout until it was too late to stop myself. Sarah took a step back. She didn't actually go pale—her blood isn't red, and her biology doesn't support things like blanching or blushing—but she may as well have; her expression told me how frightened she was. I didn't stop. "Even if she forgets about you, she *saw* me, she's going to know that there's something wrong here! You know how badly the Covenant wants to get their hands on a cuckoo. Do you want it to be you, Sarah? Because I don't!"

"Verity, you're scaring me," she whispered.

"I don't care! You *should* be scared! We have to leave, Sarah, and we have to leave now, or we're not going to be leaving at all."

Sarah stared at me for a long moment. Then, in a small, tight voice, she said, "I'll go pack." She wheeled and stomped off toward her room. It was more fear than anger. I didn't care either way. As long as I got her out of here . . .

The idea of what might happen if I didn't was unthinkable, and so I did my best not to think it.

The existence of the cuckoos wasn't proven until my great-grandfather went to Colorado to look into the movement of a local hive of Apraxis wasps. Before that, there had been rumors, but never any hard proof. One of the last communications my grandfather sent to the Covenant before cutting off all ties was a letter describing everything we knew about the cuckoos. Warning people about them was more important than hiding information from the Covenant. That's how dangerous we thought they were, and how dangerous we *still* think they are.

According to our contacts in Europe, the Covenant has been trying to get their hands on a cuckoo for research purposes ever since. It's one of those things that causes a lot of ethical debate at home, since we have a shoot on sight order on most cuckoos, but they're still sapient beings. They deserve better than the Covenant's idea of "study." If Margaret figured out who I was, and what Sarah was, she could kill two birds with one stone— take out a member of the traitorous branch of the family tree, and finally get a cuckoo they could take apart at their leisure. They'd just need to keep her unconscious. Cuckoos can only scramble your head when they're awake.

All the discussions I'd had about the danger of staying in New York had included warnings about keeping Sarah safe, and endless reassurances that of course I wouldn't let anything happen to her; of course she would be fine. She was a cuckoo. What was going to hurt her?

What, if not a Healy in the same hotel, with the potential to recognize her for what she was? Dad used to joke about Healy family luck, how sometimes it was good and sometimes it was bad, but it was always interesting. Margaret Healy clearly had that kind of luck, and she had it in spades.

Sarah emerged from her bedroom with a small suitcase in one hand and an overstuffed backpack in the other. "Let me get my laptops and my homework from the table, and we can go," she said. She didn't sound happy. I didn't blame her. We'd been planning a relaxing evening, out of the line of fire. Having the fight follow me to her door was never the idea. "Where *are* we going?"

"You can stay with the rest of us." The dragons weren't going to be thrilled about me turning their old Nest into the new Grand Central Station, but with as much as we were paying them, they could cope.

"Oh, goody. Slumber party of the damned." Sarah started for the dining room. (One thing about her taste in hotel rooms: she never gets anything smaller than a suite, and she's never had a suite smaller than a good apartment. It seems extravagant, and maybe it is, a little, but it's really one more precaution against having her brain come melting out of her ears in the middle of the night. Living as a telepath in a non-telepathic society was definitely not all wine and roses.)

Someone knocked on the door. We both turned.

"Did you order room service before I got here?" I asked, instinctively dropping to a whisper. I realized only after I spoke that I probably should have done it telepathically.

No, said Sarah, who was smart enough to do what I hadn't. There was a soft thump as she put down her bags. Then she stepped up next to me, squinting a little at the door. *I don't . . . I can't hear who's out there. I'm not sure there* is *anybody there.*

One more problem with being a telepath in a non-telepathic society: sometimes there aren't words for the things you're trying to describe. Sarah doesn't really "hear" people thinking, but there isn't any other way to say it. It gets clearer when she's attuned to a person, and strangers can sometimes be almost inaudible to her mental ear. Still, she usually knows when there's someone to be listened to. *That means it's Margaret. Maybe she'll go away.*

The knock came again.

... maybe not, I thought. I looked toward Sarah. *Okay. Here's what we need to do. You're going to say I have to jump out the window, aren't you?* she asked miserably.

No, of course not. Not that I didn't want to. Going out the window would have solved all our problems. Unfortunately, I didn't have the equipment to get Sarah down safely, and she didn't have the training to do it without help. I took a breath and thought, as reassuringly as I could, *We just need to be quiet, okay? She'll go away.*

Verity, I don't like this. Sarah's lower lip quivered, her eyes wide and frightened.

I know. I drew a pistol from inside my hoodie, gesturing for Sarah to get out of sight. She started toward the coat closet, presumably to hide herself.

There was a click as the latch released, and the hotel room door swung open. I managed to jump behind the half-wall that separated the living and dining rooms, getting myself out of sight before I could be seen. Sarah gasped.

"C-can I help you?" she asked, in a surprisingly normal tone of voice.

"Your door seems to have been left unlocked," said Margaret Healy. "Can I come in?"

Oh. Shit.

Thirteen

"Blood is thicker than water, but family isn't just about blood. Family is about faith, and loyalty, and who you love. If you don't have those things, I don't care what the blood says. You're not family."

— Alice Healy

A suite at the Port Hope Hotel, about to potentially get into a firefight

"UH, SURE," said Sarah. I heard her step back to let Margaret into her suite. "Is there something I can help you with?"

"It's an awfully cloudy night for looking at stars, don't you think?" The question was mild, just a comment on the weather.

There was nothing mild about the chill that it sent racing down my spine, or Sarah's sudden, terrified cry of, *Verity, I think this is the woman from the roof.*

Sometimes Sarah's inability to recognize people by visual cues can be a real problem. *I know,* I thought back, as soothingly as I could. *Try to convince her that you're harmless. We're going to get you out of here. It'll be okay.*

"The sky cleared for a little bit," said Sarah. "That's why I went up with Valerie to see the Pleiades."

"It's odd that you can see them at all, with all the ambient light from the city," said Margaret. "I was ever so excited, until I saw that the clouds had come back.

Quite fast, too. I've never seen a cloud cover that thick develop so quickly."

Verity, why is she asking all these questions? She should have believed us. Why can't I see her?

I don't know, I thought back. *See if you can make her leave. We need to get you out of here.*

"I guess the weather does what the weather wants to do," said Sarah weakly.

"I suppose that's true." I heard Margaret take another step. "Is Valerie still here? I wanted to see if she had any other suggestions for places where I might go to do a little stargazing."

"No, she had to leave," said Sarah. "I'll tell her that you were sorry to have missed her."

"Left? Really? That's amazing, since I had a splendid view of the front of the hotel while I was on the roof, and I didn't see her going out."

"It must have been while you were going down the stairs."

"That's still quite impressive timing. I'll have to ask my colleague who was sitting in the lobby this whole time whether he saw which way she went. I'd love to see her again." I didn't need to be able to see Margaret's face to know what it looked like. Her tone was one I'd heard before, from my sister, my mother, my grandmother. It would be accompanied by an almost feral smile, one that implied the speaker would think nothing of ripping your throat out with her teeth. A dangerous expression for a dangerous girl.

"That's probably a good idea," said Sarah, in a small voice.

"Unless *you'd* like to tell me where she went."

Verity!

I gritted my teeth, forcing myself to stay where I was. *Is she actually threatening you? Or is she just asking pointy questions and waiting to see whether you crack? Do you see any weapons?*

Not yet—it's just questions—but I still can't read her.

Shit. The Covenant has wards against sorcery, witchcraft, and the various psionic powers. Telepathy isn't common, but empathy is, and a ward against one will go a long way toward blocking the others. Sarah wasn't going to get any readings off Margaret, and Margaret wasn't going to be as affected by Sarah's particular brand of mind-fuck as she should have been.

Try and make her leave, I said, keeping my mental voice as reassuring as I could. I didn't know how well it was working. Sarah's the telepath, not me; there was no telling how much interference she was going to pick up from my own panic. *The staff will smuggle us out of here if you can make her leave.*

"I don't know where Valerie went," said Sarah. Her voice was barely shaking. I have never been so proud of her. "Why don't you go ask your friend? He can probably tell you which way she turned when she left the hotel."

"Doesn't she live around here?"

"No. New Jersey. She was just visiting me for the day."

"Ah. Well, if you see her, can you let her know that I—"

The sound of the theme from *Dance or Die* suddenly blared from my front pocket. I fumbled for my phone, hitting the "mute" button, but it was already way too late.

"What was that?" asked Margaret, all pretense of friendly curiosity gone. She was a hunter, and she had just received confirmation that her prey was nearby.

"My phone," said Sarah, hopelessly.

"If that was your phone, what's that on the couch? You have two cell phones? That seems a bit excessive, don't you think?" I heard Margaret turn and start to walk. "You sure your friend left? Seems a little odd that you'd hide her from m—"

There was a heavy smacking noise, followed by the thump of Margaret collapsing to the floor. I poked my head around the wall. Sarah was standing with her legs braced wide, a decorative vase in her hands, panting in what I recognized as terror. Margaret was sprawled face-down on the carpet in front of her. The fall had hiked both her coat and blazer up in the back, revealing the gun she had tucked between her shirt and pants.

"Get the gun," I said, moving to grab Sarah's bags. "Do you have any duct tape?"

"Why would I have duct tape?" Sarah asked. She dropped the vase. It landed without breaking, rolling to bump to a stop against the base of the couch. "Is she dead? Did I kill her?"

"No, but she's going to have one hell of a headache." I trotted over and shoved Sarah's bags into her hands before dropping to my knees next to Margaret, producing a roll of electrical tape from my own bag. "Duct tape would have been better, but this will hold her for a while. You have four minutes to grab anything else you want from this place. We will *not* be coming back here. Understand?"

"I understand," whispered Sarah, and ran for the dining room table.

I learned the basics of tying up—or taping up—an unconscious opponent when I was still in elementary school, mostly by using my siblings for practice. I flipped Margaret over and got to work, moving a little slower than I would have if I hadn't been searching her for weapons at the same time. She was armed for bear. Acid-spitting, fire-breathing bear. If I hadn't already known she was a relative, the number of knives I took out of her coat would have made me suspicious.

Even with that complication, I had her bound in less than a minute and a half. I shrugged my backpack off and began cramming her weapons into it, pausing only long enough to be sure the guns were resting on empty chambers and nothing was bugged or tagged with tracers. The last thing I did was remove her necklace: a thin disk of what looked like pure copper floating in a vial of water mixed with crushed herbs.

I heard a gasp behind me before Sarah thought, *I can feel her in the room now.*

"Swell—I was right. It's an anti-telepathy charm." I shoved Margaret's necklace into my pocket. "They're more prepared than I wanted them to be." Someone had been telling stories. Dominic was no longer a friendly.

"What are we going to do?" Sarah whispered.

"Run." I stood. "She'll be pissed when she wakes up. We'll exit through the kitchen. We can hail a cab and have them drop us at the 9th Street PATH Station."

"And from there?"

"From there, we walk." I turned to face my terrified cousin, ignoring the blood relative who was lying unconscious on the floor. At the moment, Margaret was the least of our problems. There were two more Covenant operatives in the area—three, counting Dominic—and for all I knew, they were both in the hotel. "Come on, Sarah. Let's get the hell out of here."

I managed to shove Sarah's two smaller laptops into the suitcase. She held onto the third one, hugging it like a teddy bear. We took the service elevator down to the first floor, where Sarah babbled something about an angry ex-boyfriend waiting for her in the lobby to the supervisor on duty in the kitchen. The supervisor, a tough-looking African-American woman with the sort of eyes that have seen all the dark things a city has to offer, might have believed us even without Sarah's telepathic push backing up the story. We were two women alone, and we were obviously scared, even if I was doing my best not to show it. Sarah was just the icing on the cake of conviction. The supervisor nodded at the right places, frowned at the right places, and showed us the route through the kitchen to the back door. She didn't ask why we didn't want to call the police. Odds were good that she had her own answers for that, and that they weren't much better than our reality.

Sarah was crying by the time we made it outside, huge, crystalline tears running down her cheeks. She was beautiful when she cried, since her face never got flushed and her eyes never got red. She just cried, a pale doll of a girl with eyes that seemed too big for her face. We walked along the back of the hotel—running would have attracted too much attention—to the nearest corner that wasn't visible from the lobby. A cab pulled up almost immediately. We didn't even need to hail it. Sarah's semi-audible waves of distress took care of that part.

Much as I hate cabs, Sarah's not a runner, and even if she were, we couldn't risk the Covenant having their third operative stationed somewhere at roof level. If we were followed back to the Nest, we'd be sitting ducks. I ushered her into the vehicle as quickly as I could.

"9th Street PATH," I said, once we were safely in the cab with the doors closed and the subtly tinted windows between us and the rest of the city.

The cabbie looked dubious—an unusual reaction from a New York City cab driver, but that was traveling with Sarah for you. It's harder for her to keep certain things under control when she's upset. The poor guy was probably already starting to think of her as his niece, or his best friend's daughter. "Are you sure you don't want to go somewhere safer?" he asked. "Like the police, maybe?"

"The PATH station," whispered Sarah. Then, more loudly, she added, "Please."

It was the "please" that did it. The cabbie hit the gas and we rocketed away from the curb, merging into the traffic as it flowed past the Port Hope Hotel. I gritted my teeth and forced myself to watch the sidewalks for signs of pursuit.

Sarah, breathe, I thought, as soothingly as I could. *You need to calm down, or you're going to convince this guy that you're his long-lost daughter, and we're going to wind up being taken home for comfort and casserole.*

I could have done with a little comfort, and I never turn down a good casserole. Having grandparents from the Midwest will do that. But this was not the time, and there was no reason to start dragging innocents into the line of fire.

I'm trying, said Sarah, her mental voice barely above a whisper. *That woman . . .*

I know. I put my hand on Sarah's knee. She shuddered and slumped against me, resting her head on my shoulder. I wanted to tell her to watch the street, to keep scanning for anything that looked out of place. I didn't. I couldn't. Sarah may be a part of the family, but she's not a fighter. She's never had to be. I didn't know how to tell her that was going to have to change.

The cabbie dropped us at one of the entrances to the 9th Street PATH station, making one last attempt to convince us to go somewhere safer before he allowed me to pay his fare and drove away. Sarah had a tendency to stiff cabbies—not intentionally; she just never thought about needing to pay them—but I didn't want this guy to remember two upset girls who got a ride out of the goodness of his heart. Anything I could do to make us less unusual was worth doing.

"Now what?" asked Sarah, once the taxi was pulling away and we were alone in the inevitable crowd. She clutched her laptop to her chest like a talisman, like it could somehow protect her from what was going on around us.

"We go down," I said. I took her suitcase, hoisting it easily, and motioned for her to follow me down the steps into the station.

I didn't realize before coming to New York that the city was actually served by two different subways. There's the municipal subway, which covers the island of Manhattan and shows up in a lot of movies and TV shows. Then there's the PATH, the Port Authority Trans-Hudson train system, which connects Manhattan to the nearby state of New Jersey. Lots of people commute to work from Jersey City and Newark, allowing them to enjoy the benefits of being right by the Big Apple, without also enjoying the high cost of living.

Sarah and I paid our single-trip fares to get into the PATH system. Then we walked to the end of the platform, where I checked my phone to be sure that I had the right schedule in mind, took her hand, and pulled her down into the darkness.

Things I do not recommend trying at home: navigating an active subway system in the dark, knowing that if you're wrong about your timing, you're going to find out what it feels like to be on the losing side of a squirrel-meets-semi road kill scenario.

Things I do recommend trying when there's a chance that you've been followed by members of a pseudo-religious order that would really enjoy the opportunity to wipe you from the face of the planet: risking that road kill scenario. I knew the way along the tracks, but the Covenant didn't, and we'd have ample opportunities to escape if they did decide to pursue us into the dark. Besides, only a crazy person would walk between stops when there was a nice convenient train. If the Covenant was following us, they'd hopefully assume that we'd taken some secret shortcut down into the sewers and waste time looking for us there. In its own way, this was the smartest stupid thing we could possibly have done.

Sarah and I stuck close to the wall, walking as quickly as we dared. I didn't pull out my flashlight, much as I wanted to. That much light would be a beacon for anyone who happened to be looking for us.

"Sarah?" I murmured. She jumped a little. I squeezed her hand. "Are we alone down here? As far as you know?"

Sarah took a deep breath. I glanced back, and saw that her eyes were starting to glow faintly. That was a good sign. As long as she had something to focus on, she wouldn't dwell on the fact that we were potentially being followed by people who'd been equipped to block telepathy like hers. Margaret had lost her charm, and was hence "visible" to Sarah's specific way of looking. The others weren't.

Two hidebehinds watching us from behind the service door; homeless man asleep in an alcove; family of bugbears passing through, Sarah reported finally. *And rats. Lots of rats.*

"Which means none of Bill's servitors have been through here recently. That's good." Servitors were the lizard-man servants of William the dragon. They used to be humans, before they were kidnapped and mutated by a snake cult. These days, they mostly skulked around in tunnels, eating rats and trying not to be seen. Nothing gets complicated like a cryptid ecosystem.

It is?

Sarah sounded anxious enough that I doubted she even realized she wasn't speaking aloud. I squeezed her hand. "It is. There's nothing down here that can't defend itself." I was including us in that statement. I had my weapons, I had Margaret's weapons, and I knew my environment. As long as we could avoid being flattened by a train, we were almost in the clear.

The tracks ahead of us were becoming easier to see; we were almost to Christopher Street. I started walking faster, pulling Sarah with me. The light from the platform was like a beacon guiding us home. We were almost there when the tracks began vibrating under my feet.

"Run!" I shouted.

We ran. When we reached the platform, I boosted Sarah up, ignoring the startled looks from the people waiting for their train home. I threw her suitcase after her. Then I grabbed the edge of the platform and vaulted myself clear, my feet moving out of the danger zone a mere second before the train came rushing into the station. My heart pounding in my ears, I bent forward and braced my hands against my knees, panting.

"Lady? You okay?"

"Fine." I lifted my head, forcing a grin. My Good Samaritan recoiled. I guess my grin wasn't all that reassuring. "Sarah, come on. We have to get out of here."

Wordlessly, Sarah grabbed her bag off the platform and nodded to me. I took her hand again, and we ran for the tunnel connecting the PATH station with the subway. If we could just catch the train, we'd be safe.

We caught the train.

The ride from Christopher Street to the Meatpacking District was short, which was a good thing, since I don't think either of us could have handled a long trip bundled into a metal box full of strangers. Sarah kept her head bowed and her eyes closed, looking for all the world like a wilted flower. I knew that meant that she was scanning the people around us constantly, looking for signs of danger. She was going to have one hell of a headache by the time we reached the Nest. I couldn't say that it wasn't worth it.

When we pulled into our final destination, I tugged her out of her seat and led her, eyes still closed, out of the train. I didn't leave the station. Instead, I walked the both of us over to the benches against the nearest wall and pushed Sarah into a sitting position, whispering, "Keep looking." Then I pulled out my phone.

Uncle Mike answered on the third ring. "Where are you?"

"Hey, Mom. I picked up that movie you wanted." Translation: I may be under surveillance, I am currently at the train station. If I'd been on the street, I would have picked up the dry cleaning; in a bus station, the groceries. It was a simple code, but it worked more than well enough for our purposes.

"Shit. Sarah with you?"

"Yes, that sounds good."

"She been compromised?"

"I'm pretty sure."

"Shit." This time, the profanity was delivered with far more feeling. "What can I do?"

"Did you check the mail today? I'm expecting a package."

"Sure thing. Hang on the line." I heard the soft clunk as Mike put the phone down, followed by the equally soft, but far more ominous "snick" of a crossbow bolt being slotted into place.

Sarah's eyes were still closed. I put my hand on her shoulder and waited, feeling like an ingénue in a bad horror movie. At any moment, the Covenant would burst out of their hiding places and take us out, and no matter how hard I fought, there was no way I'd be able to hold them all off. We'd be overwhelmed, and no one would ever find our bodies—

"Very? You there?"

"I'm here."

"The coast is clear outside the slaughterhouse. If you can get up to street level, I can cover you."

"We're on our way." I shoved the phone back into my pocket and took hold of Sarah's arm, pulling her to her feet. "Come on. We need to go."

She opened her eyes, the last of the glow dying from her pupils as she turned to look at me. "Is it safe?"

"We'll find out. This way."

I led her out of the station and up the stairs to street level. Uncle Mike was standing in front of the tiny bodega that connected to the Nest. I wanted to run to him. Instead, I walked at a conservative pace, pulling Sarah along with me. When he saw us, he nodded and stepped back inside, holding the door open until we got there. We followed him in, and he closed the door behind us. We were safe at last . . . for now. The question was, what were we going to do to make sure we stayed that way?

Fourteen

"The worst thing in the world is burying family. The second worst thing is telling somebody else that they'll have to do it."
—Enid Healy

The Meatpacking District, which is nicer than it sounds, inside a converted warehouse that's sort of beginning to resemble a clown car with all these people in it

ISTAS AND RYAN WERE WAITING for us in the main room of the slaughterhouse. Ryan looked concerned. Istas looked faintly bored, and was chewing on something that looked suspiciously like the bottom half of a rat. I decided that asking would be a bad idea if I ever wanted to eat again.

"The Covenant is staying at Sarah's hotel, so Sarah's staying with us now," I announced.

"Are you both okay?" asked Uncle Mike.

Sniffling, Sarah shook her head. Then she nodded. Then she shook her head again.

I came to the rescue, saying, "We're shaken up, but we're fine. Ryan, do you want to show Sarah to one of the open offices, so she can put down her things? She's going to be here until all of this is taken care of. It's not safe for her to go back to her hotel." It wasn't safe for her to go back to *any* hotel, if the Covenant had charms that could block her telepathy. That was the only natural defense she had.

"On it," said Ryan. He offered Sarah a faintly bemused

smile, clearly not sure why she looked familiar. "Can I take your bags?"

"Okay," whispered Sarah. She handed him the back-pack with her school books and homework in it, and I handed him her suitcase. She kept hold of her laptop, still hugging it against her chest like a talisman. Then she wandered off after Ryan, following him toward the near-est set of stairs. Istas followed them, still chewing on her probably-a-rat. That was good. I wanted a few minutes alone with Uncle Mike.

The two of us stood silently until Sarah and the others were up the stairs. Then he turned to me, and said, "Re-port?"

"I reached the roof of Sarah's hotel without incident. She came and let me in. We went down the stairs, and were met in the hall by Margaret Healy, who was warded against Sarah's telepathy. Someone must have warned her that she might be dealing with a psychic." Someone like Dominic. I should have been more suspicious from the very start—but then again, hindsight is the only perfect vision. "Margaret arrived at the door to Sarah's room while we were trying to clear out. She picked the lock, and once she was inside, she started demanding to know where I was. Sarah was trying to convince her that I was already gone when my phone rang—shit, my phone. I still don't know who called." I reached for my pocket.

"Stick to the main narrative," said Uncle Mike, hold-ing up a hand to stop me. "What happened then?"

"Margaret realized Sarah had been lying about me, and started to move deeper into the room. So Sarah hit her from behind with a vase and knocked her out." I al-lowed myself a small smile. "It was pretty darn brave of her."

"She's had some good examples," said Uncle Mike. "Then what?"

"I searched Margaret for weapons and tied her up as best I could with a roll of electrical tape from my bag." There was an empty card table nearby. I shrugged off my backpack and walked over to it. "I haven't had a chance to see what all I got from her."

"Show and tell was always my best class."

I dropped my bag on the table. "Then let's study."

Margaret had been carrying over a dozen knives, three guns—two pistols, and one mousegun that had been concealed in her sock—a garrote, a blowgun, and a variety of darts, some of which had tiny corks on them to keep her from getting scratched. I handled those with the utmost care.

"Is that everything?" asked Mike, picking up one of the knives.

"Not quite." I pulled out a set of brass knuckles and a lead-filled sap, dropping them on the pile. "That's it. Well, that, and this. She had it around her neck." I reached into my pocket and produced her anti-telepathy charm, holding it up for him to see.

Mike whistled, long and low. "That's some serious hoodoo. You think she made it herself?"

There are a few spellbooks and grimoires in the family library. Rumor has it they all used to belong to Grandpa Thomas, which explains how he was able to make a deal with one of the Netherworlds before he disappeared. No one in the family has messed around with magic since. We Prices may be foolhardy, but we're not stupid. "I don't know," I said. "If she's a witch, she didn't show it—and she was wearing the charm, which would have messed with any magic she was planning to use."

"I'd have expected a tattoo, not a necklace, if she wasn't the crafter."

"Unless they wanted her to be able to take it off," I said. "Maybe they've started using empaths to prevent more defections." There are at least eight naturally empathic cryptid species, and some of them are human enough—or harmless enough—that the Covenant might be willing to let them live if they seemed to be useful. It wouldn't be the best life for a unicorn or a cofgod, but it would be a life, and that was more than the Covenant was usually inclined to offer their kind.

"Then she'll probably be in trouble for losing it." Mike looked at the charm thoughtfully. "You sure it works?"

"Sarah started picking up on Margaret's presence as soon as I took this off her so, yeah, I'm sure it works."

"But does it work for people who aren't her?"

"Only one way to find out," I said, and looped the chain around my wrist, drawing it tight.

The effect was instantaneous. The soothing static of Sarah's close presence cut out, replaced by silence. There was a shriek of dismay from the walkway above us, and Sarah ran into view, grabbing the railing and leaning far enough out that I was briefly afraid she might lose her balance and fall. "*Verity!* Are you hurt?!"

"I'm fine, Sarah! I'm fine!" I unlooped the charm from my wrist, holding it up so she could see what was going on. The static immediately snapped back on. A mild headache came with it, like whiplash from that brief psychic silence. "We just wanted to see whether that necklace I took off of Margaret was what she used to block your telepathy."

"It was," said Sarah. She was looking at me like I was a ghost. "Please don't do that again. I thought you'd died or something."

If I'd suddenly vanished from her "view," that was an understandable thing for her to think. "I won't," I said, and put the charm back down on the table. "Did they find you a room?"

"Yes, but there's no Internet in this building." Sarah looked even more distraught. "Artie's going to be so worried."

"So call him." That would probably worry him even more, since "the Covenant found me and they have telepathy blockers but don't worry, I'm fine" wasn't the world's most reassuring statement. That couldn't be helped. "We'll get the network up as soon as we can, but none of us is a computer genius, and it hasn't been a priority."

Mike eyed me. "I work in network administration."

"Only one of us is a computer genius, and it hasn't been a priority," I amended. "Maybe you can help Uncle Mike get things set up. In the meanwhile, call Artie, tell him you're not dead. It'll probably be good for your nerves."

"Okay," said Sarah, and turned, vanishing back into the office. Ryan and Istas appeared a moment later, heading for the stairs.

"This day just never lets up," I muttered, finally fishing my phone out of my pocket. I opened it and scrolled to the missed call log. Then I blinked. "Shit."

"What?"

"The call I missed while I was at Sarah's. It was from Dominic."

"Verity—"

"No. I'm not letting him know we suspect him." Suspect, my ass. Margaret had a telepathy blocker. I was ready to lock him up and throw away the key. Still. I hit "redial," raised the phone to my ear, and waited.

Dominic picked up before the first ring had finished. "Are you all right?" he demanded.

"Yes," I said, as calmly as I could. "Barely. Is she?"

"Peter found her before she regained consciousness. What did you hit her with? A brick?"

"Actually, it was Sarah. She managed to catch her from behind with a vase while she was looking for me. Nice timing on the phone call, by the way. It nearly got me captured."

"Oh, God." Dominic sighed raggedly. I realized for the first time how worn he sounded, like he was being yanked in too many directions at the same time. "I need you to do me a favor. It may sound like I'm trying to walk you into a trap, but I swear, I'm not."

I was done believing him when he said that. I was still willing to play along. "I'll listen if you'll answer me one question."

"Anything."

"Are you the one who told them they needed to be using anti-telepathy charms?" If I didn't ask, he'd suspect; Margaret's charm was missing, after all.

Dominic's sharp intake of air wasn't quite a gasp, but it was a close cousin. "They're *what*?"

"I'm taking that as a 'no.'"

"Is Sarah all right?"

That was the only good question he could possibly

have asked. "She's shaken, but she's not hurt, and they're not going to find her again." If I'd been thinking, I would have moved Sarah the second the Covenant came to town. I didn't think. "What do you need me to do?"

"Get to Sunil and Rochak. The plan for tomorrow includes sweeping their neighborhood, looking for signs of cryptid inhabitation. They need to shut down the café and get out of there."

Shit. Even if this was a trap, it wasn't one that I could ignore. Sunil and Rochak were even more defenseless than Sarah, and they thought they were safe. Dominic and I were regulars. They *knew* us. They'd open their doors for him and welcome him in gladly.

I couldn't save their sister. If there was a way for me to save them, I had to take it.

"On it," I said.

"Thank you."

"Just take care of yourself, okay? I'm worried about you."

"You're not alone in that." Dominic laughed unhappily. "Sometimes I wish I'd never come to this cursed city. It's changed everything."

"Life does that," I said.

"Yes, but—"

He stopped mid-sentence. I waited for him to continue, only to finally realize that the silence on the other end of the phone was absolute. He wasn't even breathing. I pulled the phone away from my ear, checking the screen. The connection was dead. He'd hung up on me . . . or someone had hung up for him.

"Well," I said, with a sigh. "Isn't this going to be fun?"

"I'm going with you on whatever fuck-crazy errand you just agreed to," said Uncle Mike.

I looked up at him and smiled thinly. "I stand corrected. This isn't going to be fun. This is going to be a *party*."

Convincing Sarah to stay behind wasn't nearly as hard as it would usually have been. She'd been scared, and that was something she wasn't used to. Uncle Mike got her set up in one corner of the main room with a pile of computer pieces I didn't recognize. She settled in to connecting wires and configuring settings, looking happy as a clam. I guess we all have our comfort zones.

Traveling with Uncle Mike meant I couldn't take the rooftops, but didn't need to hail a cab, either. We rode in his sedan, blending smoothly into the traffic around us. If the Covenant was watching for me suspiciously, they'd know to be watching the high ground. Hopefully, being on the roads would keep me under their radar.

"I wish I could convince her to go home," I said, sinking deep into my seat.

Mike didn't need to ask who I was talking about. "Any chance of that died when these people got charms to block themselves from her view," he said. "No way she's getting on a plane when she won't know whether one of the other passengers is planning to kill her."

"Maybe we depend too much on her telepathy."

"We've all got our skills. There's no shame in depending on them. Just in falling apart if things don't go exactly the way you were planning. Since you're not doing that, I think we're going to be okay." Mike turned onto a one-way street without checking the sign to be sure he was traveling in the right direction. Judging by the parked cars around us, he wasn't. "So we've got a rogue Healy, and our cuckoo's benched for the duration. We still have two bruisers, you, me, and all your folks from work. What about these boys we're going to pick up?"

"They may not want to come with us, and we won't force them. They're Madhura."

"Huh," said Mike, and kept driving. After a few minutes had passed, he added, "Guess that'll save us a few bucks on spoiled food."

I smiled a little. "Guess so." Having a Madhura around retards food spoilage and decay of all types. Bread stays fresh for weeks if there's a Madhura in the neighborhood. No one's exactly sure why. Alex thinks they may be natural bacteriophages or something, but it's hard to say without a lot of invasive lab work—something none of us are particularly interested in performing, and absolutely zero Madhura seem to be interested in volunteering for.

"You really think we're driving into a trap?"

This time I was the one who was quiet for a few minutes, thinking about the question. Finally, I said, "I honestly don't know, Uncle Mike. I want to believe him. I want to believe that Margaret being at the Port Hope was just a horrible coincidence. I can't, quite. At the same time, I never gave him credit for being this good of a liar." I glanced toward my adopted uncle. "Either way, I guess we're going to find out in a little while."

"Two against four." Mike smiled. It wasn't a comforting expression. "Sounds just about fair."

"Assuming we don't plan to walk away."

"Who does?" He shook his head. "You know you can't trust him anymore, hon. He's trying to serve two masters—the Covenant, and his heart. That never works out for anybody in the long run."

I sighed. "I know. I'm just . . . I guess I'm still holding hope for him picking the right side."

"Right for him, or right for you?"

This time I didn't have any answers at all. We drove down the streets in silence, and I hoped as hard as I could that when we reached Gingerbread Pudding, we would find Sunil and Rochak alive and well, and I wouldn't have to make up my mind about Dominic De Luca. I wasn't ready for that. Soon, maybe, but not yet.

Luck was on my side for once. We found a parking space a quarter of a block from the café, and even from there, we could see that the joint was jumping. The line wasn't quite out the door, but people were pushing their way both in and out, and happy tourists with their cups of cocoa and squares of gingerbread choked the sidewalk.

Dominic freaked out when I mentioned monsters in public places. There was no way the Covenant would try to pull off an ambush with this many civilians around. Too many centuries of secrecy weighing them down.

Mike took a few quick steps forward, putting himself in front of me, and proceeded to clear us a path to the door simply through dint of walking with his elbows out and his legs a little farther apart than strictly necessary. People got out of the way without seeming to realize they were doing it. One more advantage to being a large male, rather than a small female.

Then again, being a petite woman has advantages of its own. Once we were inside, I slithered around him and flashed a radiant smile at Sunil, who was manning the counter. He blinked, looking concerned for half a second before plastering an artificially radiant smile on his face and declaring, "There you are! I was starting to worry that you'd forgotten about me, and were leaving me here to die of a broken heart."

"Never," I said flirtatiously, and worked my way around the people between us to slip behind the counter. I leaned up onto my tiptoes, close enough that onlookers would assume I was kissing his cheek, and whispered, "The Covenant is coming. We need to get you out of here."

Sunil laughed nervously. "Of course, sweetheart. Take your friend back to the break room and I'll send Rochak to bring you some gingerbread while you wait."

I nodded as I dropped to the flats of my feet. "See you soon, honey." Motioning for Mike to follow me, I started toward the back. A few people grumbled, but not many. Everyone's forgiving when romance is in the air. (Too bad it wasn't real. My parents would have been thrilled if I'd come home with a nice cryptid boy, and Sunil was sweet. Literally.) Mike trailed along behind me like a silent shadow, and I led him into the little employee break room where I once shared gingerbread and secrets with Piyusha, just hours before she died.

True to Sunil's word, Mike and I were barely in the room when Rochak arrived with a tray of gingerbread, and a white to-go bag of the same stuff. "What's going on?" he asked.

"Nothing good," I replied, taking a piece of ginger-bread. "Rochak, this is my uncle, Mike Gucciard. Uncle Mike, this is Rochak, one of the owners of Gingerbread Pudding."

"Charmed," said Uncle Mike, claiming his own piece of gingerbread.

"Likewise," said Rochak automatically. He turned back to me. "What's going on? You don't normally drop by like this."

"How quickly can you close down and get out of here?" I asked. His eyes widened. I shook my head, and continued, "Dominic—who may or may not be compromised, but that's a matter for later—just called me. There's going to be a Covenant sweep of this neighborhood tomorrow. You need to leave, and you need to leave *now*. "

"Now?" Rochak glanced at the clock over the door. "We close in an hour. If I try to clear this place out before then, it'll be a madhouse. I think the best thing to do is close normally, then put a sign on the door saying that we're doing inventory and will reopen after the weekend. That should buy us a few days."

"That sounds good," I said. "Do you have someplace to go?"

Rochak shook his head.

I could practically feel Candy's glare on the back of my neck as I sighed and said, "Well, we do. Providing you can agree to stay inside until this is over, I've got a place you can go to ground."

"Is it safe?"

"It's as safe as anyplace else in this town. Safer, if everyone stays careful and follows the rules. Kitty at the Freakshow would also be willing to give you sanctuary, if you don't mind bunking with her entire staff."

Rochak made a face. "I'd rather not. I'm unhappy enough at the idea of leaving the café without adding a bunch of strangers to the equation."

The Nest was full of strangers, too, but there would be fewer of them; maybe that would help. I decided not to mention it for the moment. "Then you come with us.

We'll stay here long enough to let you shut things down, and then we'll take you back to our current haven."

"Thank you." Rochak put the tray down and seized my free hand in both of his, holding tightly. "I don't know how I can possibly thank you enough. Thank you. You have no idea how much this means to us."

"It's my job," I said. Then I blinked, and repeated, almost wonderingly, "It's my *job*."

"Very?" Uncle Mike frowned. "You okay?"

"I'm fine. I just need to go upstairs and make a few phone calls. Rochak, can I use your apartment?"

He nodded, reclaiming his hand. "Please. What's mine is yours."

"Great. Have some more gingerbread, Uncle Mike. I'll be right back." I turned on my heel and left the room, heading for the stairs up to the second-floor apartment that Rochak shared with his brother. I didn't look back.

My dance partner wasn't home. "Hello, world. You've reached the home of James and Dennis Garcia. Leave your message at the tone, and we'll call you when there's enough of a pause in the glorious adventure of our lives." James' gleeful monologue was cut off by the sound of a shrill beep.

I cleared my throat. "James, it's Verity. You need to take Dennis on a nice vacation, and you need to go *now*. Something nice and far away. Maybe a cruise to Hawaii. Leave tomorrow, and don't come back until you hear that the city's clear." I hesitated before adding the second part of my message: "When you get back . . . I think it's time for you to start looking for a new partner. We both knew this was coming. I wish it didn't have to end this way, but it's not fair of me to keep holding you back because my heart isn't in it anymore. Thank you so much, for everything. You've been wonderful to dance with."

I hung up the phone and stared blankly at the wall of Sunil and Rochak's apartment for several minutes, waiting for my heart to start beating normally again. There it was; that was it. I was done. I could teach dance classes, I could participate in local competitions, but with one little phone call, I had finally put the nail in the coffin of my professional ballroom dreams. And oddly, it hurt less than I had expected it to. Maybe my parents were right when they said that spending a year away from home would be exactly what I needed to set my priorities straight. At the time, I'd laughed at them, saying that all a year in New York would do was make damn sure I never took off my tango shoes . . . when really, a year in New York was what it took to teach me that dancing was my heart, but cryptozoology was my soul.

I shook my head, clearing away the cobwebs, and lifted my phone again. This time, I dialed the Freakshow office. Kitty picked up, with a sultry, "You've reached the Freakshow, how may we fulfill your midway fantasies today?"

"Okay, you have *got* to stop answering the phone like that. You sound like you're running a bordello, not a perfectly respectable titty bar."

"Sometimes people can't tell the difference, and it helps bring in business," said Kitty, dropping the artificial seduction as quickly as she'd put it on. She was all business now. "What's the news, Verity?"

"I won't be coming to work tomorrow."

"I didn't expect you."

"Neither will Istas." Istas wasn't aware of it yet, but with as many noncombatants as we now had at the Nest, either she or Ryan would need to be there at all times. It was a security measure. "She's staying with me."

"That's fine. Let her know that she'll be getting paid regardless, since you wouldn't be keeping her away if you didn't really need her. Anything else?"

"There are three Covenant operatives in town." I sketched out their descriptions and provided their names, adding, "Dominic may be traveling with them. I think he's still on our side, but it's hard to be certain, and there's evidence both ways. Watch for anybody seen in his company. He doesn't know where I am, and we're keeping it that way. The new Covenant folks have telepathy blockers that may work on other forms of psychic ability and confusion charms. Keep them away from the hidebehinds if you possibly can."

"Honey, I'm keeping the Covenant of St. George away from *everyone* if I possibly can."

"That's a good approach. I'll keep you posted to the best of my ability. Things are about to get pretty messy around here, and I'm not sure how much time I'm going to have."

Kitty sighed. "Verity, you've done more than anyone could ask you to. This isn't your fight."

I looked around the perfectly domestic little apartment where, once, three siblings sat and dreamed of a new life, one that involved owning a dessert café of their very own. Below me, the two who survived would be shutting things down, getting ready to abandon their dream—even if temporarily—for the sake of their lives. They shouldn't have had to do that. No one should have to do that.

Dreams mattered. I shook my head, even knowing that Kitty couldn't see it. "No," I said. "This has always been my fight. This is everyone's fight."

"Fine, then," said Kitty. "What do we do now?"

I smiled into the darkness. It felt good. "We win."

Fifteen

"I ain't sorry. You got that? I have never regretted a single minute of my life, and I ain't sorry."

— Frances Brown

Back in the Meatpacking District (still nicer than it sounds), in an increasingly full converted warehouse

IT TOOK US almost two hours to get back to the Nest, thanks to Uncle Mike's evasive driving techniques, which included a trip through the Lincoln Tunnel. I spent most of the drive watching the mirrors for signs of pursuit. They never came.

Sunil and Rochak goggled shamelessly as we entered the Nest. Each of them had a suitcase, and Rochak was dragging a cooler filled with gingerbread, cookies, and jars of assorted types of sugar in both liquid and granular forms. I'd never realized there were so many kinds of natural sweetener. Watching a Madhura pack his kitchen was definitely an education.

Istas was sitting cross-legged in the middle of the room, carefully stitching lace around the edge of one of her seemingly endless supply of parasols. She looked up as we approached, assessing us to see whether we presented any threat. The way her posture tensed told me she didn't know what Sunil and Rochak were. I started walking just a little faster, putting myself between Istas and the others.

"Istas, this is Sunil and Rochak," I said, indicating them each in turn. "They're Madhura."

Her expression—a mixture of wariness and blank incomprehension—didn't change.

I tried again: "They're cryptids, they're harmless, and they brought cookies."

"Why did you fail to open with the word 'cookies'?" Istas set her sewing supplies aside and stood in a single fluid gesture. The smile she turned toward Sunil and Rochak contained a few too many teeth. "Baked goods are one of the primary accomplishments of civilization."

"Along with . . . ?" prompted Uncle Mike. I couldn't blame him. I'd been tempted to do the same thing.

"Waterproof mascara, conditioner, and bleach," said Istas. She cocked her head to the side, still studying the two Madhura. "My name is Istas. I am a waheela. Do you know what a waheela is?"

"No," said Sunil. He hesitated before adding, "Ma'am." Always play nicely with the predators of the world—and whether or not he knew what Istas was, she was clearly a predator. Nothing else could hold so still while staring so intently.

"I am a therianthrope from the upper reaches of this continent," Istas said, with perfect calm. "My people come from the ice and the snow and the tundra without end. I live here because I am considered a 'human-lover,' too soft and fond of people to be an effective hunter. Do you think I am soft?"

There was absolutely no good answer to that question. Sunil and Rochak shot me matching panicked looks. I sighed. "Istas, please play nicely. Sunil and Rochak are going to be staying with us while the Covenant is in town."

"We bake," said Sunil. "Constantly. And we share."

"Hm." Istas considered them. "I will extend my protection to you in exchange for cookies."

"Deal," said Rochak.

I rubbed my forehead with one hand. Between Istas and the mice, it was probably a good thing we were importing our own dedicated bakers. Probably. "Okay, guys.

Any open office is available for you to use as a bedroom, and we're going to get more inflatable mattresses. You've met Uncle Mike, and Ryan is—Istas, where's Ryan?"

"He has gone to the Freakshow to collect some things, and to confirm that Kitty does not require our services." Istas bent and picked up her parasol. Then she paused, sniffing the air. "I smell gingerbread."

"Like I said, they brought cookies." I gave Rochak a meaningful look.

I like smart people. He opened the cooler, grabbing one of the medium-sized bags of gingersnaps and tossing it to Istas. She caught it one-handed. It took her less than five seconds to open the bag, snatch out three cookies, and cram them into her mouth.

"Okay, that's Istas taken care of, and you can meet Ryan when you get back. I should probably introduce you to the mice. That'll go better if you're willing to give up some more gingersnaps. That just leaves one more person. Hang on a second." I cocked my head, "listening" for the telepathic static of Sarah's presence. As soon as I started looking for it, I found it, lingering at the back of my mind like so much white noise. *Sarah?* I thought, as loudly as I could. *Can you come to the main room for a minute? There's someone I need you to meet.*

I'll be right there, she replied. *I just need to get off the phone.*

If she was on the phone, that meant she'd managed to reach Artie. That was a good thing. She'd be calmer after talking to him, and I didn't want to introduce her to her new roommates while she was still all worked up about losing her hotel room. Sarah was funny about privacy. That telepath thing again. She liked putting space between herself and other minds, the more, the better. I made a mental note to tell Sunil and Rochak not to take the office directly next to hers.

They were frowning at me, looking confused, while Istas did her best to eat her way through the entire bag of cookies without pausing for air. I offered an apologetic smile. "Sorry," I said. "My cousin is coming down to meet you. Her name's Sarah. She's a telepath, but she's a very polite one, and she won't poke around in your head without permission."

Somehow, they didn't look particularly reassured. Rochak put down his suitcase and coughed into his hand before indicating the cooler, and asking, "Is there someplace we can put all this? A cooler isn't exactly ideal for long-term storage."

"There's a kitchen," said Uncle Mike. "Come on, I'll show you. There's even some masking tape so we can label the stuff you don't want anybody else touching."

"Thank you," said Rochak. He glanced to Sunil. "Will you be all right here with Verity?"

"If she were going to kill us, we'd be splattered all over the inside of the café by now, not standing in this godforsaken excuse for a refuge," said Sunil. He sounded tired. "Go on. Make sure everything is put away. I'll get us a room."

"All right," said Rochak, and followed Mike out of the room. Istas glanced between us and the cooler, and then went after the cooler, choosing the potential for more cookies over company. I couldn't exactly say that I was surprised.

"So," said Sunil.

"So," I agreed. I spread a hand, indicating the slaughterhouse around us. "This is home for the duration. The dragons lived here for centuries without getting caught. It should work for us for a few weeks."

"You really think this will be over in a few weeks?" asked Sunil dubiously.

"If it's not, I think it's unlikely to be my problem anymore, because I'll be dead," I said, and shrugged. "It's a hazard of the job. When you decide to be the immovable object standing in front of the unstoppable force, you'd better pray that you're right about being immovable, and they're wrong about being unstoppable."

"Otherwise, you'll wind up like a bug on a windshield," said Sarah. She sounded exhausted. I turned to see her coming down the stairs from the second floor walkway. Her hair was loose, and her feet were bare, but apart from that, she was dressed exactly as she'd been when I left to get the boys from Gingerbread Pudding. "I don't want to be the one explaining that to your mother, you know."

"So hopefully, you won't be. Sarah, this is Sunil. Sunil, this is Sarah."

"Hello," said Sunil. His eyes were a little wide. Not unusual in men meeting my cousin for the first time—or in anyone meeting her for the first time. It's not that she's pretty, although she is. It's that her cuckoo mojo goes to work with word one, trying to find a way into their heads. If Sarah wasn't careful, she'd have him thinking that they'd been friends since childhood. Or that they were dating, or married, or who knows what else.

"Sarah . . ." I began.

She flinched a little. "Sorry. I relaxed while I was on the phone, and I just . . . sorry." Her eyes flashed white as she clamped her shields down tighter. The telepathic static increased in volume at the same time, like keeping herself from changing the minds of people around her meant that it was harder for her to stay out of "sight." That was good to know.

Sunil blinked and shook his head, like he was trying to clear away cobwebs. His expression changed, going from bedazzled curiosity to fear as he took a large step backward. Then he bowed deeply toward Sarah.

"What the hell?" I asked.

"I don't know," said Sarah. Louder, she asked, "Um, sir? Do you think you could stand up, maybe, and stop being weird?"

"My lady Johrlac, if you allow me to take my brother and depart your hive, I swear, we will never darken your door again." Sunil was talking almost too fast for me to understand him. It didn't help that he was facing the floor. "I did not know. I am sorry. I did not realize."

"What are you *talking* about, Sunil?" I asked. "Sarah's my cousin. This isn't her 'hive,' it's our hiding place. If it belongs to anyone, it's mine, since I'm the one renting the place from the dragons."

He lifted his head enough to shoot me a deeply apologetic look. "I can't save you. I'm so sorry."

Right. "Okay, I think I see what's going on here. You called her 'lady Johrlac.' That means you know what Sarah is, doesn't it?" The Covenant of St. George never figured out that the cuckoos existed. That didn't mean the other cryptids weren't aware—and "Johrlac" was the proper name for her species.

Sunil's apologetic look turned panicked. "You mean *you* know?"

"Johrlac," said Sarah, sounding not only tired, but suddenly depressed. Discussion of her actual species tended to have that effect on her. "No one knows where we come from, no one knows how to send us back there, and most people don't know how to kill us. Everybody calls us 'cuckoos,' because a thing can be less scary when you have an easy name to hang on it. We steal lives, and then we end them. Is that what you think I am?"

"Please, I meant no offense," whispered Sunil.

Sarah closed her eyes. "Verity . . ."

I stepped closer to her, putting a hand on her shoulder. "Sunil, Sarah is my cousin. Not by birth, maybe, but by adoption. *Voluntary* adoption. My grandmother—her mother—is also a cuckoo. She raised my Mom. So my whole family is sort of resistant to the instinctive brainwashing. We like Sarah because she's Sarah. We love her because she's family. And she's not going to hurt you. She's here to hide from the Covenant, just like the rest of us."

"I've always done my very best not to take advantage of the people around me," said Sarah, opening her eyes and looking plaintively at Sunil. "It's hard sometimes. You can't even imagine how hard. But I swear, I'm not going to mess with your head."

"This is . . ." Sunil frowned, finally straightening up. "I've never heard of a Johrlac deciding to live among others as one of them, and not as their master."

"I do dishes, too," said Sarah.

"Sunil!" Rochak reappeared from the direction of the kitchen, Mike tagging along behind him. Istas was nowhere to be seen, possibly because the kitchen now contained a great deal of unguarded gingerbread. I hoped that Mike had asked her to leave some for the rest of us. "Who's this?"

"My cousin, Sarah," I said, and braced for the explosion that was sure to follow.

It didn't. Rochak stopped next to Sunil, looking speculatively at Sarah. Then he turned to me, and asked, "Your cousin is a Johrlac? How is that even biologically possible?"

"See, I'm a little more curious as to how you're identifying her on sight, but yes, she is," I said. "Is that going to be a problem?"

"No. I'm fully mature. She can't get inside my head." He put a hand on Sunil's shoulder, turning back to Sarah. "If you hurt my brother, I will destroy you. Then I will find the rest of your hive, and destroy them as well."

"I'm not going to hurt your brother, and I don't have a hive," said Sarah. "I just want this to be over before I miss too many classes."

"Then we're in agreement," said Rochak.

I blinked. "Mature? What?"

"Madhura are immune to the lure of the Johrlac once we pass our third molt," said Rochak. He nodded toward Sunil. "My brother has only passed his second."

"Thanks for announcing that to the world, Rochak," said Sunil, looking mortified.

"Don't worry; the world has no idea what it means," I said. "Uncle Mike, can you show them to an empty office? Not one of the ones to either side of Sarah, please, I think we'll all feel better if we're not stacking people on top of each other." And maybe later, when all this was over, I could sit down with Rochak and grill him on exactly how the Madhura were able to resist the call of the cuckoo—something no other known species was able to do, except for possibly the Apraxis wasps, and those weren't something we could sit down and talk to. Not unless we felt like being stung to death and used to feed the hive's larvae.

"I'm on it," said Mike. "If you two gentlemen would follow me, I'll show you to your quarters—and to the bathroom, since you're probably going to want that eventually." He started toward the stairs. Sunil and Rochak followed him.

In a matter of seconds, Sarah and I were alone. I looked toward her. "You okay?" I asked.

She laughed unsteadily. "Oh, I'm dandy. This has been the *best* night. The Covenant of St. George has telepathy blockers on their people, so I won't be able to hear them coming. I had to leave my hotel before I was ready, and I didn't have time to finish my homework first. I'm going to miss class tomorrow, Artie's freaking out and wants to fly to New York to panic at me in person, and now there are people who know what I am living in the same building as me."

"I know what you are," I protested. "I've always known."

"You don't look at me like that, Verity. You've *never* looked at me like that."

I sighed. "Okay, fair. Look, you don't have to stay here. You can go and stay with the dragons down in the sewers. You know William would be happy to have you."

Sarah shook her head. "I can't. Even if I was comfortable leaving you alone, which I'm not—"

"You don't have to stay for my sake. I can take care of myself."

"I don't care if you think you can take care of yourself. I'm *not* leaving you," Sarah repeated, more firmly. "But even if I was, there's no Internet or cell service in the Nest. The dragons don't consider it a priority. All their calls are made on an old landline the city put in for the municipal workers, and they'd slit their wrists before they paid for smart phones. If I drop off the grid like that, Artie will be on the next plane out of Portland, and I'm not going to be the reason he puts himself in danger. I can't."

"Right." I sighed, rubbing the back of my neck with one hand. One day, those two are going to admit that they're in love with each other. Until then, we're all going to stay stuck in the middle of their not-a-relationship. "Well, then, I guess we're all just going to have to cope."

"Yeah," agreed Sarah miserably. "We are."

I got Sarah settled back in her room-slash-office, largely by promising to pick up some tomato juice the next time I had to go out of the Nest. Which was going to be soon; my feet were already starting to itch with the need to go, to run, to *move*. I'd been sitting still for hours—and being in the car while Uncle Mike drove us around New York didn't count. It just made me feel even less like I was in control of the situation. Holing up and laying low might be the smart thing to do, but doing the smart thing has never been a Price family tradition. We're more interested in running straight into the jaws of danger and daring it to bite down.

(There might be more of us among the living if danger weren't so very willing to take us at our word and bite. That doesn't change the fact that somebody has to do the job we do, and we're uniquely qualified for it. We've been breeding to die this way for generations.)

The mice were still enjoying their celebration—or maybe they'd started a new one; it can be hard to tell with them. I peeked through the office window long enough to reassure myself that they weren't about to set the place on fire or anything. Then I started moving again, heading for my own makeshift bedroom. I needed to know what was going on out in my city, and that meant I needed to be *out*, not dealing with evacuating the resident cryptids or getting my relatives out of the line of fire.

First things first: I stripped off the clothes I'd been wearing to go see Sarah and changed into my usual night-running gear: a skintight gray bodysuit that would render me virtually invisible in the shadows, a belt that always made me feel a little bit like Batman, since he's sort of the platonic ideal of "person running around in spandex with their weapons around their waist," and a cotton hoodie only slightly darker than the bodysuit. With the hood pulled up to hide my hair and face, I could disappear on the rooftops, becoming part of the scenery.

Combat boots and a backpack full of ammo, replacement knives, and climbing gear completed my preparations. I was loaded for bear—literally—and if I was lucky, that would translate into being loaded for Healy. If I was really lucky, the question would never come up.

I went thumping back down the stairs to the ground floor of the slaughterhouse. There was no one there. I took that to mean that they were still where I'd left them and walked toward the kitchen, using the stroll as an excuse to test the weight of my backpack. It was a little heavier than I would have liked, but it was perfectly balanced, and in the end, that mattered more than a few extra pounds. It's not how much you're carrying; it's what you do with it. And I was planning on unleashing a world of hurt on anyone who got in my way.

"Uncle Mike?" I stuck my head into the kitchen. Sunil and Rochak were at the stove, frying something that smelled like taffy while Istas looked on appreciatively. Uncle Mike was sitting at one of the card tables, sharpening his knives. From the assortment he had spread out in front of him, he'd been at it since he left me alone with Sarah, and was planning to be at it for quite a while longer.

"What is it, Very?" he asked, looking up. "Everything okay with Sarah?"

Sunil and Rochak stiffened at the question. Wow, I could already tell that we were entering a new era of fun times here in our hidey-hole. Good thing I was planning to get the hell out for a little while.

"She's miserable, but she'll cope," I said, as casually as I could. "I guess being judged by her species makes her unhappy."

"I am very sorry," said Sunil, in a soft voice. "It was instinctive."

I paused and took a breath before saying, "Just try to keep it cool until all this is over, please? My whole family vouches for Sarah. She's one of us. And just like everyone else here, she's stressed enough not to need an extra dose of feeling terrible about herself. She didn't choose her species." Any more than I chose to be born a Price, or Dominic chose to be born into the Covenant. We were all of us dealing with the hands we were dealt.

"We will treat her with as much kindness and respect as she treats us," said Rochak.

"I can't ask you for more than that." I turned back to Uncle Mike. "Can you please help Sarah finish getting us on the Internet? I'd feel better if I could check my email, and Sarah's a lot less likely to freak out if she can chat with Artie."

"I'm on it." Mike stood, leaving his knives on the table. "Heading out?"

I smiled a little. "What was your first clue?"

"Call it intuition. You'll be careful out there?"

"As careful as I can be."

"I don't like this."

"You don't have to." I needed to move, or I was going to scream. "Keep an eye on things here. If anything goes wrong . . ."

"I'm here to make sure nothing goes wrong," said Mike implacably. His tone was flat, the verbal equivalent of a brick wall suddenly appearing in my path. "Call if you need help, or if you're going out of cell range for more than a few minutes. I want to be able to reach you if anything comes up here."

"Deal. Istas, Mike's in charge until I get back." The irony of telling the woman who could probably bench-press a Buick to obey the human wasn't lost on me.

It wasn't lost on Istas, either. She raised one eyebrow, looking amused. Then she nodded, and agreed, "Yes. I will listen to the man I have just met when he is making judgments regarding my safety and the safety of my mate."

"See, the sad thing is, I know you mean that." It took me a while to learn to speak waheela. After being Istas' coworker for a year, I had it pretty much down. (If it sounds sarcastic, it isn't; if it involves a threat of physical violence, it's sincere, but unless it comes with claws, it's probably friendly. Like having a pet wolverine with rabies.)

Istas smiled. "Precisely. Enjoy your hunt for things to hurt. Save some carnage for the rest of us."

"I will," I said, and turned, walking back out into the main room. I paused by the table where we'd left Margaret's weapons, picking up her telepathy-blocking charm and dropping it into one of the pockets of my backpack. If things were calm enough to allow for a few personal errands, I'd take it by the Freakshow. Bogeymen are some of the best information brokers and rumormongers in the world. Kitty might know how the thing worked, and better, how we could counter it. What's the point of having a telepathic early warning system if you can't use it?

The stairs beckoned me upward, but I forced myself to ignore them, walking instead to the door leading out to the small, enclosed courtyard. Much as I hated to start any journey on the ground, I didn't want to risk attracting attention by taking the same path too many times. That meant starting from a different rooftop. I crossed the courtyard to the abandoned bodega, and from there, made my way out to the street.

New York is the city that never sleeps, but there are still neighborhoods that quiet down after a certain hour, losing the majority of their vibrancy and life in favor of stillness and the dark. Being popular with the tourists has done a lot to revitalize the Meatpacking District. That also means that it's one of the areas that clears out quickly after midnight. A few well-dressed people on their way home from the bars lingered, but the streets were otherwise left to the homeless, the taxi drivers, the lost, and of course, the cryptids. I recognized them by the way they wore their hats, pulled low over their faces, and the quick anxiety of their steps. The Covenant had everyone on edge, most of all the people who inhabited this shadowy slice of the Big Apple.

I kept close to the buildings as I walked, looking for a good route upward. I found it about three blocks away from the Nest, at a corner that seemed to be in deeper shadow than most of the others, where the cornices of the building formed an almost perfect series of handholds. I glanced around once, making sure that no one was looking at me. Then I reached up, and started to climb.

There's a security on the rooftops of a major city that I never feel anywhere else, a feeling like I could run forever if I had to. The city limits always loom, but no one can chase in a straight line across the slope of that much disparate architecture; there's always a chance to double back and find another way. It would take an army to take me out when I'm that far above the street.

With no real idea of where I was going or what I was going to do when I got there, I took a long step backward, tensed, and ran.

Running helped to clear my head, allowing me to review the events of the night so far in a clearer, more rational light. Bad: Margaret Healy had seen me, and even if she didn't know for sure who I was, she knew I was someone who wasn't on her side. Not even an idiot could wake up facedown on the carpet of someone else's hotel room, wrists and ankles taped together, and not realize that something was probably up. Good: even if she'd seen me, she didn't know for sure who I was, or that I had anything to do with Dominic. She might be furious—she *would* be furious, if she was anything like every other member of our mutual family—but she wouldn't know where to start looking for me.

Bad: Sarah's cover had been blown, and Gingerbread Pudding was no longer safe. Good: I'd managed to get Sunil, Rochak, and Sarah all to safety before the Covenant could reach them, and under the circumstances, that was a victory. Better yet, the Freakshow was still secure. We had options. They might not be as diverse as I would have liked them to be, but at least they existed.

Bad: Dominic was with the Covenant, at least for the moment . . . and that was good at the same time, because he'd called to warn me about Sunil and Rochak, and there'd been no ambush waiting for me. Maybe I was wrong. Maybe Margaret had just been at the Port Hope for the normal reasons, and he hadn't betrayed us. When this was over . . . it wasn't impossible to think that maybe when this was all over, he'd be standing with me, not against me. Covenant members had chosen to walk away from their duty before. I was living proof of that.

I was so lost in thought that I misjudged the drop as I leaped from one roof to another. I landed harder than I intended to. I caught myself with my hands before I could face-plant on the roof. The gesture cost me a lot of momentum, and rather than trying to get started again, I let myself skid to a stop, turning my feet to the side to increase my friction. Once the last of my inertia had bled off I straightened, looking around.

I was near the Freakshow, in one of those weird New York neighborhoods that mixes commercial and residential buildings in a patchwork of brownstone, concrete, and glass. I walked to the edge of the roof, looking down. There were a few people on the street, and the ubiquitous taxis slid endlessly by, but everything was silent, or as close to silent as New York ever gets. It was a real cinematic moment, the sort of thing that normally only exists in movies.

The sound of a gun being cocked somehow managed to fit right in. I stiffened. "Hello," said Margaret from behind me, her sharp British accent somehow turning that single word into a threat. "I was wondering when you'd arrive."

Then her gun caught me across the back of the head. I had just enough time to realize that I'd done something completely stupid—and that wasn't like me, what the *hell* was I doing?—before I fell. The last thing I heard was the sound of my own body hitting the rooftop, a heavy, wet thud, like a sack of cement being dropped. Then there was nothing.

Sixteen

$$\pi_2(n) \sim 2C_2 \frac{n}{(\ln n)^2} \sim 2C_2 \int_2^n \frac{dt}{(\ln t)^2}$$

"Damn."

— Alice Healy

A converted slaughterhouse in the Meatpacking District, resuming narration with the assistance of Sarah Zellaby

THE CEILING in my temporary room was water stained enough that it sort of looked like a Magic Eye puzzle, one of those pictures that's supposed to resolve into three dimensions if you stare at it long enough. It was a far cry from the kind of hotel where I usually stayed. It was even a far cry from the Port Hope, where I could probably have found a few water stains if I'd been willing to look hard enough.

It was better than being dead. I stretched out on the air mattress with my hands folded behind my head, squinting up at the ceiling. Maybe it would be a sailboat. Or a functional solution for the Riemann Hypothesis. Either one would be fine with me.

I was starting to relax when pain flared into sudden life at the back of my skull, as intense as if I'd somehow slammed my head into the concrete floor. Only I hadn't moved. I cried out, too startled to do anything else, and sat up, clapping a hand over the spot. The pain got worse . . .

. . . and then it was gone, disappearing as suddenly as it had come. One second, pain, the next second, no pain. I lowered my hand slowly, waiting for the pain to come back. It didn't. Everything was silent.

That was when I realized that the sense of Verity's presence—a low constant, as long as we were within a few miles of each other, even if I normally couldn't "hear" her when we weren't in the same building—was gone. *Verity?* I thought, as hard as I could. At this distance, she shouldn't have been able to answer me, but there should have been *something*.

There was nothing.

I staggered to my feet, trying to make sense of the silence. It was the loudest thing I'd ever heard. I've had family around me for as long as I can remember, people I was so telepathically attuned to that I could hear them without trying. It was disorienting, like blowing out the last candle in the middle of a blackout. It was also terrifying, because I didn't know what it meant . . . but I suspected.

"Uncle Mike!" The words came out in a wail as I turned and bolted for the door.

The main room of the slaughterhouse was empty. I practically flew down the stairs, following the vague sense of "people this way" to the kitchen where Istas and the Madhura were sitting around a table. I grabbed the edge of the doorframe to keep myself upright, aware that I had to look half insane with worry, and not really giving a damn. "Where's Mike?" I demanded.

Istas blinked. "You are distressed," she said. "Why? Are we under attack?"

"I don't know," I said. "Where's Mike? I need him. Tell me where he is." I couldn't resist giving a telepathic "push" at the end, trying to make her tell me. I encountered nothing—no resistance, no response. Istas might as well have been a rock for all the effect that I had on her mind. That was what I got for trying to push someone who wasn't human. I'm more attuned to humans than I am to any other species, even my own. Istas was the only waheela I'd ever met, and I had no idea how to make her do what I wanted. I couldn't even pick up on her thoughts, just her emotions, and even those were blurry, like I was reading them through thick fog.

Luckily for me, she felt like playing along. "He is in

what was originally the foreman's office," she said. "I believe he is attempting to make the Internet function, so you can communicate with the outside world, and I can go shopping." A brief scowl crossed her face. "I hope this is resolved soon. Verity will not allow me to have things shipped here, and Kitty becomes annoyed if I receive more than one package per day."

I stared at her. The Covenant was in town and Verity had gone silent in my head, but Istas was worried about the mail. Verity would probably have called that proof that trivial desire endures no matter what, allowing our minds to find stability under the most chaotic conditions. Then she would have made a bad dance pun. All it made me do was want to scream.

I swallowed my first three responses before asking, "Where is the foreman's office?"

"He said that he would be in the office in the leftmost corner," said the younger Madhura. I could feel him at the edge of my mind, a little static melody against the louder, less delicate noise generated by Istas. I couldn't feel his brother at all. If I hadn't been looking at the table, I would have assumed that only two people were there. "Are you well, lady Johrlac?"

The older Madhura hissed, "Sunil! Do not insult her."

"I'm sorry." Waves of stricken embarrassment that I didn't understand washed off the younger Madhura. "I meant no offense."

Exhaustion swept over me, washing the Madhura's incomprehensible embarrassment away. I shook my head. "It's fine. I need to go talk to Uncle Mike." He would know what to do. He would know what to tell me. Standing in this kitchen with three relative strangers, the only thing I could think to do was crawl back into my bed and wait until all this blew over, and I knew that wouldn't help anyone. "Thanks for your help," I said. Then I turned and left the kitchen.

Somehow I managed not to start running again until I was out of their sight. This time, I looked for the sound/feeling of a human mind nearby, and followed it to the office where Uncle Mike was setting up a cable router on another of the folding card tables that seemed to be everywhere around the Nest. He didn't look up when he heard my footsteps, but his thoughts tensed, going from calm to on alert without visibly changing his posture. I glanced toward his hand. He had a knife that I was pretty sure hadn't been there a moment before.

"What's going on, Sarah?" he asked.

His question was calm, reasonable, and the last straw for my overstretched nerves. "I can't find Verity!" I wailed.

"What?" Uncle Mike lifted his head. Concern baked off him like heat off pavement in the summer sun. "Verity went out for a run, to clear her head. She should be back in a little while. Is there something I can help you with?"

I took a deep breath. Sometimes humans can be so *slow*. Choosing my words carefully, I said, "I don't mean 'she's not in the building'—I knew that. I mean I can't find her anywhere in the city. I should be able to find her no matter where she is in this city, and if she left, I should have had time to realize that she was moving farther away. I was in my room when my head started hurting like my skull was busted. Then the pain went away, and Verity was just *gone*."

Uncle Mike stood slowly, putting both modem and knife down on the table. "Sarah, are you telling me Verity's dead?"

Those were the words I'd been most afraid of hearing. Tears suddenly burned in the corners of my eyes. I managed to swallow and forced myself to shrug, whispering, "I don't know. I've never been connected to anyone who died before. I don't know what it would feel like. Maybe she's dead. I don't know."

"Shh, Sarah, shh." He closed the distance between us in three long steps, putting his arms around me and gathering me close to him. It was a human gesture, and not one I was entirely comfortable with, but I let myself be gathered, pressing my face against his chest and sobbing. At least there was a layer of fabric between his skin and mine. He stroked my hair with one hand. "You need to calm down, okay? Can you do that for me? Because if Verity's out of the picture, we have to figure out what we're going to do, and I need you to be with me for that. So let it out, and let yourself calm down."

How can you say *that?* I demanded, my throat too full of tears—and snot, since mucus production is one of the biological traits that cuckoos are "lucky" enough to share with the human race—for me to speak.

Mike didn't respond. He just kept stroking my hair. Slowly, I realized that he hadn't heard me. I can only communicate telepathically with people I'm attuned to, and that requires spending a certain amount of time in my physical company. Uncle Mike and I only saw each other at holidays, if then, and I usually spent Christmas and Thanksgiving hiding in my room, if we were in Columbus, or hiding in Artie's room, if we were in Portland. Without Verity, there was no one left who could hear me when I didn't remember to talk out loud.

Swallowing to try and clear some of the stickiness from my throat, I pushed away from Mike and said, "Verity's not out of the picture, okay? She's just missing. I don't know how, or why, but she's not out of the picture. She's not gone. Don't you let yourself think that she is, not for an instant, or I swear, I will make you regret it."

"I'm not saying she's dead, Sarah, but if you can't find her, and you hurt before she disappeared, there's a pretty good chance that she's not in fighting shape right now. We're going to need to find her, and you've been here a lot longer than I have. So what do we do?"

The word "panic" rose to the tip of my tongue. I swallowed it, and said, "We need to call the Freakshow. Kitty will know if anyone saw anything."

"Bogeymen aren't always happy to share information. Kitty had a relationship with Verity. What makes you sure that she'll talk to us?"

He was already referring to Verity in the past tense. I didn't think he even realized he was doing it. I swallowed again, this time to stop myself from screaming, and said, "Kitty's relationship with Verity is *why* she'll talk to us. Kitty and Verity have an understanding, and Kitty and I know each other." Calling us friends would have been too much of a stretch, but "allies by necessity" was a pretty accurate description.

Kitty would want Verity to be okay. If there was any way for her to help us out, she would.

"Okay," said Uncle Mike. "So you go call the Freakshow."

"What are you going to do?"

"Check the defenses, make sure there's a lot of traps set, and change anything Verity would have known how to get around." His tone was apologetic, and his words were accompanied by a wave of sorrow and determination so emotionally loud that I could have picked it up from a complete stranger. "We gotta assume she's compromised, kiddo, and that means we batten down the hatches and we get ready for the siege to begin. Now get Kitty on the phone, and find out if there's anything she can do to help us get Verity back. You're the one who comes closest to knowing what happened to her, and I've got work to do."

With that, he turned and walked out of the room, leaving me standing alone, staring after him, with absolutely no idea what I was supposed to do. No; that wasn't true. I pulled my phone out of my pocket and started scrolling through my contacts. I would call the Freakshow. Kitty would know what to do. *Someone* would know what to do, because I didn't have a clue.

"You've reached the Freakshow," said the bored, half-attentive voice of Angel, the bar's only human bartender. "We're closed right now, but if you'd like to come see us tomorrow night, we'd be happy to make all your dreams come true." It might have been easier to believe her if she hadn't punctuated her words with the sound of gum being noisily snapped.

"Angel, this is Sarah Zellaby, Verity's cousin. Is Kitty available?"

"Who?" Angel's tone changed over the course of that

single syllable, going from distracted to fully focused on the phone. "You're the blue-eyed girl, right? The one that comes in with Very some nights." I could practically hear her thoughts rearranging themselves, making me important to her. My telepathy doesn't work at a distance, but Angel had been in my sphere of influence before. Cuckoo tricks can linger. "Is everything okay?"

"Not really, no," I said. "Is Kitty available?"

"Yeah, yeah. Hang on." There was a soft scraping sound as she cupped her hand over the receiver. She may as well not have bothered; I heard her clearly when she shouted, "Hey, Carol! Tell Kitty she's got a priority call on line two!" The scrape repeated as Angel took her hand away. Then she said, in a more reasonable tone, "She should be with you in a second. Sorry about the wait."

"It's okay." I started walking in a circle around the card table, trying to calm myself down. It wasn't working very well. I tried another tactic: "You're still working? Even with the . . . even with everything that's going on?"

"I like it here," said Angel. "The Covenant of St. Stupid isn't going to chase me off a job I actually enjoy just because they've decided to get judgmental about my co-workers. Kitty said I could have the time off without penalty, no problem, and I told her I'd rather stick with my friends. Some assholes want to come in here and start hacking, I'll be right there with my pepper spray."

A nervous giggle welled up in my throat. "That's a really good attitude. Thanks."

"Don't thank me. It's the right thing to do."

There was a clunking noise, followed by Kitty saying, "Thanks, Angel. You can hang up now."

"Anytime, Kitty. Sarah, hope everything gets better for you. You sound stressed." A click, and a change in the quality of the sound over the line, told me that Angel had hung up on her end.

"Hello?" I said.

"Sarah Zellaby," said Kitty. Her voice seemed to come from next to me, rather than through the phone. That's a classic bogeyman trick. They can throw their voices anywhere they can hear—which includes the other end of telephone lines. Just one more way nature and technology combine to make the world a creepier place. "Verity's little adopted cousin with the big blue eyes and the clear antifreeze for blood. What brings a cuckoo like yourself to my virtual door?"

Humans have only known about cuckoos for a few generations. The bogeymen have known for centuries and, surprise surprise, they don't like us much. That's something they have in common with every other sapient species in the known world. "It's Verity," I said. "I can't find her."

There was a pause. Knowing what cuckoos were meant that Kitty also understood what we could *do*. "I'm listening," she said.

I gave her the same explanation I'd given Uncle Mike, dwelling a little longer on the static, and the way it had gone away completely when the pain did. I finished by saying, "I'm scared. I think something terrible may have happened to her."

"Before we start jumping at sunbeams, let me ask you this: is there any chance you're having the cuckoo equivalent of a muscle cramp or something? Maybe you can't feel her because you've got a problem, not because she's not there."

"I can feel everyone else in the building." Everyone except the older Madhura—Verity said his name was Rochak—but his thoughts had been hidden before Verity disappeared. Bringing him into this would just confuse things. "Besides, this isn't the sort of silence I get when someone blocks me out. I mean, it is. But that never starts with pain. I've never felt anything like that before."

Kitty made a small, frustrated sound. "Which means, if I believe you, that the damn Covenant probably got her. Fuck. Do you think they killed her quick, or did they take her prisoner so they could torture her first?"

My breath caught in my chest, wedging there like a stone. I struggled to force it out, trying to get my voice back. Finally I said, "How can you even ask me that?"

"Look, Sarah. For you she's family; I get that, I really do, and it sucks that you're the one making this call, almost as much as it sucks that I'm the one taking it. But if she's dead, she's dead, and I have living people to worry about. If the Covenant knows what Verity knows, they can clean this city *out*. You follow me? Nobody's safe if they're torturing her—and don't try telling me that she won't break. Given enough time, and enough knives, *everybody* breaks. It's just a matter of finding out how hard you have to push." Kitty spoke with a soft assurance that whispered of experiences I'd never had, and never wanted to have. I found myself wondering which end of the knife she'd been on. I realized just as quickly that I really didn't want to know. That sort of thing was Verity's territory, and she was welcome to it.

Kitty listened to the silence for a few seconds. Then she sighed. "Look, Sarah . . . if they took her prisoner, that sucks for us, because we don't know what she's going to tell them. We have to be prepared for the worst. But it could be awesome for her."

"How is being taken prisoner by the *Covenant* awesome for anybody?" I asked.

"People usually keep their prisoners alive for at least a little while before they kill them. If she's been taken prisoner, there's a chance that you can get her back."

"But how am I supposed to—"

"I'm sorry, Sarah. I really am. I know she's your cousin, and I know you love her. I owe her a lot. I wish it hadn't gone down like this. But you're the one who has to worry about getting her back. I'm the one who gets to worry about getting my people through this alive. Good luck."

Kitty hung up after that. She didn't say good-bye. There wouldn't have been any point.

Mike and Istas were in the main room when I emerged. The Madhura I could detect was still in the kitchen; I assumed the older Madhura was there with him. Having someone in the building that I couldn't "hear" made me profoundly uncomfortable. I was used to people being hard or even impossible to read. Them being invisible was something entirely different. It was like when—

I stopped where I was, eyes going wide. Uncle Mike looked away from the deadfall he'd been arranging over one of the windows—Istas was holding the rope that supported the deadfall's weight with one hand, like it was negligible to her—and frowned at me. "Sarah?" he asked. "What did Kitty say?"

"That charm." I started briskly toward the table where Verity had dumped Margaret Healy's possessions. Midway there, I broke into a run. When I reached it, I started rummaging frantically through the knives, ammo packs, and things I didn't know the uses of. "Where is it? Why can't I find it?!"

"Hey. Hey! What are you trying to find?" Uncle Mike's hand settled on my shoulder. His thumb grazed the skin above my collarbone. As always, the skin-to-skin contact did what it would normally take months of close contact to do: his mind snapped into sharp relief, a picture seen through a window blind that I could open if I needed to. Touching people does that for me, especially when it happens repeatedly in a short period of time. It's why I try to avoid it whenever I can when I'm not dealing with people I'm already attuned to.

Uncle Mike was petrified. He *knew* Verity was dead. Not because he had some fact that I was missing; just because he'd been in situations like this one before, and he knew the odds had been against us from the start. *Should never have let her go out alone, no matter what she was used to,* he was thinking, blame and self-loathing dripping off every thought/word and sense/impression. *This is my fault. How am I going to tell Kevin that I let his baby girl go out and get herself killed? Hell, how am I going to tell* Evelyn? *She'll never be able to look me in the eye again. This is all—*

I shrugged his hand off, breaking the endless loop of his thoughts before it could drag me even further down. If he wanted to put on a brave face and pretend that he thought everything was going to be okay, I'd let him. As long as I made sure not to touch him again, it might even make me feel better.

"The charm. The one the Covenant uses to block telepathy." I looked up at him. "Margaret was a hole when we met her. She wasn't a human, she wasn't an individual, she was a *hole*. When Verity put the thing on to test it, she was a hole, too. She vanished completely from any sort of nonvisual spectrum."

Uncle Mike nodded slowly. "So you're thinking that, if she's wearing one of those things, that might explain her disappearing the way she did?"

"I've never been attuned to someone who died, but I can't imagine it's as easy as 'ow that hurts oh I'm gone.'" I stood up a little straighter, trying to ignore the waves of curiosity emanating from Istas. At least she hadn't come over. That probably had something to do with the rope she was still holding, and the desire not to drop Uncle Mike's deadfall on the slaughterhouse floor. "She's not *dead*. She's just missing."

"So can you track holes?"

"No. I can follow dead spots, maybe, if I see people with my eyes who don't appear to my mind, but . . ." I shrugged helplessly. "There are two Madhura in the building. I only know that because I've seen them both. If the one I can't read decides to leave, I won't know about it. He'll just be gone, and I'll have no idea."

"Your ability to observe the minds of others seems exceedingly limited in scope," commented Istas. She switched the rope to her other hand. "Of what use are you?"

"I'm really, really good at calculating how much I need to leave for a tip when I eat out, even if I never pay for my actual meals," I said flatly.

"So what you're saying is that you won't know you've found someone you can't read until you see them with your eyes," said Uncle Mike. "Okay. That's not as convenient as it could be, but it's something. You saw Margaret, right?"

"She forced her way into my hotel room."

"Could you describe her well enough for the mice to draw her?"

I bit the inside of my cheek to keep myself from saying something I'd regret later. Then, carefully, I said, "My eyes don't work that way. Or, well. I guess they do, since I see on a human wavelength, but that's not how I process visual information. There's no way I could describe her."

Cuckoos can see—we're not blind, and I'm glad, since that would make answering my email really hard—but our brains aren't wired to register the same things that human brains are. We don't need to recognize individuals by their faces when we can recognize them by their thoughts, the unique mixture of ideas and emotions that make them who they are. All those shows about mistaken identity and identical twins or cousins are lost on me, because to my eyes, pretty much everyone looks cosmetically alike, and it's totally impossible to mistake anyone for anyone else. Oh, hair and eye and skin colors differ, but faces? They're just faces. It's what's behind them that's unique.

Uncle Mike nodded again. "If that won't work, we'll have to think of something else. What did Kitty have to say?"

"She's afraid the people who have Verity will torture her and get her to reveal secrets regarding our plans and whereabouts," said Istas, sounding bored. Mike and I both turned to face her. She shrugged. "It is a logical concern. The current situation presents great potential for mayhem, and very little for a peaceful resolution." This said, she yawned broadly, displaying teeth that were twice the size of the human norm. The laconic waves of thought drifting off her were almost entirely focused on the idea of destroying things.

"I'm not going to just sit around waiting for Verity to die," I said hotly. "I don't care if she's being tortured. If she's alive, we have to find her."

"We have a duty to the cryptids of this city," said Mike.

I scowled at him. "I *am* a cryptid of this city, remember? And I have a duty to my family. We can't call them and tell them that she's been—" I paused. Duty. Family. "Wait a second. I think I have an idea."

"What?"

"The dragons. Females are basically indistinguishable from human women. We know Dominic didn't tell the Covenant about the dragons—if he had, they'd have come long before this, and they'd definitely have sent more than three operatives—so that means the Covenant won't be treating every blonde woman they see as a potential threat."

"So you want to what, use the dragons as spies? Sarah, they're not going to go for that. Dragons are only interested in personal gain."

"That was before they had a male, and before they owed Verity for making sure they were there when he woke up." I smiled thinly. "They're going to pay what they owe, and they're going to pay it *now*."

"Oh, good," said Istas, letting go of the rope. "This will almost certainly afford opportunity for carnage."

The deadfall made a horrible crunching noise when it hit the floor.

Seventeen

$$\pi_2(n) \sim 2C_2 \frac{n}{(\ln n)^2} \sim 2C_2 \int_2^n \frac{dt}{(\ln t)^2}$$

"There were advantages to growing up with a cold-blooded telepath for a mother. The ability to lie about why I was out past curfew was not among them."

—Evelyn Baker

The sewers below Manhattan, heading for the lair of the only known male dragon left in the world

AFTER SOME PERFUNCTORY ARGUING—Uncle Mike knew I wouldn't listen, I knew he wasn't really trying to convince me to stay, we both knew he had to make the effort if he was going to live with himself—I was allowed to grab a city spelunking kit from Verity's supplies and head for the nearest concealed manhole. I left the weapons behind, taking only a flashlight, some rope, and a backpack full of assorted individually wrapped snacks. There's almost nothing that lives in a sewer that will attack a cuckoo who looks like she's just passing through. There's defense of your territory, and then there's being suicidal.

Besides, who needed weapons when I had Istas? She was shorter than me in her human form, and she'd never met a pair of practical shoes in her life, but she could take on just about anything that I couldn't mentally shield us from. We were an unstoppable team, or would have been, if I'd had the first clue how to talk to her. Verity always made it look so *easy*, while I found communication with most other cryptids really, really hard. Even

when I could read their minds, I couldn't always understand what I found there.

With Istas' help, I was able to get the manhole levered
out of the way—by which I mean "Istas picked up the
manhole and tossed it off to one side, because she is not
the most subtle brick in the wall"—and descended the
ladder to sewer level. Istas skipped the ladder in favor of
simply stepping off the edge, landing next to me without
even bending her knees. Even Verity would have
crouched to absorb the impact. Istas just dropped.

"Come on," I said, and pulled the flashlight from my
belt. She followed amiably after me as we started walking into the dark.

The waheela minced through the sludge covering the
sewer floor like she was strolling down Broadway on a
summer afternoon. She had added a parasol and a min-
iature top hat to her ensemble before we left the Nest;
the hat was perched jauntily just above her side-swept
ponytail. From the feelings of contentment emanating
from her mind, she was convinced she looked absolutely
fabulous, and also anticipating the opportunity to show
her fabulousness to anything that might decide to take a
shot at eating us.

"I don't think there are any alligators down here, you
know," I said, playing the beam from the flashlight over
the sewer wall. A rat ran by on urgent rat business.

Istas watched it go, emotional weather briefly shifting
to "hungry" before swinging back to her usual calm contentment. "No, there are not," she agreed. "There used to
be, before the bugbears, servitors, and other carnivores
removed them. There is, however, always the potential
for a pleasant surprise. There have been rumors which
indicate that a sewer kraken may be making its home
downtown. I would enjoy the opportunity to battle
something with that many limbs."

Given the way Istas was dressed, the idea of her fighting a sewer kraken was disturbingly like something from
the kind of anime Artie liked to pretend he never
watched, and I liked to pretend I didn't know about. I
gave her a sidelong glance. "Um, Istas, it was nice of you

to insist on coming with me and everything, but you *do* know what we're doing down here, right?"

"I am not stupid, Sarah Zellaby," she said, in a voice that was much quieter than the one she'd been using only a moment before. "I realize I wear frilly clothing and impractical shoes, and that by many people's standards, I am odd, but I am not stupid. You are here because you want to ask the dragons to assist in recovering your cousin. I am here because Verity is my friend, and would look on me with sadness if I were to allow you to come to harm. Friendship is a rare thing among my people. We do not practice it often, and most of us do not practice it very well. I am hoping to be a better friend to Verity than my brothers and sisters were to me."

"Oh." I kept walking. Beside me, Istas did the same, spinning her parasol lazily with each step. Finally, I said, "I forget sometimes that I can't treat you like you're human. I mean, I don't forget, exactly, but . . ."

"Your mannerisms and reactions are human enough, despite the fact that you are biologically even less human than I am, that you sometimes forget not all hominids will follow the same behavioral patterns." Istas shook her head. "It is a common, if unfortunate, trap of the mind. I am sorry you have fallen prey to it. I will not take offense at your ignorance."

The worst part was that she meant it: for Istas, the matter was already forgotten. I had made the mistake of treating her like a human being, she had corrected me, and as long as I didn't do it again, there was nothing left to discuss. Being a waheela had to be pretty simple compared to being a cuckoo.

Then again, being a real cuckoo—an amoral sociopath who existed only for the sake of making other people miserable—is probably pretty easy. It's being a cuckoo like me that's hard. Sometimes I feel like neither nature nor nurture did me any favors. Here, Sarah. Have a moral and ethical code that means you'd feel bad killing people for your enjoyment, and have a set of instincts and hereditary skills that means you're not really built to do anything else. It'll be fun!

It's not fun.

The sewer floor got gradually cleaner as we walked, until the sludge was gone, and the walls showed subtle signs of having been washed recently. Dragons don't like wallowing in filth any more than the rest of us. They just lived in the sewers because William had been asleep during the construction of Manhattan, and now a good sized chunk of downtown was built over his head. Until someone figured out a way to get him out of his cavern without destroying the city, he was stuck.

Not that he was complaining. Fresh air is nice, but not being slaughtered by the Covenant of St. George is nicer, and as long as he stayed underground, he was safe from most forms of detection. Most, not all: if the Covenant had Verity, and if they were able to break her . . . the dragons wouldn't be able to move William. We weren't ready for this. We never thought we'd need to be.

Istas looked around as we moved into the final branch of the sewer. This one looked absolutely filthy, and smelled filthy, too, until we were about ten feet from the entrance. Then the smell of sewer was replaced by the smell of bleach and cheap air freshener. "The dragons have a good working relationship with the hidebehinds," I said. "It's a camouflage measure."

"Clever," allowed Istas. "I have not been here since the snake cult attempted to sacrifice me to wake their sleeping dragon. I have never met William while awake."

That explained the little hat: she was trying to make a good impression. "He's nice," I said. "He even beats me at chess sometimes." We kept walking, and the darkness around us abruptly went away, replaced by a pleasant level of soft illumination. Istas jumped, whirling so that her back was pressed against my shoulder. I kept walking. "More hidebehind tricks. They use darks for that part of the passage, so that curious sanitation employees don't wander down here." I personally doubt that anyone would be curious enough about a dark, smelly tunnel that isn't part of the currently in-use sewer system to wander down it, but Verity swears I should never underestimate human curiosity. Humans are weird.

"I do not like this," proclaimed Istas.

"That's part of the point." The tunnel ended at a bare wall eight feet, five inches across. I knocked lightly at a point exactly four feet, two and a half inches from either wall, stepped back, and motioned for Istas to wait.

A few minutes passed. Then a door—a simple, normal, wooden door—swung open in what had appeared to be solid stone, and a blonde woman in a baggy New York Giants sweatshirt peered out through the opening. I smiled pleasantly, reaching out with my mind just far enough to tap the surface of her thoughts and confirm her identity.

"Hi, Priscilla," I said. "Is Candy here? I need to talk to her."

Priscilla's ever-present frown deepened as she looked past me to Istas, who was doing her best to look through the open door into the Nest beyond. "Why did you bring the waheela?" she demanded.

"Because Verity was unavailable, and it's not safe for anyone to go out alone right now." Most of the female dragons picked up shifts at the Freakshow every now and then, and several of them worked there full time. There was no way Priscilla didn't recognize Istas. She was just being prickly, which was something the dragons specialized in. "Now please, can we come in before we attract attention standing here?"

Frowning even more, Priscilla said, "Fine," and opened the door the rest of the way, beckoning us inside.

"Thank you," I said, and led Istas into the Nest.

Some clichés exist for a reason. Dragons and gold, for example. They love it. It's biologically and psychologically vital to their well-being, and consequentially, they collect the stuff the way Artie collects comic books. Since male dragons are larger than Greyhound buses when fully grown, they serve as guardians of the hoard, while the females find ways to go out and get more gold. That used to involve highway robbery, infiltrating kingdoms, and occasionally mining. There are a lot of female dragons living in California, thanks to the Gold Rush. These days, about half the "cash for gold" franchises out there are operated by dragons, while the rest work tirelessly at whatever jobs they can get, immediately turning around and converting their paychecks into more gold for the Nest. As for what they *did* with all that gold . . .

We walked through the door into Willy Wonka's chocolate factory as reinterpreted by King Midas and Salvador Dali. Cardboard structures scavenged from closing Halloween specialty stores were studded around the room, all covered in a thick layer of genuine, structurally-reinforcing, 24-karat gold. It made a weird maze of haunted houses without backs, abandoned tunnels, and crooked graveyard fences. William enjoyed metalworking, and he was his own forge, so he just let the girls bring home whatever they thought would go well in the Nest. If it didn't work out, he could always re-melt the gold and try again.

More normal furniture from thrift shops and Ikea was scattered around the gold sculptural pieces, along with the better part of a playground. There was a slide, a jungle gym, even a swing set—and all of it was plated with still more gold. Gold bars, coins, chains, even gold leaf littered the floor of the cavern, making our footing a little unsteady. We were standing in the midst of several hundred years of concentrated penny-pinching, and oh, how it glittered.

Istas looked around without shame, lazily twirling her parasol. Finally, she said, "It is very sparkly."

"It is at that," I said, just before a swarm of young dragon girls—none of them older than eight—came running from the direction of the jungle gym, waving their arms in the air and shouting my name. I didn't recognize any of them, and when they came at me in a pack like that, I couldn't pick out individual minds. That didn't particularly matter. I stooped and swept up the first one to reach me, swinging her up into the air and draping her over my shoulder like a potato sack. This put her nose-to-nose with Istas, who surveyed our sudden ocean of giggling preteens with bemusement.

"Hi!" said the dragon on my shoulder. "I'm Eva. I'm a dragon. Who're you?"

"I am Istas," Istas replied gravely. "I am not a dragon."

"I knew *that*," said Eva. "But you're not a cuckoo either, 'cause you have the wrong eyes, and you're not a human, because Aunt Priscilla wouldn't have let you in without calling for Aunt Candy. What are you?"

"Istas is a waheela," I said, and put Eva down. "Go find your Aunt Candy for me, okay?"

"Okay!" said Eva, and the swarm moved on, running easily over the uneven floor. A few of them ran backward so that they could wave. I waved back, and tried not to look relieved. Sometimes the little girls would spend an hour or more making me do parlor tricks before they got bored, and when you've read one preteen dragon's mind, you've read them all.

I resumed walking. Istas did the same, looking at me while confusion wafted off her thoughts like smoke. "If you have sent them to retrieve Candy, why are we not waiting?"

"Because I have a landmark to say hello to." I gestured toward the far wall of the cavern, where one of the only things that was neither blonde nor covered in gold was waiting for us.

William raised his head as we approached, opening enormous eyes the color of electric jack-o'-lanterns. His lips turned upward in an eerily human smile, considering that he was a giant fire-breathing semi-saurian cryptid. "Sarah!" he said, his crisp British accent somehow making things all the more incongruous.

Even dragons have to come from somewhere. William came from England, back when the United States of America were still the thirteen original Colonies. In a very real way, this country was built on top of him.

"Hey, Billy," I said, waving. "You remember Istas? She was here when you woke up."

"But she was unconscious at the time, as I recall." William lowered his head, putting Istas at eye level. That wasn't necessarily a comfortable place to be; his head, after all, was the size of a VW bus. "A pleasure to properly make your acquaintance, Miss Istas. I truly do appreciate your efforts on my behalf."

Undaunted, Istas looked him in the eye. Then, solemnly, she curtsied. "It is very nice to meet you."

I will never understand people, no matter how long I live. And that could be a very long time, if the Covenant of St. George doesn't kill me—cuckoos have an extremely high life expectancy. "We're here to talk to you, and to Candy," I said. "It's about Verity."

William's smile faded, replaced by an expression of profound concern. "Oh, dear. Has Miss Verity's unsuitable swain finally turned against her?"

"Not that I'm aware of, thankfully, but that's sort of the problem." I could hear Candy's thoughts clearly enough to know that she was pissed about us being here. Also that she was coming up behind me. I turned. "Hi, Candy."

The current Nest-mother stopped and folded her arms over her chest, glaring so hard that even I could recognize it. Candy *hated* the fact that I could always recognize her, since she knew I didn't do faces. What she never quite understood was that I do minds, instead, and hers was distinctive.

"What are you doing here?" she demanded, turning her glare from me to Istas, who looked impassively back. "What if you were followed?"

"We weren't followed," I said.

"What if you *were*?"

"I would have ripped and torn and broken the bodies of our pursuers, and it would have been glorious," said Istas. She sounded so calm that we all turned to look at her, even William. Heedless, Istas gave her parasol a spin, and added, "I would have brought you their heads. I think it would have made a suitable subterranean cavern-warming present."

The silence that followed this announcement lasted for several seconds. I was the one to break it, turning to

Candy and saying, "We're here because we need your help."

"Did Verity send you because she knew I'd tell her no?" asked Candy. "She already has our slaughterhouse. She doesn't need any more help from us."

"Verity didn't send me," I said. "Verity's gone."

Candy paused. William snorted out a small puff of smoke.

"Gone?" he asked.

"Gone. Something knocked her out about an hour ago. It hurt like hell, and I haven't been able to reach her since."

Candy's thoughts turned alarmed. "Oh, God, what if she's not dead?"

"Candice," said William chidingly. "That isn't a nice thing to say in front of her family."

"But it's true! What if she's not dead? What if the Covenant has her? She knows where we are! We can't move you!" Candy put her hands protectively over her belly, starting to cry. That was an expression even I could read without second-guessing myself. "We can't lose you. I can't leave you."

"I don't think she's dead, but I don't think she's told them anything, either," I said. Seeing Candy cry made it oddly a little easier to stay calm. It was like she was freaking out on my behalf. "They haven't had her long enough, and I don't think there's any torture they could subject her to that would make her give you up in less than a day."

"If they have a telepath—"

"They're using anti-telepathy charms. If they had a telepath, they'd have to remove those charms from Verity in order to get any kind of information out of her, and I'd know where she was. Since she hasn't been appearing and disappearing from my radar, they aren't removing the charms, and they don't have a telepath. Human methods of getting information aren't good, but they're not going to break Verity Price in less than a day. We have time to find her if we start moving now."

"We can't—" Candy began.

"Anything you need," said William. She stopped, turning to look at him. Her eyes were wide, and her confusion was a raw wound on her emotional landscape. He blew a puff of flame in her face, sending it dancing along her hair. It wasn't the aggressive gesture it would have been with anything but another dragon: Candy was fireproof. For her, that was an affectionate peck on the cheek. "I would not be with you now if not for Verity. We owe it to her family to do what we can to bring her home. Moreover, you're correct: she knows where I am. If the Covenant has her, she has to be taken from them, or you'll lose me again." He ducked his head enough to nudge her belly, ever so gently, with the tip of his snout. "I want to meet our baby. I want to see how many of you are carrying fine, strong sons to bring joy to the other golden ones waiting lonely around this world. How can we deny these women the aid they need?"

Candy sniffled. Then she sighed, turning back to me, and asked, "What is it you want from us?"

Candy listened attentively as I explained my plan. She even suggested a few things I hadn't considered, like using the kids—in a swarm, and with the help of some of the adults—to canvas parks and playgrounds, since they'd be able to ask really blatant questions without anyone thinking it was strange. Little girls can get away with a lot just by looking cute and clueless when they're doing it.

When we were done talking, William and Candy had promised to dispatch every available female dragon—omitting the pregnant ones, the ones assigned to tend the eggs that had already been laid, the ones under five years of age, and the babysitters—to start searching the city for my missing cousin. They'd phone the Nest if they found anything, and then Candy, who was staying put because of her pregnancy, would call me. If they actually found *Verity*, as opposed to just finding information that might lead us to her, they'd bring her back to the old Nest.

"Thank you," I said for the eighth time, as Candy walked us to the door.

"Thank my husband," she said. "I understand why he wants us to help you, but if we didn't have to stay here and protect him, we'd be *gone*."

"I know."

"You have a lovely home," said Istas amiably.

That seemed like a good place to end things. We walked out the door, which closed behind us, blending seamlessly back into the stone wall. Istas spun her parasol.

"I think that went quite well, despite the lack of carnage," she said.

"I hope so." I started walking. "There are a lot of dragons. They can cover a lot of ground. I just hope none of them get hurt."

"If they do, we will avenge them," said Istas.

Once again, that seemed like a good place to end things. I didn't say anything for the rest of our trip back through the sewer to the manhole where we'd made our descent. It was still uncovered—probably because Istas had thrown the lid too far away for anyone with normal human strength to drag it back into position. I made a note to ask her to put it back where it belonged just as soon as we were aboveground, and started up the ladder.

I was almost to the top when a figure loomed above the opening and a hand was thrust down into the darkness, grabbing my forearm. I squeaked, and was about to scream, when the static kicked on and I realized who had hold of me.

Fighting wasn't going to help. I let myself be pulled the rest of the way up into the light.

Dominic released me as soon as I was on solid ground. We both stepped back to let Istas out of the hole. She looked at Dominic, sniffed the air, and frowned.

"You are unwell," she informed him. "I will end you if you have harmed Verity."

"I know," said Dominic quietly.

Even I could tell that he wasn't looking good. His hair was uncombed, and there were dark circles around his eyes. He looked like a man who'd just realized he was in the middle of fighting a war.

"Dominic?" I said.

He turned to me. "Sarah." He sounded relieved. "I need your help."

"Is Verity alive?" I didn't know what I was going to ask until the question was out, and then there was nothing else I could have asked him. Nothing else in the world.

"Yes." He nodded. "But I don't know how long she will be. We need to move."

"You know I can't trust you."

"Yes, you can." He held out his arm in silent invitation.

I didn't say anything. Dominic knew what he was offering me, and how much stronger I would be if I were touching him. Before either of us could change our minds, I reached out and grabbed his wrist, diving into his psyche as hard and deep as I could without pausing to make the process easy on either one of us. This wasn't the time to be gentle. Dominic gritted his teeth, and he didn't pull away.

Telepathy—cuckoo telepathy, anyway—is usually a passive thing, polite and noninvasive. Sure, I may learn a person's deepest, darkest secrets, but it doesn't hurt them, and it doesn't hurt me. This . . . wasn't like that. This was a home invasion of the soul, and it made me feel dirty even as I was doing it.

Dominic's mind was filled with cluttered rooms packed with thoughts and memories even he wasn't fully aware of anymore. He didn't think he remembered what his mother looked like. He did; he just had the memory walled off by so many other things that it only came to the surface when he slept or, oddly, when he ate German chocolate. He was in love with Verity. He hated the smell of violets in the rain; that was connected to his mother's death, and was part of the wall between him and the memory of her face. He wasn't a part of the plan that captured Verity; the rest of the Covenant agents in town hadn't even told him they suspected she existed. He thought they suspected him of being a traitor. He didn't care. After we got Verity back, he was done with the Covenant of St. George.

Dominic de Luca was finally picking a side, and it wasn't theirs.

I let go of his wrist, breaking the telepathic contact at the same time. He gasped, and I realized just how pale he'd gotten. *Sorry,* I said mentally. *I know that can be rough.*

"It's all right," he said. Then he paused. "You . . . didn't speak."

I smiled a little. "I didn't have to. After that kind of excavation, we're attuned. Welcome to the family. Now let's go and get my cousin back from your ex-allies."

Eighteen

$$\pi_2(n) \sim 2C_2 \frac{n}{(\ln n)^2} \sim 2C_2 \int_2^n \frac{dt}{(\ln t)^2}$$

"The trouble with the Covenant of St. George is that it encourages loyalty through ignorance, zealotry, and fear. I wonder sometimes . . . what would they have accomplished if they'd tried doing it all with love?"

—Enid Healy

A converted slaughterhouse in the Meatpacking District

ISTAS WALKED into the warehouse ahead of us, her parasol resting against her shoulder. She looked utterly relaxed, which may be the only reason no one attacked Dominic on sight. They were too busy staring at the muck-encrusted waheela. "Dominic is not responsible for Verity's disappearance, and is no longer affiliated with the Covenant of St. George," she announced. "The telepathic girl without a proper circulatory system says so, and as she has no reason to lie, I am choosing to believe the story which presents the highest odds of future carnage."

"That's my girl," said Ryan—but his voice was several octaves lower than normal, and he seemed taller as he got up from his seat. Uncle Mike didn't bother standing. He just produced a gun from somewhere inside his jacket and raised it to shoulder level, the muzzle trained on Dominic's throat.

"I admire the efficiency, but can you at least *try* not to get arterial spray in my hair?" I asked.

"Hello, sir," said Dominic. "I assume you're Verity's father. I wish we were meeting under better circumstances."

Uncle Mike blinked, looking nonplussed. "Excuse me?"

"Dominic, this is our uncle, Mike Gucciard." Telling him Uncle Mike's last name was a warning that the choice Dominic was making was irrevocable: if Dominic so much as twitched in the direction of the Covenant after this, he'd find himself stuffed into a dumpster somewhere in midtown. There are things we don't screw around with, and that includes the covers of our friends and allies. "Uncle Mike, this is Verity's boyfriend, Dominic De Luca. He's here to tell us how to get her back, and to discuss the many fabulous advantages to defecting to the side with the sense of humor."

"The sense of humor, and the many, many unmarked body disposal sites," said Uncle Mike. I'd never heard his voice that devoid of warmth.

"Please go easy on him," I said quietly. "He's our best shot at finding Verity."

"Or he's lying to you," Uncle Mike shot back. "Did you consider that?"

I sighed heavily. "Okay, so is it time to have the talk about lying to the telepath again? I say 'don't lie to the telepath, it never works,' and you all say you won't. And then I point out that the corollary to this is that when the telepath says someone isn't lying, she's probably right. That's when you look sheepish and say you're sorry and hey, look, I just shortcut about ten minutes of awkward conversation, go me. Now can we get on with saving Verity from the Covenant, or do I have to get annoyed?"

There was a moment of silence before Istas said, "I was unaware the telepathic girl possessed a temper. This is pleasing. Temperamental people are more likely to participate in carnage."

"Sweetie, what have we talked about?" asked Ryan.

Now it was Istas' turn to sigh. "Humans are discomforted by excessive discussion of their squishy interiors."

"Which means . . . ?"

"No referencing carnage more than once in a single conversation."

"As the dominant human in the room, that rule is hereby suspended until we get my niece back," announced Uncle Mike. Now he stood, stalking toward Dominic with the calm, predatory assurance of a man who knew damn well that he was armed to the teeth and ready to kill anything standing in his way. I knew I wasn't in danger. I still took a step away from Dominic, just in case. Uncle Mike kept walking until the two of them were almost nose-to-nose, lowering his gun at the last minute as he looked the younger man square in the eye.

To Dominic's credit, he stood his ground. Then again, maybe that was a sign that he was too stupid to live.

"Sarah's vouching for you, and that would normally be good enough for me, but my niece's life is on the line," said Uncle Mike. His tone was absolutely level. That was another warning sign, and I took another step away from them. "If you're lying to us—if I find out you're using some Covenant trick to lie to us—I won't just kill you, I'll hurt you. I'll make you sorry that you ever came to America, and then I'll make you even sorrier to have tangled with my family. Do I make myself clear?"

"Yes, sir," said Dominic. "And if I may be blunt, sir, I'm already sorry to have encountered your family."

Uncle Mike's eyebrows shot up. Then they lowered again, coming together as he scowled. "What is that supposed to mean?"

"Before I met your niece, I was content to be ignorant of the true nature of this war, and my place in it. Without her influence, I might have been able to spend my entire life believing 'monster' was the word for cryptid, and 'traitor' was the word for Price. I would have been unaware of how incomplete my understanding was. I would have continued to think that I was happy." Dominic gave a small shake of his head. "I want to find Verity more than anything else. I want to bring her home, and never let her go. I want to learn everything there is to know about this maddened mirror image of the world where I grew up. But here and now, I am frightened, and she is missing, and part of me is sorry I ever got involved."

"He's telling the truth," I said. "In case anyone cares."

Once again, every head turned toward me. Uncle Mike radiated disapproval. "I didn't expect you to take his side, Sarah. Do I need to remind you of what his kind does to yours?"

"Uncle Mike, I love you, and I know what you're trying to say, but I'm a cuckoo. Killing cuckoos isn't a sign of evil, it's a sign of sanity. Killing other sapient cryptids is another matter—and that's something I've never seen Dominic do. Plus he's in love with Verity. That sort of puts him in my good graces."

"I am in love with her, and would prefer she remain among the living," said Dominic. "Please. I don't know what I can possibly do to prove myself to you, and I doubt that we have time for anything that you might name. Verity is alive, but that doesn't mean she's not in danger. Time is short. I need your help."

"Goddamn kids," muttered Uncle Mike. Then he stepped away from Dominic, moving out of the other man's personal space. "Okay, Covenant boy. Tell us what you know."

"Margaret Healy loves her duty and hates your branch of the family in equal measure," said Dominic, apparently counting both myself and Uncle Mike as official members of the Price-Healy clan for purposes of this debriefing. It made sense. Even if we weren't related by blood, we were tainted by the ideology that led her actual relatives astray. "I was honestly surprised to see her with the review team. The last time we spoke, she was still barred from activities in North America."

"Why?" asked Ryan.

"Margaret never believed that the Michigan incident had truly eliminated all survivors of the family on this continent. She wanted to investigate in person. Our superiors felt this was a personal vendetta with no immediate benefit to the Covenant."

"You mean they were worried she might be right, and that she might set off a war," said Uncle Mike.

Dominic nodded. "I think that was a factor in their decision, yes. If she was wrong, she would be wasting her time and the Covenant's resources on a wild goose chase. If she was right, and she was unable to eliminate or capture all hostiles in her first attack, she could very easily have caused the remaining members of the family to turn their efforts against the Covenant."

"But there are like, eight of them," said Ryan. His thoughts were confused, chasing each other around his head like puppies chasing their tails. "I don't know how many, since Very was always pretty cagey about that, but I know they all live in the same house when they're at home."

"If there's one thing you should know about the Prices, it's that odds rarely work the way they should once the family decides to get involved." Dominic smiled. "The Covenant had them outnumbered ten to one in Buckley, and they survived. Margaret could easily have triggered a chain reaction no one was prepared for."

"Maybe she just did that anyway," said Uncle Mike. "Verity dies, I can guarantee you that the Covenant of St. George isn't going to like what comes next."

"Sir, while I respect the destructive power of your family more than you may believe, I can guarantee you in turn that if Verity dies, the Covenant will regret their actions long before any of her relations can get here."

"We get it," I said. "If Verity dies, everybody's sorry. You know who's probably going to be sorriest? Verity. If this Margaret person wasn't allowed to be in North America, why is she here *now*?"

"I was told that it was a test for her, to see whether she could focus on the mission at the exclusion of her personal vendettas," said Dominic. A sudden wave of regret, blame, and self-loathing rushed off him like it was trying to fill the entire room. It took everything I had to stay where I was. None of the others were telepathic, but they shouldn't have needed to be. He was practically screaming his pain. "Please forgive me. I believed them."

"There was no reason for you not to," said Uncle Mike. From his tone, I could tell that he'd picked up on the same emotional weather I had. I relaxed a little. "Whatever lies the Covenant may have told you about the cryptids, they raised you. They trained you. Did they ever lie to you about anything but dogma before?"

"I don't know," said Dominic.

"I hate the Covenant as much as anybody, but I'm willing to bet they didn't, because truth is the best way to guarantee obedience. The more lies you're told, the harder it gets to keep the stories straight. When your bosses told you Margaret was here to test her obedience, you had absolutely no reason to think that they were lying to you. You got me? You warned Verity as soon as you had the chance. You did everything you could."

"I didn't do enough."

Istas yawned more widely than a strictly human jaw would have been able to support. There was an audible cracking noise as the bones shifted to accommodate the gesture. Dominic went very still, and I had the brief impression from his thoughts that he had managed, temporarily, to forget that humans were the minority in this room.

"This is dull," Istas announced. "Are we going to stand here and debate blame while Verity is slaughtered? Vengeance carnage is often satisfying, but it takes longer to perform properly than the kind which does not require a death to begin."

"That's my girl," said Ryan. "A delicate flower."

Istas snorted.

Dominic took a breath, seeming to center himself. "Margaret Healy hates Verity's bloodline for daring to leave the Covenant," he said, returning to his original conversational thread. Smart boy. "She didn't accompany the investigative team because they thought her hatred might have dimmed."

"They sent her here because somebody suspected

you'd been compromised, didn't they?" asked Uncle Mike. He sounded almost gentle. Dominic's obvious distress was getting to him. It was definitely getting to me; it was rolling off him in waves, making the air seem thick and heavy. Some emotions are harder to handle than others.

"Yes." Dominic looked from me to Uncle Mike. "I don't know how. I don't know what I did, or didn't do, or said, or didn't say. I was so careful . . ."

"Kiddo, they've got charms and telepathy barriers on these people. They're loaded for metaphysical bear. For all we know, they've got a witch or something back at headquarters who did some remote viewing on you when you didn't even realize you were being watched. That would explain why they were able to drop Margaret at Sarah's hotel. But just because they got suspicious, that doesn't mean you did anything wrong." *Beyond joining their goddamn cult in the first place.*

I try not to eavesdrop on other people's minds most of the time; it makes me feel a little sleazy, like I'm living down to their expectations of my species. Still, that thought was loud enough that there was no way I could miss it. "Uncle Mike, he didn't join," I said. "He was *born* into the Covenant, the same way all of us were born into our lives. Please don't take that out on him. Not right now."

Uncle Mike flinched a little, glancing in my direction. There was a brief flicker of apology in his emotional state. Then he focused back on Dominic, and said, "What matters now is that you're here with us, not there with them, and you're going to help us get her back. As far as I'm concerned, if you're on the up and up, we're cool, you and me."

A small throat was cleared from the center of the folding table, audible only because it was timed to come at the exact end of Uncle Mike's statement. I turned to see one of the Aeslin mice standing there, waiting to be noticed. It was the one Verity referred to as the Head Priest. He was wearing a sequin-spangled cape that used to be part of one of her dance costumes, and his whiskers were as white as if they'd been baby powdered. They hadn't been. This was a very old mouse. Two other mice, younger, wearing unspangled capes, crouched a foot away from him. They must have been sent to assist him on what would be, to a mouse, a very dangerous journey.

"I come to speak the Will of the Colony," announced the mouse priest.

"Hello, mouse," said Istas calmly, looking entirely unsurprised by the sudden intrusion of talking rodents on the conversation.

"Hello, carnivore," said the mouse priest. He turned and bowed to Uncle Mike and Dominic. "Hail to the High Priest of Goddammit Eat Something Already, and to the God of Hard Choices in Dark Places."

Ryan blinked. "What?"

"It's a mouse thing, just roll with it, you'll be happier that way," I advised. "Hail," I added, to the mouse.

He sat up a little straighter, wrapping his pink thread of a tail around his feet, and adjusted his grip on the carved pencil he was using as a staff. "The Colony has discussed the disappearance of the Arboreal Priestess," he said. "We have further discussed the words of the Priestess before she was Taken from us, and have decided that we will Abide by her Wisdom."

"What?" I asked.

Uncle Mike blinked. "Are you sure?" he asked the mouse.

The mouse priest nodded, the squirrel skull perched atop his head making it look like he was going to topple over. "We have served in this capacity before. We will serve in this capacity again. We are at your disposal."

"Before Verity left, she talked about using the mice as spies," said Ryan. "She even said that they were pretty good at it. Being mice means they can get into a lot of small spaces."

"We do not wish to leave our Priestess in the grip of the false Priestess who has taken her," said the mouse priest. "We understand that it will be dangerous. We do not mind the risk."

"None of us do," added Ryan. "Verity's not my family,

but she's my friend. Whatever has to be done, I'm going to do it."

Dominic nodded. "Then perhaps there is a chance after all. But we need to move, and we need to move quickly."

"Then what are we waiting for?" asked Uncle Mike. "Let's get started."

We all stopped interrupting Dominic after that—even the mice were quiet—as we allowed him to get down to the business of properly explaining what he knew. According to Dominic, Margaret had been working on her own when she set the trap that eventually snared Verity: the anti-telepathy charm we took off her unconscious body was laced with a compulsion spell that forced Verity right back into her nasty little clutches. It was a neat trick. I might even have been impressed by it, if it hadn't been so likely to get Verity killed.

Dominic only knew that Verity had been taken because he'd been with one of the other Covenant agents— Peter Brandt—when Margaret called and asked for backup. Peter had gone without him, and Dominic had followed at what he guessed would be a safe distance. "Thanks to Verity and her maddening insistence on taking the rooftops whenever possible, I had a whole set of routes open to me that they barely realized existed. I was not seen."

Privately, I wasn't so sure, but I didn't interrupt. We were out of time for interruptions.

There are times when I wonder how humans get anything done. Talking is so *slow* compared to the speed of thought. I could have told everyone everything Dominic knew in a few seconds, if I'd been attuned to them all and willing to risk bruising their brains a little bit. And then I realize that thinking like that just proves that I'll always be a cuckoo, no matter how hard I try not to be, and I have to force myself back into the slow, comforting safety of speech.

"Where's Verity being held?" asked Uncle Mike.

"An old warehouse that the Covenant purchased during the last purge. Much like this locale," Dominic indicated the Nest, "it has been in private hands for so long that most have ceased viewing it as a building. It has become a part of the landscape."

"Well, then, I guess we're landscapers," said Uncle Mike. "We're going to need some muscle for this."

Slowly, Ryan smiled. "I think I can help you with that."

Istas looked up at him, her thoughts turning quizzical. Then she smiled as well. "Oh, lovely," she said. "I do so enjoy spending time with my coworkers in a social setting."

Ryan was on the phone with Kitty, explaining why he needed to borrow half her staff for a potentially deadly mission, when my own phone started ringing. Phones are tricky. They have no minds for me to read, which makes them a good exercise in telling what people mean from nothing but tone. That also makes them frustrating as hell, and a bad idea when I'm already stressed. I pulled it out of my pocket, checking the display to see who was calling. I was about to press "ignore" when Uncle Mike's hand landed on my shoulder.

"Take it," he advised. "You need to talk to him, and it's not like you're going anywhere dangerous."

"Right," I said, not sure whether I should be annoyed with him for meddling or grateful for the excuse. I pressed "answer" instead, bringing the phone to my ear as I started walking away from the others. If I was going to have this conversation, I was going to have it in "my" room. "Hi, Artie. What's up?"

"I hadn't heard from you in a few hours, and you're not online. You've got the Covenant in town, Verity's not answering her phone, I got worried, hey-presto, I'm calling you." Artie's voice was a warm, familiar presence in my ear, conjuring images of afternoons spent lying on his bedroom floor arguing about whether Wolverine's claws could pierce Captain America's shield. (They *so* could, assuming Wolverine cared enough to try. And the fact that I know that is why Artie and I get along so well, and why Verity despairs of me ever going on a real date, with a non-virtual boy.)

Those comfortable thoughts were followed by a chill sliding down my spine, chasing all the warmth away. Artie didn't know that Verity was missing. Uncle Mike knew, but apart from that, no one in the family had been notified. "It's good to hear your voice," I said, with utter sincerity, and closed my eyes as I walked up the stairs. Maybe if I looked at nothing, I wouldn't feel so bad about lying by omission. Maybe. Probably not, though.

I always tell people not to lie to the telepath. It sucks to realize that my rules don't swing both ways.

"Yours, too, Sars," said Artie. He paused. "Everything okay with you? You sound tense."

"Covenant's in town, remember? We're bunking in an undisclosed location with what feels like half the cast of *The Muppet Show*, since Verity doesn't want any of us to wind up dead. And Uncle Mike is here, which means everything's been booby-trapped."

"I bet Antimony would love it there."

I laughed at that, opening my eyes. I was at the top of the stairs by then; I needed to be able to see if I wanted to find my room. "She'd be sawing holes in the floor so she could make actual pit traps, and we'd never get our security deposit back."

"I said she'd love it, not that she'd be useful." Artie sounded like he was buying my story, which helped me relax even more. "Any chance you'll be back online tonight?"

"Well . . ." I glanced guiltily down at the slaughterhouse floor. Everyone seemed very busy getting ready for battle. Uncle Mike was deep in conversation with the mice on the table; Ryan was on the phone; Istas was relacing her boots. None of them appeared to have particularly noticed that I was gone. That didn't mean I was off the hook. "No, I don't think so. We're doing a field thing, and Uncle Mike wants me to be there."

"*You're* doing 'a field thing'? You hate field things."

"That doesn't stop Very from making me do them every other weekend."

"No, but you always complain about them, and you're not complaining now." It's impossible to pick up thoughts through the phone, and for once, I was glad; the anxiety in Artie's voice was loud enough without any help from my telepathy. "Why aren't you complaining, Sarah? Are you really okay?"

"I'm *fine*, Artie," I said, and stepped into the barren little office that was, for the time being, my bedroom. I sank down onto the air mattress, sighing in time with the little hiss it made as I settled. "I'm stressed, and I'm scared, and I'm afraid somebody's going to get hurt before this is over, but I'm fine. Honest. I'd really rather hear about how you are, if that's cool. I need to not think about things here for a little while."

"Have you been to the comic book store yet this week?"

A smile tugged at my lips. "No, I have not," I said. "Things have been a little too hectic around here for me to get down to Midtown Comics. Have I missed anything important?"

"Not important, necessarily, but definitely cool. See—" Artie began telling me about the latest developments in the Marvel and DC superhero universes, speaking with the enthusiastic shorthand of the true aficionado. That wasn't a problem for me. I've been reading comics for as long as I can remember; seeing faces drawn on paper helps me recognize them in real life, or at least helps me recognize the emotions they're trying to convey. The encyclopedic knowledge of mutants and superhumans is really just an unexpected bonus.

I curled up on the air mattress with one arm tucked beneath my head as a makeshift pillow while I listened to Artie talk. When he paused, I made the appropriate encouraging noises, getting him started again. In the comic books, the good guys might lose for an issue, but they always won by the end of the story arc, and death was never forever. I liked the comics. I couldn't live there, but for a little while, I could pretend.

Not for long enough. Someone knocked gently on my doorframe. I sat up, the phone still pressed against my ear. Uncle Mike was standing there, and I didn't need to be good at reading faces to understand how grim his was.

"It's time," he said.

"Okay," I whispered.

"Sarah?" asked Artie. "What's up?"

"Nothing—Uncle Mike just needs me. It's time to go. Stay safe, okay? I'll call you soon." If I was alive. If any of us were still alive.

"Okay, Sars. Miss you."

"Miss you, too," I said, and hung up the phone.

Fun facts about cuckoo biology: we can't bleed, not the way mammals do. But we can cry. I got up and followed Uncle Mike out of the room, and I cried the whole way.

Nineteen

$$\pi_2(n) \sim 2C_2 \frac{n}{(\ln n)^2} \sim 2C_2 \int_2^n \frac{dt}{(\ln t)^2}$$

"You know what, honey? You're right. It's time to change my approach. Can you give me one of those nice concussion grenades?"
—Alice Healy

The Freakshow, a highly specialized nightclub somewhere in Manhattan

WE LEFT SUNIL and Rochak behind when the rest of us left the Nest. There was no way of knowing whether Verity had given up our location, and so Kitty was calling some of her relatives to come and take the Madhura away to someplace Verity didn't know. The brothers Madhura weren't happy about spending quality time with the city's bogeyman population, but they understood that it was the only way we could keep them safe, since taking them into battle with us would have been an even worse idea.

It was a good thing the Madhura weren't coming, since Uncle Mike's car was barely big enough as it was. I got the front seat—no one really wanted to snuggle up to the touch-activated telepath—while Istas, Ryan, and Dominic were crammed into the back. It would have been funny, if the situation hadn't been so dire. I couldn't stop thinking about how much Verity would have laughed if she'd seen her boyfriend wedged between two therianthropes like that. She probably would have taken a dozen pictures with her phone and threatened to use them for her Christmas cards.

Thinking about Verity's laughter helped me keep my shields up, which kept me from picking up on the thoughts of the people around me. That was good. The vague dread filling the car was stomach-churning enough without adding any stronger signals. Being a telepath in a largely non-telepathic society means the onus of not reading people's minds is entirely on me. Almost no one maintains a decent mental shield on purpose, and the ones who do it accidentally are rare enough to be a miracle.

At least Istas wasn't worried. Her emotional state was pure excitement, and a particularly bloody sort of anticipation. It said something about the day I'd been having that this was reassuring.

"We're here," said Uncle Mike.

The backseat emptied like a clown car at the circus, everyone hurrying to be the first one out. Uncle Mike moved at a more leisurely pace, still efficient, but aware that no amount of hurry was going to make up for an assload of support and ammunition. I was somewhere in the middle, clearing the car while Uncle Mike was still setting the alarm. The other three were almost to the Freakshow doors. I hurried to catch up.

The ticket booth was empty when I got there, and the doors themselves were closed and locked. According to the posters advertising the Freakshow's virtues, the club should have been open, even if this wasn't anything like peak business hours. I guess when your friendly neighborhood cryptozoologist gets herself taken by her less friendly relations, staying closed starts looking like the better option.

"Now what?" demanded Dominic.

"Chill," said Ryan. He knocked four times, paused, and knocked twice more. There was an answering knock from inside. Ryan knocked again.

"This code is stupid," said Istas. "We should simply allow whomever is manning the door to eat anyone unwelcome. People we do not want coming around would quickly cease."

"Or they'd come back with tanks," said Ryan. "Strategic thinking means not eating your enemies *all* the time."

"I hate strategic thinking," grumbled Istas.

Kitty opened the door. I blinked.

She was wearing the modern equivalent of bogeyman cultural dress: dark gray leggings and a knee-length dress a few shades lighter, cut to accommodate the length and flexibility of her limbs. Her hair was loose around her face, accentuating the strangeness of seeing her like this. Kitty could never pass perfectly for human—very few types of cryptid can. A lot of the ones who come close, like Kitty, resent me for how easily I can move through the human world, even if they forget why they resent me the second I'm out of their sight. Still, she normally wore human clothing, and kept her hair neatly styled. The monster-under-the-bed look wasn't normal for her.

If she was wearing a bogeyman's array, she meant business.

"Come on in," she said. "Everybody's waiting."

"Thank you again, Kitty," said Uncle Mike, and stepped into the Freakshow. Ryan and Istas followed.

Dominic moved to do the same. Kitty stepped between him and the opening, setting her hand flat against his chest. She wasn't exerting nearly enough pressure to hold him in place, but he still stopped, looking at her gravely.

"This is your fault," she said. "I'm going to bet that you've already been threatened to within an inch of your worthless life, so I'm not going to bother. I'm just going to make you a promise. If the Price girl dies, that's sad, but she knew this job was dangerous when she took it. If a single cryptid who didn't choose to walk into this fight dies? Just one? I will be the monster in your closet for the rest of your life. If not me, then my cousins, and their cousins, until you've paid for your sins. Do I make myself clear?"

A bogeyman threatening a trained operative from the Covenant of St. George should have been funny. It wasn't, because I didn't have to be a telepath to know Kitty meant it. If Dominic failed, she was going to throw the weight of her entire species at destroying him.

I almost felt sorry for the man, but Dominic didn't waste time with anything as useless as self-pity. He just nodded, and said, "I understand, and I accept your punishment as just."

Kitty blinked, surprise rolling off her like fog. She dropped her hand. "Well, then," she said, sounding bewildered. "As long as we've got that straight." Then she stepped aside, letting Dominic into the Freakshow.

I moved to follow. Her hand flashed up again.

"Hold it," she said. "Who are you again?"

Oh, fudgesicles.

This is life as a cuckoo: sometimes your allies will cease to be your allies in the middle of a bad situation, because your distress signals are overwhelming the low-grade "we should be friends, let's be besties" beacon that cuckoos put out at all times. Bogeymen are more resistant than humans, maybe because they made easier targets in the days before they learned to lock their doors against us. Easier, not preferred—cuckoos are happiest when they blend in, and we blend in best with humans.

"Sarah Zellaby," I said, and quoted her own words back at her: " 'Verity's little adopted cousin with the big blue eyes and the clear antifreeze for blood.' Does that ring any bells?"

Kitty's eyes widened, a response I didn't have to be good with faces to understand. "You're a cuckoo."

"Yes, but I'm a good cuckoo, I swear, and we've met before like a dozen times. You usually remember me. I'm sorry, I'm so freaked out that I'm broadcasting." I tried to focus on building a mental wall between us. It was harder than normal. Stress was making everything slippery.

Kitty's suspicion slowly gave way to recognition. "Sarah?"

"Yes," I said, and smiled a little, hopefully. "Sorry for the whammy, I didn't know it was going to be that bad."

"Just try to keep it under wraps while we're inside," she said, lowering her hand. "I don't want you starting a riot."

It was a lot more likely that I'd start a new branch of the "everybody protect Sarah" club, but I didn't say anything. I just stepped past Kitty. She closed and locked the door behind me. I waited for her to finish, and we walked together down the canvas-draped corridor to the main room where, by the sounds of things, there was quite a party going on. The mental noise hit a second after the audible noise did: at least two or three dozen people, almost as many different species, and all of them doing their best not to panic.

I gasped. I couldn't help myself. The wall I'd built to keep from broadcasting to Kitty was good, but it was nowhere near good enough to withstand the assault waiting at the end of the hall.

"Are you okay?" asked Kitty.

"What?" I hadn't even realized that I wasn't walking anymore. My legs had stopped moving without conscious command, taking themselves out of the equation while I did the complicated mental math of self-protection. I needed better walls, bigger walls, walls that could keep me from becoming so overwhelmed that I whammied everyone in the room just to keep them from hurting me.

"Are you okay?" repeated Kitty. "You look like you're about to throw up."

I was considering it. "I'll be fine," I said. "There's just a lot of focused anxiety in here." And it was all about my cousin, or at least about the people who had her; that, coupled with my having met everyone in the Freakshow at one point or another, explained the severity of my reaction. "Give me a second."

"Those are in pretty short supply, cuckoo girl," said Kitty . . . but she waited with me while I got myself under control, and I was grateful for that. It's easier to build a telepathic wall when you have someone nearby you can build it *against*, and Kitty was a lot less angry than some of the people in the main room. Once I was sure I wouldn't fall apart, I nodded, and Kitty led the rest of the way into the Freakshow.

The room looked strange, seen during the daylight. The lights were turned up to full, exposing the scuffs on the floor and the well-repaired tears in the upholstery. I could see scars on the ceiling where the old stripper poles had been removed. On the whole, though, the décor stood up pretty well to being visible—probably because it was designed by Kitty, and Kitty, like all bogeymen, could see perfectly well in the dark. She might be willing to live with a little wear and tear, but who wants to own a club they can't be proud of?

I wasn't surprised by the number of people who were turned toward the door, waiting for us; I'd already detected their presence, and my head still throbbed a little from the shock of it. I was, however, gratified. They could have run. They could have hidden themselves away and let Verity take whatever punishment the Covenant wanted to dish out. Instead, when the call for help was sounded, they came. Sure, some of them were probably like Istas, who would take any excuse to hurt things without getting in trouble for it, but I didn't care. They came. That was enough for me.

Kitty clapped her hands, walking ahead and leaving me standing in the doorway. "Okay, people. Nothing to see here, and we have a rescue mission to mount." She looked to Dominic. "That's your cue, Covenant boy. Impress us with your willingness to sell out your former allies."

"Think you could've made that sound any worse, Kitty?" asked Ryan.

"Oh, trust me, I could still make it sound worse," said Kitty. "I have a gift."

Dominic listened in silence, his posture impassive and unyielding. I was pretty sure his expression was meant to match. Internally, he was a different story, broadcasting anxiety and remorse so loudly that it was leaking through my shielding. I took a breath, focusing on shoring up the walls between me and the rest of the room a little bit better.

"Before we go any further with this, and yes, knowing that we have very little time, I need to be sure you understand that I did not make the decision to come to you lightly," said Dominic. There was a slight quiver to his voice. Anyone who didn't know him would probably miss it. I couldn't stop hearing it. "I was raised to believe that almost everyone in this room was a soulless monster, and that the humans among you were traitors to their species. I was misled, and I allowed it, because it was all I knew. I'm sorry."

Muttering greeted the first part of his statement, replaced by silence and a general feeling of surprise as he continued. I stepped out of the doorway, moving to stand next to Kitty.

"I was willing to let the Covenant come and go unhindered, helping Verity protect you and your families until the danger had passed. Unfortunately, that ceased to be an option when they took her. I understand that I am asking you to challenge an organization that wants nothing more than your extinction. I have nowhere else to turn, and Verity has no other options."

"Will they kill her?" asked Carol. She wasn't wearing her wig, and the snakes atop her head hissed and writhed in response to her agitation.

"Sadly, no," said Dominic.

Ryan took a step toward him, seeming to get almost a foot taller in the process. My eyes weren't deceiving me; the therianthrope was growing. Never a good sign. "What did you say?" he growled.

"If they were going to kill her, we could create a gas leak in the building and blow them all to Kingdom Come," said Dominic. If having a shift-primed tanuki menacing him was a problem, he wasn't letting it show. "Since they're not going to kill her any time soon, we have to come up with a solution that doesn't include killing her ourselves."

"Oh," said Ryan suspiciously. He didn't shrink back down to his original size. I guess some things take time.

"As I was saying: no, the Covenant will not kill her. It would be, if you will forgive me an unpleasant turn of phrase, wasteful. Verity Price represents something they have not had in generations. She is a source of information about her family, and about the cryptids of North America. They will break her, through whatever means necessary, and then they will drain her dry." Dominic shook his head. "I love her. I do. But believe me when I say that the Covenant of St. George is extremely good at breaking people. She will do her best to withstand them, and I believe she'll be able to hold out much longer than many people could. In the end, she'll break. In the end, everyone breaks."

"So what do we do?" asked Angel.

"The Covenant is using a dockside warehouse as their temporary headquarters while here in town. Their hotel rooms have already been abandoned; presumably all three of them have moved into the warehouse to supervise their prisoner, and to fortify their defenses against me." Now Dominic's voice turned even grimmer. "I didn't tell them Verity existed; I vanished when she was taken."

"And our family has a history of converting Covenant agents to our way of thinking," I said. "They've probably already decided that Dominic is no longer on the right side."

"This is true," said Dominic. "In their eyes, I am as much of a monster as any of you, if not more. After all, I saw the light, and turned it aside."

"Congratulations," said Istas primly.

Nervous laughter spread through the room like a stain. Uncle Mike allowed it for a moment before stepping forward, saying, "Okay, folks, get it together. My niece needs saving." He glanced to Dominic, who nodded. Uncle Mike nodded back before he continued, "We know where they are, and we know how many of them we're going up against. We also know they may have bitten off more than they could chew when they took Verity. If they're hoping to get information out of her, that means they're keeping her awake and reasonably aware of what's going on. Now, I don't know about the rest of you, but I've seen that girl kick a boundary imp's ass when she had a concussion and a broken arm. If they think she's just going to sit there and let them ask their questions, they're going to find themselves with a nasty surprise. That works in our favor."

"If things are so slanted in our favor, what are we still doing here?" asked a Pliny's gorgon I vaguely recognized as being one of the newer members of the staff. He crossed his arms, posture daring Dominic and Uncle Mike to come up with an answer he'd believe. The snakes on his head hissed ominously, twining themselves together in a sinuous braid which undid itself just as quickly. I thought his name was Joe. Maybe. Whatever his name, he was tall, unfriendly, and crowned with venomous snakes. That alone made him worth listening to, if only so his hair didn't start biting people.

"Because there's this little factor called 'the unknown,'" said Uncle Mike. "We need to worry about what we don't know."

"The three Covenant operatives are highly skilled in their own areas, and are not going to be inclined to go gently on us," said Dominic. "Peter Brandt is a demolitions expert. Robert Bullard is a tactical specialist. Between the two of them, they're very likely to have turned the warehouse into a death trap for anyone coming in without knowing how to avoid the trip wires. Margaret . . ." He hesitated.

"Margaret is a Healy," I said. Several heads turned toward me, like everyone had forgotten that I was there. Sadly, they probably had. Stupid cuckoo powers. "For those of you who don't know what that means, she's like an evil Verity. She won't stop hitting you just because you say you're going to be good, you changed your mind, and you'd like to go home now. That means that no matter how heavily weighted we think this equation is in our favor, we have to be better than the probabilities. We have to be absolutely certain of what we're walking into."

"Nobody's absolutely sure of anything, cuckoo girl,"

said Kitty, sending mutters through some of the staffers who had managed to forget what I was. Stupid, *stupid* cuckoo powers. Sometimes I get tired of apologizing for my species to the same person a dozen times. "How are we supposed to know that we're not all walking into a trap?"

"We employ spies," said Uncle Mike, dipping his hand into a pocket.

When he pulled it out again, one of the younger mouse priests was standing proudly on his palm. "Hail!" squeaked the mouse.

Silence reigned.

No one's sure whether Aeslin mice are extinct except for the family colony, or whether they just like their privacy. Whichever the answer, most people have only heard of them in passing, and they're largely regarded as a weird sort of fairy tale, Cinderella's mice without the vegetable transport and poor footwear choices. But they're the only species of talking mouse that anyone has found so far, and so there wasn't much question about what Uncle Mike was holding. The only question was how.

"Hello, mouse," said Istas, sounding pleased.

"What the . . . ?" said Kitty.

"Is that an *Aeslin mouse*?" asked Joe.

"My hair is hungry," announced Carol.

That brought the conversation to its second screeching halt in as many minutes, as everyone turned to stare at the gorgon. Carol blushed, ducking her head slightly while radiating embarrassment. She was telling the truth about her hair; the individual snakes were stretching toward the mouse, their mouths open and their tongues scenting the air.

"This just gets better and better," muttered Ryan. I didn't disagree.

Uncle Mike ignored them all in favor of focusing on what mattered—the plan—rather than what didn't—everything else. "We've got half a dozen volunteers from

Verity's resident Aeslin colony. They're going to go in, scout the place for traps, and report back. That lets us get a feeling for the lay of the land before we put ourselves in harm's way."

"You mean she wasn't just bragging when she said she had a colony of Aeslin living with her?" asked Kitty.

Dominic snorted. "Bragging? No. Complaining vociferously? Almost certainly. While she is quite fond of her resident rodents, she seems to enjoy complaining about them as she does little else."

"The family has coexisted with Aeslin mice for generations, which brings us to the one possible flaw in this plan," said Uncle Mike. "We don't know for sure that this Margaret woman doesn't have a colony of her own. It seems unlikely, given the Covenant's stance on cryptids, but the original colony was harbored before the family defected."

"If we encounter heretics while on the search for our brave Priestess, we will smite them down with the Fury of a Thousand Angry Rolling Pins!" squeaked the mouse.

"Don't know what that means, really. I've got to assume it's pretty dire, since it's coming from a talking mouse," said Uncle Mike. "Now I don't know about the rest of you, but I'm going to go and rescue my niece from the Covenant of St. George. Who's with me?"

"I am," said Dominic.

"It will be a pleasing diversion," said Istas.

"Verity's my friend," said Ryan.

"These people give humans a bad name," said Angel.

"We're with you," said a voice from the back of the room. I turned to see Priscilla standing in the door to the hall. She must have been speaking for the dragons while Candy's pregnancy kept her confined to the Nest. More dragons stood to either side of her, both the European and Chinese varieties. Several of the lizard-like servitors that Verity insisted on calling "Sleestaks" were behind them. All of them were holding weapons.

"All right, then," said Uncle Mike. He sounded pleased. Who wouldn't be, when they had just been handed their very own cryptid army? "Now we're cooking with gas. Let's go get Verity back."

This time, when the mouse cheered, so did everybody else. One way or another, it was time to go and face the Covenant of St. George. *Hang on, Verity,* I thought, wishing there was any chance at all that she was in a position to hear me. *We're on our way.*

Just hang on . . .

Twenty

"I'll never understand why people think kidnapping is a good way to solve their problems. Near as I can tell, it just makes more problems that you need to solve, and who are you going to kidnap then?"

—Frances Brown

An unknown location in the city of Manhattan, returning to our original narrator, who has just regained consciousness after a nasty blow to the head

I KNEW THREE THINGS even before I opened my eyes: that I was somewhere enclosed, probably no larger than a bathroom stall, that someone had changed my clothes—nothing was riding the way it should have, which probably meant my weapons were also gone—and that I was in serious trouble. Then I raised my aching head, opened my eyes, and added a fourth thing to the list: wherever I was, it was pitch-black. No natural *or* artificial light, and I'm not a bogeyman, I can't see in the dark.

Well, shit, I thought. I was smart enough not to say it out loud. There was no point in letting my captors know I was awake before I absolutely had to.

The last thing I remembered was Margaret Healy's gun slamming into the back of my head, and the meaty, deadweight sound of my body hitting the rooftop. Not the sort of thing I like to go to sleep on. I'm more of the "dance until you can't feel your knees, two or three rounds of really fun sex, wine cooler, bed" school of thought. Still, we all have to work with what we're given in this life, and what I'd been given was a crazy cousin from England who seemed to think my skull was a piñata.

At least she hadn't managed to hit me hard enough to make the candy come out. I could turn my head easily enough, and while I couldn't see a damn thing, I was reasonably confident that it was due to a lack of light, not because she had somehow knocked my optic nerves offline. I sat up a little straighter. The gesture caused the chains holding my wrists to the wall to pull up tight, clanking faintly.

"Damn," I whispered, not bothering to internalize it this time. I hadn't even realized I was chained until I tried to move. That was an amateur mistake—I should have assumed I was bound the second I woke up, and planned accordingly.

Not that there was much I could have done in the dark, presumably unarmed, and with a head sore enough to make me suspect concussion. Maybe I was being hard on myself . . . and maybe that didn't matter, since Margaret and her goons weren't going to go easy on me just because I wasn't feeling at the top of my game. I took a deep breath, ignoring the sick swimming sensation in my head, and tugged against the chains that bound me. There was barely a foot of give, and by chaining me to a wall, rather than tying me to the chair that I was sitting in, the Covenant had managed to deny me the leverage I might have otherwise used against them.

My left leg was free. My right leg wasn't. That made sense, too. It didn't totally immobilize me, and if they wanted me to stay functional for any length of time, they were going to want me to have some capacity for movement. Enough to keep the blood flowing at least, since bedsores and gangrene are nobody's friends.

That was a sobering thought all by itself. People who plan to kill you quickly don't worry about tying you up so that you can still move enough to keep your circulation good. People who plan to torture you for everything you can tell them about your family and the cryptids you've spent your whole life protecting do. And if what I knew about the Covenant was accurate, they wouldn't view torturing me as a bad thing. God told them it was all cool, as long as when it was over, they got to kill a dragon or two.

Antimony suggested once that we should all carry suicide pills, just in case a situation like this one came up. Alex and I both laughed at her. I told her that there was no way I'd ever let a situation like this one be a problem. "I'll die before I let myself be taken that way"—those were my exact words. Yet here I was, captive for the second time since I arrived in New York, and this time it wasn't just a harmless little snake cult intending to use me as a virgin sacrifice. This time it was the Covenant of St. George.

Worse, this time it was family. And as many people have pointed out over the years, there's nobody in this world who can hurt you like family can.

I took a few deep breaths to calm myself down before carefully tugging on each of the chains in turn, looking for differences in how they moved. The Covenant was pretty good at chaining people up; I had to give them that. I doubt I could have done a better job. (Antimony probably could, but that's because Antimony focused on keeping people as far away from her as possible, and when she couldn't do that, she liked to be sure they'd stay where she put them.)

Okay: so I was chained up, in the dark, with no idea of where I was. I shifted a little, feeling loose fabric around me, and added "wearing a bathrobe instead of real clothing" to my list of problems. The material was rough enough to be cheap, meaning it had probably been purchased from a gift shop, not stolen from one of Sarah's high-end hotels. My feet were bare. If they'd taken my clothes, they'd taken my weapons. I was as close to helpless as I was ever going to get, and that pissed me off.

Taking another slow breath, I closed my eyes and thought, as hard as I could, *Sarah? Can you hear me?*

There was no response, and I realized that even the

low-grade telepathic static of her presence was gone. I pushed back a surge of panic. There was no reason to suspect that they'd managed to track Sarah down while I was unconscious, and that meant one of two things. Either I was still under the influence of Margaret's telepathy-blocking charm, or the Covenant had already moved me out of New York, and I was outside Sarah's normal broadcast range. She'd be looking for me—they all would—but if I was too far for her to find telepathically, she wouldn't know what to do. She wouldn't have another way to start looking. If she was smart (and Uncle Mike would *make* her be smart, if he had to), she was already on a plane back to Ohio to hole up with her parents. Two cuckoos in one house meant the Covenant would never find them, no matter how hard they were looking. Sarah and Angela have been the family escape plan for a generation now.

I realized I was thinking like I was already lost, and I embraced it. It wasn't the same as giving up; I didn't expect the Covenant to kill me fast, and the longer they kept me alive, the better my chances became. But if my family thought I was out of reach, they might give up on me, and we might be able to minimize the damage.

There was no way they were going to do that. But it was a nice thought.

There was a soft click from one wall, like a lock was being turned. Nice as it would have been to stare defiantly at the door as it opened, I wasn't in the mood to have my retinas seared after sitting in the dark for this long; I turned my face to the side. It was a bad choice. The actual door was in the wall I was facing now, and as it swung open, a blast of industrial white light streamed into the room, framing the outline of Margaret Healy.

"I see you're awake," she said pleasantly. That was more frightening than any threats she could have made. "That's good. We've got quite a lot to talk about, you and I."

"You could have invited me to coffee," I said, squinting as I waited for my eyes to stop watering. "I don't know how you do things in Europe, but here in America, we usually start our family reunions with something a little less high-impact than assault and kidnapping."

"You hit me first," Margaret shot back. Her pleasant tone didn't waver. "Besides which, you're not much of one to talk, since the first thing you ever did was lie to me. Where did you leave that girl who was with you? Sandy, I believe you said her name was?"

There was no way I was going to remind her that Sarah was the one who hit her, not me. "She has nothing to do with this," I said. "She's just someone I met at a dance class. Leave her alone."

"That's the thing about traitors and liars. You can't believe a word they say. She lied for you. She tried to cover for you. Now why would she do that if she had nothing to do with this?" Margaret flipped a switch next to the door. The overheads came on, filling the room with more light. This didn't hurt as much. My eyes were adjusting. "Your name isn't even Valerie, is it?"

"Does it matter?"

Margaret smiled. "Oh, it matters. It matters a great deal. We'll need to know what name to bury you under, when we're finally done with you. If you're worried for your life, don't be. You'll be with us for quite some time."

"I gathered." I forced myself to relax, trying to look unconcerned. "What makes you think I'm going to talk?"

"I have a better question for you: what makes you think you've got a choice?" Margaret lunged across the small distance between us, grabbing my hair before I had a chance to move. She yanked my head back, making it pound even harder. "No one knows you're here. No one's coming to save you. You're going to get what you have coming to you, finally, and you're going to tell us where to find every other stinking rat in your hole."

The pain in my head helped me focus on what mattered: she was right. I was her captive, and I was pretty sure the Covenant wouldn't slap her wrists for using excessive force on me. All the advantages were hers. I put on my best tolerant reality television smile, trying to look like I wasn't even a little bit concerned about my situation. "Oh, Christ, you're a metaphor villain, aren't you? You're the ratcatcher, I'm the rat, you're here to exterminate the vermin, is that it? Wow. Do they have a cliché course that they make you guys go through before they release you into the field? Or maybe you're naturally talented. I mean, that happens, right?"

Margaret's eyes widened in confused indignation before she let go of my hair and shoved my head hard to the side. My neck audibly cracked. I somehow managed not to squawk. "You may think you're funny now, *heretic*, but you won't be laughing for long."

"You may as well kill me," I said, aiming for boredom rather than bravado. I wasn't sure that I was managing either. "I'm not going to tell you anything."

"Aren't you?" Margaret smiled. "You've already told me plenty."

My stomach sank. "Oh?" I asked.

"You're a traitor from a bloodline of traitors, but no Healy has ever been a coward. You wouldn't be telling me to kill you if you didn't have something to hide." Margaret's smile grew, chilling me. "You're not the last of your family. And you're going to tell me where to find them all before I let you die for your sins."

I was so busy watching her face that I didn't see her tense her arm until her hand lashed out, her fist catching me square in my unprotected jaw. The lights went out— for me, at least—and for a little while, the world went away again. My last thought before I lost consciousness was that I really, *really* hated this girl.

The sound of the door opening again woke me. I cracked my eyes open just enough to see that the lights were on, and that the person standing in front of me wasn't Margaret. It was a man, slim, dark, about my height. *Dominic.* The sight of him made me sit up a little straighter and open my eyes all the way, my heart thudding painfully in my chest. Thankfully, I managed to bite my lip before I could say his name.

It wasn't him. This man was the right height; that was where the resemblance ended. His hair was dark red, not brown verging on black, and his eyes were a cool, implacable blue. His skin was pale, spattered with freckles . . . and he was smiling.

"Why do you people smile all the damn time?" I asked, and was instantly ashamed of how shaky my voice sounded. Head injuries and unknown periods of captivity without food or water will do that to a girl.

"Because, love, you're our unicorn," he said. His accent was Irish, and heavier than Margaret's. "Never thought I'd see the day."

"Wait, so first I'm a rat, and now I'm a unicorn? If you're going to be metaphor villains, maybe you should have a meeting first. Come up with a nice theme and stick to it."

The man clucked his tongue, looking amused. "Oh, you've got a mouth on you, don't you? I hoped you would. You look enough like the family standard that I assumed some other bits might breed true." He leaned closer and murmured, with evident satisfaction, "You may have thought you were hiding, but you never stood a chance. You look too much like your ancestors."

"And yet you people lost track of us for two generations. That sounds like a pretty good chance to me."

"It was always borrowed time." He leaned in and grasped my chin, turning my head so that he could study my profile. "You've got the Price blood in you, too. Oh, won't those stuffed shirts be horrified to realize that their little disappearing scion really did marry the American Healy girl? You get to disappoint both sides of your heritage before you die, love. There's people who'd love the chance to horrify their families like that."

He was standing close to watch me squirm. My left leg was free. And I'm a trained salsa dancer.

My leg swept upward at a speed that would have seemed superhuman to anyone who'd never watched competition ballroom dance, catching the man from the Covenant squarely between the legs. The squishing feeling of his scrotum compressing against my knee was more satisfying than it probably should have been, but I didn't worry about it much. When someone chains me up and tries bargain bin intimidation tactics on me, I figure I'm allowed to take a little pleasure in their pain.

"Ack," said the man from the Covenant, his eyes going wide and glassy. His mouth dropped open as his hand fell away from my chin, letting me pull my head out of his grasp.

"Is that so?" I asked, dropping my leg slightly before ramming it back up into his balls.

His answer this time was much less coherent, and substantially higher in pitch.

"Huh. Think that's something I can discuss with my long-lost family?" I dropped my leg, preparing for a third hit. You know what they say—third time's the charm.

"I wouldn't do that if I were you," said a male voice.

I froze, leg still held straight out between the Irishman's legs, and looked toward the door. The older of the two men from the Covenant was standing there, regarding me contemplatively. There was something that looked almost like sympathy in his eyes.

"It's just that Peter doesn't care for having pretty girls smash his testicles, and while two hits you might be able to write off as having been scared and disoriented, three sort of implies premeditation." The man—Robert, by process of elimination—had a Welsh accent, and was wearing wire-rimmed glasses, hiding the color of his eyes. His hair was a nondescript shade of sandy blond, slowly fading into gray. I could easily have lost sight of him in a crowd. That just made him more unnerving. Covenant representatives should be easy to spot, and easier to avoid.

I let my foot drop to the floor.

"Thank you." Robert walked over to Peter, putting his hands on the other man's shoulders and pulling him backward. Peter went willingly, dropping his hands to cup his crotch as he moved.

"Ack," he said.

"I think that's the right response, mate, but you shouldn't have been harassing the lady. You know she's

Maggie's kin, and Maggie requested quite properly and deferentially that I not allow you to mess about with her. She understands chain of command." Robert led Peter to the wall, where he let him go. Peter promptly leaned against it, folding forward as he continued to clutch his wounded genitals. "Sorry about all this, miss . . . ?"

It was a leading question, designed to give him my name. I had to admire that, even as I had to question the wisdom of a good cop/bad cop routine that put the bad cop in a position where he needed to take a nut-shot. "Nice try," I said. "I appreciate you stopping me from making an enemy out of an enemy. But I'm not going to tell you my name."

"Your last name is 'Price,' like your paternal grandfather; your first name starts with the letter 'V,' which rather limits the possibilities, since there aren't that many names for women that start at that end of the alphabet." I must have stiffened. Robert smiled a little. "We all have our training. You give yourself away every time you open your mouth, every time you move. I'll sort you out from top to bottom while you still think you're restricting yourself to noncommittal answers and sassing back. I'm sorry about that."

"If you're sorry, don't do it," I said. "Unlock these chains and let me the hell out of here."

"Even if I wanted to, I couldn't do that. The Covenant has a need for your services, Miss Price, and your family took an oath many generations ago to answer when they were called upon. You may not uphold your oath willingly, but you *will* uphold it. Now please. This would be so much easier if you worked with us, rather than against us."

"I'm going to kill her," said Peter. He still sounded strained, but at least he was managing words now, and sentences. I probably hadn't done any permanent damage. He turned a glare on me. "I'm going to kill you."

"I heard you the first time," I said dismissively, and looked back to Robert. "You're not going to win. You can intimidate me as much as you want, but you're not going to win."

"I'm sorry," said Robert. "We already have."

He supported Peter with one arm as he led the other man out of the room, and closed the door behind them. Once again, the sound of the lock engaging came from the wrong wall, like they had some sort of speaker set up just to disorient me. I waited for the click, and then forced myself to mentally replay the first verse and chorus of Lady Gaga's "Lovegame"—roughly thirty seconds of music. When that was done, I allowed myself to glance up, and smile.

The lights were still on.

Don't get me wrong: I can get a *lot* done in total darkness. Blind fighting is a part of the standard training package where I come from, and there was a whole summer where I wasn't allowed to eat any meal I couldn't prepare blindfolded. (Lessons from that summer included "never let Verity make spaghetti with a blindfold on" and "never eat *anything* Antimony prepares with a blindfold on." How she got the blessed cedar ash into the oatmeal is something the world may never know.) But at the end of the day, I prefer working in the light, and it's hard to case a room that you can't see.

Robert Bullard said that I was giving myself away with every word I said—or didn't say. Fine. This room was doing the same thing, and I didn't even need to ask it questions. All I needed was the luxury to look around.

For one thing, the walls were matte white, with no staining or discoloration of any sort. My chains weren't bolted to anything that I could see; they passed through holes cut into the wood. That, combined with how little leverage I had, told me I was in a false room, probably constructed in the middle of something much larger. Each wall was about five feet long, giving my captors room to move, but not giving me much opportunity to get away.

I hadn't been able to see much through the open door when Peter and Robert arrived, but what I'd been able to see gave me the impression of industrial gray. Either my false room was in a shipping container, or we were in some sort of unused factory or warehouse. I'd never actually been shipped anywhere—that was one exciting life opportunity I'd worked hard to avoid—but I was reasonably sure that I would have been able to feel the pull-and-roll of the tides moving the ship if we'd been at sea. So no matter which option turned out to be the right one, we were staying in one place.

For now. If there was one thing I knew for sure, it was that complacency is a killer. I had to assume that they'd be moving me at any moment, and putting me in a false room opened the potential for moving my surroundings with me. I needed to get these chains undone. But how? Most of the common cons wouldn't work on these people; they were the ones who taught them to my family in the first place. If I faked a stomach ache, they'd force charcoal and Pepto-Bismol down my throat until I stopped. If I faked demonic possession, they'd just dump holy water over my head. And so on, and so on. Getting them to untie me was going to take something totally new and original, something they'd never seen before.

It was really a pity that I had absolutely no idea what that something was.

As for fixtures, there weren't many; this wasn't a place they were planning to keep me long-term, not if they wanted me to stay functional, and the setup argued for them wanting me to last. The chains were thick and solid—they must have brought those with them, because the chair I was sitting on was a piece of crap that looked like it was originally from Ikea. It was bolted to the floor. I leaned forward enough to study the bolts. They were generic hardware store issue, nothing special or unique. The Covenant was improvising. That was good for me. I can improvise with the best of them, and I've always gotten high marks for my freestyle.

The lights on the ceiling were more generic hardware. The false room had taken work, but they hadn't been ready to put someone into it. Not yet. There was bound to be a weak spot somewhere, and I would find it . . . later.

My head hurt. I was chained to a wall. I was going to need to eat, and pee, before too much longer. But for the moment, there was nothing I could do, and so I closed my eyes, cleared my mind, and let myself slip slowly into the restorative arms of sleep. Never fight tired if you don't have to, and never let a captive recover their strength if you have any other choice. I was following the rules. Margaret wasn't. And when she came back to resume her little question-and-answer session, she was going to find out just how important some rules really are.

Twenty-one

"Blood is one thing, but that's not all that goes into family. The family you choose is the family that really matters. They're the ones who'll keep you standing."

—Evelyn Baker

An unknown location in the city of Manhattan (but it's probably a shipping container or a warehouse)

THE SOUND OF FOOTSTEPS woke me from my doze. I cracked my eyes open just far enough to test the quality of the light. It hadn't changed. There were no windows in my little room, so the passage of time wouldn't affect things, but they also hadn't turned off the lights, or tried setting up an interrogation rig. That was good. I stayed comfortably limp, waiting to see who was approaching me, and what they wanted. I didn't have to wait for very long.

"Are you *asleep*?" demanded Margaret. She sounded incredulous. Out of all the things she was expecting from me, this was apparently at the bottom of the list.

I raised my head, yawning. "I was," I said. "Now I'm not. Maybe you should try it sometime. You might be less cranky."

"I am not cranky," said Margaret.

"You could've fooled me." She was dangerous, employed by the Covenant of St. George, and I was totally at her mercy. I probably shouldn't have been taking pleasure in tormenting her. At the same time, she sort of reminded me of my sister—a shorter, slimmer, more potentially murderous version of my sister—and I hadn't been able to torment Antimony in person for way too long.

And as long as I kept thinking of things in those terms, I wouldn't completely lose my shit. Maybe I was going to get away. Maybe I wasn't. Either way, I could keep irritating the Covenant until they killed me. It was a small thing. It was the only thing I currently had.

Margaret narrowed her eyes. "Your continuing insolence won't do you any good. You're going to pay for your sins, and I will personally commend you, body and soul, into the arms of the Lord."

"What sins are those, exactly?" I leaned back in my chair. "I'm sorry I hit you and stole your stuff, but you're the one who picked the lock in the first place. I was just acting in self-defense." I wasn't the one who'd hit her. I didn't feel like reminding her of that fact.

"You are charged with consorting with demons, conspiracy to betray the human race, and corruption of the innocent."

"That's a whole lot of 'C,'" I said, through lips that felt suddenly numb. I'd been expecting two of her trumped-up charges. The third . . .

"Consorting with demons" meant "working with cryptids, rather than shooting them on sight." "Conspiracy to betray the human race" meant basically the same thing, with a side order of not shooting any cryptid who looked like they might someday accidentally be a danger to humanity. Like Istas, who had never hurt anyone who didn't hurt her first—that I was aware of, anyway, and I try to judge people by what I see, not what I suspect—but had been perfectly happy to slaughter snake cultists with extreme prejudice. By the standards of the Covenant, I was a traitor just for letting her kill the people who'd been intending to kill *us*. But "corruption of the innocent . . ."

Dominic had been on my side all along. I was an idiot.

Margaret pressed her lips into a thin line, glaring at me. "That's right, you succubus, we know. We know you led Dominic De Luca from the paths of righteousness, just as your ancestress led Thomas Price into sin. *He* may still be forgiven, but *you* are beyond saving."

"You know, if you're comparing me to Grandma, the one thing we have in common is that we're both descended from the Healys," I said, trying to push aside the cold, sick feeling in my stomach. "What does that say about your family, huh? Have you seduced and betrayed anyone recently?"

She didn't punch me this time. Instead, she slapped me, her palm landing hard and stinging against my cheek. I rocked back in my chair. The manacles dug into my wrists, and I barely managed to bite my lip hard enough to keep from crying out.

"You're a selfish little bitch, just like everyone else in your tainted bloodline," spat Margaret. She sounded like she was about to cry. I blinked at her, not saying anything, and she continued, really getting her rant on now: "Do you have any idea what it's like to grow up knowing you're descended from *traitors*? That once you would have had this amazing family legacy, this endless parade of heroes and saviors and saints, but some self-absorbed idiots had to take all of that away from you? You're an aberration, a monster-loving plague upon the human race! Your parents are no better than you, and we're going to find them, and we're going to make them pay until my family name is clean! Do you understand me?"

"I understand that you're upset," I said carefully. *Also a little obsessive,* I thought. "But I'm not your redemption. I'm just a woman who happens to be distantly related to you, and whatever hell the Covenant may have put you through for being a Healy, it's not my fault. Okay? It wasn't me who chose to leave, or my parents, or my grandparents. Hell, it wasn't even my great-grandparents. Isn't there a statute of limitations on the sins of the father?"

"Yes," said Margaret coldly. "Even to the seventh generation. You are still responsible for the things they did to our family, and as they can't pay for them, you will."

This time, when she slapped me, she was a lot less gentle about it—and she hadn't been pulling her punches the first time. A thin trickle of blood ran down from my nose, pooling along the top of my lip. I couldn't wipe it away, and so I simply sat there, glaring helplessly.

"You're going to tell us *everything*," she spat. "How many of you there are, where we can find you, what your defenses are like—*everything*. And then, when your blasted family is safely in our custody, we can discuss whether or not you should be held accountable for what our ancestors have done."

"You need a hug," I said. "Or maybe therapy. Or maybe—I know—you need to be kicked in the throat. How about you unchain me, and I'll hug you before I kick you in the throat?"

"You're a violent little thing, aren't you?" she asked. "Peter told me how shamefully you treated him. I honestly expected more ladylike behavior from you." As she spoke, I realized that even when she was slapping me, she'd been careful to keep most of her body at an angle that would be virtually impossible for me to kick. She was smart. She learned from the mistakes of others. That just meant that I couldn't give her time to take notes when the time came for her to make her own mistakes.

"What can I say?" I asked. "Some of us grow up in the care of global terrorist organizations. Others aren't so lucky."

For a moment, Margaret actually looked sorry for me. I itched to slap that expression right off her smug little face. "We're not terrorists. We're the good guys. And now it's time for you to start earning that redemption." She stepped away from me. "Gentlemen, she's ready. We can begin the interrogation."

The Covenant's definition of "interrogation" wasn't nice. It wasn't gentle. It also wasn't going to leave any scars, so I suppose I ought to thank them for that—although it's hard to thank anyone who thinks that, say, beating the bottoms of my feet with a wooden baton is a sociable thing to do. They weren't interested in my long-term dance career. They weren't even interested in my being able to walk normally the next day. What they wanted was information, and they were more than happy to hurt me if it would help them get it.

As I had suspected, Robert was the most efficient of the three. Margaret was happy to help Peter hold me down, and Peter grinned disturbingly the whole time, but it was Robert who kept producing common household tools from his little box. He looked disappointed every time he had to get a new one, like I was letting them down by refusing to break.

"You could end this now, you know," he said, pulling what looked like a blood pressure cuff out of the box. "All you need to do is tell us your name. That's all I'm looking for today, is your name. We know your surname is 'Price.' Why not buy yourself a bit of a rest, and tell us what your first name is?"

"Go to hell," I said.

"I'm afraid you're going to beat me there," he said. Margaret took the blood pressure cuff, fastening it tight around my upper arm. I tried to squirm away. Robert raised a finger. "This will hurt less if you hold still."

"Why the hell would I start believing that now?" I demanded.

"Because I might be telling the truth, and wouldn't it be wonderful if I were?"

I didn't say anything. I just glared mutely, willing him to fall down dead. Maybe that would have worked, if I'd been Sarah and he hadn't been wearing an anti-telepathy charm and oh, right. If we lived in a comic book universe where the rules said that the bad people would be punished, and the good people would always come out on top. Too bad we didn't live in that kind of world. Too bad we never had.

And then the cuff around my arm began to expand, and the needles I hadn't previously been able to feel began piercing my skin. After that, I forgot about everything but screaming for a little while.

"What's your name, love?" asked Peter.

I screamed.

"Just tell us your name and this can all be over for now. What's your name, love?"

I screamed. The more they inflated the cuff, the more the needles dug into my arm. The fact that it was designed to let air slowly out again meant that I never achieved equilibrium; the cuff would inflate, the needles would dig in, the cuff would deflate, the needles would shift positions, and then it would all start again. It was a new, exciting way of hurting someone, and I wanted nothing to do with it.

"What's your *name*, love?" asked Peter.

I screamed, and kept screaming, until the sound ran out and I slumped, practically boneless, in the chair. Robert stopped inflating the cuff, letting it collapse with a soft hissing sound. Then he leaned in, wrapped his hand around the now-deflated cuff, and *squeezed*.

Somehow I found it in myself to scream one last time, wailing like someone's family *beán sidhe*. Robert kept squeezing, grinding his hand against the cuff so that the needles danced inside my flesh. His expression was sad, almost disappointed, like he hadn't wanted any of this to happen.

"What's your name?" he asked, almost in a whisper.

"V-Verity," I replied. "Verity Price."

"It's a pleasure to meet you, Verity Price," he said, and took his hand away. The needles were still there, but the sudden reduction in pressure was such a blessing that I started to sob. "Take it off. We have what we need for right now."

"How is that what we need?" Margaret asked.

Robert smiled. "Verity's seen the light. She'll be willing to help us, now, won't you?"

I couldn't say anything. I could only sob, and keep sobbing as they gathered their things and left my tiny artificial prison. This time, they remembered to turn off the lights on their way out, and I was left alone again. Well, almost alone; the pain was still there, and was more than happy to be my companion in the dark.

Professional dancers learn to work through pain. It's a part of the job. We dance on sprained ankles, we dance with broken ribs, we dance on blisters and bunions and broken toes. We are expected to be beautiful machines, capable of holding our form no matter what injuries we're hiding. All my training told me that I should be able to compartmentalize the pain, and so as soon as I was alone—and as soon as I stopped crying—I began to do exactly that.

First up was an assessment of my injuries. The puncture marks in my right arm were probably the worst; they were still bleeding, and I couldn't move my arm enough to tell whether there were tears in the muscle. For the moment, I had to assume that they were all superficial, and that I'd be able to climb if I needed to. Anything else was unthinkable.

My feet were in worse shape. I didn't think any bones were broken, but both soles were badly swollen and probably just as badly bruised. I wasn't going to be running anywhere any time soon. I'd just need to find another way.

Apart from that, all I had was a split lip, a bloody nose, some abrasions on my scalp where the hair pulling had gotten overly enthusiastic, and some extremely sore fingernails. They hadn't pulled any of my nails off, which was a small mercy, given how enthusiastic they'd been about driving slivers of bamboo underneath them. My whole life, I'd been hearing about how torture doesn't work; torture is never the answer. Well, apparently, our cousins at the Covenant never got that particular lesson. They thought torture worked just fine.

I took a breath, held it until my lungs ached, and breathed slowly out. I could function. I was hurt, but not too badly, and I could function. That was a good thing, because I needed to get away the second I had the opportunity to do so. These people were willing and eager to hurt me in the name of their cause, and when they started asking for information more sensitive than my name, they'd probably be more than happy to move on to more advanced methods of extracting answers. I liked my fingers, and my toes. I wanted them all to stay attached to my body.

And I could no longer be sure I wouldn't give them what they asked for when the cutting started.

I don't know how long I sat there in the dark, just breathing, waiting for the throbbing in my feet and arm to die down. When the door finally opened, I didn't twitch, even though the light burned my eyes. I just stayed in the same position, chin down, slumped as far over as the chains allowed.

"Not so mouthy now, are you?" asked a voice. Peter Brandt.

I allowed myself a brief moment of satisfaction. Of the three, he was the one I'd been hoping would come to check on me. Margaret had a holy crusade. Robert had a job to do. And Peter? Peter had a grudge.

"Please," I whispered.

"Please? Please what, love? Please mercy? You didn't show much mercy when you thought you had me. Why should we show any mercy to you now?" Peter crossed the room to my chair. My leg twitched with the urge to be reintroduced to his balls, at speed. I forced myself to keep still. "There's not any mercy here for the likes of you. We're going to beat the devil right out of you."

"Please," I whispered again. "I need to use the bathroom. I don't . . . I mean, I don't want to . . ." I started crying again. It wasn't hard. All I had to do was press my feet a little harder against the floor and the tears came practically on their own.

Claiming to need the bathroom was an old trick, which meant it had a pretty high chance of failure. But you never succeed if you don't try, as my dad always says, and it became an old trick because it worked so often. Most people don't want to deal with prisoners who come pre-soiled. Tears always helped with that sort of thing. Being tiny and blonde means that most people are looking for excuses to underestimate me, and Peter was from the Covenant. He had to consider me inferior, or he'd be admitting that the Covenant might not have the best training program out there.

"What's to stop you pulling a fast one and trying to get away from me, hmm?"

He was smarter than I'd expected; damn. I sniffled, and said, "My feet hurt so bad I'm not even sure I can walk. How am I supposed to pull a fast one when I can't even *walk*?"

"What's in it for me?"

I almost dropped my subservient posture in favor of taking another shot at his groin. I managed to suppress the rage—barely—and whispered, "Anything you want." Hopefully, if I couldn't escape, his "anything" wouldn't be anything that forced me to kill him any more than I was already planning to.

Peter hesitated. Then, finally, he made up his mind. "Stay there," he said, and laughed as he walked out of the room.

Oh, I was *definitely* going to kill that man when I got the opportunity, or at least hurt him a lot. I stayed in my half-hunched position, listening intently to the noises coming from outside my little room. First came the clinking of metal, and then the soft sound of a hasp being turned. He was undoing my chains. My wrists and ankle were still cuffed, but the chains themselves were no longer attached to whatever was outside the walls.

Peter stepped back into the room a moment later. "All right, love. Let's get you out of here."

"But how?" I whispered, raising my head. "I can't . . . I mean, I'm still . . ."

"I'm the man with the solution to your problem." Peter held up a key, grinning.

I grinned back. "Awesome."

"What?" His grin faltered, replaced by confusion. "Don't you get any ideas, now. You're still—"

"Chained? Yeah, I know," I said, and lunged.

The chains had approximately a foot of give when they were attached to their anchor. If the false room was at floor level—which it was, because none of my captors had stepped up to enter—that meant that the anchor had to be a minimum of a foot from the opening. I had at least two feet to play with, and I was going to play.

To my surprise, my estimates had been off, a lot, and in the direction that worked *for* me, rather than against me: I had four feet of slack to play with. The chain was still unspooling when my elbow hit Peter in the chin, followed less than a second later by my knee slamming into his stomach. I wasn't kidding about how difficult it would be for me to walk on my bruised-up soles, but what I hadn't mentioned was that they'd been focusing on my instep, not the balls of my feet. As a dancer, the balls of my feet are where I live.

Peter went down like a sack of arrogant Irish potatoes, and I finished the job by slamming my balled-up, manacle-weighted fists into the back of his head. There was a risk I could kill him—that's always a risk with blows to the head—and somehow I couldn't find it in me to care very much. He'd been willing to do a lot worse than killing me.

The key was on the floor only inches from his hand. I grabbed it, unlocking the manacles on my wrists and ankle, and shoved it into the pocket of my bathrobe. Then I grabbed his belt, feeling frantically around until I found what I was looking for: the hilt of a knife.

"Thank God," I muttered.

I took the knife and his shoelaces. Then I turned, and I was out the door.

The false room where I'd been held was set squarely in the middle of a large warehouse that had clearly been used for storage before it was converted into a temporary Covenant base. Old boxes still lined the walls, and there were hooks hanging from the ceiling. They looked disturbingly like giant meat hooks. I paused only long enough to be sure that neither of the remaining Covenant members were coming for me. Then I ran for the nearest wall, moving as fast as my aching body and battered feet allowed.

It's amazing what a little adrenaline can do. I beat my own personal record for the twenty-yard dash, reaching one of the stacks of boxes and ducking behind it a split second before I heard voices coming from the far end of the warehouse.

"—talk," said Margaret, her irritation clear even at a distance. "She simply won't. We don't work that way."

"You must stop regarding this woman as a member of your family," said Robert. "Her limits are not the same as yours."

"She's held up fairly well so far," said Margaret sourly. "Who's to say she won't hold out until we get her back to England?"

"If she does that, she's not our problem anymore. I know you want to be the one who breaks her, but what matters is that she's broken, not who does it."

"Don't talk to me like I'm a child. I know what's at stake here." They were getting closer. I pressed deeper into the shadows behind my concealing wall of boxes, trying to assess my options in the rapidly decreasing time I had available. The bathrobe was white, or mostly; the front was more bloodstained than it had been when they first put it on me. It would show up against the gloom like a beacon. Grimly, I untied the belt and slipped the terrycloth off my shoulders. Naked may not provide much protection from the elements, but a bathrobe never stopped a bullet. I needed to disappear more than I needed to preserve my feeble sense of modesty.

"Do you really?"

I tied Peter's shoelaces hastily around the hilt of his knife, creating a makeshift cord that would hopefully keep me from going unarmed. I needed both my hands free. I also needed the knife. This was the best compromise I could come up with on short notice. Once I was reasonably sure the knots would hold, I wrapped the cord around my right arm, using it to secure the knife to my bicep. The knots held.

"Of course I—" Margaret's voice cut off mid-sentence, followed by a shout that was half-wordless exclamation, half-profanity. I heard her running toward the false room. Only one set of footsteps; Robert wasn't moving, and until he moved, neither was I.

"So we lost you already, did we? Clever little thing. I'll have to arrange for additional containment measures when we get you back. And we *will* get you back, Verity

Price. You can be certain of that." He spoke like he knew
that I could hear him—and maybe he did. If there was
only one way into the warehouse, he'd have noticed me
going by. That meant I had to be in the main room, somewhere.

That didn't mean I had to make things easy for him. I
slipped farther back behind the wall of boxes, hooked
my fingers onto the first available handhold, and started
climbing.

Most humans think flatly. It's not a criticism: humanity evolved when monkeys left the trees, and—as a
whole—we haven't been all that eager to go back. Most
people rarely look much higher than their own line of
sight. More importantly, most people stop climbing when
they get out of elementary school. Robert might expect
me to seek higher ground, but he wouldn't expect me to
do it silently—and if there's one thing I've learned from
years of free running, it's how to ascend without making
any noise.

I stopped once I was ten feet off the ground, moving
sideways until I found a cleft between two boxes that I
could wedge myself into without making myself visible.
And then I waited.

It wasn't a long wait. "She's gone!" shouted Margaret.

"I gathered as much," said Robert. His voice was
closer now. I didn't move. "What happened?"

"I can't be sure—Peter's out cold—but it looks like
she somehow convinced him to unchain her, and then
walloped the holy hell out of him."

"She improvises well. We'll have to remember that."
Robert stepped suddenly around the edge of the wall of
boxes, visible from my current position only as a flicker
of motion in my peripheral vision. I froze in my hidey-
hole, trying not to breathe. "Her robe's here."

"She left her robe?" Margaret sounded incredulous.
"What good did she expect that to do her?"

"It's white. White would stand out in here. It was the
right choice, assuming she's not worried about running
around naked." Robert raised his voice, calling, "You can
come out. We understand why you ran away, and we're

not angry, but there's no way you're getting out of here. You may as well make things easy on yourself, and stop hiding before we come looking for you."

Biting back the snarky replies took an almost physical effort. I succeeded. The pounding ache in my feet helped. If they'd done this to me when they weren't angry, what would they do if they got me back?

Robert sighed audibly. "It's going to be like that, is it?" He started walking away, presumably moving toward the boxes along the next wall. "You know, I'd really hoped that we were making progress, Verity. I know we'll never be friends, but I wanted you to know that we respect your willpower."

I held perfectly still as I began counting down silently from ten. Sure enough, I had just reached four when a flicker of motion betrayed Margaret creeping cat-silent into the narrow space between the boxes and the wall. She was looking for me, and so I did the one thing that I could do: I didn't move. Without my bathrobe and in this degree of shadow, my hair and skin would look like they were all one color. I just hoped that it would be the color of the box that I was huddling against. I could climb—climbing was mostly a matter of digging in with my toes and forcing my way past the pain—but I wasn't going to place bets on my being able to run any time soon.

"Where is she?!" Peter's voice blasted into the warehouse, loud and sudden enough that I nearly flinched. I managed to restrain myself, the large muscles in my thighs jumping frantically as I struggled not to panic. "Where's that little Healy bitch? I'll strangle her with my bare hands!"

"Your interest in doing things with your bare hands is how we lost her in the first place," snapped Robert. His voice was a whip crack in the quiet of the warehouse. Margaret was still creeping along, moving like she thought there was no chance I'd have seen her. I pressed myself deeper into the crevice, barely allowing myself to breathe as I watched Margaret inch her way along.

In the movies, this would be where I inevitably had to sneeze, triggering an exciting chase scene. In the movies,

I wouldn't be stark-ass naked, and I'd have a machine gun or something, not a single stolen knife. I didn't sneeze, and below me, Margaret moved on by, still searching for my hiding space. When she looked up, the shadows—faithful to the last—made me look like just another part of the wall. God bless the limitations of the human eye.

She passed out of my sight, her footsteps moving to join the others.

"She must be in the upstairs," said Robert.

That was news to me. I hadn't realized there *was* an upstairs.

"Well, let's go get her," snapped Margaret. "We need to get her back into custody, *now*."

"I'm going to kill her," said Peter.

"No," said Robert. "You're not. We're going to enlighten her. I think you'll find that she enjoys that far less."

The three of them moved off together. Their footsteps faded into silence, until I finally heard a door close in the distance. I still stayed where I was for another five minutes, measuring the time by counting off the steps of a proper Viennese waltz in my head. Finally, I was satisfied that I was alone, and I allowed myself to unlock my shoulders, sagging into a sitting position on the box where I'd been standing.

I was alone, naked, practically unarmed, and terrified. I might not have much time, but I had long enough. Bending forward to press my forehead against my knees, I closed my eyes, and cried silently until the tears ran out.

When I was sure that I was done leaking, I unfolded and stood, not bothering to wipe my cheeks. These assholes from the Covenant wanted to play? Oh, we'd play. And they'd lose.

Twenty-two

"Never forget that I loved you, and I did the best by you I could. You can forget everything else about me, but please. Don't forget that."

—Enid Healy

Hiding from the Covenant of St. George in a warehouse somewhere in Manhattan

THE FIRST THING I needed to do was find a way out that didn't involve going past the Covenant. There's nothing dignified about racing naked across the rooftops of Manhattan—for one thing, without a bra, I was going to wind up in a world of pain, and that didn't even start to go into the situation with my feet—but that wasn't going to stop me. If I had an exit, I was going to take it. The trick was going to be finding that exit without coming out into the open.

I carefully extracted myself from my position between the boxes and began climbing again. Higher ground helped my nerves. Margaret and the others wanted me alive, for the moment, and that meant they'd be reluctant to shoot me; it's never a good idea to shoot someone you're not intending to kill, no matter how good of a shot you think you are. That's something I learned from my grandmother, and she's the best shot I've ever known. "Even when you're aiming for the hand, you'd best assume you're shooting to kill," was what she'd said, and she was right. Shooting to wound was only a few inches from missing your target entirely, and a different few inches from killing them. Assuming the Covenant had similar training (a big assumption, but I had to go with *something*), they'd try to use other means of getting me down.

Besides, once I was high enough, they'd be even less likely to see me without my wanting to be seen, and there was something to be said for that. I didn't want them to take me alive. I didn't want to die, either. That meant I needed to escape.

The boxes were piled high enough that I could see the rafters overhead, but not so high that I could reach them. I couldn't even jump with any assurance that I'd hit my target—not with my feet in their current condition—and a misjudged landing could send the entire stack of boxes toppling. That wouldn't be exactly what I'd call "subtle," and it would bring the Covenant rushing back to find me, instead of wasting more time searching the upstairs.

I wish to hell I had some backup, I thought grimly, frowning at the unreachable rafters. That triggered a whole series of thoughts I'd been trying to avoid—like why couldn't I feel Sarah if we were still in Manhattan? I should have been able to tune in on her "static," even if she was too far away to communicate telepathically. I wasn't wearing Margaret's anti-telepathy charm anymore. Hell, I wasn't wearing *anything* anymore. It wasn't likely that Sarah would have left town while I was unconscious. So where was she?

If Sarah was unlikely to have left town, the Covenant was even less likely to have found her without me to lead them to her hiding place. She was a cuckoo. She was probably terrified by whatever feedback she picked up when Margaret knocked me out. That would have been enough to activate her automatic defenses, and once those were up, they'd never be able to catch her. That meant they were still blocking her telepathy somehow. It was the only explanation for her ongoing radio silence.

There was no way they'd have been able to telepathically shield an entire warehouse. The resources required would have been massive, and it would have meant bringing in several witches, if not a witch, a sorcerer, and some variety of exorcist. So they had to be telepathically shielding me. I wasn't wearing anything . . .

But that didn't mean I hadn't been forced to swallow anything. I put a hand on my stomach, feeling suddenly queasy. *Okay, Verity, settle down,* I thought sternly. *Even if you ate it, it's not poisonous. They wanted to bring you back to the Covenant alive, and that means they're not going to have fed you any mercury-based charms.*

Oh, I hoped I was right about that. Sure, keeling over because I'd been poisoned would be a dandy way to prevent myself from telling them any of the family secrets, but it wasn't exactly on the top of my "to do" list for the day. (It wasn't a guarantee of my silence, either. The phrase "dead men tell no tales" doesn't hold that much water in my family. We know a lot of ghosts. My Aunt Mary died years before I was born, and no one, living or dead, has any idea how to shut her up.)

I took a deep breath, trying to calm myself down, and went back to looking for things that could help me get up into the rafters. The boxes weren't high enough, and I didn't want to start rearranging them—there was no telling how heavy they were, or how many of them were rotten on the inside. That left the hooks that hung from the ceiling. I looked at them, assessing the distance I would have to leap. If I could just grab hold before I fell, I could climb the chain to reach the rafters. Tetanus would be a risk, but hell, in my line of work, tetanus is *always* a risk.

"Only die once," I muttered (that wasn't quite true, either), and started climbing back down the boxes. It was a stupid plan. It was a potentially suicidal plan. It was the only plan I had, and so I intended to go for it. Never allow for the possibility that you might fail, and you'll succeed just because the universe is too embarrassed to admit that it painted you into a corner.

My feet hurt worse than ever by the time I reached the floor. Every bend of my toes was agony, and putting my weight down on my heels was like standing on hot coals. Ballet helped with that. After years of pointe classes, where bleeding toes were considered a status symbol, a little bruising wasn't going to slow me down. I hit the ground running, a naked blonde streak heading as fast as I could for the false room that had been my prison, and would now hopefully be my salvation.

As long as I didn't slow down, I could use the pain in my feet to motivate me. I was going to pay for that as soon as I stopped—the limits of the human body are something that I am intimately familiar with—but for the moment, adrenaline and inertia were both on my side. I assessed the pain as I ran, letting it serve as its own diagnostic engine. The bruising was as bad as I'd thought it would be, maybe a little worse, but that was all. It didn't feel like they'd actually managed to crack any of my metatarsals, which was a relief. Bruising was going to be a lot easier to work around than broken bones.

I didn't slow down as I approached the side of the false room. Instead, I aimed myself for the doorway, leaping at the last moment to grab the top of the frame. I let my own momentum carry me into a forward jack-knife, then whipped myself backward and flipped up onto the roof. I landed silently, my bare feet actually helping with the action.

"If you wanted to keep me, you shoulda broken my fingers," I murmured. Then I straightened, turned, and started running again before my feet could fully realize that I had stopped. This time when I jumped, I launched myself into empty air.

For a moment, I was flying, arms outstretched, like a Lady Godiva superheroine aiming for the sky. Then my hands hit the big metal hook dangling from the ceiling. I grabbed hold, clinging as tightly as I could while the force of my leap sent the whole chain swaying. The extra ten feet of height I'd been able to gain from the false room had been enough to boost me to the necessary level. Thank God. If this hadn't worked, I probably would have wound up with a broken leg, and that would have been a *lot* harder to work around.

The chain creaked as it swayed, but quietly; it was too

heavy to get up any real momentum, and that was keeping the noise down. For the moment.

"Gonna need a tetanus shot when all this is over," I muttered, and began climbing up the still-swaying chain, heading for the ceiling. It was time to get out of sight.

The less said about my trip up the filthy, rusty, incredibly cold length of chain, the better, except that the whole experience left me with a lot of respect for Antimony's trapeze classes. Not that she was usually into climbing chains—ropes were more her thing—but my arms were aching by the time I reached the rafters, and my shoulders felt like they'd been scooped out and replaced with mashed potatoes.

Once I was at the top of the chain, I had to actually pull myself up onto the main support beam, another task that was easier said than done. It was bigger around than the span of my arms, the sort of old, solid construction that was supposed to outlive the city itself. I finally managed to hook my foot into the loop that secured the chain to the beam, scrabbling up the side of the wood and collapsing, facedown, onto it. What were a few splinters in sensitive places after everything I'd already been through?

Answer: damn uncomfortable. I stayed where I was for longer than was probably a good idea, wincing as the feeling came slowly back into my arms. Once I was sure that I could move without sending myself plummeting to the floor, I sat up and looked around me.

The beam where I was seated was covered in a thick layer of grime, cobwebs, and rat droppings. I was naked in the middle of a major health hazard. The filth was at least reassuring, confirming that no one else had been up here in years, if ever. The Covenant wasn't likely to start looking for me in the rafters until they got really desperate, and by that point, I would hopefully be long gone. There was less than seven feet of space between me and the ceiling; if I stood on my tiptoes, I could have brushed my fingers against it. Assuming I would have *wanted* to.

The cobwebs were even worse up there, creating a hanging shroud of grime.

The big beams, like the one I was starting to think of as mine, were spaced evenly down the length of the warehouse. Smaller beams connected them, creating almost a network of catwalks that someone without a fear of heights could use to traverse the building easily. Best of all, they connected to the windows that were set high into the walls. All I had to do was get there, get the windows open, and get out. Emboldened by what looked like the nearness of my escape, I stood.

Only years of hard training and harder discipline kept me from screaming as I put my weight back on my bruised feet and promptly fell down again. I managed to grab the edge of the beam before I could roll off into space. I clung for dear life, curling into a ball and sobbing into the dirt. This moment had been coming since I escaped; I'd known it was coming, had seen and cataloged the signs. You can only keep running on a bruise for so long. Still, I had refused to believe that my body would betray me like this while I was still in danger. Like the idiot I sometimes was, I'd allowed myself to believe that I could just keep running, and fall down when it was safe.

It wasn't safe. It was a long damn way from safe. But I was still falling down.

My tears turned the grime against my cheek into a horrible, foul-smelling mud that smeared on my face. I struggled into a sitting position and tried to wipe it away, but only succeeded in smearing it down my chin and all over my hand. That just made me cry more. I was dirty, I was alone, and I was hurt too badly to be doing this by myself.

It was funny, really. I'd always known that I wasn't going to have a long and peaceful life; that sort of thing is reserved for people who think the monster under the bed is just a story, and who run away from the sound of screaming, not toward it. Somehow I'd always expected to die so fast that I wouldn't even realize it was happening—a broken neck, like my great-grandmother, or a swarm of Apraxis wasps, like my great-grandfather.

Maybe even sucked into a portal to another dimension, like Grandpa. But no, my choices had to be "tortured to death by the Covenant" or "starved to death in the rafters of an old warehouse." Talk about a rock and a hard place.

My tears gradually ran out, replaced by a hollow feeling in my chest. My parents would never know what happened to me. My mice wouldn't even be able to give a full accounting. I'd be one more branch lopped off the family tree, with nothing to show that I'd ever been alive.

Well. Almost nothing. I'd managed to sway a Covenant agent over to our side, and that was something we hadn't done for a couple of generations. Grandma Alice was the last one to accomplish it, and she'd used similar tactics. being cute and blonde and persistent. It was weird to think that she would probably outlive me.

Unbidden, the image of my grandmother rose in my mind's eye, hair spiked with some unnamable goo from some equally unnamable hell-thing that she'd just killed, a sour expression on her face. "You call yourself a Price girl? Get up. Fight. Don't you give up like this. That's something a Covenant trainee would do, and you're better than them."

When all else fails, talk to yourself. "My feet hurt," I informed her.

"I carried my father's dead body out of the woods when I was bleeding out from Apraxis stings," she countered. "If you can't walk, you crawl. Show me what you're made of, girl, or I'll start thinking you're a cuckoo left in place of my real granddaughter."

It wasn't really Grandma, but my imagination definitely talked like her. "Yes, ma'am," I said, and shifted to my hands and knees. My imaginary grandmother smiled before she disappeared. I smiled back.

And then I started crawling.

The beam was rough and splintery in addition to everything else; I'd barely gone five feet before my knees were bleeding. I was going to need more than a tetanus shot when this was all over. Still, I was moving, and that was better than I'd been managing a few minutes before.

Infection was something to worry about after everything else was taken care of, like the three Covenant agents who knew my name and face.

I was going to have to kill them. I couldn't see any way around it. Maybe not right now—right now, escape was a bit more of an immediate priority—but there was no way I could let them live. I'd never be safe again if they were out there, and if I wasn't safe, I couldn't go home. I might be able to go and hide with Grandma Baker in Ohio, but the rest of my family would be lost to me. The Covenant has taken too much away from us since the day that we decided we had to leave. I wasn't going to let them add me to the list.

Maybe it was a flimsy justification for murder, but we've always argued that cryptids deserved equal treatment with humans, and I was raised to believe that a cryptid who represented a clear and present danger to another sapient species had to die. Predators don't get a free pass just because it's in their natures. The Covenant agents were predators. I was their prey. Fighting back didn't make me a bad person. It made me someone who was willing to practice what I preached, and treat them like any other dangerous creature. If they lived, I, and a lot of innocent cryptids, would die. So they had to die. End of story.

The beam terminated where it met the wall, joining with the rest of the building's support structure. I stood again, gritting my teeth against the pain in my feet, and pressed my hands against the wall as I leaned sideways to examine the window. My heart sank as I realized that there were no latches, no hinges, no way to open it at all. The windows were made to let in light, not fresh air. It made sense; who would be climbing up here to open them? I mean besides a naked girl with bruised feet and a stolen knife, of course

I looked up to where the window frame met the ceiling. The Covenant was up there, searching for me. Somewhere above them, the roof was up there, too.

I only had one shot at getting out of here, and that meant finding a way up. Assuming I could manage it. That was a big assumption: I knew nothing about the warehouse where I was being kept, other than that it had a large downstairs, and a second floor . . . I paused, suddenly feeling like an absolute idiot.

I knew nothing about the warehouse, except that it was a *warehouse*, and it was built before they had cheap and dependable elevator technology. That meant all the floors would need to be connected by some sort of hatch system, to enable them to move things from one floor to another. I turned and started scanning the ceiling, looking for the telltale outlines of a removable panel. I found what I was looking for about halfway across the room: a square where the cobwebs didn't quite match the ones around them, maybe due to drafts blowing down through the ceiling/floor. More tellingly, that was one of the only patches not used to anchor anything at all, and there were no beams crossing in the space below it. That had to be one of the transportation hatches.

Now the only challenge was getting to it. I could crawl and risk shredding my hands and knees further when I might still need them, or I could try to walk. Neither option seemed like it was a particularly good one, and so I went for the better of two evils: I would walk. Maybe that would make my feet go numb enough that I'd be able to escape without tripping. If it didn't work, well. I'd find another way. I took a deep breath, centering myself as I found my balance, and began walking slowly down the beam toward the hatch.

Balance beam was a part of my earliest gymnastics classes. I always excelled, because I had no fear of falling. This was different. If I fell, there was nothing I could use to catch myself, no convenient handholds or ways to redirect my inertia. I walked slowly, all too aware of how much space stretched between me and the floor. I didn't look down. That would have been suicide, and all appearances to the contrary, I've never particularly wanted to make a splash when I died.

Step by painful step, the hatch came closer. I was almost there when a door slammed behind me and I froze, only long practice at navigating rooftops and high places keeping me from losing my balance.

"—she not be there? There's no way she made it out of this building!" The voice was Margaret's.

"You're right, and she's not going to get past us." Robert. That was actually a good thing. Peter might be the one who'd been most willing to harass me, but he wasn't the planner of the bunch. If he was the one guarding the second floor, my odds had just improved. "The front door is locked. The back door is locked. The basement has been sealed off for years. She's trapped."

"I hate her." There was a note in Margaret's voice that might have been grudging respect, under different circumstances.

Robert actually laughed. "Not for nothing, but I bet she's not too fond of you, either."

Please don't look up. Please, please don't look up. I remained frozen on my beam, listening as they passed below me. I was filthy enough that I would probably blend into the ceiling by this point, but that didn't mean I needed to start tempting fate. I was so focused on keeping still that I was barely even breathing. *Just keep going.*

"Has there been any sign of De Luca?" Robert asked the question calmly, almost casually, like it was of no real importance.

"No. You were right. The little whore turned him traitor," snarled Margaret. "He's just as bad as she is."

"Peace, Margaret. We'll catch him next, and deliver them both to our superiors. He'll have a great deal of explaining to do." The footsteps stopped almost directly below me. I forced myself not to move. In a way, my damaged feet were almost a blessing. If I hadn't been hurt, I would almost certainly have run.

"What is it?" asked Margaret suspiciously.

"I just don't understand how we could have lost her like this." The footsteps didn't resume. "There's no way out of this room. There's nowhere she could have run. But she's gone, all the same. It's impossible."

"Nothing's impossible," said Margaret.

"Apparently not," said Robert.

The footsteps started again. I waited until I heard a door slam on the far end of the room before relaxing enough to start breathing. I still counted silently to a hundred before I peeked over the edge of the beam . . .

. . . and found myself looking straight down into Robert Bullard's smiling face.

"Gotcha," he said.

I straightened up, and bolted for the hatch.

Pain is a powerful motivator. So is panic, and when the panic is extreme enough, even pain can find itself set by the wayside. I forgot about the ache in my feet, the distance between me and the ground, and everything else in my hurry to reach the only chance I had of getting to the second floor. Below me, Robert was barking orders to Margaret, who was no doubt figuring out her own route to the rafters. But since neither of them could fly, I still had a few minutes, and I was going to use them for all that I was worth.

The beam didn't run directly under the hatch—that would have made it difficult to use—but it came close enough. I grabbed one of the vertical supports, leaning out as far as I could without losing my footing, and thrust my other hand into the cobwebs until it banged against the ceiling. The wood shifted slightly. I hit it again, harder, and felt it lift up.

That was all I needed. When I hit it the third time, I twisted and rammed my fingers into the opening I had created before the hatch could fall back down. Then I let myself swing out, praying frantically to every god that I could think of as I scrabbled to get a grip with my other hand. Robert was still shouting, and I could hear a rattling, scraping sound that meant Margaret was probably halfway to the top of the chains by now. This was my only shot. I swung, grabbed for the narrow lip created by my fingers—

—and caught it.

There was no time to dangle, no matter how stunned I was. I immediately began pulling myself upward, digging my nails into the wood and shoving as hard as I could to bump the hatch out of my way. It left splinters in my wrists and arms. I kept shoving. At this point, after everything, a few splinters were among the least of my worries.

Cobwebs filled my mouth and eyes as I pushed the hatch open enough to get my head through. That was the last bit I needed to get sufficient leverage; I twisted around, grabbing the top of the hatch, and blindly pulled myself up into the second floor. The hatch slammed shut as soon as I pulled my feet loose. Choking and gaping, I clawed the cobwebs out of my eyes, trying to clear them. I was filthy. I was almost free.

I was wiping the last of the cobwebs away when I heard the characteristic sound of a gun being cocked from directly behind me. "Now isn't this a lovely little turn of events?" asked Peter Brandt.

Shit.

Twenty-three

"Don't you worry about whether you failed your family. Family loves you, no matter what. Worry about whether you failed yourself. As long as the answer's 'no,' then there's still a chance that everything else will be okay."

— Alice Healy

On the second floor of a warehouse somewhere in Manhattan, facing down a member of the Covenant of St. George

PETER'S EYES TRAVELED the length of my naked, filthy body, a smirk twisting up his lips. He lingered on my breasts for a moment before flicking to my right bicep. "Nice knife," he said.

"Yeah, I got it from a real asshole," I said. I didn't move. The gun—*my* gun—in his hand told me that moving would be a bad idea. "I have an idea. How about you look the other way while I jump out the nearest window?"

"I have an idea. How about I hold you here while my colleagues come up the stairs, and this time, we make sure you don't get away?" His smirk turned dark around the edges, transitioning from an implied threat to a very real one. "We want to take you home alive. But 'alive' doesn't mean the same thing as 'intact,' and you'll do a lot less running away without feet."

"Mutilation? Really? That's where you're going with this? I guess you people have stopped thinking of yourselves as the good guys." I glanced around while I spoke, looking for something I could use as an escape route. There were windows on the wall, no more than twenty feet away. All I had to do was reach the windows, and I'd be scot-free.

I made my decision in that moment. Maybe it wasn't the bravest decision I could have made, but it was the only one that made sense. If the Covenant took me back to Europe, I'd tell them everything, and I'd be lucky if they killed me when they were done. No matter what else happened, I couldn't leave this warehouse in their custody. I gathered what little strength I had left, saying one more silent prayer to whoever might be listening, and launched myself at Peter.

He shouted something that I didn't quite make out, distracted as I was by the sound of the gun in his hand going off at the same time. A sharp pain punched through my stomach, sending duller shock waves through the rest of me. I did my best to ignore it. I had more important things to worry about, like yanking the knife off my bicep—cutting the shoelaces I'd been using to hold it there in the process—and jamming it into his shoulder as my momentum carried me into him. It wasn't a fatal wound, but it distracted him for a few precious seconds as he shouted, grabbing at the blade. I grabbed the sides of his head, breathing in to steady myself.

He had time to give me one last, utterly stunned look before I was twisting hard to the left, turning his face away from me. There was a sharp snapping sound, and then he was collapsing, the dead weight of his body pulling him out of my hands. He took the knife down with him. I didn't try to retrieve it.

I did scramble to grab my gun from his suddenly limp fingers, clamping one hand over the hole in my stomach to keep anything I needed from sliding out. It was a relatively small hole, thank God; if I'd been packing something with a larger caliber, I'd probably already be dead. As it was, the gut wound would definitely kill me if I didn't get it taken care of fast, but for the moment, it was definitely a distraction from the pain in my feet. Maybe I'd get *really* lucky, and shock would set in.

Maybe not.

Robert and Margaret must have heard the gunshot. I didn't know where the door was, or whether it even had a lock, so I didn't bother looking; I just turned and started half-running, half-limping toward the nearest window. I'd shoot it out if I had to. I'd do whatever it took to get out of this damn building. I'd die in the open air. If that was the closest I could get to a happy ending, then so be it. It was better than the alternative.

The door banged open when I was still only halfway there, accompanied by the sound of running footsteps. "Freeze!" snarled Robert.

I didn't freeze. What was the worst thing he could do, shoot me? I was losing blood fast, and the room was starting to go dark around the edges. One more gunshot wouldn't do anything but finish the job. As long as he couldn't take me alive, I won.

"No," said Margaret. Her tone was different, much more anxious . . . and her accent was gone. She sounded American. "You freeze."

"Margaret?" Robert, on the other hand, sounded utterly puzzled. The footsteps stopped. Thank God. "What are you doing?"

"I'm holding a gun to your head," said Margaret reasonably. No—not Margaret. It was Margaret's voice, but it wasn't Margaret speaking. The tones and accent were all wrong. "Verity? Stop running. I don't know how long I can hold her."

I stopped running. I was so tired I could barely breathe. I still managed to turn and smile wanly at the scene behind me: Margaret Healy, the woman who'd lost her anti-telepathy charm, holding a gun against the temple of Robert Bullard.

"Hello, Sarah," I said.

Sarah contorted Margaret Healy's lips into a wan smile. "You know, if you were bored, we could have gone to the ballet or something." Servitors appeared from behind her, making their serpentine way into the room. Robert's eyes tracked them, his expression never changing.

"I'll keep that in mind for next time." I raised the gun I'd reclaimed from Peter Brandt, aiming it squarely at Robert's chest. My hand was shaking so badly that I was afraid I'd miss my target, something I hadn't needed to worry about since elementary school. I removed my other hand from my stomach, using it to steady my elbow.

Margaret—Sarah—gasped. "Verity, you're *hurt*."

"Yeah, single gunshot wound to the abdomen. It hurts like a bitch and I'm losing a lot of blood here, so if you're not the only member of the cavalry, this would be a great time to bring in reinforcements." The servitors were good for looking intimidating, but without a dragon to give them orders, they weren't going to be good for much beyond that. I didn't know why she didn't have a dragon with her, and I didn't have time to worry about it. Spots were starting to appear around the edges of my vision.

"You're going to die here," said Robert. He sounded surprisingly calm, considering the situation he was in. "All of you. And you, witch, wherever you are, we'll find you. You'll pay for what you've done."

It took me a moment to realize that he was talking to Sarah. I actually laughed a little, snorting indelicately through my nose. "Oh, dude. She's not a witch. Witches are *way* less dangerous."

"Cuckoo to you, too," said Margaret/Sarah, digging the barrel of her gun a little deeper into Robert's temple. "Verity, can you walk?"

"I don't really know." Honesty is sometimes the best policy. "I do know I wouldn't get very far if I tried. So I'm sort of opposed to trying."

"Verity!" She sounded genuinely upset. No real surprise there. "I can't hold her for much longer. She's *fighting* me!"

"I didn't know you could hold someone like this at all. It's a new trick for you."

"It was Kitty's idea." Margaret/Sarah's face contorted like she'd been punched. "She's fighting me *hard*, Very. Come on. We have to get you out of here before I lose her. Please."

"Yes, do run," said Robert. "You've killed one of us already. You've shown us where our weaknesses are. We'll find you. And when we do, you'll wish to God that you'd let us take you here and now. Or you could surrender. Let us treat your wounds, tell us where to find your witch, and submit to the mercy of the Covenant."

"I wasn't aware that we were in the business of mercy," said Margaret, all cold fury and hate. Her voice was her own again, all traces of Sarah gone as she pulled her gun away from Robert's temple and swung it toward me. I widened my stance, trying to cover both of them at once. It wasn't going to work, and I knew it. From the satisfied gleam in her eyes, so did she. "You've befouled my mind, you little bitch. Do you know what that means?"

"It means you lose," said Uncle Mike, stepping through the doorway behind her and aiming his crossbow at the back of her head. Istas was only half a step behind him, deceptively sweet-looking in a little pink pinafore. Her hair was pulled into girlish pigtails and tied off with white bows. She was smiling. That's never a good sign with Istas.

"You're outnumbered," I said, with as much bravado as I could muster. "Drop your weapons. I promise we'll be more fair to you than you were going to be to me."

"No," said Margaret, and cocked back the hammer on her gun—

—only to freeze as Istas calmly reached forward and fastened one rapidly expanding hand (already better classed as "a paw") over the gun, completely engulfing both it and Margaret's hand. "You may fire," said Istas, as if she were conferring some great favor. "I will remove your entire arm a moment later, but you may fire."

"I'd really rather she didn't," I said. The black spots were spreading. I teetered, catching myself at the last minute, and kept aiming my gun at Robert. "We have to . . . we gotta . . . this has to end. They can't walk away from this."

"But we can't kill them, either," said Dominic. He appeared in the doorway behind Uncle Mike. His face was set in a blank, expressionless mask. It didn't waver as he looked past the heads of the Covenant agents to me, filthy, naked, and bleeding all over the warehouse floor. "If we kill them, the Covenant sends more."

"We win," said Robert.

Istas squeezed Margaret's hand. Margaret yelped, unable to help herself. "I am not so sure of that," said Istas. "There is a difference between 'living' and 'retaining all your limbs.'"

"They can't leave," said Uncle Mike. "They know who Verity is. It's not safe to let them go."

"So they can't live and they can't die." It was taking everything I had just to keep myself upright. "Oh, and here's one more for you: Dominic can't stay here if we send them home. They'd never forgive another defection." There was no way to win. There was no way to get out of this with everyone still standing.

"No. But they might be willing to bury a traitor." Dominic stepped around his former colleagues and crossed to where I was standing. He took the gun from my hand, aiming it at Robert as he slid an arm around my waist, holding me up. I let myself sag into him.

Then I realized what he'd just said. "What? No! No. We're not going to kill you." I wanted to pull away and glare at him. I didn't have the strength.

"I wasn't going to ask you to," said Dominic. "Sarah?"

"I'm here." Sarah stepped up behind Uncle Mike, moving into the room on silent feet. "Istas, let go of Margaret's hands. Robert's anti-telepathy charm is attached to his medal of St. George. Take it off him."

"Yes," said Istas. She released Margaret—although she didn't release Margaret's gun, and from the way Margaret groaned as Istas yanked it away, she broke at least one of Margaret's fingers in the process—and turned toward Robert. To his credit, he didn't flinch when Istas reached for his throat with her vast, taloned paw. The chain on his medal snapped easily when she pulled on it. Istas looked at the medal curiously for a moment, then shrugged and tucked it into the neckline of her dress.

"Sarah . . ." I said.

"It's all right, Verity." She smiled at me, uncertainly. "I can do this."

"I don't know . . ."

"We have no choice," said Dominic softly. He tightened his arm around me. "They have to live. I have to die. I can't let them endanger you, or your family. This is the only way."

"But Sarah . . ."

"Trust her," said Dominic.

I closed my eyes. "Okay."

Cuckoos are natural memory manipulators. It's part of how their power works. They fit into the world without leaving a seam, and that means they have to insert themselves, retroactively, into the lives of every person they meet. It's an autonomic function most of the time, something that just happens around them, as easy and as natural as breathing. Sarah spent her days working to keep that very thing from happening; she wanted to be known and cared about for who she really was, and not because everyone she met decided that she was their long-lost sister, daughter, or best friend from college.

Even autonomic functions can become intentional, if you're willing to work for it. I opened my eyes to see Sarah standing in front of Margaret and Robert, her eyes glowing such a brilliant white that it actually chased the black spots away from the edges of my vision. Margaret looked terrified. Robert looked resigned, like this was the fate he had been preparing himself for since the day he reached American soil.

"You'll pay," he said, in a calm, quiet tone. "We found you once, and we can find you again. Eventually, your whole stinking family will have to pay for your crimes against the Covenant, and against humanity."

"Maybe that's true," I said, letting myself slump against Dominic. "But you know what? You won't be the ones to come looking for us."

"Hold them up," said Sarah. I think I'm the only one who heard the tremor in her voice.

Istas grabbed Robert while Uncle Mike lowered his crossbow and grabbed Margaret. Sarah reached out and touched their foreheads, making skin contact. Skin contact always made it easier for her. The Covenant agents went limp.

That seemed like a good idea. I couldn't feel my feet anymore, and I was so tired. I stopped fighting to keep myself upright at all. Staying awake and on my feet didn't matter. We'd done it. The Covenant didn't know— wouldn't know—that the family survived. There would be no purge of Manhattan. We'd won, and that meant that I could rest.

The last thing I heard was Dominic shouting my name. Then there was nothing but the white glare from Sarah's eyes, chasing away the shadows, and I fell into the light . . .

. . . only to fall back out again as Dominic shoved me away, grabbing the gun from my hand in the same motion *(didn't he already have my gun? Something was wrong, and I couldn't tell what it was anymore . . .).* Sarah was on the floor, clear fluid leaking from a hole at the center of her forehead, and Margaret was somehow free, her own gun aimed at Dominic's chest. "Traitor!" she shouted, and fired.

For some reason, the servitors were gone. For some reason, nothing moved to stop her when she pulled the trigger. Something should have stopped her. Instead, Dominic staggered back, making a sharp barking noise as the bullet slammed through his collarbone. Then he raised my gun and fired three times, aiming for Margaret, who ducked easily out of the way. One bullet went into Uncle Mike. The other two went into Istas. I knew from past experience that two bullets weren't going to do much but slow her down.

Slowing her down was more than enough. The force of the bullets knocked her backward and allowed Robert to break free. He spun around, pulling a knife from his belt, and drove it into her throat. Istas keened like a wounded animal, and fell. And all this before I could hit the floor.

I landed hard, my head bouncing off the wood before I managed to catch myself. I raised my head, squinting, in time to see Margaret shoot Dominic again. This time, her aim was better, befitting a Healy girl: she grouped her shots at the center of his chest, three holes appearing in the fabric of his shirt. He looked surprised. Then he fell, too.

(This is wrong, this is wrong, we don't lose like this, this is wrong *. . .)*

I tried to scream, but the air wasn't there. Margaret smiled as she turned toward me, raised her gun, and pulled the trigger again.

And then there was nothing at all.

Twenty-four

"Don't you dare leave me, baby girl. There's been enough dying. Mind your momma, now, and stay."

— Frances Brown

Waking up in an unknown location—but at least it isn't a warehouse somewhere in Manhattan, being held captive by the Covenant of St. George, which makes it a definite improvement (also, not dead)

"NOTHING" LOOKED a lot like the glaring white of an active cuckoo's eyes. I opened my eyes. The unrelenting whiteness didn't go away, although it did change forms, becoming the overhead lights which were shining directly down into my face. I groaned and tried to block the light with my arm, only to discover that the various tubes connected to my body made that impossible.

They don't usually connect tubes to dead people. Not unless they're preparing them for embalming, and this wasn't a funeral home. It didn't smell right for that. I blinked, abandoning my efforts to cover my face. The glare got a little more manageable as my eyes adjusted. Only a little, though. I blinked again, finally settling for squinting through my eyelashes as I tried to get a handle on where, exactly, I was—other than "not dead."

The memory of being shot the first time, by Peter, was still very vivid and real. The memory of being shot the second time, by Margaret, was already fading like a bad dream. "Dammit, Sarah," I muttered, and twisted in the bed enough to look around.

It was a small room, with walls painted a cheery shade of eggshell blue and trimmed in even cheerier yellow. Various machines beeped quietly to themselves, monitoring my vital signs. I followed one of the tubes in my arm up to an IV stand, where a bag of clear liquid was presumably responsible for keeping me hydrated. That also explained the weird pinching sensation at my groin; I'd been out for long enough that they'd needed to catheterize me to keep me from wetting the bed. Always the sort of thing a girl wants to wake up to.

On the plus side, nothing hurt. Maybe that meant that I was flying on morphine, but at the moment, I'd take it. It was better than the alternative. Better still would be having some vague idea of where I was. I started looking around for something that looked like a call button.

I was still looking when I heard footsteps. I turned to see Dominic standing in the room's doorway, white as a sheet and holding onto the lintel for balance. "You are an *insufferable* woman," he said, barely above a whisper. "You slept for three days, and then you simply had to wake up during the five minutes that I was out of the room, didn't you?"

My heart leaped, even as my lungs gave up working to pull air into my body. "Hi," I managed, forcing the word out despite my lack of oxygen. That was enough to get my lungs working again, at least. "You're okay. Are you okay? You're okay." I was babbling. I didn't care. Just seeing him, alive and standing on his own two feet, was more than enough. I half-remembered him dying, bleeding out on the warehouse floor, and—

—and—

—and that had never happened. The memory was shredding like a cobweb even as I tried to look at it. I shuddered all over, trying to wipe the false events out of my mind. "Whoa," I said. My voice quavered. I hated it for that. "I thought I was protected by that anti-telepathy charm."

"It turns out that when your cousin really, ah, 'turns

on the juice,' she punches rather harder than any of us suspected she was capable of," said Dominic, as he came to stand by the side of my bed. "Even Istas—who claims to possess a natural resistance to Sarah's manipulations—got somewhat confused about what had actually happened, which could have been rather unpleasant, as it seems that she dislikes zombies. Strongly. And when she saw me up and moving about, despite having seen me 'die,' she was sure I was a zombie. I very nearly found myself put down as a menace to the public health."

I laughed at that. I couldn't help myself. It was a small, strained thing, but it still made Dominic smile.

"I didn't think the irony would be lost on you," he said. "The former cryptid hunter, killed by a cryptid, *as* a cryptid. You would doubtless have been disappointed that you'd missed it."

My laughter died. "No, I wouldn't have been disappointed," I said. "I already saw you die once today."

"Ah, yes. I was spared the strain of seeing you shot down; I fell first, after all." Dominic walked over to the bed, where he sat down gingerly on the very edge of the mattress. "Your Uncle Mike informs me that Sarah put together a thoroughly rational and believable scenario."

"Peter?" I asked.

"According to the memories she gave them, I killed him myself, when I broke in looking for my false 'Price girl.' You were a cocktail waitress that I was cultivating to look like an enemy of the Covenant, so that I could rally the cryptids of Manhattan to my side." He leaned over and pressed a kiss against my forehead. "Even when you're not allowed to be a true representative of your family, you're dangerous."

"Yeah, well." I sniffled. It was getting hard to keep from crying. "I guess some things never change."

"No, I guess they don't."

"But why would you—?"

"Turn traitor? It's happened before, Verity, and it will happen again. Bogeymen and dragons offering wealth and knowledge, succubi and Oceanids offering love . . . it happens. Most traitors simply die quickly. Few are as successful as your family at thwarting us." He paused, grimacing. "Thwarting the Covenant. I suppose I need to adjust my thinking."

There was nothing I could say to that. Leaving the only place he'd ever called his own was still a raw wound in his voice; any words of comfort would have just been salt rubbed into it.

Dominic sighed, and continued, "I killed Peter, and Margaret killed us both, while Robert took out our allies. As for the bodies, there was an unfortunate collision between a stray bullet and a gas pipe, and the warehouse was lost. All remains were destroyed."

I closed my eyes. "That's convenient."

"True. But they both believe it with all their hearts." I felt his fingers on my forehead, brushing back my hair. "They'll return to England and give their report to the Covenant. By the time another team can be dispatched, the cryptids of the city will be ready to disappear as if they'd never existed."

"The dragons can't move."

"The Covenant still believes dragons to be extinct, and dragon princesses are on the books as too difficult to tell from humans to be worth hunting. They're to be killed if encountered, but a waste of resources to search for unless the coffers are getting low." Dominic stroked my hair back again. "Manhattan will be safe. Margaret and Robert uncovered a conspiracy by one of their own. All the trainees and journeymen will be kept under closer attention for a while; I doubt they'll be sending anyone any time soon."

"Wait." I opened my eyes, staring up at him. "They really believe you're dead."

"Yes. And as they were the target of your fair cousin's 'whammy,' they're going to keep believing it." Dominic grimaced. "Remind me never to make her angry."

"Smart man." I looked around the room again. "Where am I?"

"In the recovery ward of St. Giles' Hospital," said a familiar, if unexpected, female voice. "Welcome back to the land of the living, Very-Very."

"Grandma?" Eyes wide, I turned toward the voice. "Grandma!"

The black-haired, blue-eyed woman standing in the doorway smiled. "Hello, sweetheart. How are you feeling?"

"Surprisingly good, given the whole 'shot in the gut and lost consciousness' thing and— Grandma! What are you doing here?" I glanced to Dominic. "Have you met my grandmother?"

"Yes." Dominic stood, offering a nod to my grandmother. "Ma'am."

"Dominic," she said.

He looked back to me. "I'm going to let Mike and Ryan know that you're awake. Please. I know you're a madwoman, but try to stay still and take it easy." He pressed a kiss to my forehead before turning and leaving the room before I could react. Grandma Angela stepped aside to let him pass.

Once he was gone, she stepped fully into the room, pausing to close the door behind herself, and started walking toward my bed. "I'm glad you're awake."

"So am I."

Angela Baker is my mother's mother, and we're not related by blood: Mom was adopted, since Grandma wasn't willing to spend enough time with a member of her own species to have a biological child. She looks more like Sarah than anyone else in the family, with pale skin, black hair, and improbably blue eyes that sometimes go white around the edges. She's old enough to be my mother's mother by birth, not just adoption, but she looks like she's barely Mom's age. I have long since resigned myself to the fact that I won't look nearly as good as either of my grandmothers when I'm their age, since Grandma Alice spends most of her time in dimensions where time runs differently, and Grandma Angela isn't human.

She adopted Mom because cuckoos can only have children with other cuckoos, and—like all sane individuals—Grandma hates pretty much every cuckoo she's ever met. She adopted Sarah because Sarah was just a little girl who needed a home, and she wanted to find out whether cuckoos were really innately sociopathic.

I looked at her face, so grim, so serious, and felt a chill run down my spine. Maybe she was here because we finally had the answer. "Grandma," I said. "What are you doing here?"

"Mike called me once they managed to get you and Sarah both here and stabilized," said Grandma. She pulled a chair from against the wall closer to the bed, sitting down in it. "It was pretty touch and go for the first twenty-four hours.

I bit my lip. "How bad?"

"Your doctor will tell you exactly what the bullet perforated that wasn't supposed to be perforated, and all those other nasty things. All I know is that if you didn't have a Caladrius working on you, you probably wouldn't have lived. *Please* don't get shot like that again. I don't think my heart could take it." She smiled weakly at her own joke. Cuckoos don't have hearts. Their circulatory systems are entirely decentralized, controlled by micropulses of muscles throughout the body.

Cryptid humor is weird sometimes. "Why didn't Uncle Mike call Mom and Dad?"

"He did, but I was the only family member who could get here before you were out of surgery . . . and given the circumstances, I was the only one for the job."

The Bakers lived in Columbus, Ohio, the same city where my brother was doing his research project on basilisk breeding. I frowned. "Is Alex here?"

"No. I couldn't reach him when the call first came, and I told him he didn't need to come once we were sure that you were going to live." Her smile was fleeting, and strained. "I didn't see any point in filling this hospital with anxious relatives before we had to. Not when Mike and I are already filling that role, and your various cryptid friends are coming and going at all hours."

She wasn't mentioning Sarah. The chill intensified. "Grandma, what aren't you telling me?"

She took a deep breath. When she let it out, she

seemed smaller somehow, like she had deflated. "Verity, it's important you understand that I am not angry with you. I'm not angry with *any* of you. You were in an impossible situation, and it was a choice between doing . . . what you did . . . and endangering the whole family. I might have done the same thing, if I were in your position. Sarah made her own choices."

Alarm bells were ringing in my head. I sat up a little straighter. "Where's Sarah?"

"She's asleep." Grandma's lips thinned into a hard line. "She's been asleep since I got here. I made her sleep, because it was the only way to make her stop screaming."

"Oh, God," I whispered, slumping against the pillows. "Is she going to be okay?"

"I'll be honest with you, Verity: I don't know. I don't have any way of knowing. Cuckoo psychology is such a strange thing, and Sarah didn't start out like me."

I swallowed hard, looking at her as levelly as I could. "You mean Sarah didn't start out knowing right from wrong."

Grandma didn't say anything.

By human standards, cuckoos are born sociopathic. They get it from their mothers. Literally: when a telepathic sociopath carries a baby for nine months, that baby is going to be born with a radically skewed moral compass. Grandma Angela was born "normal" by human standards, because she's not a receptive telepath. So she didn't get the in-utero conditioning to teach her that other people existed only to be pawns and playthings. Sarah, on the other hand . . . did. Grandma adopted her when she was seven years old, after her human foster parents died, and spent years after that carefully removing the deep conditioning Sarah had received from her biological mother.

Sarah is a sweet, thoughtful, empathic person. She didn't start out that way. And there was no way of knowing whether Grandma had managed to get all the little mental land mines out of Sarah's head. That was a large part of why Sarah always arranged to audit courses at schools near one of her cousins. If she ever went back to her cuckoo roots, she wanted one of us close enough to kill her before she did too much damage.

My mouth was suddenly dry. I swallowed several times before I managed to ask, "Is there anything I can do?"

"What she did . . ." Grandma shook her head. "I couldn't do that if I wanted to. If you'd asked me, I would have told you it wasn't possible. But she managed it, and now she won't stop screaming. She hurt herself, Verity. She hurt herself very badly. Not in a physical way, although that would have been easier. Somewhere inside her mind."

"Like pulling a muscle?" I ventured.

"Something like that." Grandma sighed, very briefly looking every one of her years. She reached over and patted my hand. "I'm glad you're all right. And I truly don't blame any of you for what happened. But Sarah's going back to Ohio with me, and I don't know how long it's going to take her to recover."

Or if she was going to recover. Grandma didn't say that part; she didn't need to. It was written in the tension of her mouth and the defeated slant of her shoulders. "I'm sorry," I whispered.

"Don't be sorry. Just get better." Grandma leaned forward and hugged me tight. "You had us all scared, Very-Very, and you know Sarah wouldn't have done it if she didn't love you more than anything."

"I know," I said, and returned the hug as best I could with the tubes sticking out of my arms. "If there's anything I can do . . ."

"Just get better," Grandma repeated, and let go, standing. "I don't want to tire you out. You're supposed to be still recovering."

"Okay." I sighed, sagging deeper into the mattress. "I love you, Grandma."

"I love you, too, Very-Very." She leaned in and tapped me gently on the forehead. "Now get some rest."

Grandma wasn't a receptive telepath, but that didn't mean she couldn't push. I was asleep almost before I felt myself getting tired, and I didn't hear her leave the room.

I awoke to the sound of cheering.

"HAIL THE RESURRECTION OF THE ARBO-REAL PRIESTESS!"

Normally, waking up to the mice will elicit a groan and maybe a flung pillow. This time, I just smiled and said, without opening my eyes, "Amen."

The mice went nuts, shouting hosannas and praising the hospital room, the bed, the pillows, and everything else they could think of to high Heaven. One enterprising acolyte even began praising my bedhead, calling it "the tousled proof of our glorious Priestess' trials." I'd have to remember that one the next time there wasn't enough mousse in the world.

Next to the bed, Uncle Mike snorted and said, "You know, they're not going to shut up for like a week."

"I'm looking forward to it." I opened my eyes and turned to face him, a process that was greatly simplified by the fact that most of the tubes—and the catheter—had been removed while I was sleeping. "Hi, Uncle Mike."

"Hi, Very-girl. You planning to stay awake for a little while this time?"

"That's not fair," I protested. "Grandma knocked me out before."

"Because you needed it. If you're awake, you don't need it anymore. The doctor says you're just about fully recovered at this point. I knew you were too stubborn to stay injured for long." Now Uncle Mike smiled, relief underscoring the expression. "You scared the crap out of me, you know."

"HAIL THE FAMILIAL TERROR!" exulted the mice.

"Hey, this is a hospital," I said, sitting up to see the congregation gathered on my bed. There were only about a dozen of them present. It had sounded like more. "Keep it down."

"Yes, Priestess," said one of the mice, sounding abashed. The others cheered. Very softly.

"That's better." I looked back to Uncle Mike. "I didn't exactly sign up to get kidnapped."

"I know, I know." Uncle Mike scowled. "When we got that anti-telepathy charm back, Kitty took it to some hidebehinds for a look-see. They said it had a homing compulsion on it. Once you picked it up, you had to return it to Margaret."

"Well, that's one bit of stupidity explained," I said. "When you say 'got it back,' you mean . . ."

"That you had swallowed it, yes. And no, I'm not the one who had to do the actual retrieval."

"Thank God for small favors," I muttered, before asking, in a normal voice, "How did you find me?"

"Dominic. That boy's crazy about you, you know. He'd better be. The Covenant will never take him back now."

"Good thing I'm crazy about him, too." I tried to say it lightly. I failed. "Uncle Mike, about Sarah . . ."

"She's the one who made sure we kept looking for you, right up until Dominic showed up to help us out," he said. "She's the one who got the dragons looking for you, and it was the dragons who followed the Covenant back to their base and confirmed you were being held in that warehouse. She's the one who transported the mice to the area to survey the ground floor and give us the all clear. Sarah knew what she was doing. I know it's hard for you to believe right now, but she had her eyes wide open through this whole thing. None of it happened to her without her knowing it was a risk, just like you didn't get shot without knowing it was a risk. Am I clear?"

"Crystal." I sighed. "I still feel awful."

"Good. You should feel awful."

I blinked at him. "Way to pep talk, Uncle Mike."

He looked at me implacably. "I'm serious. If a member of your family gets hurt, you feel bad. You figure out why it happened. You make sure it doesn't happen again.

Feeling awful is the first step. Everything after this is up to you."

"Pep talk received," I said.

"Good," said a new voice from the doorway. I turned to see a man in scrubs and a lab coat, with broad white-feathered wings. He was looking at a clipboard. Then he looked up, and smiled. "I'd tell you that mice in a hospital were unhygienic, but as they're Aeslin, I believe we can count them as family members and let this one slide. How are you feeling, Miss Price?"

"Totally better," I said. "Can I get up?"

"Given that your injuries should be completely healed by this point, yes, you may get up whenever you like." He lowered the clipboard. "I'm Dr. Morrow. I've been responsible for your care while you were here."

Recognition sparked. "You're the one who contacted me about the manananggal," I said.

"Yes, and we very much appreciate you taking care of that for us. My mate and head nurse spoke very highly of your handling of that matter, which is why I was willing to take your case. We don't treat many humans at St. Giles'."

"Well, I really appreciate you taking the time to look after me."

"The pleasure was all mine, Miss Price." Dr. Morrow smiled. "I know how much you've done for this city. Thank you."

"You're welcome," I said.

"I brought some clothes for you," said Uncle Mike. "You want me to take the mice so you can get dressed?"

"Please." It wasn't like the mice hadn't seen me naked before—that was sadly unavoidable, no matter how much I might try to avoid it—but I still had standards.

"Thought so." Uncle Mike handed me a folded bundle before standing, making a sweeping motion with his hands. "Come on, you lot. There's cheese and cake in the waiting room."

Cheering and hailing his name, the mice scampered from my bed and streamed across the tiled floor, disappearing between Dr. Morrow's bare, vaguely-taloned feet. He watched this with an air of vague discomfort, finally saying, "We don't treat many human patients, but the ones we do treat rarely come with their own traveling biosphere."

"My family is special," I said, with a smile.

"I'm getting that idea. Please don't leave without speaking to me, Miss Price." With that, the doctor stepped out of my hospital room. Uncle Mike paused long enough to kiss my cheek, and then he was gone as well, shutting the door behind himself.

I waited a few minutes to be sure that no one was going to come barging in before I stretched slowly and folded back the covers, finally moving into a full sitting position. I was wearing one of those pale green hospital gowns. It was almost a relief to realize that those were just as much standard issue in cryptid hospitals as they were in human ones. I took a breath, steeling myself, and pulled the gown up to get a look at my stomach where Peter had shot me.

Dr. Morrow was telling the truth: the gunshot wound was gone, and while the skin there was slightly paler than the skin around it, there was no scar. I touched it lightly with the tips of my fingers, feeling the first tears wet my cheeks. I was going to be okay. I was going to be better than okay, in fact. And that meant that whatever came next, it was going to be something that I needed to deal with.

Uncle Mike had chosen well, where clothes were concerned: he brought jeans, a tank top, a flannel shirt, my loosest hip holster, and a brace of throwing knives for me to hide wherever it would make me most comfortable. For shoes, he had a pair of broken-in trainers and some thick wool socks. By the time I had the last of the knives secured inside my clothes, I felt almost like myself again.

I tried to hold onto that feeling as I walked to the door, opened it, and stepped out into the hall. Remembering the promise Uncle Mike had made to the mice, I paused for a moment to listen before making my way toward the sound of cheering.

When I reached the waiting room, there was a full-scale dance number going in the middle of the floor, with the mice literally waltzing around with their slices of cake and chunks of cheese. Uncle Mike was watching with detached amusement; Ryan and Istas with something approaching awe. Dominic wasn't watching at all. He was staring fixedly at the hall, waiting for me to appear. He straightened as I came into view, and by the time I reached the doorway, he was standing, stepping around dancing mice as he made his way toward me.

Ryan turned to see where Dominic was going, and his face split in a wide smile. "Verity. You're up and moving again."

"I am," I agreed. "Hey, Istas."

"The mice are performing a dance of thanks," she informed me, frowning. "You should observe the mice."

"All right," I said. I let Dominic gather me into his arms and leaned up against him, my shoulders to his chest, as we stood and observed the mice. Istas clapped her hands, happy as I'd ever seen her, while Ryan looked tolerantly on. Uncle Mike caught my eye and smiled. This was it, then. This was my life. Since it was going to continue, I might as well get used to it.

There are worse fates.

Twenty-five

"Family, faith, and knives. Those are the things that last in this world. Everything else is essentially extra."

—Evelyn Baker

St. Giles' Hospital, an establishment for the care of cryptids

THERE WAS ONE THING I had to do before I could leave the hospital. Everyone knew I had to do it. And so when I said that I was going to go and talk to the doctor, they all let me go. Even Dominic. Even the mice.

There are some things that we have to do alone.

Grandma Angela was sitting next to Sarah's bed when I came into the room. She looked up at the sound of my footsteps, and smiled. "Hello, Very-Very," she said, making no effort to be quiet. There was no reason for it. Sarah was deeply unconscious, and from the slow, shallow rise and fall of her chest, she was at no risk of waking up. She was dressed in a pale green hospital gown, just like I'd been. She was flat on her back, like a princess in a bad Disney remake of some ancient fairy tale. Only it was going to take more than a kiss to wake her up.

"Hi, Grandma," I said, walking over to the bedside. "How's she doing?"

"Asleep, mostly, but I think she's getting better, a little bit at a time. It can be hard to tell, since I can't pick up what she's projecting." Grandma reached over and smoothed Sarah's hair back from her forehead.

I swallowed hard. "Are you shielding the rest of us right now?"

"Yes." Grandma nodded. "I didn't want to risk it being something that wasn't . . . well. That wouldn't go over well."

"But it could be important. Maybe we need to know." I stood a little straighter. "Can you unshield me? Just long enough for me to tell you what she's projecting at the rest of us?"

Grandma looked unsure. "Verity . . ."

"Please. This is partially my responsibility, even if it's not my fault, and I've had Sarah screaming in my head before. I'm a big girl. I can take it."

"If you're sure . . ."

"Will it help?"

Very slowly, Grandma nodded. "I think it will, yes."

"Then do it."

"All right." She looked at me gravely. The edges of her irises went white, the lack of color spreading into the blue like frost—and just like that, the static buzz of "telepath nearby" returned, Sarah's presence once more making itself known to my mind. I hadn't realized how much I'd missed it until I finally had it back again.

Then her thoughts came flooding in, hot on the heels of the static. There were no words: just an emotional slurry of images and feelings and panicked reactions. I staggered, eyes going wide. Grandma half-stood, and I gestured for her to sit back down as I braced myself and started trying to sort through what I was receiving. It wasn't easy.

"She's scared," I said finally. "She doesn't know how she did what she did, she doesn't know whether it's something she should have been able to do. She volunteered, but she didn't think it would be quite that easy, or quite that strong. So she's scared. And she's afraid that because it was easy, it's going to be something she wants to do again. Like this is something she'll just *do* now." *But you won't,* I thought fiercely. *Sarah, do you hear me?*

You won't do anything like that unless you don't have any other choice, because you're one of the best people I know, and good people just don't do *that kind of thing. So don't be scared of something that's never going to happen. That's just silly.*

There was a brief pause in the overwhelming flood of guilt. I didn't know for sure whether that meant she'd heard me, but I still took it as a good sign.

"What else?" asked Grandma.

"She really did hurt herself. It was easy, but it was a strain at the same time, like those people who get hopped-up on adrenaline and throw cars around. She's afraid to be awake, because if she's awake, she might manipulate people just to avoid straining herself further."

Grandma nodded. "That's what I was afraid of. Well, we can keep her out long enough to get her home, where there's nobody she can do that to." Grandma didn't receive; Grandpa was a Revenant, and having died once, he was basically immune to telepathic influences. My Uncle Billy might have had more issues, but he wasn't living at home at the moment, and he could stay away while Sarah recovered.

"She's going to get better, right?" I bit my lip as I waited for her answer.

To my deep relief, Grandma nodded. "If she's projecting clearly enough that you can hear her, but not so strongly that she's knocking you unconscious, then yes, I think there's a very good chance that she's going to get better."

"Good." I looked sternly at Sarah's still, pale form. "You hear that? You're going to be fine. And if you're not, I'm going to kick your ass." *I mean that. Whether you can hear me or not, I mean it.*

"You're a good cousin, Very-Very," said Grandma.

"I'm a terrible cousin who leads Sarah into the path of danger because I think she needs to get out more," I said. "I'm also a terrible granddaughter."

Grandma blinked. "Oh? How's that?"

"I'm going to let you be the one who tells Artie."

Much to my relief, she laughed. "Oh, you *are* a terrible

granddaughter." She paused. "There is one thing you could do to make it up to me."

"Name it."

"Can you watch Sarah while I go and get myself something to eat? I haven't wanted to leave her unattended for long, but it seems to me that you have a pretty good handle on things."

I smiled. Grandma might not be a receptive telepath, but she knows how to read people, and she knew that I wanted some time with Sarah alone. "Take as long as you need," I said.

Grandma hugged me before she left the room. I took her seat next to Sarah's bed, reaching over to take Sarah's hand in mine. Her skin was cool, but no more than usual. Cuckoos run a little cold compared to humans.

"Hey, Sarah," I said, trying to mentally project the words as I said them. I wanted her to hear me with her ears, as well as with her mind. "I just wanted to say thank you. I mean, you saved my ass back there. If you hadn't shown up when you did ... well, this would be a really different scene, and I don't make nearly as good of a Sleeping Beauty as you do. Not that you're a Sleeping Beauty. More of a Snow White, with your coloring. Too bad Artie isn't here. He could kiss you awake. You'd like that, wouldn't you?"

Silence from Sarah. There was no change in the mix of thoughts and emotions rolling off of her.

I sighed. "I know you're feeling pretty rotten right now, but seriously, you found the best solution. You found the answer where everybody walked away. How many cuckoos would have done that? Most of them would have just reached for the matches and watched the whole thing burn. You did the right thing. You did the *best* thing. You did the thing that saved the most lives, and that's why I love you."

Silence from Sarah ... but I thought, for just a second, that I felt her fingers tighten on mine.

I closed my eyes. "So Grandma says that you get to go back to Ohio for a little while. You like it there, right? You'll have all your books, and you can pick up your comics from the comic book store for the first time in like, a year. Lots of spandex drama for you to catch up on. Speaking of drama, you realize we're stuck with Dominic now, right? The Covenant won't be coming back for him . . ."

I talked until I ran out of words, and then I just sat there and held her hand, "listening" to the mixture of thoughts and images that came pouring off her. This, too, was a part of my life; remembering that everything costs, and sometimes, what it costs is more than we want to pay. But we pay anyway, because that's the right thing to do. Sarah would get better. She had to.

I was still sitting there, holding Sarah's hand, when Grandma came back into the room. She came and stood next to me, putting her hand on my shoulder, and the three of us stayed that way for quite some time.

Epilogue

"Any ending where you're still standing on
your own feet is a happy one."
— Alice Healy

A semilegal sublet in Greenwich Village

Three days later

WITH THE COVENANT out of Manhattan, it was safe to
return to my apartment ... and with the apartment's actual owner returning from her year-long sab-
batical at the end of the month, it was also time to start
packing my things. It was time for me to go home.

Uncle Mike was already on the way back to Chicago.
He'd taken Grandma Baker and Sarah with him when he
left, promising to drop them in Columbus, where
Grandma would be able to focus on nursing Sarah back
to a reasonable facsimile of normal. Sarah was still
asleep when they left. As far as I knew, Grandma was
planning to keep her that way all the way home. I didn't
question it. She knew better than I did what was safe for
cuckoo biology.

Kitty had accepted my resignation with a minimum of
argument once I explained that I was leaving the city.
New York was too dangerous for me, at least for a little
while. My parents and I were both right when we said
that my time in Manhattan would determine my future.
I was just wrong when I said that my future was going to
be in ballroom dance. That was a good world. It was one

that I enjoyed visiting, and would probably be a part of for the rest of my life. But it wasn't *my* world.

I was a Price. I was a cryptozoologist. I needed to accept that, with all the good things and bad things that it included, and that meant that I needed to focus on my training. If I was going to be a serious cryptozoologist, I needed to get better. I needed to make sure that I would never be caught flat-footed again. It was time to approach my real calling the way I had always approached dance: with total dedication, and my whole heart.

Well. Most of my heart, anyway. I could save a few bits out for special purposes.

The mice scurried around my feet, carrying small items and articles of my clothing to the appropriate boxes. The Sacred Ritual of Packing All the Crap was one that they knew well, and they were surprisingly good at not getting stepped on.

I was packing my collection of perfume bottles filled with holy water in sheets of eggcup foam when there was a knock at the front door. I straightened. I'd been waiting for that knock all day, but my hands still shook when I heard it. Slowly, I walked to the door, and called, "Who is it?"

"Let me *in*, you infuriating woman," said Dominic.

Smiling, I undid the locks and opened the door.

Dominic De Luca was standing in the hall, wearing his oh-so-classic black duster, holding a paper sack of what smelled like fried chicken in one hand. He held it up. "I thought you might be hungry."

"Starving," I said, and stepped to the side. "Come in."

He did, stepping past me before turning to look in my direction. "Verity—"

"I would have called, but I didn't have your number." I closed and locked the door. "That's going to have to change, you know. You can't be the mysterious disappearing boy anymore if we're going to do this thing."

"Do what?" he asked. There was a hopeful note in his voice that told me I was doing the right thing. I'd already been almost sure, but it was still nice to hear it confirmed.

I turned to offer him a shrug and a smile. "I'm leaving

for Oregon in the morning. Renting a U-Haul and everything, since I can't exactly ship the mice across the country via FedEx, and it would be nice to have a little time to just drive. I thought you might want to come with me. There's a lot more to America than New York, you know."

"You would want me to come with you?"

This was it, then: this was the moment of truth, for both of us. I reached out and carefully took the bag of chicken from his hand. He let it go without resistance, and didn't look in the least bit surprised when I chucked it into the kitchen. A river of mice followed the bag, cheering. I stepped closer to him, closing the distance between us.

"You said you loved me, before," I said. "Did you mean that?"

"With all my foolish heart," he said.

I put my arms around his shoulders, offering him a very small smile. "Then yes. I want you to come with me. I want you to come to Oregon; I want you to meet my family. You chose me over the Covenant of St. George, so I guess that means I need to show you that you did the right thing."

"Really?"

There was something I hadn't said to him yet, even though he'd said it to me. Realizing that I was doing this all out of order—who invites a guy to come meet their parents before they tell him whether they love him or not?—I leaned in close, and whispered, "I love you."

Dominic didn't say anything. He just tilted his head to close the distance between us and kissed me, hard and desperate. He was shaking. I hadn't realized it until that moment, but so was I. I clung to him, returning his kiss with all the force of my own fear behind it—the fear that I had lost him when the Covenant came and made him choose between us, the fear that I had lost everything when they took me. There was so much fear, but some things are stronger. Like love, and like the knowledge that sometimes, you can win.

The scorching-hot kisses don't hurt, either. Dominic

wrapped his arms tight around my waist, literally lifting me off the ground as he started walking backward down the hall. I pulled my mouth away from his long enough to shout, belatedly, "Food for privacy! Food for privacy!"

The cheering of the mice accompanied us all the way into the bedroom, shutting off only when Dominic kicked the door shut behind us. We could finish packing in the morning and still be on the road by noon. There was a whole country out there for us to cross before we got to Oregon ... and for once, I had a guy I wouldn't need to warn about my family. Maybe I'm naïve, but if that's not a happy ending, then I don't know what is.

Price Family Field Guide to the Cryptids of North America
Updated and Expanded Edition

Aeslin mice (Apodemus sapiens). Sapient, rodentlike cryptids which present as nearly identical to noncryptid field mice. Aeslin mice crave religion, and will attach themselves to "divine figures" selected virtually at random when a new colony is created. They possess perfect recall; each colony maintains a detailed oral history going back to its inception. Origins unknown.

Basilisk (Procompsognathus basilisk). Venomous, feathered saurians approximately the size of a large chicken. This would be bad enough, but thanks to a quirk of evolution, the gaze of a basilisk causes petrification, turning living flesh to stone. Basilisks are not native to North America, but were imported as game animals. By idiots.

Bogeyman (Vestiarium sapiens). The thing in your closet is probably a very pleasant individual who simply has issues with direct sunlight. Probably. Bogeymen are close relatives of the human race; they just happen to be almost purely nocturnal, with excellent night vision, and a fondness for enclosed spaces. They rarely grab the ankles of small children, unless it's funny.

Caladrius (Angelos dhalion). The Caladrius are some of the most skilled healers in or out of the cryptid world, which explains why they were hunted almost to extinction by people seeking miracle cures to incurable illnesses. They are attractive, white-winged humanoids, and are often mistaken for angels. The few Caladrius who have survived into the modern day often run secret hospitals for cryptids and their allies. We owe them our lives. Protect theirs.

Chupacabra (Chupacabra sapiens). True to folklore, chupacabra are bloodsuckers, with stomachs that do not handle solids well. They are also therianthrope shape-shifters, capable of transforming themselves into human form, which explains why they have never been captured. When cornered, most chupacabra will assume their bipedal shape in self-defense.

Dragon (Draconem sapiens). Dragons are essentially winged, fire-breathing dinosaurs the size of Greyhound buses. At least, the males are. The females are attractive humanoids who can blend seamlessly in a crowd of supermodels. Capable of parthenogenetic reproduction, the females outnumber the males twenty to one, and can sustain their population for centuries without outside help. All dragons, male and female, require gold to live, and collect it constantly.

Ghoul (Herophilus sapiens). The ghoul is an obligate carnivore, incapable of digesting any but the simplest vegetable solids, and prefers humans because of their wide selection of dietary nutrients. Most ghouls are carrion eaters. Ghouls can be easily identified by their teeth, which will be shed and replaced repeatedly over the course of a lifetime.

Johrlac (Johrlac psychidolos). Colloquially known as "cuckoos," the Johrlac are telepathic hunters. They appear human, but are internally very different, being cold-blooded and possessing a decentralized circulatory system. This quirk of biology means they can be shot repeatedly in the chest without being killed. Extremely dangerous. All Johrlac are interested in mathematics, sometimes to the point of obsession. Origins unknown; possibly insect in nature.

Lamia (Python lamia). Semi-hominid cryptids with the upper bodies of humans and the lower bodies of snakes. Lamia are members of order synapsedia, the mammal-like reptiles, and are considered responsible for many of the "great snake" sightings of legend. The sightings not attributed to actual great snakes, that is.

Lesser gorgon (Gorgos euryale). One of three known subspecies of gorgon, the lesser gorgon's gaze causes short-term paralysis followed by death in anything under five pounds. The bite of the snakes atop their heads will cause paralysis followed by death in anything smaller than an elephant if not treated with the appropriate antivenin. Lesser gorgons tend to be very polite, especially to people who like snakes.

Madhura (Homo madhurata). Humanoid cryptids with an affinity for sugar in all forms. Vegetarian. Their presence slows the decay of organic matter, and is usually viewed as lucky by everyone except the local dentist. Madhura are very family-oriented, and are rarely found living on their own. Originally from the Indian subcontinent.

Manananggal (Tanggal geminus). If the manananggal is proof of anything, it is that Nature abhors a logical classification system. We're reasonably sure the manananggal are mammals; everything else is anyone's guess. They're hermaphroditic and capable of splitting their upper and lower bodies, although they are a single entity, and killing the lower half kills the upper half as well. They prefer fetal tissue, or the flesh of newborn infants. They are also venomous, as we have recently discovered. Do not engage if you can help it.

Oread (Nymphae silica). Humanoid cryptids with the approximate skin density of granite. Their actual biological composition is unknown, as no one has ever been able to successfully dissect one. Oreads are extremely strong, and can be dangerous when angered. They seem to have evolved independently across the globe; their common name is from the Greek.

Sasquatch (Gigantopithecus sesquac). These massive native denizens of North America have learned to embrace depilatories and mail-order shoe catalogs. A surprising number make their living as Bigfoot hunters (Bigfeet and Sasquatches are close relatives, and enjoy tormenting each other). They are predominantly vegetarian, and enjoy Canadian television.

Tanuki (Nyctereutes sapiens). Therianthrope shapeshifters from Japan, the tanuki are critically endangered due to the efforts of the Covenant. Despite this, they remain friendly, helpful people, with a naturally gregarious nature which makes it virtually impossible for them to avoid human settlements. Tanuki possess three primary forms—human, raccoon dog, and big-ass scary monster. Pray you never see the third form of the tanuki.

Tooth fairy (Pyske dentin). Tooth fairies are small—no taller than the length of a tall man's hand—and possess dual-lobed wings. Their dietary habits are unpleasant, and best left undiscussed. Do not leave unsupervised near children.

Wadjet (Naja wadjet). Once worshiped as gods, these sapient, highly-venomous cobras can reach seventeen feet in length when fully mature. They spend their lives in pair-bonds with human servants who enjoy extended lifespans thanks to the venom of the wadjet, and whose thumbs can come in extremely useful. Given recent discoveries about dragon biology, we are not discounting the possibility that these servants are another form of the wadjet themselves.

Waheela (Waheela sapiens). Therianthrope shapeshifters from the upper portion of North America, the waheela are a solitary race, usually claiming large swaths of territory and defending it to the death from others of their species. Waheela mating season is best described with the term "bloodbath." Waheela transform into something that looks like a dire bear on steroids. They're usually not hostile, but it's best not to push it.

PLAYLIST:

Here are a few songs to rock you through Verity's adventures.

"Superheroine" . . . . Liz Nickrenz
"Here It Goes Again" . . . . OK Go
"I Know Where You Sleep" . . . . Emilie Autumn
"He Said, She Said" . . . . Maldroid
"Pot Kettle Black" . . . . Tilly & the Wall
"The Cave" . . . . Mumford & Sons
"No Spill Blood" . . . . Oingo Boingo
"Ever Fallen In Love" . . . . Peter Yorn
"One Engine" . . . . The Decemberists
"Beautiful, Dirty, Rich" . . . . Lady Gaga
"Catwoman" . . . . Shakespear's Sister
"If Looks Could Kill" . . . . Heart
"Basket Case" . . . . Green Day
"Uninvited Guest" . . . . Marillion
"Fight Fire With Fire" . . . . Kansas
"Shootout at the Candy Shop" . . . . Jess Klein
"I Am the One Who Will . . . . Dar Williams
   Remember Everything"
"The Places You Have . . . . . . Dashboard Confessionals
   Come to Fear the Most"
"The Ghost in You" . . . . Matthew Puckett
"Sentimental Heart" . . . . She & Him
"Break In" . . . . Halestorm
"93 Maidens" . . . . Rachael Sage

"The Adventures of ...... The Red Hot Chili Peppers
   Rain Dance Maggie"
"All the Stars in Texas"........................ Ludo
"Stay Young, Go Dancing" ...... Death Cab for Cutie
"Fairest of Them All".................. Slaid Cleaves
"And We'll Dance" ....Thea Gilmore

ACKNOWLEDGMENTS:

So here we are again, as *Midnight Blue-Light Special* takes the floor, and Verity takes a well-earned break: the next two books will focus on her brother, Alex, as he deals with some problems of his own. Thank you all so much for reading, and for supporting this series so enthusiastically. Cheese and cake for everyone!

Betsy Tinney, to whom this book is dedicated, remains my ballroom pixie godmother, explaining all the nuances of dance culture. Phil Ames is still to blame for a surprising amount of this whole mess, while my webmaster, Chris Mangum, continues to tolerate my introducing cryptids into every single conversation we have.

As always, the machete squad provided proofreading and editorial services, doing everything in their power to make this book as good as it could possibly be. Kory Bing illustrated my fantastic Field Guide to the Cryptids of North America, which you can visit at my website—I want a fricken of my very own. Tara O'Shea continued to design amazing wallpapers, icons, and internal dingbats for these books, helping to create a large, unified world. I couldn't be more thrilled.

My agent, Diana Fox, remains my personal superhero and one of my favorite human beings. My editor at DAW, Sheila Gilbert, looked at my first draft, saw what needed fixing, and made everything better. Huge thanks to everyone at DAW, and to my cover artist, Aly Fell, who continues to bring these people to life in an amazing new way.

Thanks to my Disney World girls—Amy, Brooke,

Patty, Vixy, Rachel, and of course, Mom—and to Barfleet, for service above and beyond the call of duty. Thanks to Borderlands Books, for tolerating my large, often chaotic book events. And of course, thank you. I couldn't write these books without you.

Any errors in this book are my own. The errors that aren't here are the ones that all these people helped me fix. Thank you.

"*Silence* is a solid, interestingly-told YA novel that seems, superficially, to be just another wave in the current flood of YA supernatural. Being a wave isn't bad; I write urban fantasy, I am basically sponsoring a surfing competition. But there's something wonderful about diving into a wave and discovering infinitely more.

Read *Silence*. Read it because it's awesome, and read it because any author who includes a complex, well-written, believable, believably autistic central character deserves our applause, and book sales are the best form of clapped hands, for an author.

My hat is off to Michelle Sagara."
                                        —Seanan McGuire

Coming in May 2013
in a DAW mass market edition
from MICHELLE SAGARA

SILENCE

Read on for a special preview

EMMA

EVERYTHING HAPPENS AT NIGHT.
The world changes, the shadows grow, there's secrecy and privacy in dark places. First kiss, at night, by the monkey bars and the old swings that the children and their parents have vacated; second, longer, kiss, by the bike stands, swirl of dust around feet in the dry summer air. Awkward words, like secrets just waiting to be broken, the struggle to find the right ones, the heady fear of exposure — what if, what if — the joy when the words are returned. Love, in the parkette, while the moon waxes and the clouds pass.

Promises, at night. Not first promises — those are so old they can't be remembered — but new promises, sharp and biting; they almost hurt to say, but it's a good hurt. Dreams, at night, before sleep, and dreams during sleep.

Everything, always, happens at night.

Emma unfolds at night. The moment the door closes at her back, she relaxes into the cool breeze, shakes her hair loose, seems to grow three inches. It's not that she hates the day, but it doesn't feel real; there are too many people and too many rules and too many questions. Too many teachers, too many concerns. It's an act, getting through the day; Emery Collegiate is a stage. She pins up her hair, wears her uniform—on Fridays, on formal days, she wears the stupid plaid skirt and the jacket—goes to her classes. She waves at her friends, listens to them talk, forgets almost instantly what they talk *about*. Sometimes it's band, sometimes it's class, sometimes it's the other friends, but most often it's boys.

She's been there, done all that. It doesn't mean anything anymore.

At night? Just Petal and Emma. At night, you can just be yourself.

Petal barks, his voice segueing into a whine. Emma pulls a Milk-Bone out of her jackct pocket and feeds him. He's overweight, and he doesn't need it—but he wants it, and she wants to give it to him. He's nine, now, and Emma suspects he's half-deaf. He used to run from the steps to the edge of the curb, half-dragging her on the leash—her father used to get so mad at the dog when he did.

He's a rottweiler, not a lapdog, Em.

He's just a puppy.

Not at that size, he isn't. He'll scare people just by standing still; he needs to learn to heel, and he needs to learn that he can hurt you if he drags you along.

He doesn't run now. Doesn't drag her along. True, she's much bigger than she used to be, but it's also true that he's much older. She misses the old days. But at least he's still here. She waits while he sniffs at the green bins. It's his little ritual. She walks him along the curb, while he starts and stops, tail wagging. Emma's not in a hurry now. She'll get there eventually.

Petal knows. He's walked these streets with Emma for all of his life. He'll follow the curb to the end of the street, watch traffic pass as if he'd like to go fetch a moving car, and then cross the street more or less at Emma's heel. He talks. For a rottweiler, he's always been yappy.

But he doesn't expect more of an answer than a Milk-

Bone, which makes him different from anyone else. She lets him yap as the street goes by. He quiets when they approach the gates.

The cemetery gates are closed at night. This keeps cars out, but there's no gate to keep out people. There's even a footpath leading to the cement sidewalk that surrounds the cemetery and a small gate without a padlock that opens inward. She pushes it, hears the familiar creak. It doesn't swing in either direction, and she leaves it open for Petal. He brushes against her leg as he slides by.

It's dark here. It's always dark when she comes. She's only seen the cemetery in the day twice, and she never wants to see it in daylight again. It's funny how night can change a place. But night does change this one. There are no other people here. There are flowers in vases and wreaths on stands; there are sometimes letters, written and pinned flat by rocks beneath headstones. Once she found a teddy bear. She didn't take it, and she didn't touch it, but she did stop to read the name on the headstone: *Lauryn Bernstein*. She read the dates and did the math. Eight years old.

She half-expected to see the mother or father or grandmother or sister come back at night, the way she does. But if they do, they come by a different route, or they wait until no one—not even Emma—is watching. Fair enough. She'd do the same.

But she wonders if they come together—mother, father, grandmother, sister—or if they each come alone, without speaking a word to anyone else. She wonders how much of Lauryn's life was private, how much of it was built on moments of two: mother and daughter, alone; father and daughter, alone. She wonders about Lauryn's friends, because her friends' names aren't carved here in stone.

She knows about that. Others will come to see Lauryn's grave, and no matter how important they were to Lauryn, they won't see any evidence of themselves there: no names, no dates, nothing permanent. They'll be outsiders, looking in, and nothing about their memories will matter to passing strangers a hundred years from now.

Emma walks into the heart of the cemetery and comes, at last, to a headstone. There are white flowers here, because Nathan's mother has visited during the day. The lilies are bound by wire into a wreath, a fragrant, thick circle that perches on an almost invisible frame.

Emma brings nothing to the grave and takes nothing away. If she did, she's certain Nathan's mother would remove it when she comes to clean. Even here, even though he's dead, she's still cleaning up after him.

She leaves the flowers alone and finds a place to sit. The graveyard is awfully crowded, and the headstones butt against each other, but only one of them really matters to Emma. She listens to the breeze and the rustle of leaves; there are willows and oaks in the cemetery, so it's never exactly quiet. The sound of passing traffic can be heard, especially the horns of pissed-off drivers, but their lights can't be seen. In the city this is as close to isolated as you get.

She doesn't talk. She doesn't tell Nathan about her day. She doesn't ask him questions. She doesn't swear undying love. She's *done all that*, and it made no difference; he's there, and she's here. Petal sits down beside her. After a few minutes, he rolls over and drops his head in her lap; she scratches behind his big, floppy ears, and sits, and breathes, and stretches.

One of the best things about Nathan was that she could just sit, in silence, without being alone. Sometimes she'd read, and sometimes he'd read; sometimes he'd play video games, and sometimes he'd build things; sometimes they'd just walk aimlessly all over the city, as if footsteps were a kind of writing. It wasn't that she wasn't supposed to talk; when she wanted to talk, she did. But if she didn't, it wasn't awkward. He was like a quiet, private place.

And that's the only thing that's left of him, really.

A quiet, private place.

CHAPTER
ONE

AT 9:30 P.M., CELL TIME, the phone rang. Emma slid it out of her pocket, rearranging Petal's head in the process, flipped it open, saw that it was Allison. Had it been anyone else, she wouldn't have answered.

"Hey."

"Emma?"

No, it's Amy, she almost snapped. Honestly, if you rang her number, who did you *expect* to pick it up? But she didn't, because it was Allison, and she'd only feel guilty about one second after the words left her mouth. "Yeah, it's me," she said instead.

Petal rolled his head back onto her lap and then whined while she tried to pull a Milk-Bone out of her very crumpled jacket pocket. Nine years hadn't made him more patient.

"Where are you?"

"Just walking Petal. Mom's prepping a headache, so I thought I'd get us both out of the house before she killed us." Time to go. She shifted her head slightly, caught the cell phone between her chin and collarbone, and shoved Petal gently off her lap. Then she stood, shaking the wrinkles out of her jacket.

"Did you get the e-mail Amy sent?"

"What e-mail?"

"That would be no. How long have you been walking?"

Emma shrugged. Which Allison couldn't see. "Not long. What time is it?"

"9:30," Allison replied, in a tone of voice that clearly said she didn't believe Emma didn't know. That was the problem with perceptive friends.

"I'll look at it the minute I get home—is there anything you want to warn me about before I do?"

"No."

"Should I just delete it and blame it on the spam filter? No, no, that's a joke. I'll look at it when I get home and call you—Petal, come back!" Emma whistled. As whistles went, it was high and piercing, and she could practically hear Allison cringe on the other end of the phone. "Damn it—I have to go, Ally." She flipped the lid down, shoved the phone into her pocket, and squinted into the darkness. She could just make out the red plastic handle of the retracting leash as it fishtailed along in the grass.

So much for quiet. "*Petal!*"

Running in the graveyard at night was never smart. Oh, there were strategic lamps here and there, where people had the money and the desire to spend it, but mostly there was moonlight, and a lot of flat stones; not all the headstones were standing. There were also trees that were so old Emma wondered whether the roots had eaten through coffins, if they even used coffins in those days. The roots often came to the surface, and if you were unlucky, you could trip on them and land face first in tree bark—in broad daylight. At night, you didn't need to be unlucky.

No, you just needed to try to catch your half-deaf rottweiler before he scared the crap out of some stranger in the cemetery. The cemetery that should have bloody well been deserted. She got back on her feet.

"*Petal, goddammit!*" She stopped to listen. She couldn't see Petal, but he was a black rottweiler and it was dark. She could, on the other hand, hear the leash as it struck stone and standing wreaths, and she headed in that direction, walking as quickly as she could. She stubbed her toes half a dozen times because there was no clear path through the headstones and the markers, and even when she could see them—and the moon was bright enough—she couldn't see enough of them in time. She never brought a flashlight with her because she didn't need one normally; she could walk to Nathan's grave and back blindfolded. Walking to a black dog who was constantly in motion between totally unfamiliar markers, on the other hand, not so much.

She wondered what had caught his attention. The only person he ran toward like this was Emma, and usually only when she was coming up the walk from school or coming into the house. He would bark when Allison or Michael approached the door, and he would growl like a pit bull when salesmen, meter men, or the occasional Mormon or Jehovah's Witness showed up—but he wasn't much of a runner. Not these days.

The sounds of the leash hitting things stopped.

Up ahead, which had none of the usual compass directions, Emma could see light. Not streetlight, but a dim, orange glow that flickered too much. She could also, however, see the stubby, wagging tail of what was sometimes the world's stupidest dog. Relief was momentary. Petal was standing in front of two people, one of whom seemed to be holding the light. And Emma didn't come to the graveyard to meet people.

She pursed her lips to whistle, but her mouth was too dry, and anyway, Petal probably wouldn't hear her. Defeated, she shoved her hands into her jacket pockets and made her way over to Petal. The first thing she did was pick up his leash; the plastic was cool and slightly damp to the touch, and what had, moments before, been smooth was now scratched and rough. Hopefully, her mother wouldn't notice.

"Emma?"

When you don't expect to meet anyone, meeting someone you know is always a bit of a shock. She saw his face, the height of his cheekbones, and his eyes, which in the dim light looked entirely black. His hair, cut back over his ears and shorn close to forehead, was the same inky color. He was familiar, but it took her a moment to remember why and to find a name.

"Eric?" Even saying the name, her voice was tentative. She looked as the shape in the darkness resolved itself into an Eric she vaguely knew, standing beside someone who appeared a lot older and a lot less distinct.

"Mrs. Bruehl's my mentor," he said, helpfully. "Eleventh grade?"

She frowned for a moment, and then the frown cleared. "You're the new guy."

"New," he said with a shrug. "Same old, same old, really. Don't take this the wrong way," he added, "but what are you doing here at this time of night?"

"I could ask you the same question."

"You could."

"Great. What are *you* doing here at this time of night?"

He shrugged again, sliding his hands into the pockets of his jeans. "Just walking. It's a good night for it. You?"

"I'm mostly chasing my *very annoying* dog."

Eric looked down at Petal, whose stub of a tail had shown no signs whatsoever of slowing down. "Doesn't seem all that annoying."

"Yeah? Bend over and let him breathe in your face."

Eric laughed, bent over, and lowered his palms toward Petal's big, wet nose. Petal sniffed said hands and then barked. And whined. Sometimes, Emma thought, pulling the last Milk-Bone out of her jacket pocket, that dog was so embarrassing.

"Petal, come here." Petal looked over his shoulder, saw the Milk-Bone, and whined. Just . . . whined. Then he looked up again, and this time, Emma squared her shoulders and fixed a firm smile on lips that wanted to shift in entirely the opposite direction. "And who's your friend?"

And Eric, one hand just above Petal's head, seemed to freeze, half-bent. "What friend, Emma?"

But his friend turned slowly to face Emma. As she did, Emma could finally see the source of the flickering, almost orange, light. A lantern. A paper lantern, like the ones you saw in the windows of variety stores in Chinatown. It was an odd lamp, and the paper, over both wire and flame, was a pale blue. Which made no sense, because the light it cast wasn't blue at all. There were words on the shell of the lamp that Emma couldn't read, although she could see them clearly enough. They were composed of black brushstrokes that trailed into squiggles, and the squiggles, in the leap of lamp fire, seemed to grow and move with a life of their own.

She blinked and looked up, past the lamp and the hand that held it.

An old woman was watching her. An *old* woman. Emma was accustomed to thinking of half of her teachers as "old," and probably a handful as "ancient" or "mummified." Not a single one of them wore age the way this woman did. In fact, given the wreath of sagging wrinkles that was her skin, Emma wasn't certain that she *was* a woman. Her cheeks were sunken, and her eyes were set so deep they might as well have just been sockets; her hair, what there was of it, was white tufts, too stringy to suggest down. She had no teeth, or seemed to have no teeth; hell, she didn't have lips, either.

Emma couldn't stop herself from taking a step back.

The old woman took a step forward.

She wore rags. Emma had heard that description before. She had even seen it in a movie or two. Neither experience prepared her for this. There wasn't a single piece of cloth that was bigger than a napkin, although the assembly hung together in the vague shape of a dress. Or a bag. The orange light that the blue lantern emitted caught the edges of different colors, but they were muted, dead things. Like fallen leaves. Like corpses.

"Emma?"

Emma took another step back. "Eric, tell her to stop." She tried to keep her voice even. She tried to keep it polite. It was hard. If the stranger's slightly open, sunken mouth had uttered words, she would have been less terrifying. But, in silence, the old woman teetered across graves as if she'd just risen from one and counted it as nothing.

Emma backed up. The old woman kept coming. Everything moved slowly, everything—except for Emma's breathing—was quiet. The quiet of a graveyard. Emma tried to speak, tried to ask the old woman what she wanted, but her throat was too dry, and all that came out was an alto squeak. She took another step and ran into a headstone; she felt the back of it, cold, against her thighs. Standing against a short, narrow wall, Emma threw her hands out in front of her.

The old woman pressed the lantern into those hands. Emma felt the sides of it collapse slightly as her hands gripped them, changing the shape of the brushstrokes and squiggles. It was *cold* against her palms. Cold like ice, cold like winter days when you inhaled and the air froze your nostrils.

She cried out in shock and opened her hands, but the lantern clung to her palms, and no amount of shaking would free them. She tried hard, but she couldn't watch what she was doing because old, wrinkled claws shot out like cobras, sudden, skeletal, and gripped Emma's cheeks and jaw, the way Emma's hands now gripped the lantern.

Emma felt her face being pulled down, down toward the old woman's, and she tried to pull back, tried to straighten her neck. But she couldn't. All the old stories she'd heard in camp, or in her father's lap, came to her then, and even though this woman clearly had no teeth, Emma thought of vampires.

But it wasn't Emma's neck that the old woman wanted. She pulled Emma's whole face toward her, and then Emma felt—and smelled—unpleasant, endless breath, dry as dust but somehow rank as dead and rotting flesh, as the old woman opened her mouth. Emma shut her eyes as the face, its nested lines of wrinkles so like a fractal, drew closer and closer.

She felt lips, what might have been lips, press themselves against the thin membranes of her eyelids, and she whimpered. It wasn't the sound she wanted to make; it was just the only sound she *could*. And then even that was gone as those same lips, with that same breath, pressed firmly and completely against Emma's mouth.

Like a night kiss.

She tried to open her eyes, but the night was all black, and there was no moon, and it was *so damn cold*. And as she felt that cold overwhelm her, she thought it unfair that this would be her *last* kiss, this unwanted horror; that the memory of Nathan's hands and Nathan's lips were not the ones she would carry to the grave.

Seanan McGuire

The October Daye Novels

"...will surely appeal to readers who enjoy my books, or those of Patrica Briggs." —*Charlaine Harris*

"I am so invested in the world building and the characters now.... Of all the 'Faerie' urban fantasy series out there, I enjoy this one the most."—*Felicia Day*

ROSEMARY AND RUE
978-0-7564-0571-7

A LOCAL HABITATION
978-0-7564-0596-0

AN ARTIFICIAL NIGHT
978-0-7564-0626-4

LATE ECLIPSES
978-0-7564-0666-0

ONE SALT SEA
978-0-7564-0683-7

ASHES OF HONOR
978-0-7564-0749-0

CHIMES AT MIDNIGHT
978-0-7564-0814-5
(Available September 2013)

To Order Call: 1-800-788-6262
www.dawbooks.com

DAW 142

Diana Rowland

"Rowland's delightful novel jumps genre lines with a little something for everyone—mystery, horror, humor, and even a smattering of romance. Not to be missed—all that's required is a high tolerance for gray matter. For true zombiephiles, of course, that's a no brainer."

—*Library Journal*

"An intriguing mystery and a hilarious mix of the horrific and mundane...Humor and gore are balanced by surprisingly touching moments as Angel tries to turn her (un)life around."
—*Publishers Weekly*

My Life as a White Trash Zombie
978-0-7564-0675-2

Even White Trash Zombies
Get the Blues
978-0-7564-0750-6

White Trash Zombie Apocalypse
978-0-7564-0803-9
(Available July 2013)

To Order Call: 1-800-788-6262
www.dawbooks.com

Gini Koch

The Alien *Novels*

TOUCHED BY AN ALIEN
978-0-7564-0600-4

ALIEN TANGO
978-0-7564-0632-5

ALIEN IN THE FAMILY
978-0-7564-0668-4

ALIEN PROLIFERATION
978-0-7564-0697-4

ALIEN DIPLOMACY
978-0-7564-0716-2

ALIEN vs. ALIEN
978-0-7564-0770-4

ALIEN IN THE HOUSE
978-0-7564-0757-5
(Available May 2013)

To Order Call: 1-800-788-6262
www.dawbooks.com

DAW 160

Katharine Kerr

The Nola O'Grady Novels

"Breakneck plotting, punning, and romance make for a mostly fast, fun read."   —*Publishers Weekly*

"This is an entertaining investigative urban fantasy that sub-genre readers will enjoy...fans will enjoy the streets of San Francisco as seen through an otherworldly lens."
                                        —*Midwest Book Review*

LICENSE TO ENSORCELL
978-0-7564-0656-1

WATER TO BURN
978-0-7564-0691-2

APOCALYPSE TO GO
978-0-7564-0709-4

LOVE ON THE RUN
978-0-7564-0762-9

To Order Call: 1-800-788-6262
www.dawbooks.com

DAW 180

Tad Williams

The Dirty Streets of Heaven

"A dark and thrilling story.... Bad-ass smart-mouth
Bobby Dollar, an Earth-bound angel advocate for
newly departed souls caught between Heaven and
Hell, is appalled when a soul goes missing on his
watch. Bobby quickly realizes this is 'an actual, hon-
est-to-front-office crisis,' and he sets out to fix it,
sparking a chain of hellish events.... Exhilarating
action, fascinating characters, and high stakes will
leave the reader both satisfied and eager for the next
installment." —*Publishers Weekly (starred review)*

"Williams does a brilliant job.... Made me laugh.
Made me curious. Impressed me with its cleverness.
Made me hungry for the next book. Kept me up late
at night when I should have been sleeping."
—Patrick Rothfuss

And watch for the sequel, Happy Hour in Hell,
coming in September 2013!

The Dirty Streets of Heaven: 978-0-7564-0768-1
Happy Hour in Hell: 978-0-7564-0815-2

To Order Call: 1-800-788-6262
www.dawbooks.com

DAW 207